D0457422

THE
WILD
LANDS

THE WILD LANDS

PAUL GRECI

[Imprint]
MAKE YOUR MARK

NEW YORK

[Imprint]
MAKE YOUR MARK

A part of Macmillan Publishing Group, LLC
175 Fifth Avenue, New York, NY 10010

Library of Congress Control Number: 2018944992

ISBN 978-1-250-18358-3 (hardcover) / ISBN 978-1-250-18359-0 (ebook)

Our books may be purchased in bulk for promotional, educational, or business use.
Please contact your local bookseller or the Macmillan Corporate and Premium Sales
Department at (800) 221-7945 ext. 5442 or by email at
MacmillanSpecialMarkets@macmillan.com.

Book design by Heather Palisi

Imprint logo designed by Amanda Spielman

First edition, 2019

1 3 5 7 9 10 8 6 4 2

fiercereads.com

This book stays in the owner's hands.
Steal it and you'll be banished to burnt-out lands.
With nothing to eat and nowhere to hide,
You'll be in for a grim and ghastly ride.

For my wife, Dana

PART
ONE

CHAPTER
1

"WITH ANY LUCK, WE'LL BE gone by tomorrow," Dad says.

I nod and keep stuffing the tent into its sack, looking forward to getting out of this ash bucket but not to the four-hundred-mile walk north. And not to cramming my six-foot frame into a small tent with my mom, dad, and sister.

We've been living in the cement basement of a burnt-out house for about a year now in the hills above what used to be Fairbanks, Alaska.

An expanse of gray runs to the horizon—ash from the fires that ravaged this place the past two summers. The first fires, which the government set intentionally after classifying Interior Alaska as a "Sacrifice Area," burned Fairbanks and the two military bases east of town, but spared most of the houses in the hills. It used to be that only places the military had trashed were labeled as Sacrifice Areas, but now the government was using the term for places it couldn't support anymore. And it was destroying those places so other countries couldn't benefit from what was left behind.

But no one knows who started the fires the second summer. Those fires reburned the town, blazed through the hills, and scorched the land as far as the eye can see.

Trees are memories. Buildings are memories. We inferno

survivors, however many or few, are all living in basements. Tiny ribbons of green, spindly stalks of fireweed pushing through the ash, spaced far and wide, are the only signs of plant life I can see from our place.

I wanted to leave three years ago, when most everyone else fled this wreck of a place, when the United States government said they could no longer support Alaska due to the scarcity of resources worldwide. They'd been pulling back for years now, ever since the oil ran dry up here. They couldn't keep pumping energy into a far-away place that wasn't giving any back. Never mind that they'd sucked every ounce of oil from the ground and shipped it south.

But they offered everyone an out three years ago when they withdrew statehood status: a bus ride north from Fairbanks to the Arctic Coast on the last road that was actually drivable with the last gas available. Then a journey in a ship east across the Arctic Ocean and then south to the Maine coast, where evacuees would be resettled.

Way back, it used to be that heading north meant heading into a wilderness where you'd bump up against an ocean that was frozen most of the year. But for years now, the Arctic Ocean has been ice-free in the summer.

But if you stayed, you were on your own.

"Travis," Dad says, "how's the cache coming?"

I pull the drawstring tight on the tent's stuff sack. "I should have it finished today."

Dad stops cleaning his shotgun, his three remaining slugs lined up on the floor. "Should have?" The edge to his voice makes my stomach go raw. "You better have it finished today."

I want to tell him to finish it himself if he's not happy with how long it's taking me, but I know he's under a lot of pressure.

Pressure he could've avoided if he wasn't so freaking stubborn. And it's not like digging the cache is the only thing I'm doing. Every time I breathe he gives me something else to do. "It's just taking a little longer than I thought," I tell him.

"I'll finish packing up in here," he says. "Just go. Finish that cache. Christ."

My head slumps. Whatever I do, and however fast I do it, it's never enough.

The cache is just a big hole about a quarter mile from our basement. Six feet deep, six feet long, four feet wide. Coffin-sized. Our plan is to bury some of what we can't take with us in case we have to come back. Food, clothing, tools, packs. But we'll leave some stuff out in the open so when the looters come, hopefully they won't look any farther. And if they do discover evidence of something buried, hopefully they'll think it's a grave and leave it alone.

Yeah, looting is standard practice. Whenever anyone leaves or dies, their stuff is up for grabs. Not that there's much of anything left since the fires.

There was lots of food that first winter because all the people who'd abandoned their houses and taken the government up on getting the hell out of here left it behind. They left everything.

Now I don't even know how many people are still in the area. Walking is the only way to get anywhere, and with miles of burnt land separating you from the next family living in the basement of a burnt-out house, you might not see anyone for days, and when you do see someone, you don't know how dangerous they are, how desperate they are.

* * *

"Jess," I say to my little sister, "hand me another jar." I could do the job myself, but I want Jess with me at the cache. I want her to see where it is and what's in it. Embed the location in her mind in case something happens to me or Mom or Dad—or all three of us. My mom has an endless amount of energy, which she's poured into our survival, but somehow it hasn't hardened her like it has my dad.

I take the quart jar of salmon from Jess and place it in the cache. We're on the back side of a hill behind our basement in the remains of a stand of birch trees—charred, lifeless snags poking up from the ash and ready to be blown down by the next big wind.

Jess is ten years old. Seven years younger than me, and only seven herself when the government decided it could no longer support Alaska at all. They'd pulled their support from the western and northern parts of the state a few years before that, which brought a wave of people into Fairbanks. And the southern coast had been wracked by a couple of big earthquakes with no help to rebuild. Rumor was that a lot of people had starved on the coast after the quakes, and Anchorage had been pretty much leveled, but we didn't know for sure what went on down there.

Most people up here got on the buses headed north, and we never heard from them again.

Others walked south, attempting to cross the mountains and then the endless forest to the coast, looking to start a new life down there despite the destruction from the quakes.

My girlfriend, Stacy, and her family walked south. I don't know if they made it or died along the way, but they never came back.

I cried and cried the day they left. No phones. No email. No regular mail. Stacy was as gone as gone could be, and so were all my other friends, too.

Used to be you could drive south from Fairbanks to Anchorage, and to the small town of Valdez, too. But even way back, before the oil ran out, the shifting ground and melting permafrost kept destroying sections of road. Then the glaciers in the Alaska Range, that's the mountain range south of here, went on a melting rampage and that caused the rivers they fed to spill their banks and cut new channels, and the routes the roads took pretty much became memories.

But we'd stayed, obviously. My dad was already paranoid about the government. He loved Alaska because he felt like Uncle Sam wasn't looking over his shoulder all the time, telling him what to do.

Now Uncle Sam's a memory.

Jess hands me another jar. "Trav, I'm hungry."

"Sorry, but you're gonna have to wait until dinner. You know the rules."

"But look at all this salmon." Jess sighs. "We should at least be able to have a jar. We're doing all the work and we'll probably never see this food again." She smiles at me, and her rosy cheeks, spotted with ashy fingerprints and framed by her blond hair, make me smile, too. My sister is beautiful.

Then she sucks her cheeks in and pretends she's a fish and says, "Feed me. Feed me." I let out a laugh. Right now the only thing I want is to protect her and make her happy.

And she has a point: We probably won't see this food again. But if word gets back to Mom and Dad that I broke into the supplies, they'll be pissed. I want them to be able to count on me, even though it's their fault we're still here.

Really, it's mostly Dad's fault. He wanted to stay, Mom wanted to go. Maybe if she'd threatened to leave without him, he would've caved and we all would've left on the buses. I still would've been separated from Stacy, but at least we wouldn't be trapped here on the brink of starvation.

But I want Jess to be able to count on me as well. I don't want to be the one to tell her "no." She's hungry. She isn't faking it. I mean, she's not asking for a candy bar. Not that there are any candy bars, except in our memories. She's begging for nasty, spawned-out salmon that my mom boiled until it turned even more mushy than it was when we caught it. Lucky for us, we fished and fished a couple years ago, because last summer the salmon didn't return, and so far this summer our nets have turned up nothing. Not one fish. Our one reliable source of protein—gone. And there's no way to know if it'll ever be back. That's why we're finally leaving.

* * *

"You see that?" Dad points.

Me and my mom both look. She takes a step closer to me so we are standing shoulder to shoulder. I hear her take a deep breath and exhale.

Down in the flat land below our place, about a mile away, ash is puffing up from the ground.

"You think they're coming this way?" I ask. Luckily, I've just finished the cache and brushed out the footprints leading to it. My mom puts her arm around me, but says nothing.

When goods started getting scarce after that first winter, some people banded together while my dad took us farther from town, isolating us. Then, after surviving the second summer of fires, we found this basement of a small house that had burned and moved in. Our place sits on top of a hill, and since the trees are all gone we can see for miles across the valley.

When we first got here, we roamed the area, looking for abandoned houses. Places where goods may have survived in a basement or a crawl space.

If we came upon a place that was occupied, sometimes the people would just tell us to move on. Or sometimes they'd wave hello and we'd talk from a distance. And they'd say, *You won't find anything around here.*

"Just keep an eye on them," Dad says, nodding at the rising ash. "If they start coming up our hill . . ." Dad pauses. "Damn, I think they just turned our way." He turns to my mom. "Time for you and Jess to hide."

My mom says softly, "I know." Then walks to the doorway and disappears down the stairs.

When she's gone, my dad turns to me and says, "If only you'd finished that cache on schedule, we could've left yesterday."

I want to tell him that it takes more time than he thinks to dig a grave-sized hole and then fill it back in and make it look like the ground hasn't been disturbed. I want to tell him that just because he thinks something should be a certain way or take a certain amount of time that doesn't mean it will. But there's no time to argue right now. Someone is coming and we need to be ready.

CHAPTER
2

WE CAN MAKE OUT INDIVIDUALS now, six of them in single file snaking their way through the ash and approaching the base of the hill. Soon they'll be out of sight, and then if they keep coming they'll probably pop up about fifty yards down from our place.

"Dad," I say, "what are we gonna do?"

My dad shifts his shotgun from one hand to the other. "We'll see what they do."

"But what if they have guns?" I ask. "Or knives. Or whatever. What happens if we let them walk all the way up here and they turn out to be bad people?"

Dad chews on his upper lip, then says, "I can't just shoot someone because they're walking this way. Maybe they're nice, like us. Or at least reasonable. And if they are, I don't want to waste ammo that I could use for hunting, much less kill someone who doesn't deserve it."

"But Dad, I—"

"Just let me do the talking," Dad says. "And don't show your knife. If we do need it, then it'll be more effective if they don't see it right off the bat."

I pull my shirt out so it covers the knife in the sheath on my belt. I've never stabbed anyone. A raw spot forms in my stomach and I taste salmon at the back of my throat.

Then we wait. And wait some more, but no one piles over the hill. I scan the valley to see if the group changed course but don't see anything. They have to be just below us. My eyes sweep the edge of the hillside. We expect them to come up the center because that's the way they've been moving, but now I realize they can come up anywhere in a 270-degree arc.

Dad's voice echoes in my head: *If only you'd finished that cache on schedule, we could've left yesterday.*

I see a little movement, some ash puffing off to the right. Then some more off to the left. Then straight on. And all of a sudden there are six heads poking up in a semicircle, surrounding us.

"What do you people want?" Dad says. He's holding the shotgun forward but pointed down.

I can feel my arms shaking. I watch their shoulders appear. Then they're fully in view, all men, covered in ash from the crawl up the hill.

"What does anyone want?" the man straight ahead says. "Food. You got any?"

I hear Dad take a breath. "Just enough for me and my boy." He nods his head toward me.

I'm not a boy. I'm seventeen years old and tower over Dad by a few inches. I even have a beard. But I know what he means.

My eyes are darting from man to man. Six on two. This is going to suck, especially if they have any guns.

"I got mouths to feed." The man sweeps his arm left, then right.

The two guys on the ends look young, about my age, but the

other three are older than the guy doing the talking, who is maybe Dad's age, in his forties or fifties. Stocky build and bald.

"We've all got mouths to feed," Dad says. "Maybe the salmon will come back this year. Summer's not over yet."

The man spits. "And if they don't?"

"Look," Dad says. "I don't want any trouble. I don't want to shoot anyone, but I will if I have to. Now just move on."

Some thunder rumbles in the distance.

"You know what it's like to watch your own kids starve?" the man asks. "To feed your family a few fireweed sprouts that you know will make no difference? To watch your wife die because you can't provide for her?"

The man takes a step forward and Dad raises his gun ever so slightly. "I don't want any trouble," Dad repeats. "I don't like to kill, but I'll protect what I've got. I've had to do it before."

"I'm not out to rob anyone." The bald man smiles. "I just want to feed my people." He holds his hands up, palms out at shoulder height.

"Travis," Dad says. "Go get two jars of salmon. Now."

I hate leaving my dad out there alone, but I can't start arguing with him. Can't do anything to distract him. I run down the stairs and hear movement from Mom and Jess's hiding spot.

"Not yet," I whisper to them.

An arm reaches out from behind a curtain and a warm hand strokes my beard. "Be careful," my mom whispers. Then she withdraws her hand.

I can hear Dad and the man talking but can't make out what they are saying. I grab two jars of salmon from one of the backpacks and run back upstairs.

Without turning, Dad says, "Trav, set the salmon down about halfway. And nobody moves until he's back with me."

I walk forward, a quart jar of salmon in each hand, my feet puffing in the ash. Another rumble of thunder fills my ears.

I stop about halfway, set the jars down, then back up until I'm next to Dad.

The man moves forward, scoops up the jars, and just holds them. "Not much for six."

"Time for you all to be on your way," Dad says. "I've been more than generous."

The man just stands there. "You must have quite a supply if you've got salmon from two summers ago."

We shouldn't have given them anything. But Dad, he helps people if he can do it without putting Mom and Jess in danger. And I agree with that. But it's hard to tell what might put them in danger.

"Time to be on your way," Dad repeats, then raises the shotgun to shoulder level.

"Four more jars," the man says.

The first drops of rain sink into the ash. I feel my stomach tighten. The guy on the far right puts his hand into his sweatshirt pocket. In an instant everyone but the guy holding the fish has a baseball-sized rock in his hands.

"You might be able to kill a couple of us," the man says. "That is, if that gun's got any bullets."

"Slugs," Dad says. "Blow a hole in your chest as big as your heart."

"Prove it," the man says. "Fire one into the air."

"If I shoot," Dad says, "it'll be to kill."

I've never seen Dad kill a man, but he's done it before. At the last place we lived, I heard the shot and came running. The guy had attacked him with a knife. Dad used the last bullet in his pistol from close range.

My eyes jump from person to person, trying to see if there are any more surprises, but they all just stand there like they've rehearsed this a thousand times and are now playing it out.

The rain comes harder, and I can feel it starting to soak through my shirt. If this had been the first year after the mass exodus, we would've invited these guys in and fed them. Maybe we even shared a meal with them a couple of years ago. Maybe I went to school with the two guys on the ends—back when there used to be school. But it seems like everyone is the enemy now.

I hear the sneeze behind me, muffled through the basement walls. Damn it, Jess.

The man smiles. "You're hiding more than salmon."

"And I'll kill for them," Dad says. "Count on it."

"I don't want your women," the man says. "Just more food. Four more jars and we'll leave and never come back."

Bullshit, I think. I know that the more we give, the more they'll press us for.

I also know that none of these guys want a hole in their chest or their head completely blown off. Dad has three slugs, and he really does want them for hunting in case we do see a moose or a bear, or some caribou up north.

That first year after the government pulled out, everyone was hunting. Even before that, when the shipments of food became sporadic, more people turned to the land for moose and bear. And then the fires came through, which usually meant you'd eventually have more moose habitat, but these fires burned so hot that the plants were slow to come back. We haven't seen a bear or a moose in over a year. Not even tracks.

Lightning flashes from the hills on the other side of the valley, followed by thunder. The ash is turning to mud at our feet.

"We'll set our rocks down," the man says. "Just have your boy get four more jars."

Dad keeps the gun at shoulder height and pans the group with it. The man with the fish takes a step back. Everyone else drops their rocks in the mud and does the same.

"Trav," Dad says. "Get the fish."

I want to grab the gun and fire it, show these people that they can't do this. That they don't have this kind of power, but if I struggle with Dad that'd just give them a chance to attack. And even though it'll take less than a minute to get the fish, I don't want to leave him alone. And four more jars—that's a lot of our food for our trip. And if we give it to them, what will they ask for next?

I run down the steps and grab four more jars out of the pack. As I turn around, the blast of a shotgun slams my ears.

"Dad," I yell as I take the stairs two at a time, cradling the jars against my chest.

Out in the rain Dad stands with his head bowed, the gun at his side. From the edge of the hill, I see five figures running toward the valley through the ashy mud.

The kid on the far right, the first one to pull out his rock, lies crumpled on the ground.

We walk over to the body. I feel my heart pounding against the jars of salmon.

"He left me no choice. He pulled a pistol on me." Dad reaches down, picks up the pistol, clicks it open, and spins the cylinder.

"Empty," he says. Then he slams it on the ground.

CHAPTER
3

"COME ON, JESS," I SAY. "We've got to keep walking." Truth is, I'm growing tired of coaxing her along, but Dad assigned me the task of keeping her moving.

At least now we can feel the surface of the old road under the ash.

We went cross-country to get to the road because we wanted to steer clear of everyone, especially the guys who threatened us with rocks. A neighbor from five years ago could be your worst enemy now.

The crumpled, bloody body of the kid Dad shot, the rain soaking him, ash splattering on his face, keeps popping into my mind. Why would he point an empty pistol at someone holding a shotgun? Maybe he was calling Dad's bluff. He thought if Dad hadn't fired already, then he probably didn't have any bullets. And maybe they could muscle more food from us with the pistol.

The thing about Dad is he'll only hurt someone as a last resort. These days, most people would've pulled that trigger when the rocks came out, or before.

We aren't the first people to walk north this summer; there're some tracks on the road. The people who headed north on foot the second summer never came back, so that gives me hope that if we can get ourselves up to the Arctic Coast something good could happen. That the boats are still running or sailing across the Arctic Ocean, going wherever they go. I'm pretty sure it's already July, but I'm not certain. I had a watch that showed the date, but it stopped working a couple of winters ago.

"I just want to rest a little longer," Jess says. "My feet hurt." I look for that sparkle in her eyes, but it's not there.

I'd carry her partway, but I have a pack on that weighs ninety pounds, just like Dad's. And Mom's pack is at least sixty pounds. Jess has a smaller pack, but I bet it weighs thirty.

Mom and Dad have stopped just up the road. Talking too quietly to hear. They turn and keep going up the road.

"Let's catch up to Mom and Dad," I say, "and see if we can have a real rest, with some food." The one nice thing about traveling the road north is that the farther from Fairbanks we get, anyone we do run into will most likely be searching for a better life like us, not just roaming around looking for someone to rob.

Since the sun is up practically all the time, we're just resting for a couple of hours here and there, not stopping to sleep a whole night. Even at home when we slept, someone was always up— keeping watch.

I don't know what we'll find up at the coast. What if there are no boats? Four hundred miles is a long way to walk, not even counting the possibility of having to turn around and walk back.

The farther north we go, the more we start seeing little stands of trees that escaped the fires. Most of them are in the middle of swamps, but it gives me hope that maybe there'll be some game soon. A moose or a bear, or beaver, or caribou. Even if the boats don't show up, it might be a lot easier to live off the land up north, since it probably isn't a burnt-up wasteland like Fairbanks.

Jess finally pushes herself up from the ground, her clothes covered in ash, her blond hair coated with gray. I'm just glad she stood up on her own without any more arguing.

On top of the next hill, Mom and Dad stop and we catch up.

Jess plops down in the ash next to them. "I'm hungry. And my feet hurt." She puts an oversized frown on her face.

Mom smiles. Her blond hair has turned completely white these past couple of years. "We'll just rest here awhile." She takes her pack off and squats next to Jess, then touches her beneath the chin. "Where's that pretty smile?" Mom pulls a jar of salmon out of her pack. "We'll have a little snack."

Jess makes her fish face but you can still see the frown in her eyes.

Dad slips out of his pack. I copy him and just stand there. I hope this plan to head north is going to work.

* * *

"It looks deep," I say. We've just crossed a boulder field and are standing on the bank of a river. A silty creek really, only fifty feet wide. If I had a map I'd know what its name was, not that it matters. And it's tiny compared to what's coming. But still, it's cruising along, cutting a swift path through the ashy hills, running like it's in a race.

"I don't want to cross another river," Jess says.

"Jess, honey," Mom says. "Sometimes we do things we don't want to do." She glances at Dad, but he doesn't say anything. "Sometimes we have to."

I hear Jess sigh.

"Jess," Dad says. "It'll be fun. I'm going across first, and I'm gonna carry a rope and Trav is going to have the other end. Then

16

when you cross, you get to hang on to the rope. The only rule is that you can't let go."

"But I'm dry," Jess says. "And I want to stay dry." She crosses her arms over her chest.

Jess has really come through. She's already walked for five or six days, working her way across some slower-moving streams in water up to her armpits. And I can see it in her eyes: She isn't scared of getting wet, she's scared of that fast-moving water.

"Make a deal with you, sis," I say. "You can cross right in front of me. One hand on the rope and one on my arm. And if you make it without putting your head under, I'll give you a piece of my salmon next time we eat."

Jess rubs her feet in the ash. "Okay, but my head's gotta go all the way under for me to lose." She makes a quick fish face.

I laugh. "You drive a hard bargain, but okay. Deal." Mom mouths the words *thank you* to me and I nod in acknowledgment.

Dad unstraps the waist buckle on his pack and hands me one end of the rope. "Keep it tight." Then he steps into the current. When he's in up to his knees, he turns and yells, "I might drift downstream a bit, but just keep giving me the line little by little."

I tell him okay and he keeps going. When he gets into the middle, the water is waist-high and pulling him downstream. I can tell he's working hard to stay upright, driving into the current. Without the rope he'd be bouncing downstream. I keep paying the line out, straining against his weight, trying to give him just enough so he can move forward but not so much that he doesn't have a pivot point. The outside of my forearms are starting to burn and my upper arms are shaking, but I keep it steady.

Then Dad slips, and I'm yanked in up to my shins. Dad disappears underwater and my heart jumps to my throat. I keep pulling on the rope, my shoulders and wrists screaming for relief. Mom and Jess are shouting. Dad's head pops up once but then he's back down.

I haul harder, my whole body straining against the weight and the current, and Dad pops up again closer to our shore but downstream about thirty feet. Then he's on his hands and knees, his pack halfway on top of his head, and he's crawling out of the water.

He makes it to the shore. I let out a breath that I don't even know I'm holding. I don't agree with Dad about how he does things a lot of the time, but I don't know what I'd do without him.

Dad takes his pack off, sets it in the ash, and stands up.

"Clipped my knees on a big rock and lost my footing," Dad says. "Would've made it otherwise." I see him starting to shake from the cold.

Jess has her arms wrapped around Mom's waist. She's tough but she's only ten. Mom's stroking her hair.

"You ready for round two?" Dad asks. Before I can answer, he grabs his pack.

We start downstream from the last spot, and this time he makes it across.

I hand the rope to Mom and she pulls it tight with Dad on the other end.

I lift Jess's pack and sling it over my shoulder until it bumps into my pack. I wink at her. "You're next, kiddo." And she gives me this tiny smile that makes me smile.

Then I grab the rope and step into the water. The cold starts working on me right away, chilling my feet. About halfway across, I suck in a breath when I dip in over my waist but just keep going. I drop the packs on the bank and then recross. I grab the shotgun, carry that across, and go back again.

"Time for a swim." I smile at Jess, but this time she doesn't smile back. "Forget the bet. How about you just ride piggyback while I hang on to the rope?"

Jess jumps on my back and off we go. The thing about the cold water is once I'm in, I'm in, and as long as I keep moving I'm okay, especially since I know that the quicker I get everything across, the sooner I can get out of the water and warm up. Jess has her legs scrunched up, trying to keep her feet out of the water. If it wasn't such a fast-moving stream, I would've put her on my shoulders. I used to carry her around like that for fun. I'd ask her, "How's the view from up there?" And she'd tell me what she saw.

I drop Jess on the bank, tickle her ribs until she squeals, then go back across before Mom can argue. I don't want her coming across on the loose rope.

The wind chills me some as I hold the rope for Mom. She's moving slow since she has a pack on, but she makes it across no problem.

I step into the water, staring at the silty swirls, and start going hand over hand on the loose rope. I've got to work harder to keep my footing because the current is dragging me downstream.

Jess screams my name and I jerk my head up. Dad drops the rope just as Mom grabs it, and I stumble back a step. Then Dad has the shotgun pointed right at me, and I know there has to be some-one behind me, so I drop the rope and dive headfirst into the water and hear the muffled report of the gun.

The current carries me downstream. I know I should be going down feetfirst and try shifting my body. My lungs are screaming for air. Now I'm sideways with the current. I feel my fingers touch the air. Then my side slams into something. My ribs are on fire and I'm stuck, the water piling up and flowing around me. I push away from the huge rock that presses against my ribs, get my head above the surface, and suck air.

"Trav," I hear Jess call. "Trav, Trav, Trav!"

I turn toward the bank and catch a glimpse of her and Mom. Then something slaps my cheek.

"Grab it," Dad yells. "Now. Christ." He must be behind me because I can't see him. I grip the rope with both hands, and my legs are swept downstream and I feel my arms being pulled from my shoulder sockets as Dad reels me in like a snagged fish.

Onshore, kneeling, I cough up some water, then lie down and grab my throbbing side. My mind is a jumble of thoughts. The gun pointed at me, the blast, bashing my ribs into the rock.

I feel a hand on my back. "I had to do it," Dad says. "He was coming at you. Would've grabbed you if I hadn't shot him."

I turn and stare up at my dad. He looks me in the eye and says, "I don't think I could live with myself if something happened to you."

CHAPTER
4

ABOUT FIVE DAYS LATER WE'RE standing on a hill overlooking the half-mile-wide yellow-brown highway of water called the Yukon River, our first major obstacle. Rumors flew about what had happened to the bridge, the most popular one being that the government blew it up after the last bus going north crossed it. Another was that some of the people who stayed behind destroyed it to keep the government from coming back.

I don't know what to believe. And it doesn't really matter. What matters is right now. How are we gonna cross the river?

The people who headed north on foot the second summer never came back, so somehow they'd made it across. And even after we cross we have to walk another two hundred freaking miles, so we need to start working on this problem now.

On the far side of the river, trees stretch out in deep green like they used to on this side. "We've got to be extra careful by the river," Dad says.

"Anyone who makes it this far has to want the same thing we want," I say.

"Any people we see," Dad says, "I'll make the call."

"What Travis says makes sense," Mom responds. "Whatever we do, we'll have to talk things over." Before Dad can respond, Jess starts to whine about her feet hurting and my mom turns toward her. Jess throws her arms around my mom's waist and buries her head in my mom's chest, and they walk a few paces away from me and Dad.

We haven't seen anyone since that guy tried to grab me at the creek crossing, and that was still close to Fairbanks. Just some desperate person trying to take whatever he could. We watched two guys dressed in light blue jackets dragging him away from the bank while two more stood and watched, their guns at their sides.

I'm just glad it was me and not Mom who swam that creek last and that those guys didn't shoot back. My ribs have mostly settled down. I still feel a sharp jab every time I lift a heavy pack off the ground, but the bruise is fading.

The last three years, the tougher things got, the more of a dictator Dad became. And that wasn't necessarily a bad thing. It's probably what's gotten us up the road this far. And I know he feels bad about not leaving when Mom wanted to, when it would've been easy.

But still, people aren't made to live so isolated. We have to meet up with someone at some point whether we get across the river or not. What would be the point of the four of us living in isolation until we died? I guess it'd be better than nothing, but I want more out of life than that. Put me on a freaking boat and take me to a safe place. To a place where there'll be people my age. Girls my age. And Jess, she needs kids her age to play with. To be a kid before she grows up.

Maybe there's a better world across the sea. I want to find out. I'll do whatever I can to get out of this burnt-out land. Before it burned there'd been a chance at a good life. But so many people died in the burn, and of the ones who were left, we hadn't met many we could trust.

"Dad," I say, pointing to the Yukon, "it's a big river. How are we going to cross the damn thing?"

"We're gonna study the situation and then make a plan. Build something. A raft, probably, unless we find an abandoned boat on the shore."

One of the good things about Dad is that when he focuses on a problem, he doesn't let it go until he solves it. After Mom agreed to stay, he threw himself into surviving in the new conditions when suddenly, the only thing your money was good for was starting fires. The new playing field demanded you bring your brain, your heart, and your physical strength, and luckily for us Dad scored big in all three.

I always tried to keep up with him, especially after the buses had left and he'd taken me aside and said, *I want a good life for your mother, your sister, and you. But you, Trav, you're gonna be key in helping me make it happen.*

"Just what are we going to build a raft with?" I ask. All the trees we've seen so far have been on the other side of the river, or in the middle of swamps on this side and miles away from the riverbank.

"Downriver." Dad points. "See that bend?"

I nod. About two miles away, I guess, the river makes a sweeping bend to the north.

"There's a clump of trees," Dad says. "I think they're actually on this side of the river. Either that or they're on a gravel bar close to this side."

I squint and tilt my head side to side. I can't see what he's seeing, but I hope he's right.

CHAPTER
5

"DAD, HOW LONG ARE WE gonna just watch?" We've been on this hill for at least half a day watching smoke rise from that clump of trees at the bend, so we know people are down there, but that's where we need to be, too.

"Can't be too careful," Dad says.

And I think, *Yeah, you can. You can be so careful that moss will mistake your boots for tree roots and start colonizing.*

"We just need to go down there," I say. "They've got to be doing the same thing we're doing. We can help each other."

Mom is inside the tent with Jess. I can hear her voice, telling Jess a story, probably. Mom tries her best to keep things normal for Jess. To make sure she has some playtime or story time even though we are struggling to survive.

"Trav, your optimism is gonna kill you," Dad says. "Who have you run into in the last year who's helped us?"

I shake my head. "You've kept us so isolated the only people we've run into have been out scavenging. There's gotta be other people like us. But if we don't look, we'll never find them."

"What if they're short of food?" Dad says. "We can't afford to give them any."

"But if we just sit here, then we'll be short of food." I know there's no easy answer. That it's risky either way. I step closer to him and speak softly. "You wanna see Jess going hungry? That's what'll happen if we just sit here."

"The threat of starvation changes people," Dad says. "What if they've got guns and take our food? You wanna deal with that?" He takes a breath. "We plan for the worst and go from there. That's how we've made it this far."

I sigh, but my blood is boiling inside. "Then maybe we need to sneak down there and spy on them. See just who these people are who've made it as far as us, instead of sitting here and watching our food supply shrink."

* * *

I'm surprised when Dad agrees to let me go alone, insisting I carry the hatchet for protection in addition to my knife. He would've given me the shotgun if we had another. But I don't want to look dangerous if they spot me. If they have guns, they might shoot first and ask questions later.

"Travis," Dad says, "at the first sign of trouble, you get yourself out of there."

Mom steps forward and hugs me. "You be careful," she whispers into my ear. And then she lets me go.

I point to the tent where Jess is sleeping and ask, "What are you going to tell her about where I went?"

"Don't worry about that," Mom says. "I'll think of something."

Now, I'm at the edge of the trees. Just like Dad thought, the trees are on this side of the river.

How the fires bypassed this spot, I don't know. That next summer after the buses left, some people said the government intentionally started the second round of fires but I don't know if there's any truth to that rumor. I mean, why would they come back to torch a place again? But if the government could abandon a state, well, who knows what else they might do and why.

I stand flush with the biggest spruce I can find and just listen. I hear the plunge of an axe into wet wood, and the back-and-forth grinding of a handsaw. I peek from behind a tree but only see more trees. I take a breath. I need to move closer, but now that I'm here I'm thinking about what Dad said. How can I really know if these people are friendly?

When people kick into survival mode, they change. Dad's a gentle person, but he shot two people in the last couple of weeks. If he could pull the trigger, then just about anyone could.

I take a few steps around the tree and a squirrel starts chattering. I haven't heard one in a couple of years. The chopping and sawing stops. No way can they see me, but they know that squirrel isn't chattering for nothing. I feel my heart pounding in my ears, my stomach cramping up. Maybe Dad's right. Maybe this is a stupid idea. But then why did he let me try it?

Maybe he knows there's no other option if we want to cross the river.

I think about turning around, creeping out of the woods, and beating it back through the ash to the top of the hill, but that'd just reinforce that I was up to no good. I'm pretty sure Dad watched me enter the trees. I wonder what he's thinking now. And I wonder what he'd do if he was in my position. I wish he was here with me.

"You just turn around real slow now, and drop that hatchet," a deep voice says from behind me. "Unless you want some lead in your skull."

My heart jumps into my throat and I try to swallow it down. I let the hatchet fall, turn, and see a man holding a pistol, a beard flowing halfway down his chest, white hair pulled back in a pony-tail and stretched tight.

I think about my stringy long blond hair and scraggly beard combined with the hatchet I'm carrying, and I know I must look like an axe murderer. I wait for him to say something else, but when he doesn't, I say, "Me and my family want to cross the river. We knew someone was down here. Saw your smoke."

The man glances around. "Where are they? How many?"

"Upriver, on top of a hill. Four, including me. My mom and dad, and my little sister." I wish he'd quit pointing that gun at me.

"We've got nothing to spare," the man says. "How come you're snooping around like a thief and carrying that hatchet like you're looking to use it on someone?"

I feel my legs shaking. "I didn't know if you'd be friendly. We've run into a lot of people trying to rob us lately."

"We don't take anything that's not ours," the man says, still pointing the pistol at my chest. "But we'll protect what we've got. Just turn around and walk toward the river. We'll see what Clint says."

There are three green dome tents tucked into the woods fac-ing the river. I count six people including the guy with the gun to my back. The river is rushing by, an endless yellow-brown barrier.

"Clint," the man behind me calls out.

A short guy with a salt-and-pepper beard down to his belly, his eyes coming up to my chin, approaches me. "So you're the disturbance."

"Like I told your friend," I say, "me and my family just want to cross the river."

Clint spits on the ground. "The last person who said that tried to kill me."

* * *

"Travis," Clint says, "I don't know why but I trust you. Maybe because I told you to sit down by that tree and you did it. Maybe it's just something about your eyes that tells me you're not lying. Or maybe I'm just stupid."

Mark, the one with the pistol, keeps an eye on me while the others work on the raft, and now we're all talking. There are two women. I guess one is Clint's wife and the other is Mark's, but I'm not sure. And there are two girls a little taller than Jess, their daughters, maybe, but I don't really know.

One change that I like since all the fires is that there are a lot fewer mosquitoes. I remember reading that if a female mosquito has an unlimited supply of blood it can lay a couple hundred eggs every few days, but with no blood it can only lay about ten eggs every two weeks. But sitting under this tree is like old times. I'm slapping them left and right.

"I took a chance coming down here," I say. "A chance that I'd meet some people who at the very least wouldn't try to hurt me." I tell Clint about the guys with the rocks and the guy who tried to grab me at the creek crossing. And I tell him again that we're not after their food.

Clint nods. "Sounds like you've had to fight some battles. You march back up that hill and bring your family down here. Make a raven call when you get to the edge of the forest, and wait."

"Okay," I say. Ravens are one bird that we still see. Not many but they're scrappers. If anything can survive in the Sacrifice Area, they can. Back in the day, ravens used to fly to town and feed around dumpsters and then roost at night out in the forest. We used to see them flying over our house, going to and from.

On the way back through the forest, I grab my hatchet. My feet feel light with possibility. Jess can play with the two girls. Maybe Mom will make friends with the women, and Dad with Clint and Mark. And me, I'll take any company I can get as long as it's friendly and moves us in the right direction. I hope Dad will agree to the plan.

CHAPTER
6

WE'RE STILL A HALF MILE from the edge of the trees when Dad makes us stop for a conference and says, "I don't want anyone making any noise."

"But Dad," I say. "I told Clint we'd make a raven call, then wait. If we don't do that, how's he gonna trust us?"

"But why should we trust him?" Dad asks.

"They could've killed me. Had a gun to my back."

"It could still be a trap. Thanks to you, they know we have food."

Mom looks at him and shakes her head. She puts one arm around Jess. "We have to cross the Yukon. Soon. Or else we won't have enough food for the rest of the journey. We've got two weeks' worth left." She grinds one of her feet into the ashy ground.

The sun is peeking through some thin clouds. It's one of those hot, muggy days. Once we get to the trees—if we get to the trees—there'll be mosquitoes.

"Dad," I say. "What else are you going to do? What can you do?"

He looks at me, then at Mom, then at the trees in the distance. He huffs. "I don't know."

"These people seem different to me," I say. "Trustworthy."

"It could all be an act," Dad says. "Just like the guy with the knife."

Dad had met this guy who seemed friendly. He'd even offered my dad food and some of his matches, which we were in need of. Said he'd come from down the Tanana River. He'd been checking for salmon and had a place like ours, only farther out. His wife had left him when he refused to take the bus north with her. We don't know if the whole thing was a story. All we know is that he tried to kill Dad after appearing generous.

"Have you lost all faith in humanity?" Mom asks. "Look at us." She sweeps her arm in an arc. "We're not looking to hurt anyone. Why can't you believe that there are at least some other people left in this disaster area you wanted to live in who feel the same way?" Mom returns to stroking Jess's hair. Jess's eyes are closed and she's leaning her head against Mom's side. "Did you listen to what Trav said? They've got two little girls, just like Jess."

Jess opens her eyes and pushes away from her. "I'm not little."

Mom squats beside Jess. "Oh, Jess. That's not what I meant. Of course you're not little. I'm sorry."

Jess says, "I'm tired of standing here. It's too hot." Tears form in her eyes and she wipes them away before they have a chance to run down her cheeks.

I see Dad grinding his teeth together. He takes a breath and sets his pack on the ground. "You three stay here. Even if you see me wave, stay until I come back."

I nod once. At least he's going to do something.

"One more thing, Travis," Dad says. "Inside my pack is a green stuff sack with some food and a fire starter." He glances at Mom, but she looks away. "Take it out and bury it by those rocks." Dad points to some chest-high rocks set back from the river a quarter mile or so.

"Okay," I say. Bury this. Bury that. He always has to make things more complicated than they are. I'm about to ask why, but I don't want to slow him down, because he might change his mind about approaching Clint at all.

Then Dad hands me the gun. "Only one slug, remember."

I consider saluting him but don't think he'd appreciate the humor right now. Instead, I look him in the eye and say, "You can count on me."

He touches my shoulder and replies, "I know I can." Then he leans in close and whispers so only I can hear. "You see any other men while I'm gone, you protect your mother and sister."

"I will," I say.

Dad gives Mom and Jess hugs, then turns and walks away. I swing my foot and kick a fist-sized loose rock. It plows through the ash for several feet and then stops. I can't remember the last time he's hugged me.

If we cross the Yukon, maybe we'll find a moose or a caribou. Or maybe the whole place has been hunted out by all the people who headed north before us, and all the people who turned toward the land when the food shipments from the south dried up.

I watch Dad walking toward the trees, unarmed and alone. Maybe heading north was a mistake. Maybe it's just all one big sacrifice area.

*　*　*

"There's no guarantee that anyone is going to be at the coast," Clint says. "You might walk all that way for nothing. And then have to walk back, because you sure as hell don't want to spend the winter up there."

"Staying in Fairbanks is a death wish," Dad says. "I thought we could make it work. But after the second fire, there wasn't much left. And it seemed like the longer we stayed the only people we ran into were so desperate they'd do anything. We couldn't trust anyone. I should have listened to my wife and left on the buses."

And you should have listened to me when I told you these people were nice, I think, *then I wouldn't have had to bury some of our supplies, which I'm sure I'll be told to dig up later before we leave.*

Dad peels off his outer shirt so he just has his red long underwear shirt on, and then tells Clint about the guys with the rocks, and the guy with the knife, and the guy in the light blue jacket he shot who tried to grab me at the creek crossing, and Clint tells him about the guy that tried to kill him at this very spot about a week ago. He's somewhere downriver, probably dead.

And while we talk, we work at notching logs so they'll fit together to make a solid raft. Another half day of work and Clint thinks we'll be ready to float.

Jess is a little ways away, playing with Clint's twin daughters, Sara and Molly. And Mom is with Clint's and Mark's wives, cooking something up in a big pot over an open fire.

Clint's plan is to float down the Yukon until he finds a suitable spot and then build a cabin. Just like the old days, he says. Nature's turned back the clock.

I get what he's saying, but I don't want to live that way. I want to go where people are, not just live in some cabin in the middle of nowhere. Plus, the reason we're leaving, at least according to Dad, is that he doesn't think we can make it living off the land. The land is too tired, too abused, too burnt. It's been mistreated for so long he thinks it may never heal.

Clint is more hopeful. He thinks there's big pockets that survived the burns, and in those pockets there'll be enough fish and game and berries to support a few people who don't mind hard work and simple living. And that over time the burnt land will heal, and the moose will move in to feed on the new growth. He has some seeds for a garden, too. And Clint welcomes anyone who shares his vision and work ethic. I can tell Dad is considering it, but I know Mom would never go for it, even though Jess would have some playmates. Dad had his chance and failed. Now we're giving Mom's plan a try.

Clint can just drop us on the other side and we'll keep walking.

CHAPTER
7

IT'S JUST BLIND LUCK THAT Jess and I are downriver when the shooting starts. Jess had a little tiff with Molly and Sara and stormed off, and at Dad's request, I followed her.

Now, I grab Jess and pull her into the river. If whoever is shooting doesn't know the two of us exist, I want to keep it that way.

I try to stay by the shore as the current sweeps us away and the bottom drops out from under me. I have one arm encircled across Jess's chest and am paddling with my other arm while kicking with my legs, just trying to keep our heads above the surface. The water is knife-stabbing cold, pricking me everywhere. I hear more shots and just keep paddling and kicking.

Jess starts to squirm and I tighten my grip. I tilt my head and speak softly into her ear. "Be still. And don't talk." She stops moving for a moment but then starts squirming again and my head goes under. I come up choking, river water spewing from my mouth. Jess coughs up some water right into my ear. At least I know she's still breathing. She's flailing her arms and I catch a pointy elbow in the eye. I turn my head and use my good eye to focus on the shore. I need to get her out of the water before she kills me.

We round a tiny bend and I kick toward shore, hoping the bank will hide us.

Jess is shivering as I pull her out of the water.

My teeth knock together and my eye burns. "We've got to stay here and stay quiet and stay down."

"Trav," Jess says, "are Mom and Dad dead?" She shivers. "Are they?"

I pull her close and say into her ear, "I don't know." But in my mind I know. Somehow I know.

I feel the sun on my back and shift, exposing Jess to some of the warmth. "We're gonna be okay," I say, trying to make myself believe it. And then I repeat it over and over in my mind.

We're probably a half mile away from the patch of trees on the river. If I stand up, I'll be the tallest thing around. All I can hear is the rush of the river and Jess's soft weeping. I wonder if any of the shots were from our guns, if anyone even had a chance to shoot. And why didn't Mark detect their presence and sound a warning? I wonder how many there are. The shots came so fast. There had to be more than one shooter.

I flip onto my stomach. I rub my eye and keep opening and closing it until I can see out of it.

"Jess," I say. "You stay here. I'm going to scoot my head above the bank and see if I can see anything." She doesn't respond, just keeps crying softly. I touch her arm, and then crawl up on my elbows.

I poke my head over the riverbank. My right eye goes blurry again so I close it and just look with my left. I can see smoke rising from the patch of trees but that's all. No movement by the river. I make out the raft on the shore but can't tell if there are bodies lying beside it. I can't see the tents from this angle either. And all I hear is the river.

I scoot back down and put my arm around Jess. "We're gonna stay right here for now. The sun should help dry us."

Jess sticks her face into my side and puts her arm over my chest. She was running alongside the river with Sara and Molly just a little while ago, laughing and shrieking, her hair flying behind her. I don't know what the fight was about, but it saved her life.

As I lie there with her snuggled up against me, I catch a glimpse of an arm in a red shirt and the top of a head floating by, then the river claims them and they are gone. I feel vomit in the back of my throat and swallow it down. *Dad,* my mind screams. *Dad.* I pull Jess closer and keep peering into the river with my good eye, imagining all the bodies being sucked downriver. I feel my heart thumping through my wet shirt and Jess's heart pounding on my side.

Every so often another shot splits the air. Then it's quiet for a while, and then we hear another one.

We are going to need to move soon. But to where?

CHAPTER
8

"I'M HUNGRY," JESS SAYS. THE whine in her voice causes the hairs on the back of my neck to lift.

The sun is in the northwest sky. It goes around in a circle this time of year this far north, rising in the northeast and twenty-two hours later setting in the northwest, but it never dips too far below the surface. That's why it never gets dark in the summer.

I remember the bag Dad insisted I bury. "We'll be able to get some food soon. But we've got to be careful." I hope whoever ambushed us didn't also find the bag. I still can't believe that Dad is gone. I mean, I'm pretty sure that was Dad's body I'd seen floating by. And Mom, I don't know for sure. But if she's alive, then where is she? She knew I'd followed Jess downriver.

I peek over the bank. My right eye throbs some, but at least I can use it now. There's still smoke coming from our camp. And by the raft I count four people total. All men with beards. And they're wearing blue jackets, just like the guy who tried to jump me at the creek crossing.

I crawl back down the bank. "Jess, we're gonna have to wait here a little longer and stay real still."

I thought it couldn't get any worse after the fires last summer.

A yellow-black smoke had covered the land. And the air was pasty-hot. The kind of hot where every time you took a breath your mouth dried out.

"Unnatural," Dad said. "Something about this isn't right. The color, the taste."

Back in the day we would've turned on the radio or TV or got on the internet and found out what was going on. Or made a call. But since the buses had left last summer and the fires had burned the town, everything had jumped back a couple of clicks. No power. No communication beyond talking to someone face-to-face. No transportation beyond where your feet could carry you or a bicycle could pedal you. Occasionally, you saw someone driving a car who'd either hoarded some gas or found a vehicle with some gas in it, but that was the exception. And of course there were no firefighters and nothing to fight fires with.

"Get your mother and your sister," Dad said. "They're in the garden."

Once we were together, Dad told us we were heading to the river to wait this out. That he had a bad feeling about the fires.

We packed up the food we had. We still had some powdered milk and tea and some pasta, remnants from before the buses pulled out and we were left to fend for ourselves—or rather decided to stay and fend for ourselves. We also had the food we'd gotten from the land, salmon and moose that Mom had pressure-canned in quart jars. Some of it we took with us, but most of it we hid in the back of the crawl space under our house.

I could tell that Mom was holding back from saying, *I told you so.*

Dad focused on what to put in the packs, barking orders at me, Mom, and Jess. He was relentless, wouldn't rest or stop, except to glance out the window. The smoke forced its way into the house, between the logs and around the windows, and soon all we saw was sulfur-yellow air. My eyes burned and my throat was raw. We tied wet bandannas around our mouths and noses.

We went down to the Tanana River and, using a big piece of Styrofoam, floated our supplies out to a gravel bar. During the worst of it, we just lay in the water to stay cool and brushed hot cinders off our skin as they landed on us.

Afterward, when the houses in the hills were just memories, and charred bodies—people who hadn't made it to a river or a lake—dotted the landscape, the few people we ran into talked about how the fires were hotter than any fires they could remember, like they were burning tall and deep, like the soil itself was getting scorched.

CHAPTER
9

I CAN HEAR THEM YELLING, but don't know what they're saying. I see Jess's eyes go wide and put a finger to my lips. I'm pretty sure they don't have a clue we even exist, and I want to keep it that way.

A big splash and more yelling.

"Jess," I whisper. "We can't let them know we're here."

"Where are Mom and Dad?"

What am I supposed to say? I can't just tell her about Dad. But I have to tell her. "Jess," I say. "You saved my life by storming off and having a tantrum. If I hadn't followed you, I'd be dead."

Jess tilts her head and keeps her eyes on mine. I look away and then make eye contact again. I put my hand on her arm. "I . . . I'm pretty sure they're gone. Dead. But I'm not one hundred percent certain."

Jess just keeps those big blue eyes trained on mine, and it's all I can do to keep from breaking down and crying.

"Those voices. Those are the killers," I whisper. "We can't let them find us."

I hear another splash, then more yelling. And then a bunch more splashing. And laughter. Those murdering assholes. I feel my teeth grinding.

Their voices sound louder, like they're coming down the shore.

I grab a rock and get ready to stand up. "If they see us, just stay behind me."

Jess just nods. Then she reaches for a rock.

The sun has set and it is as dark as it's going to get, which isn't dark at all.

I hear more splashes, but they sound farther away now. And more shouting, but it's distant. Then we see them, four men crowded on the raft, with a pile of gear lashed down in the center, even with us, and about a quarter of the way across the river.

"The raft," Jess says. "Clint's raft. Our raft."

I hope they flip. Flip and drown.

I nudge Jess. "We've got to be extremely careful. Someone— one of the bad men—might still be left onshore."

"But we've got to see if anyone is alive," Jess says. "Maybe someone is hurt and not dead. Like that guy Dad found last winter. He wasn't dead yet."

Dad had come across someone who'd been shot. He rigged up a sled and dragged him home, but the guy didn't make it. He died the next day.

"You're right," I say. "Maybe Mom or some of the others are still alive."

"And Dad," Jess says.

I look away and say, "Maybe."

The raft shrinks in the distance as they work it toward the other side while drifting downstream. Maybe they'll ditch the raft and head north. Or maybe they're planning on going downriver like Clint. I don't care just as long as they don't come back here.

I turn toward the trees and pull Jess down.

"Smoke," I say. "From our camp." I don't know if it's just left over or if someone is tending it.

"My feet are cold," Jess says. "And I'm hungry." She stares right into my face. "What happened to your eye? It's all black and blue."

I don't want to give her one more thing to worry about so I say, "Must've slammed into a rock when we were crawling out of the river."

She wipes her nose on her sleeve. "Does it hurt?"

"A little." I remember she's hungry and say, "We're going back to that rock where I buried the bag, but we'll have to circle around in case someone is at the camp."

"But what if that *someone* is Mom or Dad?" Jess scrunches her face. "I want Mom."

"Okay," I say. "We'll check the camp first." She's not the only one who hopes to find Mom.

We circle around a good distance from the river and stand at the edge of the trees and can smell the smoke. Jess is just a step behind me, stopping when I stop, going when I go. I cup my hands behind my ears but hear only the flow of the river muted by the trees.

I take a step forward and Jess follows. We baby-step our way from tree to tree, pausing often to look and listen. I wipe mosquitoes from my face and neck and the back of my hands. The sun pokes up again, and long golden rays filter through the spruce.

We step to the edge of the trees and spot drag marks on the shore where the raft had been. I'm scanning for bodies, hoping to steer Jess away from any I see. We haven't spoken since we entered the woods, but now Jess nudges me and points. I follow her finger and see the outline of a person sitting against a tree facing the river and smoke rising from the firepit in front of him.

CHAPTER
10

MY HEART POUNDS THROUGH MY shirt. From where we stand I can see an arm extended toward the firepit. We can't see the person's head because it's blocked by the tree.

I keep my hand on Jess's arm and continue scanning the beach, searching for any sign of movement. I try to make out the tents in the trees off to the left, try to imagine where they are, but I can't see them.

I look Jess in the eye and point. We creep forward and to the right, toward a small clump of black spruce. Every little crunch under my feet booms in my ears like there are microphones attached to my shoes. I keep glancing toward the person by the fire ring, waiting for him to turn his head and pull out a gun.

I let out a silent sigh as we reach the clump of small spruce trees, branches hanging down to the ground. At least we've got some cover. The mosquitoes are having a feast on the back of my neck and I let them.

Then Jess grabs my arm, her nails biting through the thin fabric of my shirt. She puts her other hand over her mouth. And then I see it, see them.

Four naked bodies lying on the forest floor, facedown. Even from here it's easy to see that two are small. The other two have long brown hair; Mark's and Clint's wives. My eyes grow hot. Then my stomach constricts and I taste vomit in the back of my throat and swallow it down. I pull Jess toward me and hold her. She buries her face in my stomach and I can feel her whole body shaking. Why'd she have to see that? Why didn't I see them first and steer her away? Why didn't I leave her at the edge of the trees? But I just couldn't leave her, not for a second. I want her with me—all the time.

There has to be a better way than dragging her through all this death. But I don't know what it is. I mean, we're living in a time of death. After the second summer of fires, we all encountered burnt-up bodies. And then the following winter and spring, people who'd died of starvation. But there's something different about finding bodies that died because of a natural disaster or starvation, and finding bodies that were murdered. Bodies of girls she was playing with just hours ago.

I turn, keeping Jess pressed against me, and peer through the branches. I can see more of the man sitting by the fire, enough to know that he probably isn't alive either.

"Jess," I whisper. "I'm sorry you had to see that." My words feel so inadequate. How will I navigate her through this horror when I can barely keep it together myself?

She keeps her head pressed against me.

"I need to go look around," I say. "The guy by the fire. It's Clint. But he's . . . just like the girls."

Jess pulls back and turns her face upward. "They wanted to follow me when I walked off, but I told them to just leave me alone. I was mad, but it was stupid. They called me *little*." Jess buries her face in my stomach again.

I put my hand on her head. "You didn't do anything wrong. Nothing. You got that?"

I can feel her shaking.

"We can't change what happened to them, or to anyone." I think of Dad floating down the river. The only bodies unaccounted for are Mark's and my mom's. I blink back some tears. If anyone did anything wrong it was me. Didn't finish the cache in time. Convinced Dad that it was safe to come down here. And now, I've got Jess's life in my hands. Out here. With next to nothing.

Like she can feel my thoughts, Jess scrunches in tighter. "I want Mom."

I say, "Look. I need to search this place some more. Do you want to stay here while I look around?"

Jess takes a deep breath, then says softly, "I'm coming with you."

I'm pretty sure there's no need to be quiet but can't be absolutely certain. From our clump of trees we walk to the fire ring. Clint is bound to the tree. I don't know if they shot him before or after, but he's dead. My shoulders and head collapse forward, like something from above is pressing them toward the ground. I feel empty; I know it will all hit me later—and I dread that.

All the tents—gone. Everything is gone.

How will I ever feed her?

I put my arm around Jess and turn her away from Clint and what used to be our camp.

We find Mark's blood-soaked body at the edge of the river, the water tugging at his feet. I can't bear to look at him. I just want to erase everything that's happened here, so I roll him the rest of the way in and watch the current take him.

"Come on, Jess," I say, pulling her along. "There's nothing here for us." I just want to dig up the stuff sack. At least that's something

I can do, instead of exposing my sister to any more of this death and destruction.

"Wait!" Jess yells. "What about Mom and Dad?"

I stop and face Jess. I take a breath. "I saw Dad when we were hiding downriver."

Jess scrunches up her face. "What do you mean?"

I grind my foot into the ground and just say it. "He floated by. I saw the top of his head, and his arm. Wearing that red shirt. It had to be him. Then the current pulled him under."

"What else did you see?" Jess raises her voice. "What about Mom?"

"I was gonna tell you about Dad, but I couldn't. I just wasn't ready, and we had enough to worry about with just hiding."

"What about Mom?" Jess repeats.

"I didn't see Mom."

"You'd tell me if you did?"

"Yes," I say. "I told you about Dad, didn't I?"

"Then she could still be alive."

"Jess, I don't think—"

"Why not? We survived."

"We got lucky. We were out of sight thanks to you, and then the river took us."

The sun breaks over the trees, bathing the beach in light, making this place look so inviting. It was the perfect place to build a raft.

"Maybe the river took her, too," she says.

I don't want to sound so negative but don't want to give her false hope. "Mom was with the other women. She couldn't—"

"How do you know?"

"I don't know," I say. "All I know is that I don't see her here."
And truth be told, I'm glad I don't. If she's dead, I don't want Jess to
see her like that.

Jess folds her arms across her chest. "But don't you think she
would've been with the others if they'd caught her?"

Jess has a point. It's been hours since we hid and then worked
our way back over here to check things out. She wasn't on the raft.
I don't think it's likely that she escaped, but it's possible. It's also
possible that she tried to escape into the river and they shot her
down and the river took her. I mean, if I hadn't been looking at just
the right place and at the right time I wouldn't have seen Dad.

"What do you want to do?" I ask.

Jess just stands there. Then the tears start flowing down her
cheeks. I try to hug her but she pushes me away.

I turn to the massive river, and then to the empty forest stretching out on the other side. We're just tiny specks, specks that don't
matter to the river or the forest. Me and Jess, all we matter to are
each other.

CHAPTER
11

"JUST TELL ME IF YOU see anything," I say. "Anything at all." We're at the rocks where I buried the bag.

"Okay," Jess says.

We came here after scouring that patch of forest where we'd met Clint, searching for Mom, calling for Mom. Then we walked downriver, a couple miles past where we hid. We didn't find her. We didn't find anything else, either.

I'm scooping dirt with my hands and it's slow going. I used a trowel when I dug the hole, and I packed the dirt and ash back in tight.

"Do you think Mom could be farther downriver?" Jess asks.

I push some dirt and ash away from the hole so it won't fall back in. "I think we would've seen her by now because she would've come back looking for us."

"So you think she's dead?" Jess asks. "She can't be."

"We didn't find her." I feel my stomach heave, but nothing comes up. I take a breath and shake my head. "We've been here for hours. She's not here."

"But we never found her," Jess says. "Maybe she got away. Like we did."

I look into her big blue eyes and want so much for her to be right. Mom was good at giving Jess what she needed. They were more than a mother and a daughter. I tried to make time to play with Jess, but Dad always had me helping him scrape together our life, so Mom and Jess—because we were so isolated—were like good friends. I was envious because I didn't feel that with Dad. Whatever we were working on, there was always a push from him to do more and do it better. Like he was the boss and I was the worker. Now I'll have to be here for Jess in every way I can. Brother, mother, father, friend. My chest tightens like there's a rope around it and someone is cinching it down.

"I'm sure she tried to survive." I rub my bruised eye. "I just don't think she made it. She knew about this bag buried by these rocks. She would've come here."

I finish digging in silence, trying to figure out what to do or say that will help Jess deal with our situation, but I come up empty. I start pulling jars out of the bag, thinking some food might help.

"There's more here than just salmon," I say. Jess is sitting next to me, our backs to one of the rocks, facing downriver toward the group of trees. I take a coil of rope and three quart jars of salmon out of the bag and set them down, and I hold up the fourth jar. Inside it I see a small pistol and one of those steel fire starters that creates a rainstorm of sparks when one metal surface runs across the other. And a piece of paper, folded.

I work the tiny pistol out of the jar and click open the dial. Just one bullet. I slide the dial back into place and set the gun down, then pull the paper out and unfold it.

"Jess," I say. "It looks like a letter. To us." She scoots closer to me and I start reading out loud.

Travis and Jess,

If one or both of you are reading this, it probably means that something has happened to your mother and myself and you are on your own. I decided to write this after we made the decision to go north. I knew there were dangers involved. We discussed them and decided to go anyway because staying in the Sacrifice Area wasn't working. Instead of people banding together and forming a new community, people withdrew and fended for themselves, and I had no choice but to do the same for us if we were going to survive.

I can't say what happened or what to expect, because I am gone, but I wanted you to know that you have options. The cache in the Sacrifice Area should provide you with enough food to head south. I only mention this because your mother and I debated for a long time about which way to go. We chose north because of the old road. We thought it would be easier.

There are ways to cross the mountains south of the Sacrifice Area to get to the settlements that are rumored to be on the coast near Anchorage. Between the mountains and the settlements there is a Buffer Zone. I know people crossed back and forth the first couple of years after the government abandoned us. And it is unclear what the settlements are like, or if they even exist, but if we failed at going north, that was our next plan, to head toward Anchorage—or at least, what used to be Anchorage—in search of the settlements.

And if you are still on the south side of the Yukon and all you have is the food in this bag, then please go back to the cache and head south. It is the only way to make it. I wish I was still here with you. Just know that I am, in spirit.

Love, Dad

P.S. Trav, I was never very good at saying this, but I just want you to know that I'm God-awful proud of you for all the ways you've stood by my side and done what was necessary, and I know you'll keep rising to the challenges that you confront. And Jess, you listen to your big brother. If he's alive, he's in charge now.

I flip the paper over.

My Dearest Travis and Jess,
I hope both of you are reading this, because I can't bear to think about either of you being alone. There is nothing more I'd want than to be with you two right now. To watch you live and grow and discover. Just know that your lives are the greatest gift ever given to me and the best thing you can do for me is to go on with your lives and make the best choices you can. And please treat each other with kindness and compassion. I know if you are reading this that things are bad, probably as bad as they've ever been for you both. For that, I am sorry. Sorry that we stayed at all when we had the chance to leave. I have faith that there are places in the world where people

still treat each other like humans and I hope you find one of those places. Please don't feel sorry for me. Just knowing that you are reading this gives me hope.

Love, Mom

I put my arm around Jess and she leans into me. I feel my eyes growing hot and then the tears are flowing down my cheeks into my beard. A sob erupts from Jess and I hold her tighter as her body convulses in sadness. We sit like this for several minutes, saying nothing.

I take some slow, deep breaths to clear my mind, because I am in charge now and I need to take care of Jess.

I picture the long journey back, knowing that our house—our burnt-out basement—has probably been looted. I hope that no one has found the cache. And then we have to make our way south, just the two of us, in search of some settlements that may not even exist. As much as I disagreed with Dad these past couple of years and was totally sick of all the precautions he took, I'm already missing his driving energy. Missing him. How can I do this without him?

I think back to what he wrote in his note. He's counting on me to take charge. I want to curl up in a ball, roll into the river, and disappear.

And Mom. I was hoping that once we got out of here I'd actually be able to spend more time with her because I wouldn't have to be a continual servant to Dad's screwed-up frontier dream. I think back to the note and his words at the end of it. At least now I know that he was proud of me, that all my hard work didn't go unappreciated, even if he couldn't bring himself to tell me that when he was alive.

The sun is working its way into the northwest, just starting to shine in my eyes. I shift a little and suddenly am very hungry, like my stomach has just woken up from a yearlong nap.

I take a breath and wipe my eyes. "Let's eat a little salmon."

"I don't want to walk all the way back," Jess says. "And the other side of the river, it didn't burn. I wish we were across."

"I think going south is our best option. Maybe our only real option given how little food we have."

Jess scoots away from me, then turns and looks me in the eye. "Just because you read those letters doesn't mean that Mom's dead."

"She's not here," I say. "I wish she were, but she's not."

"Maybe she swam across, and now she's waiting for us."

I glance at the river and remember how hard it was to just stay afloat for a minute or two. No way could anyone swim that, the silt filling your clothes and dragging you down. I don't want to keep putting it in Jess's face, but don't want to lead her on either. Mom was strong, but she wasn't that strong.

"We'll have to go soon." I hold up a jar of salmon. "This food will only get us so far."

I remember Mom's words about treating each other with kindness and making the best choices we can. I don't want to drag Jess south, but I will if I have to.

Jess just sits there.

"Even if she did survive," I say, "she knows what she wrote. She knows where we'll go."

Jess stares straight into my eyes, and for a split second she looks just like Mom and I feel a shiver travel up my spine.

"We'll get through this. We'll make it," I say. "I promise." I just hope I can keep the promise.

PART
TWO

CHAPTER
12

"YOU THINK THEY'RE LIVING THERE?" Jess says.

"We'll just have to watch for a while to find out."

We're belly-down on top of a ridge overlooking our old burnt-out basement. I count at least four people standing outside the entrance, but it's confusing because they keep going inside and coming back out. Like maybe they just found the place and are checking to see if anyone is coming.

You can't see the cache from the basement because there's a little hill behind the basement you have to climb and then go down first, but it'd be risky to go there with people so close. But we need to go soon because we are freaking starving.

The long walk back was brutal. More monotonous than the walk north because we knew what was coming and knew that the longer it took the hungrier we'd be. When we rested, we took turns sleeping and keeping watch. Jess always watched back from where we'd come, hoping to see Mom kicking up some ash on the road. We hadn't seen anyone. I'm proud of Jess. We ran out of food three days ago, but somehow she found the energy to keep going. Yeah, I carried her piggyback style about a third of the time, but still, she pulled through. We filled the empty jars with water, so at least we won't go thirsty while we figure out what to do about the invasion below.

"Maybe they're friendly," Jess says. "Like Sara and Molly and their parents were."

I'm light-headed from lack of food, but grateful that this part of the journey is almost over. My eyes keep closing. I just want to sleep and pretend that my parents are still alive and that I don't have to live the rest of my life without them.

It hasn't rained in a while, and the ash has dried out, so any step anyone takes can be seen from miles around. Clouds are spilling over the mountains to the south. Mountains we have to find our way through if we are going to search for the settlements.

* * *

"Travis," Jess says.

I feel her hand on my side.

"They're coming."

I open my eyes and roll back onto my stomach. Two people have left the basement and are making their way up the hill. I hope they don't see any evidence of the cache, or if they do, I hope they'll think it's just a grave. I tried to make it look natural, so the patch of ground containing the cache would be indistinguishable from the rest of the ashy surroundings.

"Just stay down," I say. "They can't see us unless we move."

I have the pistol. One bullet. I've never shot anyone. Never even shot *at* anyone.

They are halfway up the hill now and are carrying long, thin poles. Maybe metal rods. Probably pieces of rebar from the back corner of the basement.

They keep stopping and looking around, but they are on a dead-center course for the cache. We are above them, maybe a quarter to a half mile away and off to the side.

At the top of the little hill, they stop. If they keep going down into the depression, they'll hit the cache. If they continue walking after that, they'll be climbing toward the ridgetop—where we are. Either way, we're potentially screwed.

I'm sick of sitting and watching, always waiting for someone else to make a move. Just like Dad. I know there's wisdom in not acting too fast and in studying what's happening, and there are advantages to remaining unseen. His cautiousness helped us survive. And Dad had not been a cautious person before things got tight. He adapted. A true survivalist.

It's hard to know when the right time is to show yourself. I mean, it'd be easy to just keep hiding until we die of starvation, but if we show ourselves too early, or to the wrong people, the results could be deadly.

And I have Jess to consider. I know what happened to Molly and Sara. I'd rather die than risk that happening to Jess. But I didn't walk two hundred miles just to sit back and watch two guys dig up our cache.

"Trav," Jess whispers. "What if they keep coming?"

Now I see what kind of pressure my dad was under. The macho part of me wants to stand up and tell those guys to turn around, because just lying here I feel like a wimp. But if I want us to survive, then avoiding detection for as long as possible might work to my advantage. If only I hadn't been so insistent about approaching Clint, maybe Dad would've come up with a different plan. Maybe he'd still be alive, and in charge.

"We've got the upper hand as long as they don't know we're

here," I whisper. "For now, let's just watch." But I know it's a lie. They have the upper hand. There are four of them.

They keep going down into the depression. Even though it's a sea of gray ash, we know where the supplies are buried because I positioned two rocks so they form an equilateral triangle with the cache—about fifty feet for each side. Dad taught me that trick.

Now they are walking around in little circles and they keep stabbing their poles into the ground. Every time a pole hits, it feels like a knife stabbing me.

Who are they? And how could they freaking know? What did I leave that clued them in? And where? I even brushed my footprints clean coming and going every time. Dad insisted.

How could they know?

CHAPTER
13

THEY LEAVE ONE POLE STICKING up right on the freaking spot and then walk back up the little hill toward the basement and start down the other side. It's now or never.

I stand up. "Jess, we've got to get down there before they come back. They probably went back for the shovels we left in the basement." I grab the sack with the jars and rope and start down the hill, the pistol in my other hand.

Jess catches up, but before she can speak I say, "We're going to run to the cache, grab the metal pole they left there, and run to the top of the little hill. If we can control the hill with the gun and that metal pole they left us, we can keep them away from the cache."

"But you've only got one bullet."

"They don't know that," I say. "Maybe I can even *persuade* them to give us a shovel."

"What if they have guns?"

"I didn't see them carrying any. I know that doesn't mean they don't have any for sure."

"Trav, I—"

"We need that cache—bad. And it's ours. Not theirs, whoever the hell they are."

I break into a jog and Jess keeps pace. I know those people are probably as desperate as we are. Still, we did the work to catch and can and bury that fish. Not them.

Ash is puffing up all around us, betraying where we are, but we need to get in position so we can point the gun at them from the top of the little hill above the basement. If they have guns, we can lie down and keep them from coming up. I can do that while Jess digs in safety behind me. And if we have to fight them hand-to-hand, we can break some jars and use jagged glass.

We hit a level stretch. I pick up the pace and Jess falls back a few steps, which is fine with me. I'd rather have her behind me. A little ash has worked its way into my eyes and they are itching like they used to in the spring when the birch trees would put out their pollen.

The cache is still a ways off, maybe a hundred yards, and the top of the little hill another hundred. My stomach clenches when I see two heads pop up, then two more. And all of a sudden there are four people, dressed in bulky camo clothing, like what soldiers wear. All sporting green hats like some badass military group. Three of them carry shovels and the fourth has a bow. They've topped the little hill and are heading for the cache.

I run faster. Now, I just want to get to the cache before them. Show them I mean business. But I've got to admit, they look pretty intimidating. And they just keep walking like they own the place, like I don't even exist. Part of me wishes we were back up on the ridge, watching and hiding, but it's too late for that now. The guy out front is taller than the other three.

I reach the cache and drop our green sack. I try to yell for them to stay back, but I can hear my voice cracking. My throat is coated with ash. Maybe they see my gun, because they finally stop.

Jess comes crashing in behind me, bumping my back. I stumble a little but recover.

The person without the shovel is down on one knee with an arrow nocked into his bow.

"This is ours," I yell. "We buried it. Me and my sister." I point to Jess.

The man keeps his arrow trained on me. I hope he isn't a good shot, because he's close.

The lead guy, the tall one, holds up his hand, and the person with the bow points the arrow toward the ground.

"I think these guys are starting to see things our way," I whisper to Jess. "Maybe they aren't as tough as they look." *Maybe I can even force them to hand over a shovel or two*, I think.

Jess takes a step up so she's beside me. "There's a lot of them," she whispers. "And they're kind of big." I see a few tears trickling down her cheek.

"Without the gun, we would've been sunk," I whisper.

"Listen up," I yell. "This is our land. That basement, too. We were gone but we're back now. You'll have to leave."

The lead guy with his hand raised puts it back down, and the person with the bow points it back at me. I go down on one knee to make myself less of a target. Jess steps behind me and I feel her hands gripping my waist.

I only have one bullet, and if I get hit by an arrow I don't know what will become of Jess with these green monsters. But I can't give in. We need the food and everything else in the cache.

"If it wasn't for your sister, we would've already fired," says the guy who has been raising and lowering his hand. Except it doesn't sound like a guy. "If you put the gun down, we'll put the bow down."

"The leader's a girl," Jess says.

I take a breath. Girl or no girl, we still need the food.

"We usually shoot to kill when threatened," she says.

"I don't want to hurt anyone," I say. "I just want what's mine. What's ours."

"We've got the shovels. You need the shovels," their leader says. "Can't we work together?"

CHAPTER
14

"THERE USED TO BE EIGHT of us. I won't tell you what happened to the other four before they died," Willa says. She's the tall one who was out front and seems to be the leader of their group. We've already dug up the cache and hauled it all down to the basement. Jess is inside helping to organize it. Me and Willa are on watch at the edge of the hill.

I ask her about her parents.

"Parents?" she says. "I never knew them." She scratches at the scar running across her cheek. "Gave me away right after I was born, I've been told."

I shake my head. "Where'd you live before the government pulled the plug?"

She sighs. "In a group home. It was an actual house, but it was pretty extreme. They always kept it locked and it had a big fence around it. It was a place for any girl who didn't fit in, or didn't have parents, or whatever. Just somewhere to put people they didn't know what to do with. A very restrictive place."

She tells me about how they let them out as the fires were approaching. They thought they were going to be bussed out, like everyone else who wanted to go, but instead they were abandoned.

I tell her about how my dad turned down the offer to get us out because he wanted to stay.

"I can't believe you could've gotten out, but didn't," Willa says.

"The first year was okay because there were so few people and lots of food," I say, not ready to talk about what happened to my parents.

"Maybe out here in the hills," Willa says. "But where I was, east of Fairbanks, close to the prison and the old army base . . ." She touches her scar again. "Like I said, there used to be eight of us."

*　*　*

Even though they all dress the same and have short hair, it's pretty easy to tell them apart. Willa is the tallest and has her scar.

Randie has freckles spilling down both sides of her nose. And when she takes her cap off, bright red hair sticks up about a half inch from her head. When she was seven, her parents died after their car struck a moose.

Tam always carries her bow. And she has blond hair, is almost as tall as Willa, and, as far as I can tell, never smiles. She hasn't said a thing about herself.

Maxine has dark hair. And she has a low voice and a sparkle in her big brown eyes. Jess has been sticking pretty close to her, but right now Tam and Jess are on watch and Willa is asleep in the back room. Me, Maxine, and Randie are organizing supplies.

"We lost our parents at the Yukon River," I say. "My dad was gunned down, and my mom"—my voice cracks—"we never found her body, but I'm pretty sure she was shot and then dumped into the river." I feel my eyes getting hot. I take a breath and then I tell them about our plan to head south and hopefully make it through the mountains and the Buffer Zone to search for some settlements on the coast where Anchorage used to be. All before winter.

"It will be a while before this land heals," Maxine says. "But it will come back. And when it does, so will I." She's the sole survivor after her dad tried to kill the whole family. He shot Maxine's mom, her brother, and himself. He shot Maxine, too, but she lived.

"I'll never come back," Randie says. She's putting jars of salmon in rows.

"It's not much food for six," I say. "But maybe in the mountains there'll be pockets of land that escaped the fires. Maybe fish, or other animals. And berries."

"Twenty-eight jars," Randie says. "Less than five a piece."

"If we find trees, we can make spears," Maxine says. "These will be good." She runs her hands over the collection of ancient stone spearheads we dug up from the cache.

"I made a trip to the university museum with my dad to get them," I say. "After the first fires."

* * *

"Trav," Dad said, "wood burns. Plastic and glass melt. So does metal. Rubber burns. But stone, it survives."

"Why do we even need to do this?" I asked. "Sounds like a major hassle."

We had plenty of ammo for the shotgun. And so many houses had been abandoned that everything was in abundance. So I didn't see any reason why we had to dig through a burnt-out museum, or a burnt-out anything for that matter. The entire university campus had burned in the fires the first summer, compliments of the government. We had heavy leather boots on and it was at least 90 degrees. Yellow jackets buzzed in the air and covered parts of the walls. They were everywhere. We could feel the hum, like the whole earth was vibrating.

Dad stopped walking. I swatted at a yellow jacket that was circling around my head.

"This whole place is powering down," Dad said. "I just want to be ready."

When I was little, Dad had a job at the university. He was some kind of research technician for the Anthropology Department. Then his position got axed with a bunch of others.

By the light of our flashlights we picked our way over a river of bumpy plastic in what used to be a basement auditorium for staff seminars, according to Dad.

"What you saw in the displays," Dad said, "was just a fraction of what they had."

My eyes were burning from something. Maybe the burnt plastic. My head throbbed.

We went through a burnt-out doorway. I didn't understand why the ceiling hadn't collapsed from the weight of the first floor caving in. And it's obvious that the fire had raged through here—the cement walls were blackened, but thankfully still upright.

We sifted through the ash on the floor and, sure enough, we found spearheads and arrowheads. The real things. Ancient. Made from a black stone—obsidian. The sharpest natural substance on earth.

"We may never have to use these," Dad said. "But you never know. And even if we don't, they'll be good to have. As a remembrance of how people used to live. And a reminder that we could live that way again."

★ ★ ★

Maxine picks up a spearpoint. "My ancestors traded for this black rock. It came from somewhere far away. It was valuable. The best."

"Do you think they have electricity in the settlements?" Randie asks. "And running water?"

"I don't know," I say. "All I know is that my mom and dad were going to head south and search for them if we got stopped going north. I think the earthquakes caused a lot of damage down there. Damage that they couldn't fix. But it's got to be better than this place." I look away. We were so close to crossing the Yukon.

"We'll need to go soon if we want the food to last," Randie says.

They each have a small backpack, but I'm not sure what's in them.

Besides the spearpoints and salmon, there was some spare clothing in the cache. Two wool shirts and two raincoats. Two knit caps. And two small packs. And about a hundred feet of quarter-inch-diameter yellow rope.

And in the basement there's an assortment of stuff—some tools, dishes, cups—basic household stuff. I just want to bring the essentials so we can travel as fast as possible. They want to go south. We want to go south. I know they're tough because they've survived this long. These girls are about my age, I guess. And the one that doesn't smile, Tam, looks a little like Stacy.

In my mind I flash back to Stacy, to the last time I saw her. Back then, I couldn't imagine ever being without her. I don't even know if she survived the trip south, but I want to find out.

"There's nothing stopping us from starting south today except picking the route," I say. "My dad said there are ways to cross the mountains even though the melting glaciers have made a mess of things and the rivers have cut new channels."

"Even under all this ash," Maxine says, "the land is alive. We'll just have to pay attention to it."

"The farther north we went, the more trees we saw," I say. "There were even mosquitoes."

Maxine laughs. "Where there's mosquitoes, there's meat."

"This place just seems so dead. I mean, last year when the salmon didn't come back and fires burned everything up again, it hit me just how dead it was. Big-time dead. My dad said the organic layer of the soil got burned off. And that's the main reason the plants are so slow to come back. Usually, fires don't burn that hot. The places where we see fireweed sprouting—maybe those spots didn't get totally scorched."

"The land has been traumatized," Maxine says. "It can't support much life right now. That's why we need to leave. To give it a chance to heal."

"I don't ever want to come back," Randie says.

"I'm coming back," Maxine says. "Someday."

I turn to Maxine. "All I want is to get my sister to a place where she can have a life."

Maxine leans forward and says, "She already has a life. So do you. We all do. Embrace it."

"My sister saw six dead bodies on the riverbank. That's not the kind of life I want for her."

"Travis," Maxine says. "We've all seen death. Ugly death. Up close. It's everywhere."

"No doubt," says Randie. "I just don't want to experience it personally."

"Just a safe place for my sister where she can be happy, that's all I want." *And for me too*, I think, but I don't say that.

"I don't know if anyone will ever be safe again," Maxine says.

"But that doesn't mean you can't be happy, or grateful just to be alive in this moment."

"In this moment," I say, "my parents just died and—"

"Travis," Maxine cuts in, "that sad moment has passed. This is the moment where our group has found your group." She looks me in the eye. "We're making a new family. Right now." She smiles a big smile and I feel the corners of my mouth start to curve upward in response.

I still feel a deep sadness for the loss of my parents, but I'm happy to be getting to know these new people.

Then Jess's warning whistle fills the basement.

She must've spotted someone.

CHAPTER
15

THEY ARE STILL A WAYS off but appear to be coming toward us. I have my tiny pistol and the knife on my belt. Tam has her bow. Randie and Willa are armed with seven-foot-long pieces of rebar. Maxine and Jess hold shovels. I want Jess to go inside, but seeing her with Maxine makes me pause. Jess needs the companionship. And she's part of the group. So I decide that, for now, she can stay.

I guess living people mean the possibility of food. But they also mean the possibility of death. I don't know what I'd do if I was out of food and I saw a group of people. Will some people kill you even if you just ask for food and don't threaten them? Will they just shoot as you approach? The rules of life have changed and I'm still figuring them out.

"Let me do the talking," I say.

"That all depends on what you're going to say," Willa says.

"I won't know until I see them." One thing I don't want them to know is that I'm the only guy. Not that these girls aren't capable of kicking some ass, but I don't want to deal with macho dudes getting all overconfident. Let them see my six-foot frame and four "guys" in camo clothing.

They're walking side by side but I can't tell how many. Four. Five. Six. Maybe more.

"Let's move," I say. "All the way to the edge of the hill. All of us."

"But that'll make us more visible," Willa says.

"Exactly," I say. "Last time people approached me and my dad here, we stayed back by the entrance to the basement and we didn't know where they'd pop up, and they surrounded us. Put us at a disadvantage. We need to be right at the edge of the hill so we can watch their every move."

I walk forward and everyone follows. Now I can clearly see five people down in the valley. We watch them walk for a few minutes, leaving a trail of ash in the air.

I wonder just how many people are still in the Sacrifice Area. Just these five, plus us? Fifty? A hundred? Two hundred? There is no way to know. But I do know one thing. Over time, I've seen fewer and fewer people. I'm guessing a lot of people starved to death last winter.

I put my hand to my forehead to block the sun and squint. "Anyone see anything on them? Guns? Packs? Anything?"

"The guys on the ends, they've each got a dark strap running across their chests," Maxine says. "Like maybe they've got guns on their backs."

"Yeah," Randie says. "I see that, too."

"If they have ammo for those guns, we're at a serious disadvantage," I say.

"Maybe they won't come up here," Jess says. "We've seen people just walk on by."

"Tam," Willa says, "how close before you could get a good shot?"

"About halfway up the hill," Tam says. "But shooting down a steep hill, I haven't done too much of that."

"We can't stand here and let them take aim," Willa says.

I keep my eyes on their movement. "If they reach for their guns, we can lie down. But if we back off now, they'll know we don't have any firepower."

Willa turns to me. "I don't like just standing here."

"What do you want to do?" I ask. "If we run down the hill, we lose the advantage of being higher than them. If we back off toward the basement so they can't see us, they'll take that as a sign of weakness. Plus, we won't be able to see them. And if we do get into a shouting match, I want to do the shouting. If they find out there's a bunch of girls up here, they—"

"Wait." Willa points to Tam. "That girl was gonna put an arrow through your heart until we realized Jess was a girl."

I glance at Tam and her eyes lock onto mine—like maybe she's still considering shooting me.

"All I'm saying is there's sick people out there." I pause. "I understand why you'd want to kill a guy first and ask questions later, even though in my case you would've killed the wrong guy. And I understand that you all could turn on me and take me out. It's obvious you all have a lot more fighting experience than me. But we're on the same side. Why not use my voice to our advantage if it comes to that?"

"I hear what you're saying," Willa says. "We definitely don't advertise our gender all the time. But I'll say this: We've run into groups of guys who got overconfident when they found out we were girls. Not many of them lived to tell about it."

"Okay," I say, "I get that. Maybe we should just wait and see if we even need to speak. Maybe just our presence up here—showing them that we're not backing down—will make them retreat."

The five people in the flats have stopped but are looking

our way. Besides Jess, we look like a bunch of guys. And camo can be pretty intimidating. In my mind it implies military training. Badass dudes trained to fight. Killing machines that thrive on conflict.

"Maybe they're reconsidering," Maxine says. She puts her arm around Jess. "We must look pretty buff."

"Do you have to make a joke out of everything?" Willa says.

"One life," Maxine says. "They're too far away to shoot at us. If you let the possibility of death get you down, you're just wasting your life."

"But if you don't pay attention," Willa says, "you might not have a life."

"Do you think they can see my bow?" Tam asks.

I turn toward her and say, "Maybe." But she just glares at me. I keep my eyes trained on hers for a moment and then turn away.

I wonder where she learned to shoot that thing and if she's actually any good.

The people are still standing in the flats, looking our way. We can hear little snippets of their voices carrying across the ash, but no clear words. I wish they'd either keep coming or change direction. I just want to know. At least they've paused. I doubt they'd be doing that if it was just me and Jess up here.

Gunfire explodes in my ears, and I see Willa lunge forward and fall face-first over the edge of the hill. Another shot on top of the first, and Randie is down.

I dive to the ground and feel dirt and ash splatter my face, the next shot just missing me. Confusion racks my brain. I search for Jess but don't see her, then catch a glimpse of Tam as she lets an arrow fly toward the basement behind us. It enters a man's neck and pushes him back. He drops his gun and grabs the arrow shaft with both hands. Then Tam buries another arrow into his torso and he goes down, blood seeping onto his light blue jacket.

Ambushed. Why didn't I have someone keep watch behind us? I was so concerned with what was in front of us, those guys approaching from the valley. They stopped because they saw it. They watched it happen. They must be in on it. And now, they are walking toward us.

CHAPTER
16

"JESS," I YELL. "JESS."

Tam points down the hill. I run to the edge and see Maxine lying on top of Jess. Have they been shot, too? I only remember three shots—Willa, Randie, and the one that almost got me in the face.

I take four giant steps, and I'm by Maxine's side. I shake her shoulder. "Are you okay? How about Jess? Come on. We've got to take cover."

Out of the corner of my eye, I see Tam huddling over Willa.

I pull Maxine up. Jess is shaking. I grab her with my other hand. "Jess, let's go. They're coming."

Tears are streaming down Maxine's cheeks. "This world is so messed up."

"Just go check on Randie." I point across the hillside. "And hurry. This isn't over."

"Dead," Tam calls, pointing at Willa. "I'm glad I got that swine."

I scoop up Jess and carry her up the hill, my feet digging into the ash. When she sees the man impaled by two arrows, she turns her head and pukes. I set her down, run to the dead man, and grab his gun. It's an old pump-action shotgun just like Dad's. One slug in the chamber and two in the magazine. I frisk him, searching for more ammo, but find none. Maxine and Tam top the hill. Maxine has the two shovels in her hands.

I make eye contact with Maxine, but she just shakes her head.

"Maxine," I say, "you and Jess go inside and stuff as much as you can into four packs. Quick. I want to be up on the ridge behind us by the time these guys reunite with their dead friend."

I tap Tam's arm and we crawl to the edge of the hill and peer down into the valley. The guys are closing in, slow and steady, the two on the ends carrying shotguns in their hands.

Randie and Willa lie crumpled below us. I wish there was something I could do for them. Something to show them respect. Bury them. Anything. But we don't have time.

We don't need this place. Any place, I decide, is a trap. We need the food in our packs, whatever else is useful, and we need to keep moving south, all the way to the coast. But first we have to get up on the ridge and regroup, before more bullets start flying.

Tam glances back toward the basement, then says, "They are taking too long. I'm going to go help them."

"Great," I say. "I'll keep watch here. We need to move."

Tam runs to the basement and down the steps. I turn back toward the guys in the flats. They are almost to the base of the hill and are starting to spread out. The two guns are all I can see among the five of them. I've used Dad's shotgun a couple of times, but I'm no expert. And if they knew how many bullets their buddy had, then they know I don't have enough from him to get all five of them. Or maybe they don't even know that their man is dead. I mean, Tam killed him with arrows right in front of the basement. No way could they have seen it, or heard it.

I hear footsteps and turn. Maxine appears, then Jess, each with a pack. Then Tam carrying two packs.

I shoulder the pack Tam offers. Then I kick the dead guy in the head because I have to do something to show respect for Willa and Randie. "Everyone kick him, then we're off."

I know it's kind of stupid and sort of warped, but I want everyone to have some closure, unlike what Jess and I had with Dad's death and Mom's disappearance.

They all kick him like it's the most natural thing in the world, and then we're snaking our way down the depression behind the basement, past the empty cache, and up the ridge.

From the top of the ridge, the same place Jess and I sat just two days ago, we watch the five guys swarm the basement entrance like a bunch of agitated yellow jackets.

Jess curls into Maxine.

Tam sits with her knees pulled to her chest. "If only I'd seen him sooner." Tears run down her cheeks. "That bastard." She keeps rocking back and forth.

"It's my fault," I say. "I should've had someone watching our backs."

"Travis," Maxine says, "quit acting like you're in charge. Any of us could've decided we needed a back watch."

"Yeah," I say. "But I convinced everyone to move to the edge of the hill. And now . . ." I dig my feet into the ash. I'd convinced Dad to team up with Clint, too. That made three dead, and one missing but probably dead, based on my plans. I suck.

I turn to Tam. "If it weren't for you, we'd all be dead."

"Willa," Tam says, talking to the sky. "And Randie. I'm sorry." Then she bows her head.

"I know I screwed up." I kick some more ash. Lives. I cost us lives. I gave orders that killed two people that I'd just met.

Huge clouds are piling up to the south. A crack of thunder invades my ears.

No one says anything, so I keep on talking. "Those guys might come this way, and we need to decide what we're going to do. Stay and fight, or just start heading south."

Maxine says, "We survived by fighting when there were no other options. I'm not proud of how many people we've killed, but—"

"I've got two arrows left," Tam says. "What's in the gun?"

"Three slugs," I say. "And one bullet in the pistol."

Maxine pulls Jess closer. "We have to think."

"Okay," I say. "Here's what I think. As much as I'd like to waste those guys down there, I don't think they're worth the ammo unless they're threatening us. I mean, I'd love some revenge, but not at the expense of being helpless later."

"Ditto that." Tam nods and sniffles. "I'd love to kill them all, but it'd leave us with next to nothing for protection." Then she starts rocking back and forth again.

"Maxine? Jess?"

Jess leans into Maxine. "I'll do what Maxine wants to do."

"Girl," Maxine says, "we're gonna make some serious tracks through this ash."

But that's the problem. If they want to follow us, it'll be easy.

The ridge we're walking on angles southwest on a steady incline with a few dips. Before the fires those dips would've been boggy and thick with black spruce, but now they're just boggy. On a few protected slopes the remains of birch trees still stand, charred and lifeless.

Most of the white spruce died from beetle infestations and the poplars from the leaf miners years ago. Yeah, this place was changing even before the fires.

Warmer winters meant greater insect survival. And some summers the yellow jackets were thicker than the mosquitoes. We'd put out five-gallon buckets half-filled with soapy water and some salmon on a piece of floating wood. In a day or two there'd be a few thousand drowned yellow jackets in each bucket. And it'd be like that all summer. Now you still see some, often on dead bodies, but they haven't recovered from the fires either. Nothing has.

The first drops of rain splatter in the ash.

Tam and I stop on a little knob, the high point of the ridge, and wait for Maxine and Jess. I'm pretty sure we're standing on top of Ester Dome. The oldest marathon in Alaska was in Fairbanks, and the high point of the race was Ester Dome. Dad used to run it, and when I was little, my mom and I would meet him at different points along the course. I was going to run it with him someday, but that was back when people were still running for fun. Once the government pulled out, you ran when it was practical—to accomplish a goal.

"When Jess and Maxine catch up, we should head toward the Tanana River," I tell Tam. Off in the distance a yellow-brown swath of water carves its way through the burnt-out land. A few ribbons of green highlight the places where fireweed has sprouted. "The Tanana makes a big bend and flows into the Yukon, which means we'll have to cross it to go south."

Tam stares at me but says nothing, and for a split second her blue eyes remind me of Stacy's. Except Stacy's eyes were soft and inviting, not icy and hostile.

Maxine pulls Jess the final few feet to the top of the knob. "My people used to hunt that country." Maxine points west, where there are hundreds of depressions that used to be ponds before the permafrost melted and they drained into the ground. "Ducks, geese, beaver. Black bear. Moose," Maxine says. "A magical place I've only heard stories about."

When the permafrost started melting, some places drained, and other places that were dry turned into swamps. Bridges buckled. Buildings sagged. Trees leaned and slowly uprooted themselves and then either totally collapsed or grew at acute angles. Anything putting weight on what used to be frozen ground just tilted or sank.

"I'm hungry," Jess says. She gets that pouty look on her face and I wish Mom were here to deal with her so I could focus solely on keeping us moving, like Dad used to do.

We've walked maybe three or four miles. I don't know how many days it'll take to reach the coast around where Anchorage used to be. Twenty-eight jars of salmon, I remember Randie saying. I realize that I don't even know what else is in the pack I'm carrying. Had it been Willa's or Randie's?

We have about 360 miles to cover in straight-line distance, but I know our route won't be straight.

"How about the four of us split a jar of salmon, then keep going until we hit the river? Jess, see if there's a jar in your pack." I figure the lighter her pack, the better. Trying to keep up with people seven or eight years older than her can't be easy.

After we eat the salmon, we head down the back side of Ester Dome. We hit a stretch of willows that burned but are still standing and crash our way through the blackened brush, leaving a trail of snapped-off branches. The rain keeps starting and stopping like it can't decide what to do. The ridge is bumpy, and in the saddles ash has collected, blown by the wind or pushed down by water run-off. It's over a foot thick in some places, but up on the bumps it's just an inch or less. A few birch stumps poke up through the ash—little dead islands in an even deader sea.

In the flats of the river valley we pass some human bones. Charred skeletons really, partially covered by ash. A lot of people died in the fires that second summer. The ones in the flats right here had probably been on their way to the river. Just a few more miles and they would've made it.

The sun breaks through the clouds. It's low in the northwest sky, projecting our shadows for twenty or thirty feet.

I stop and so does Tam. Jess and Maxine have fallen back a little since we passed the bodies, and I want to keep us together.

My shoulders are tight, so I roll them around and they make cracking noises.

Tam points. "I—"

"Yeah," I say. "Jess can only walk so fast. We'll have to take a real break soon or she'll be so beat she—"

"No," Tam says, glaring at me. "Up on Ester Dome." She points. "Look."

I shield my eyes from the sun and squint. Sure enough there's a little bump of people up there. It's hard to disappear in the flats, especially with a trail of ash and no trees to get lost in. Our best option is to stay in front of them, but I don't know how long Jess will last. Maybe we'll have to ditch her pack or take turns carrying it.

"Maxine, Jess," I call. "Come on." They're walking side by side, holding hands.

They catch up and I say, "We're being followed." I look at Jess. "Let me have your pack for a while. We need to pick up the pace."

"I can keep up with the pack on," Jess says. "Just like Max. I promise."

I look at Maxine and say, "Max?"

She smiles. "I was telling Jess, that's what my grandma used to call me when I was little. It's nice to hear it again."

I smile. "Okay, Max it is. And Jess, we'll give it a try." I'm so proud of her. And happy that Max and Tam are with us. And torn up about Willa and Randie. And grief-stricken about Mom and Dad. And anxious about the people following us.

No one else is going to die on my watch. No one.

We're walking faster now. No one is talking, and Jess is keeping up. I can see the river up ahead, shimmering in the low-angle sun. When we hit it, we'll just have to follow it until we find a good place to cross.

Tam's a few steps in front of me. She stops and I run right into her.

"Sorry," I say, taking a step back.

She flinches but then looks me in the eye and says, "It's okay."

"What's up?" Max says.

Tam points down. "Fresh tracks."

"Damn," I say. I look in the direction they're heading but see nothing. There're a few hills in the flats to hide behind but they aren't very big.

"I don't know how old they are," Tam says. "But they don't look much different from our tracks."

"Let's walk in them for a few minutes, then cut toward the river. And when we do, we'll brush out our tracks for a hundred yards or so, and maybe our friends behind us will keep following the other tracks."

We walk for a couple hundred yards, then I stop and point to a little hill a couple hundred feet away, rising in the direction of the river. "We can go around the hill, then creep up to the top and watch."

"But if they see our trail," Tam says, "they'll be right on top of us."

"It's the perfect place to lose them. And if they do come at us, we've got the advantage of being on top of the hill."

"You mean just shoot them?" Max asks. She puts her arm around Jess.

My gut twinges. "What other choice would I have?" I look back at the way we've come. "We need to make a decision."

Tam grabs my arm. The warmth from her fingers pressing into my skin. I turn and her eyes bore into mine. "We don't shoot unless someone draws on us first," she says. Then she lets go, but I can still feel the warmth of her touch.

"Okay," I say. We just need to move. "Tam, you first, then Max, then Jess. Step directly into the footprints Tam makes. Go to the left of the hill, then circle behind it and go partway up. I'll go last and brush out our tracks."

I take my pack off and pull out a camo shirt. It must've been Willa's or Randie's spare. Then I strap the shotgun to the pack and put it back on. I step into the first set of tracks, take a couple of steps forward, then turn around.

I hold the T-shirt in both hands, bend over, and wipe away our tracks. I just keep shuffling backward, erasing our tracks. The backs of my legs tighten up. A band of pain settles across my lower back, but I just keep going, turning every so often to make sure I don't step off the trail I'm erasing.

On the backside of the hill I meet up with Jess, Tam, and Max. "Now we creep up to just below the top," I say, "peek our heads over, cover up with a little ash, and we wait."

CHAPTER
17

WITHOUT A WATCH IT'S HARD to know how long we've been waiting, but we must've been quite a ways ahead of those guys because
it feels like a long time.

Jess and Tam are sitting slightly below us on the back side of
the hill where we've stashed our packs. No way could we get caught
facing only one direction again. Me and Max are up top, lying on
our stomachs, our heads just inches apart, covered in ash compliments of Tam and Jess.

I'm grateful that Jess has taken to Max. She's even interacting
with her in ways similar to how she interacted with Mom. It's like
Jess's brain has looked to fill a gap in her life. It's the same for me,
I realize, with Tam and how she keeps reminding me of Stacy,
except for the fact that every time she looks at me it feels like she's
considering putting an arrow in my heart. Me and Stacy were only
fourteen the last time we saw each other. A boy and a girl. But Tam
is a woman.

"I think I see something," Max whispers. "But from up the
trail, not the way we came."

I squint. Off to the left I see something flicker. Then I see two
boys. They've got about a quarter mile to go before crossing in
front of our hill. The front runner is about as big as me and is carry-

ing a long pole. The boy behind him has some type of animal carcass, which totally surprises me. Where the hell has he gotten that? And what had it been living on?

"We have to warn them," Max whispers.

"We can't. It'll blow our cover."

"But those men are chasing us, not them. They're walking into a trap that we've set."

"It's too late now," I say. "They've seen each other."

From the other direction, five men, two carrying guns, stand unmoving. One of them calls out, "Spare some food for some hungry men."

The two boys look at each other, then approach the men. The tall one with the pole says, "We can cut you off a flank, but we've got people to feed."

"People," the same man says. "I don't see any people." He laughs, and then the other men laugh.

"My dad will be coming along if we're not back soon," the tall boy says.

The man laughs again. "Shit. You think your daddy is gonna stop this?" He holds up his gun. "I got people to feed, too. What makes your people more deserving than mine? One of my men was killed in cold blood. Arrows through the neck and heart. Shot by some hard-core military types. Maybe you had something to do with it. That who you're feeding?"

The two boys back up a step. "No," the tall one says. "It's just our family. We don't want any trouble. But we can't go home without any food."

"Home?" the man says. "You've got a home?" He laughs. The two men on the outside move closer and form a semicircle around the boys.

"This is our battle," Max whispers. I know she's right, but I don't want to put Jess in danger. An image of my dad flashes into my mind. He'd never kill anyone unless his family was directly threatened.

"You just leave that beaver or wolverine or whatever the hell it is," the man says. "And go on *home*."

"But—"

The man brings his shotgun up to shoulder level and the other men take a step back. "All we want is the meat, boy. You can give it to us nice and easy. Or we'll take it, and a piece of your ass, too."

"This isn't right," Max whispers.

I feel paralyzed. I want to waste these guys, but I only have three slugs and don't know how many they have, and if they shoot me, what will happen to Jess? And if they're only going to take the meat, why shoot them? But I know what they did to us. They didn't try to take our food. They just opened fire.

"Just lay it on the ground and walk away," the man says, "and no one gets hurt."

The shorter boy sets the animal on the trail.

"Maybe they won't shoot," I whisper. "But if they do, I'm firing back." I have my shotgun in my hands, the barrel pointing toward the trail. I could fire in an instant if I need to, and they're close.

"It might be too late by then," Max whispers.

The boys back away and are moving off the trail at an angle toward our hill. Then they turn and run and I know they are hoping to use the hill for cover.

The man swings his gun toward the boys, like he's taking aim. He's broadside to me. A perfect target.

I take aim and fire.

His head explodes with blood and his buddies jump back. The two boys keep running, round the hill, and scream. They must've run into Jess and Tam, with her camo clothes and bow.

The men are gathered around their friend. "Dead," one of them says.

"Gun must've backfired."

"Never heard of that happening with a shotgun."

Now another man picks up the gun. Once he checks the chamber and realizes that it didn't backfire, they will all come after us.

I tap Max and we crawl down the hill and grab our packs. I motion for everyone to follow silently. We keep the hill at our backs for cover and head for the river.

CHAPTER
18

I KEEP HEADING TOWARD THE river, but my head is a jumble of mush. I just killed a man. I imagined killing people to protect my family and thought I'd do it if I had to, but now that I really have done it I feel different. Like I've crossed a line that I can't cross back over.

I wish my dad was around so I could talk with him about it. I remember getting frustrated with him when those guys with the rocks were harassing us, wishing he would just shoot one of them. But aiming a gun at another human being and pulling the trigger is serious business. You're basically saying that your life is more important than theirs.

We scramble down an eroded bluff to the edge of the river. We don't see anyone following us so we stop. Max and Tam head back to the top of the bluff to keep watch. Jess begs me to let her go with Max and I let her. I haven't said much to the two new people I've just saved—who I've killed for—until now.

The tall guy with the spear, his name's Mike. He's about my size. His brown hair is cut short across his forehead but hangs partway down his neck in the back. And his younger brother, Dylan, has thick, wavy brown hair. He's shorter but is stocky with muscular arms and legs. I guess he's fifteen, maybe sixteen, and

Mike is nineteen or twenty. These guys tell me we're the first people they have seen in a long time. They aren't sure how long, maybe five or six months. When I tell them we're heading south toward Anchorage, they just nod.

"You guys can come with us," I say. "Supposedly, there's more people by the coast."

Mike leans on his spear. "Two summers ago I saw other people try. They'd go south and then a few weeks or a month later I'd see some of them coming back. Crossing the flats and the mountains." Mike takes a breath. "A lot of people die out there. I hear it's like a bone yard."

"If you know what you're doing," Dylan says, "if you can see a way through, you can make it." Then he smiles. "But it's risky."

"We're willing to take the chance," I say. "What are you guys gonna do in this wasteland besides starve to death or get knocked off by some lunatics?"

"We got a place," Mike says. "A hidden place. And other hideouts."

"Big deal," I say. "What about food? And what was that animal you had?"

"We've still got some salmon from two years ago. But yeah, we're running low. We don't have enough for the winter. That was a beaver. Must've come from up- or downriver, quite a ways." Mike smiles. "My little brother"—he points at Dylan—"he spotted it."

Dylan says, "I think the rivers are rearranging themselves. I'm not sure what the Tanana flows into anymore and I'm not sure what flows into it. I know a beaver can't survive around here. No trees. But it must've come from somewhere that has them."

I nod. "So it was alive?"

"Just barely."

"We need to cross the river," I say.

Mike spits into the silty water that's churning by. "There's ways to get across. But the far side, it's pretty swampy."

"We've got to cross to go south." I point at the mountains.

"You follow the river downstream," Dylan says. "In a few miles it'll make a bend. Just after the bend it'll braid out. Splits into five or six channels. You might have to swim the main channel if you don't hit it just right, but it'll be short. The rest of it you can wade. But Mike's right. It's swampy over there. Way wetter than it looks from here."

I glance back up the bluff. I can see Jess, Max, and Tam sitting next to one another.

"You guys really got family?" I ask. "Like you told those guys."

Mike shakes his head. "Used to. Now it's just us."

Dylan looks at his brother. Like he's trying to communicate something to him but doesn't want me to know what it is.

"Come with us," I say. I wonder if I'm being too trusting, or if I should have asked Jess, Max, and Tam what they think first, but these guys are all alone just like Jess and I were after we were ambushed at the river. We can't just leave them here. "What kind of life are you going to have around here? What have you got to lose? You already said you don't have enough food for the winter."

"My dad was going to stay," Dylan says. "He said that things will get better here. And when they do, it won't be crowded up with all kinds of people. Just the ones who've *made it*."

"My dad was all into sticking around and talked my mom into it," I say. "But he was wrong and he admitted it." I tell them about our trip north and what happened. Then I say again, "Come with us."

"I'll go," Mike says. Then he turns to Dylan. "But only if you agree to come, too."

Dylan stares through him and says nothing in response.

"We can always come back," Mike says. "This might be the right time for us to actually go."

Dylan nods and says, "I'll give it a try, but first we need to go upriver to our main hideout to get our stuff."

CHAPTER
19

"THIS IS LIKE A FORTRESS," I say. We're in a cave or old mine or something.

Mike nods. "Dad made us promise we'd never show it to anyone. But times change."

To get here, we walked upriver a couple of miles and then hit these big bluffs. We waded through knee-high water around a bend. Then Mike and Dylan started climbing and we followed. Faint steps had been cut into the rock, and they didn't lead directly to the entrance, which was way back in a fold. In a place where you thought you couldn't go any farther, but it just kept opening up.

"Back when there was still a little gas for driving," Dylan says, "Dad started stockpiling coal. He'd go down to Healy and load up his pickup truck from an old mine. And once the town of Nenana was abandoned, he got it from a big pile in the old shipping yards. He started fixing this place up just in case we needed to hunker down for a while, or longer. He knew something was going to happen. He could see. And then . . ." Dylan just shakes his head.

I don't know what to say. I mean, we all experienced some kind of raw deal that involved losing family members, some kind of personal tragedy that could just keep sucking the life out of you. And trying to respond to someone who's feeling that loss, well, sometimes words just don't cut it. So I touch his arm and say, "This place is pretty amazing. Your dad sounds like he was awesome." And Dylan smiles.

There's a metal stove with three folding chairs around it, and candles pressed into ledges on the walls, and wooden countertops that run the length of the cave, maybe thirty feet long. Underneath are rows of old milk crates filled with stuff, and other things that are loose, but it's too dark to see what's there. Especially toward the back. But on the left side at the very back the counter appears narrower, like it's missing a couple of boards, which isn't surprising. I mean, having any milled lumber at all is so rare they probably used it for something else.

"These counters survived the fire?" I ask. I put my hand on top of one. It's been sanded smooth. Someone put a lot of effort into making this place livable.

Dylan says, "We're so far down and into the bluff, the fire didn't reach in." He smiles. "Dad planned for that. High enough to avoid a flood. Deep enough to avoid a fire."

"Your dad must've been an amazing person," Max says.

Dylan looks at her and says, "He was the best. A prophet and a genius." Then he turns away.

Prophet, I think. *What's he talking about?* I try to catch Tam's eye to see her reaction but she's just staring at Dylan's back. So are Max and Jess.

Then Mike says, "There's another cave a little farther up that's stuffed with coal for the stove. Winter ain't a problem here as long as you've got enough food."

"What's the deal with that stovepipe?" I ask. It runs straight into the ceiling and disappears.

Mike glances toward the ceiling. "It goes up into the ground like you see. But the ground is kind of hollow, like there used to be a bunch of tree roots, so the smoke rises. It doesn't draw great, but once you get it cooking it does all right. Only backs up every now and then."

"No one ever found you here?" Tam asks.

"Well," Mike says, "no one who lived to tell about it. Dad. He killed a few people. But it's been months since we've seen anyone, until today. We thought we were the last people around here. The last people in the whole area."

"We got a little sloppy walking on that trail," Dylan says. "I should've known those guys were there. I should've known you guys were there."

I'm not sure what he means by that, but I figure there's plenty of time to get to know each other. "What do you guys need to get? You want some help packing, just put us to work. But one of us should keep watch."

Dylan and Mike look at each other, then Mike says, "Can all of you wait outside while we go through some stuff?"

*   *   *

"New land," Max says. "That's all people wanted for a long time. That's why white people came here. And before that, why my ancestors crossed the land bridge when the sea level was low."

We're sitting on some rocks just outside the entrance to the cave, waiting for Dylan and Mike, the rusty-yellow Tanana River flowing about a hundred feet below.

"My dad loved the land," I say. "He was actually kind of happy when most everyone left on the buses."

"My people lived here a long time," Max says. "I—"

"But you're only like one-eighth native," Tam says.

"It's the eighth I relate to."

I see Tam roll her eyes. Then she lets out a sigh. "Everyone's been mixed together. I've probably got a sixteenth in me. But face it, there's no such thing as native anymore."

Max smiles. "Maybe not full-blooded. But the white part of me sleeps while the native part dances and prays."

Jess taps Max on the shoulder. "I like to dance. My mom used to dance with me. Back when we had music. And after it was gone, sometimes she'd sing so we could dance." Jess snaps her fingers and sways her body.

Max puts her arm around Jess and squeezes her.

Jess is so resilient. I mean, she'd seen those two girls, her newest and only friends, dead on the banks of the Yukon. Lost her mom and dad. And then saw Willa and Randie killed. But she kicked the murderer just like the rest of us. I don't think I would've done that when I was ten. But when I was ten, there were still schools. People had jobs, and they used money to buy things. I actually got to be a kid.

Yeah, she's tough, but she's still small and vulnerable. On our trip back from the Yukon, she'd woken up calling out for Mom in her dreams. And then Jess cried when she remembered Mom was gone. I feel my chest tighten and just want to get her across the river and put some distance between us and this place.

"I hope Dylan and Mike don't take too long," I say. "Those guys following us might've found our trail."

Pulling that trigger and seeing the guy's head explode keeps popping into my mind. Mike and Dylan had given them that beaver, and the guy was still going to shoot them in the back.

Some people are just whacked. Or maybe the burnt-out land makes them crazy. It can be so monotonous. Miles upon miles of gray wasteland. Sure, you see some stumps and snags and a bit of fireweed here and there, but mostly it's gray. Dead and gray. You'd never guess this cave was here. The land is so burned you couldn't even see it in your imagination.

"I kind of hope we do run into them," Tam says. "I want to kill anyone and everyone responsible for Willa and Randie's deaths."

"I feel responsible." I look at Tam. "If it weren't for you, we'd all be dead."

"Travis," Tam says, "I don't mean you. What happened, happened. You didn't think about keeping a back-watch. None of us did. Let it go."

"Stay in this moment," Max says.

I feel my eyes getting hot. I think of my dad and my mom. I can't just let it go.

Max tilts her head toward the cave, then whispers, "Can we trust those guys?"

I notice Tam has positioned herself so she's facing the cave's entrance at an angle, her bow beside her.

"Hope so," I say. "Why would they lead us all this way and show us their hideout?"

"Spoken like a guy," Max says. "I saw them checking us out." She nods in Tam's direction. "Once they put a fence around the group home and locked us in, guys would walk by and say all kinds of sick stuff."

Tam nods. "If I had had my bow then." She picks it up, draws an imaginary arrow, and fires. "Some of those guys deserved to die." Then she sets down her bow.

"I don't think these guys are like that," I say. "They're like me.

And anyway, how could they check you out when you're wearing those bulky camo clothes?"

"Trust me." Tam shakes her head. "It doesn't matter what we're wearing."

I glance at Max and then at Tam. They are both beautiful girls. Truth is, I can see that even with the bulky clothes. "You're right," I say, "it doesn't matter. But they—"

"You don't know anything about them," Max says.

Tam pulls her bow closer. "You can't trust anyone absolutely." She turns her head away from the entrance to the cave and toward me. "Especially guys."

"You trust me, right?"

Tam shrugs. "If it weren't for Jess, I don't know what would've happened. You were just another guy pointing a gun at us. And if Willa had given the signal, I would've skewered you." Then she turns back toward the cave.

I touch my stomach, picturing an arrow sinking into my flesh, and my gut muscles instantly contract. "They're like us," I say. But I don't know. I don't really know, but I feel it. Just like the way I felt that Clint and Mark were good people.

Max leans into Jess and rests her head on Jess's shoulder and looks at me. "I hope you're right."

CHAPTER
20

"MY DAD KNEW THIS COUNTRY better than anyone," Dylan says. "But it's changed a lot since . . ." And his voice trails off like it floated away on the wind.

We're standing on the riverbank, several channels separating us from the other side. The side we need to be on.

"Once we're across," I say, "we should have a pretty clear path to the mountains."

Mike laughs. "How do you know?"

"I remember the maps. No major rivers flowing west on this side of the range."

"The land is the land," Max says. "We can't control it."

Tam stands with her back to us, scanning for movement. Jess has taken her pack off and is sitting on a rock.

"Based on how much the Tanana River has moved, and the earthquakes moving things around," Dylan says, "I don't think we can count on anything."

"Okay," I say. "But we still need to get across this freaking river before someone sees us."

"It's not gonna be easy over there," Dylan says.

I take a step toward him. "I'm not looking for easy. I'm looking for safe." I glance at Jess, then turn back to Dylan.

Dylan smirks a little, then runs a hand through his wavy hair and looks up at me. "Just chill. You scared?"

"Do you remember what happened back there? I saved your sorry ass." I hold up my gun. "I killed a guy for you and your brother."

"Sorry ass?" Dylan says. "Yeah, I remember. And now I'm trying to save yours. Dumbass."

I turn to Mike. "Try to talk some sense into your little brother."

Dylan laughs. "I may be younger, but that doesn't matter. Not out here. Not anywhere." Mike doesn't say anything, doesn't even acknowledge that I've spoken to him.

A gust of wind lifts some silt from the gravel bar we are standing on and swirls it around. High water in the spring has washed all the ash from the gravel bars, but the sand and silt are dry and the wind could kick up nasty clouds fifty or sixty feet high. The stuff can sting your eyes, get inside your ears and nose, up your sleeves, and into your shoes and socks. I know the wind will get stronger the later in the day it gets—until the sun reaches toward the horizon—and then it'll die down. But I don't want to wait. I want to go. Now.

"Dylan, he knows his stuff," Mike says. "He can sense things, just like my dad used to."

This is starting to sound hokey or weird or something. I remember that Dylan referred to his dad as a prophet. I'd never asked about that. Does Dylan consider himself a prophet, too? And what exactly does that mean to him? Does he think he can communicate with God? God definitely doesn't exist around here. I mean, this place is an abandoned wasteland. If Dylan's hearing voices, maybe they're just in his own head.

"Let's just cross the river and be done with it," I say, "before we have to contend with a dust storm, or those guys that tried to kill us. Or both."

Max steps forward and Jess follows her. "I want to hear what Dylan . . ." She hesitates. "What he can sense."

"Okay, Dylan," I say. "What's the problem with crossing here, right now?"

"I think there's a better spot downriver, just a few more miles." He looks at Mike. "And we've got a hideout down there on another bluff. Something to fall back on."

"I don't want to fall back on anything," I say. *This is just what Dad did*, I think. He kept hesitating until it was too late. He waited so long to act that all he could do was react.

Dylan kicks the silt and it puffs out and the wind takes it upriver. "There's just something I don't like about crossing right here, right now. I'm not sure what it is, but I can't ignore it."

"You guys can cross here if you want," Mike says. "Me and Dylan, we'll cross downriver and meet up with you." He points out across the gray flats. "You won't be hard to spot."

"I think we should stay together," Tam says. Then she turns back around to keep watch.

"Me too," Max says. "Let's all stay together."

"Okay," I say. "If the quickest way we're all going to get across the river is to go to the next crossing spot, then let's get going."

Dylan just stands there, staring across the river. "Something . . ." he says. "Something's changed since we've been here."

"The wind has picked up," I say, pointing at the dust in the air over the gravel bars.

Dylan smiles. "Not just that, genius. Something else. All the way across." He points. "In that bumpy area."

A series of small mounds sit just across the river and downstream. It's hard to tell their size because of the distance, but if I had to guess, I'd say they're as big as the dome tent we had on our trip north. Maybe they're boulders covered with ash. Or just little bumps on the land.

Now we are all peering across the river, except for Tam, who keeps watch behind us.

"Something's moving around in those hills," Dylan says.

"I see it," Max says. "On the far left."

I shift my eyes and try to focus. Some dust blows across the gravel bar and then it's clear again. "I see it, too," I say. "No freaking way. It looks like a bear."

"Not just any bear," Mike says. "A grizzly." He pats Dylan on the shoulder, but Dylan moves away from him.

I don't know where a bear would've come from, but it'd be hungry. Meat-starved.

We have our jars of salmon, but anything fresh would mean that we can save our food for later. But it'd take ammo to kill a bear. I only have two slugs left, and they're our major protection against people.

"The land *is* coming back." Max puts her arm around Jess, then faces Dylan and says, "How did you know that bear was there?"

Dylan just smiles and raises his eyebrows at her. Max smiles back, and now Jess is smiling at Dylan, too.

I don't know how Dylan knew about the bear. And somehow, he'd found that beaver. But something still bothers me about him, about how controlling and uncompromising he's been. And about how he and Max smiled at each other like they've got some secret between them, or that they understand each other and no one else does. Back at the shelter, Max hadn't even trusted him. Now she's all in.

I think of Jess and her connection to Max and then I worry even more about Dylan. If Max is quick to follow Dylan, and Jess follows Max the way I've encouraged her to, then Dylan's got some influence over Jess.

"We need to move," Tam says. "There's someone on our trail."

CHAPTER
21

"WALK IN THE WATER," I say. "Then they won't know if we've crossed or gone downriver."

I lead the way through shin-deep water and keep glancing across the river, catching glimpses of the bear moving around in the hills. I just don't get it. It must have come from the south, across the mountains, but why?

Years ago people found a beluga whale hundreds of miles up the Yukon River. And polar bears, before they died out because of the sea ice melting, had survived for a while by migrating inland. There's even evidence of polar bears mating with grizzlies.

And who knows what the state of the land is east of here. I mean, Northern Canada might not have burned. Once we didn't have power, there was no way to communicate. We only knew what was happening as far as the eye could see. And that closes you in, but it also forces you to look closely at what's around you, because what's around you is now your whole world.

We're approaching another set of bluffs now as the river meanders west. No one is talking. Just forward, single-file movement as our feet shuffle through the silty water, sliding on top of rounded rocks that we can't see.

"The water's gonna be deep under those bluffs," I say. "Probably over our heads."

Mike steps up beside me. "There's a way into the folds, some tiny steps my dad cut, just as we start around. I'll lead."

*　*　*

"Jason and Patrick," Tam says, "we wouldn't have survived the fire without them. We wouldn't have survived. Period."

Max and Jess are on watch at the entrance to the cave—another one of Dylan's dad's hideouts—in the side of the bluff. And Tam is telling us some wild stuff.

"They had a yurt they'd stolen from the Air Force Base before the government pulled out. We were wandering. Only four of us were left out of eight from the group home. We had nothing and were heading east, scavenging from abandoned houses as we went. We were starving.

"You could see the burnt-out hulk of the Air Force Base, but behind it, way back in the hills, before they burned, was this circular brown structure. We headed for it, hoping it was abandoned, but it wasn't.

"Jason and Patrick had solar panels compliments of the Air Force, and a wall of big batteries. They'd found an old truck with a little fuel. Packed it full of supplies and drove it into the hills and no one came after them. No one cared. Most of the enlisted men and women just wanted to leave on the transport planes while they had the chance. Just like most everyone else left on the buses except for the people who were intentionally left behind, like us. But not Jason and Patrick. They wanted to remake their life up here.

"We stayed with them for a couple months. They shared everything. Invited us to stay indefinitely to form a family. But when the fires got closer, Willa wanted to leave. She had a bad feeling about the place. Patrick and Jason gave us our packs and clothes, and my bow, which I'd practiced with the whole time, and took us to a gravel bar in the river a few miles from the yurt. They'd cut all the trees down around the yurt for a couple hundred yards and had a water pump they were running off the solar panels, pulling water from a small lake. They were sure they could protect the yurt.

"But those fires, they burned everything. Patrick and Jason didn't have a chance." Tam pauses. "We had to lie in the water, and even then we could feel the heat. Hot coals rained down on our wet clothes and we'd brush them off over and over.

"The yurt turned into a tiny black lump on the land. The lake boiled dry. Patrick and Jason had a little piece of paradise going with those solar panels. A ton of freeze-dried food from the military. A big garden, too. But where could you get solar panels after the fire? Where could you get anything after those fires?

"We couldn't even find their remains."

*   *   *

Jess walks into the cave and says, "Those guys that were following us walked over the bluff."

Max crowds in behind her and says, "They probably walked right on top of us, but they're downriver now. It looked like the same guys, minus one."

I know it was necessary to pull that trigger, but it still bugs me. There has to be a better way than killing, but when someone is going to kill you or someone else who doesn't deserve to die, what choice do you really have?

I scoot over and make room for Max and Jess to sit down.

Mike and Tam get up and leave the cave. It's their turn to go on watch.

I take an oily strip of salmon and pass the jar to Max.

"Real food," she says. "It powers the body and the spirit. You eat the land. You become the land."

"You *see* the land," Dylan says. "You become the land."

"Exactly," Max says, then passes him the jar and smiles.

I don't know if he's just saying stuff to impress Max or if he really means it. But Jess is sitting there, too. Absorbing every word.

If those guys keep going south and bypass the braided area downstream a couple miles, we're going to follow them, but then cross the river.

"Trav," Jess says. "Do you think there'll be schools in the settlements? And stores? And houses? Real houses?"

"I don't know what's there," I say. "No one does. I don't even know if they actually exist, but I hope they do."

"Then why are we going?" Jess asks.

"So we can have a life. So we can see what's there. So we can live in a place with other people. In a place that isn't burnt-out and dead."

"But you just said you don't know what it's like." Jess sighs. "Maybe it's burnt-out, too."

"Jess—"

"She's right," Dylan says. "You *don't* know."

"I never said I knew. But look around. We're in a freaking cave eating the last food we have." I turn back to Jess. "We can't stay here. We'll die. That's why Mom and Dad wanted to leave. I—"

"But it's an adventure," Dylan interrupts, smiling at Jess. Then he turns toward me. "My dad, he wanted to stay. He was going to stay. I might still stay."

"Stay?" I laugh. "Go ahead. It's your life. Waste it however you want." If he stays, I don't think I'll miss him.

Dylan takes some salmon and passes the jar to Jess. Jess makes her fish face and Dylan laughs and makes one back at her. I feel my ears getting hot and I take a breath. I don't want to lay into Dylan too much in front of Jess because it might backfire. Jess is starting to share Max's fondness for him. So I just smile and pretend like it's funny, hoping Dylan will lay off being so combative toward everything I say.

Jess eats a piece of salmon, then lies down and rests her head in Max's lap. We sit in silence, and I can tell Jess is drifting off. I'm glad she's taking a nap now, because once we start moving there's no guarantee as to when we'll be able to stop and rest again.

Max says, "Your dad had to be quite a visionary to make shelters that would survive the fires."

"My dad had a vision," Dylan whispers to me and Max. "He believed burning the land would cleanse it. People think the government started all those fires. Maybe they started some, but my dad and a couple other people started most of them. And I helped."

Max moves one of her hands so it covers Jess's ear. Then she turns to Dylan.

He gets this glazed look in his eyes and just keeps whispering. "Dad had been stockpiling gasoline. I always thought it was to use in the boat motor or the chainsaw, or in his truck. You know, for when times got tough. But Dad, he had other plans. Big, beautiful plans.

"When the government started pulling out and burning their buildings and anything else related to serving the area, Dad just laughed. He wasn't expecting the government to help him do what he was already planning on doing. Cleansing the land. Burn it and burn it hot. Start over. Push the reset button. Let the postindustrial healing begin.

"So he hung on to his gas that winter after the buses hauled all the sissies out of here. He made the rounds when things were still abundant and people still talked to each other and shared what they had. But Dad was looking for like-minded people. People with his vision or people who'd come around to seeing things his way. He was recruiting. And he didn't tell me or Mike or Mom any of this at first.

"When he wasn't recruiting, he was poring over topo maps and street maps. And he went about this with the same gusto he'd used to build and stock these shelters along the river. I kept bugging him to tell me what he was doing, and finally, after I promised that I'd help him if he told me, he did. And his plan, it was beautiful, and pure.

"Dad waited until it'd been hot and dry. And windy. Hadn't rained in a month and we'd had a low snowfall year. And a bunch of lightning strikes had already started things burning. He sent his buddies, two guys, upriver in a canoe with instructions for when and where to set their fires. 'Start at the farthest-out point and float down, setting fires on both sides of the river,' he said. 'Then return to the shelter.' We know they set the fires, but we never saw them again.

"Dad and I started from the shelter and went downriver, setting fires. And it was cleansing. To see everything getting erased for miles around, and to be making that happen. Being part of the re-creation. To feel the land being consumed. Reduced to its basic elements. The burns got so hot that they even burned what the government had burned the year before. A deep cleansing, Dad called it. Burn the old crust off the earth. Only the purists would stay now. We could rebuild in the right way with the right kind of people. I wish he were still here. If he was, no way would I even think about leaving." Dylan lies on his back and closes his eyes. "Everything's different now. Messed up."

I glance at Max but she's just staring at the ground. I'm not sure what she thinks. I want to say something to Dylan but I'm at a total loss for what it would be. Actually, I want to bash his head into the ground. He doesn't deserve to live. I feel my arms trembling. Instead of doing anything to add to the craziness, I stand up and whisper to Max, "I'm gonna trade watch with Tam so I can talk to Mike."

* * *

The sun has swung back around and is in our faces. We can still see our friends downriver. If they disappear around the next bend, we're going to make a dash for the crossing.

"Dylan's telling some far-out stories about the fires," I say, wondering if Mike thinks his brother is nuts or if he is on board with the fire-setting, too. "Makes me nervous."

"My dad was gifted but he went nuts," Mike says. "And Dylan, he's gifted in a lot of ways most people aren't. He's supersensitive to his surroundings. Like the way he knew that bear was across the river before we saw him. And how he grabbed my spear and jabbed it into the water and came up with the beaver. I don't know how he does it."

"Yeah," I say. "But the way he talks, he thinks the fires were a good thing. Does he even know how many people those fires scorched? How many people he killed? Does he even care that he killed hundreds of people? That he burned them up? And then in the winter, masses of people froze to death and others starved. He helped wreck this place."

"Travis," Mike says softly, "you've got to let me handle Dylan. He's my brother, the only family I've got. When you challenge him, you're just pushing him further away, and we need him. We need his gift. The reason we took so long to pack up is that I had to convince him to come. If it weren't for Max, I think he would've stayed back at our place. Let me handle him."

"He could screw this up for everyone," I say. "And when you mess up these days, there usually aren't any second chances."

"You think I don't want to get out of here?" Mike asks. "But I want Dylan to make it, too. I don't want him to turn out like my dad."

"What happened to your dad?" I ask. "And your mom?"

"Forget my parents," Mike says. "They're gone. Will you just promise me you'll lay off Dylan and let me handle him?"

"As long as you do handle him, I'm willing to give that a try. But I can't have him trying to talk people into staying. That's a death sentence." I step up closer. "I'll do anything to protect my sister. Anything."

Mike just stares back at me and I think, *I'm going to have to keep a close eye on both of them.*

CHAPTER
22

"NO ONE IN THEIR RIGHT mind would cross this swamp," Dylan says.

"That explains why you're crossing it," I say over my shoulder, then keep going. I know I shouldn't have said that, but I'm sick of his negative thoughts and his let's-go-back mentality.

We crossed the river without incident yesterday, and truth be told, Dylan led the way and somehow kept us out of the deep water. And the men who had been hunting us didn't try to cross. When we reached the other side, Dylan turned and challenged them to follow. He screamed and cursed and Mike didn't even try to stop him. One of the men had yelled back, "You'll die over there."

Now we're slogging through a knee-deep slurry of ash and water, avoiding deeper holes as best we can.

Some dark peaks rise above the haze to the south. They used to be covered in snow and ice year-round, but a lot of the glaciers melted off years ago.

Dylan catches up to me and grabs my arm. "Did I read you wrong, or did you just call me a nutcase?"

Max, Tam, Mike, and Jess are about a hundred feet back.

I pull my arm toward my body and take a step back to get Dylan's hand off me. "Just keep your negative thoughts to yourself.

My little sister doesn't need to hear all that crap. This is hard enough for her as it is."

"Your sister is going to have to grow up," Dylan says. "People talk. All the time. They say all kinds of shit. As a human you've got to learn what to take in and what to let go."

I look Dylan in the eye. "That's basically true, but it doesn't mean you should be able to say whatever the hell you want anytime you feel like it."

Dylan spits into the swamp. "Hypocrite. What were you doing when you called me a nutcase?"

"I said what I said because whether you're crazy or not, you act like you are. Maybe it's all an act. Maybe that's just the way you are."

Dylan takes a step toward me. I tower over him by at least four inches but he's stocky. He runs a hand through his thick hair and says, "Did you ever think that maybe you're the crazy one?"

I laugh. "I didn't torch the land and then say how freaking great it was. Cleansing? That's total bullshit. And if you don't know that, you are full-on crazy."

"You're blind," Dylan says.

"Look around." I sweep my arm in an arc. "Blind? I wish."

"You fuck with me," Dylan says softly, "and you'll be sorry. I'll haunt you forever."

"I already am sorry."

The rest of the gang has caught up.

"Are we stopping to rest?" Jess asks, holding Max's hand.

Everyone looks at me except Dylan, who is now staring back the way we came.

"Not here," I say. "Too wet." I point south. "Just a couple more miles. In those hills, there's probably better drainage."

114

"I don't see any hills," Jess says. She's leaning against Max the way she used to lean against my mom. I know she's tired, but standing around in this slurry of ash won't revive her. She needs to sit down.

"We should keep moving," Tam says. "It's more tiring standing than walking."

Mike says, "Dylan, you ready?"

Dylan holds up his hand and keeps looking back the way we came. "The grizzly," he says, "it's following us."

I turn and look and see what Dylan sees: a brown clump of fur moving toward us.

We keep on going, but every time I glance over my shoulder the brown clump of fur seems bigger, so I know the bear is gaining on us.

I have the shotgun with two shells. Mike carries that crazy spear with the jagged-glass point. Tam has her bow with two arrows. Max has my pistol with the single shot. Dylan and Jess just have their hands. I'm not sure what's in her pack. Does she have anything to protect herself?

Besides the salmon, I don't even know what's in the pack I'm carrying. I mean, I know it used to be Willa's, but I haven't had a chance to look through it.

Back in the day, a well-fed bear would, more often than not, avoid people. I keep glancing back to make sure we don't get too spread out. We can only go as fast as Jess can walk. She's tired, and I want to keep us bunched up for protection. A bear is more likely to attack individuals than a group.

The hills still appear to be a few miles off. We've been steadily walking toward them since Dylan spotted the bear, but they don't seem any closer.

The weight of the ash slurry makes for slow going. Every step is a plow through wet cement from the knees down. My next step buries me waist-deep. I turn and force my way back a few steps, not sure which way to go. The swamp—the knee-high slurry we've been slogging across—is changing into something worse. At least it's only me who's gone in.

"It's a basin," Dylan says. "Slowly, it's filling back up. A lake before the fires boiled it dry. We should imagine the shoreline"—Dylan points east and then west—"and just follow it."

"How about if you lead us around the lake," I say.

Dylan smiles. "I could, but I kind of like watching you flounder."

"Look—"

"The bear," Mike says. "It's still coming."

Dylan shrugs, but Mike just keeps staring at him until he starts moving.

I take up the rear with Tam right in front of me. Then Mike, Jess, and Max.

I keep glancing over my left shoulder to monitor the bear.

We're making this big semicircle to the east. The water is only knee-deep, and our line of travel is taking us closer to the bear. I hope the shore will swing around to the south soon, but it just keeps dipping northward.

"The bear," I call out. "It's changed course and is angling toward us."

CHAPTER
23

THE FIRST DROPS OF RAIN sink into the swamp. It must be pushing 90 degrees. If the sun were shining, it'd be over a hundred, easy. We keep following Dylan. I keep an eye on the bear. It's only a half mile off, I estimate.

The rain comes harder. The drops creating light gray swirls in the slurry. The bear seems content to keep its steady pace instead of charging. Like it knows it can catch us if it just keeps on coming, so why waste energy running?

Two slugs from a shotgun might not drop a grizzly. I'd have to put a slug through its heart or hit it just behind the ear, and those are precision shots. And if the bear does charge, it'll be bounding—bouncing up and down. *Fifty yards*, my dad had said. *That's when you shoot. It takes a charging bear three seconds to cover fifty yards.* It'd probably be a little slower in this slurry. And if it's weak, maybe that'd affect it, too.

I feel my heart beating through my soaked shirt. *Don't shoot*, I tell myself, *until it's absolutely necessary. Until it's your only option.* I know if I shoot too soon, I might miss. But if I shoot too late, I might get mauled. Jess might get mauled.

I bump into Tam's pack. "Sorry," I say.

Tam glances back at me and says, "It's okay. I can only go as fast as them." She points forward with her bow.

"The shore," Dylan says. "It's curving back to the north even more." He points. "See the bear. It's walking the shore, too. Right at us."

Dylan's right. The shore has almost doubled back on itself. I try to picture the lakeshore below the ashy water. "We could be walking along an oxbow lake," I say. "You know, an old river channel that got cut off and turned into a lake. They can curve. Big time. It could be shaped like a horseshoe."

"I'm impressed," Dylan says. "You're not sounding as dumb as you usually do."

Before I can respond, Tam says, "Let's go back the way we came, and follow the shore to the west and see if it swings to the south."

"That would buy us a little time," I say.

Dylan laughs. "It's just a bear." Then he laughs again.

The rain is running down my nose and cheeks, dripping. It'll be even harder to take an accurate shot.

"Dylan," Mike says, "lead us back around."

But Dylan just stands there, not looking at anyone.

Mike takes a step toward him. "Do it for me."

Dylan slaps him in the face and laughs. "Do it for me," he mocks. Then he slaps him again.

Mike doesn't back off, but just keeps staring at him like the rest of us are.

"You guys are so ignorant," Dylan says. He points at Max. "Except you."

She doesn't say anything.

Then he points at Jess. "And you, too. You're too young to be ignorant."

Jess is silent. Just the constant hour-after-hour slog even without the bear has to be overwhelming to her.

Mike steps up so they are nose to nose and whispers something to Dylan.

Dylan shoves him in the chest but then says, "I'll do it. I'll walk us back the way we came."

I keep my mouth shut as Dylan walks by. I want to tell him all his bullshit has cost us some distance with the bear, but I know he'd just stop to argue and the bear would get even closer. What I really want to do is punch him in the face. If I thought it'd knock some sense into him, I'd try it.

I touch Jess's arm as she walks by and offer her a smile, but she just keeps staring straight ahead. Max is pulling her along. I try to make eye contact with Mike, but he doesn't look my way. Tam just nods. I take up my spot in the rear, watching the bear over my right shoulder.

It still amazes me that there's a bear out here. If a few people survived the fires, I guess a bear could, too. Maybe it took refuge on a gravel bar in the middle of a river just like us. And maybe it found some food in some burnt-out basements. Or maybe it lived for a while on charred human remains, or by feasting on people who had died from smoke inhalation. Even though most of the villages had been abandoned for a long time, there were places scattered all over the Alaska bush. Places people used to access by small plane or boat or a snow machine, places it would take a person half a year or more to find on foot. But a bear could've found some of those places and found food in root cellars, or feasted on the bodies of people that had died out there.

The bear keeps coming, seeming content to follow the shoreline. No one is talking. I think about trying to make a plan if it charges, but I don't want to deal with Dylan, or Mike, or anyone. I don't want to take the time and energy, especially since I know I'd probably end up telling Dylan to go screw himself if he laughed or said something stupid.

I'm not scared of him, but I don't want to fight him either. I just want all of us to get along. But it doesn't seem to matter what I say to Dylan. He always says the opposite, or finds some way to argue or to make me look stupid. What scares me is how unpredictable he is.

I'm not officially in charge of the group, but I am the force driving us south. And even though I want everyone to make it out of the Sacrifice Area, my main priority is Jess. If Dylan wants to turn around, let him. Anyone else, too. It'd be better for Jess if Max stayed, but I'd deal with it if she didn't. And if Tam left, I'd miss her. She's been steady and reliable. If it weren't for her, more of us would have died when we were ambushed.

The bear is gaining on us, only a couple hundred yards away. Less than twenty seconds if it charges. If only we would've turned west when we first hit the lakeshore. I wonder if Dylan knew that and turned us toward the bear intentionally.

"We need to do something different," I call out through the rain.

Everyone stops, and I move a few steps out from the line so I can see everyone.

"We look like prey," I say. "Let's bunch up and slowly move toward the bear. I'll shoot if I have to."

"So will I," Tam says.

"Before we try that," Max says, "how about if we move off the lakeshore, not into the lake but in the opposite direction. Maybe it'll keep following the shore and just walk on by. Walking where the walking is easiest. Maybe it means no harm."

Dylan laughs. "You people." He unclips his waist strap, slips his shoulders from his pack, and pushes it toward his brother. Mike stumbles backward from the weight of the pack and falls.

Then Dylan takes off at a dead sprint—straight for the bear.

CHAPTER
24

THERE'S NO WAY ANY OF us are going to catch Dylan, packless and with the head start he has. We all scream for him to stop, but he just keeps going.

Mike is standing up now, with Dylan's pack leaning against his knees. He shakes his head.

Dylan is about a quarter of the way between us and the bear, still running, but it looks like he's slowed a little. And the bear is still moving forward.

"Everyone," I say, "follow me and keep yelling."

I take off running at an angle away from the lakeshore into the swamp, hoping to distract the bear. Water splashes into my face. My eyes are in a permanent squint to keep the ashy drops out as I pound through the swamp as fast as I can.

Now a triangle is forming between Dylan, the rest of us, and the bear. I think Dylan can hear us. I hope he'll turn and run toward us; then we'll all be together, because running at the bear solo is freaking suicide. Truth be told, part of me doesn't even want to try to save him.

If he's intent on killing himself, let him go.

But he's survived as long as the rest of us have in this hellhole.

And even though I don't know Mike very well, Dylan's his little brother just like Jess is my little sister.

I turn and start angling toward the bear. I can hear the splashing behind me, so I know the others are following me. Dylan must've really slowed down because I'm just about even with him.

I glance behind me. Tam is on my heels. Max and Jess are back a little farther. I don't see Mike, but I know he has to be back there somewhere.

The bear stops and stands on its hind legs, its head pointed in my direction. I keep barreling forward through the rain, committed to chasing it off or trying to kill it. Why did Dylan have to screw up my plan? Why did he have to act on his own, and like an idiot? And now Dylan turns and starts backing away.

But the bear, instead of chasing him, has dropped back on all fours and is coming toward me. Not charging but walking. I stop, then feel a bump on my back. I turn and see Tam. She isn't even breathing hard. Jess and Max are about fifteen yards back. And Mike? He's still back at the starting point along the lakeshore. And Dylan is working his way back toward Mike.

I drop my pack in the knee-high swamp and Tam does the same. She nocks an arrow into her bow and I raise my shotgun. Raindrops prick my cheeks and hands.

"Maybe we won't have to shoot," I say. "Maybe it'll veer off."

"I've never shot an animal," Tam says. "Only people."

The bear stands up again. It's skinny but tall, maybe seven or eight feet. And its fur is matted down from all the rain and the swamp-walking. At least it isn't moving forward at the moment. Maybe it'll turn around and head back the way it came. I wish Mike would've followed and that Dylan had come our way instead of going back. It'd be easier to protect everyone if we were together. Plus, the bigger we appear the more likely it is that the bear will run away. That was my plan, the plan that Dylan wrecked.

"It's beautiful," Max says.

Under different circumstances I'd agree with her. But now that bear is a potential killing machine. Or, if we actually manage to kill it, a food source.

"If you do shoot," Max says, "make it a good shot. So it doesn't suffer."

"I'll do my best," I say. "Maybe it'll turn away."

"I doubt it," Max says. She puts her arm around Jess. "I thought Dylan was being brave by running at the bear. But now I don't know. Maybe it was a trick."

"Travis is the brave one," Jess says.

I try to block out their words. No way could Dylan have known that I'd lead a charge and the bear would ignore him. Maybe he just doesn't value his own life enough to value anyone else's. Or, gifted as he is, maybe he's also just plain nuts. And me, brave? I'm just doing what needs to be done. And I'm scared out of my freaking mind.

The bear drops to all four legs and starts splashing through the swamp toward us. I raise the shotgun to my shoulder. If it stands on its hind legs, I'll try to put a slug in its chest and hope for the best. If it doesn't stand, I'll just go for the head, or maybe a shoulder shot.

"When it gets within fifty yards, if it's still coming, I'm shooting," I say.

"Ditto," Tam says.

I wish there was some type of landmark to help me gauge

distances, but there isn't. If I fire too soon, I might miss. If I fire too late, the big brute will be on us.

I can hear the water being displaced by the bear's legs as it sloshes toward us. Fifty yards away? I'll just have to guess.

It rises partway up on its hind legs. I adjust my aim and fire.

The bear slams backward.

I pump my final slug into the magazine and fire. The bear's head jerks upward and all of a sudden there's an arrow sticking out of its nose.

The bear swats at the arrow with one paw as it turns, taking heavy steps away from us. I blow air out of my nose that I didn't know I was holding. My ears are on fire from the gunshots. The bear staggers onto where I think the lakeshore is, then keeps going and disappears under the water.

I watch, but it doesn't resurface. It's probably dead, or dying. No way are we going to get any meat from that carcass. At least Jess is safe, but I'm out of slugs. One bullet left in the pistol I've given Max to hold. I'll have to get it back later.

Right now, I have to deal with Dylan.

CHAPTER
25

"I DON'T KNOW WHY YOU did what you did, but it was one of the stupidest things I've ever seen anyone do," I say. "I mean, what did you think would happen?"

Dylan sticks his hands in his pockets, then says slowly, "Sometimes thinking can inhibit action." Then he laughs.

Mike's standing next to him, leaning on his spear, silent. Jess, Tam, and Max span the gap between us, so we form a little semicircle in the swamp.

"Dylan," I say, "you put everyone in danger."

"No one was in danger until you took off running and screaming," Dylan says. "I was gonna meet that bear head-on and turn it back."

"And how were you gonna do that?" I spit some ashy saliva into the swamp. "How?"

"I just was," Dylan says. "I knew it would happen. I can't explain it."

I look toward the sky, relieved to see some patches of blue in the gray. If we can get around this lake and reach those hills, we can empty our packs and dry things out.

"You can't just do whatever you want," Tam says. "Travis had a good plan, to approach the bear as a group. Max had a good plan, to move out of the bear's path. You messed them both up. We got lucky. You got *really* lucky."

Dylan laughs. "You people. You think you know everything. My dad did what he wanted. He followed his vision. And he told me, 'Always follow your vision. Always.'"

I take a step forward. "Your dad is dead. My dad is dead. We can't do what our parents did if we want to survive. They didn't make it. Their systems or visions or plans or dreams weren't good enough. My dad thought we'd be living in a stone-age utopia. That's what he called it when he was convincing my mom to stay. Few people, with enough moose, caribou, salmon, berries, and firewood to go around. We could remake the world up here, cut off from all the crap. Now your dad's vision was a little different than mine. Destroy everything, including the people, and start over." I want to add that he was just plain fucking crazy, but I know that won't be helpful.

"Cleanse," Dylan says. "Not destroy. Cleanse. Purify." Dylan turns to Mike. "Dad would still be here if it weren't for you." He thumps his brother in the chest. "You wrecked it." Dylan takes a step back. Tears run down his cheeks.

Mike reaches out, but Dylan swats his hand away and says, "You wrecked everything."

Mike steps toward Dylan and says, "If I hadn't killed him, he would've killed you, just like he did Mom."

"Mom," Dylan shouts. "He didn't kill Mom. She ran away and never came back. The bitch abandoned us."

Mike shakes his head. "That's what Dad wanted us to believe. But I found her." Mike rubs one of his wrists, and when he removes his hand, I see a scar there. "Nailed to a cross. You remember those counter boards that disappeared from the countertop?"

Dylan just stares at him.

"He used those," Mike says.

Dylan says, "You never showed me. You never told me."

"I wanted to protect you." He rubs his wrist again.

"Liar." Dylan shakes his head. "You probably killed them both. You're just trying to save your own ass now." Dylan turns to the rest of us. "Don't believe him. He's nuts."

Mike glances toward me. I don't know what to say. I mean, I believe Mike's story over Dylan's, but he just said their father killed their mother and Mike killed his father. Who are these guys?

Jess buries her head in Max's side.

"People," I say, "all we've got are each other. None of us are perfect. And it's pretty obvious that we've got a lot to learn about who we all are." I pause. "We need to act as a unit. Maybe none of us will make it to the coast to search for the settlements. But we'll have a lot better chance if we work together."

I look around the circle. Dylan is the true wild card, but if I single him out, he'll fight me the whole way. "Can we all agree to work our way around this lake together and then take a rest in those hills on the far side? And if the weather holds, hopefully, dry out our stuff."

"Who put you in charge?" Dylan asks.

"Just shut up," Tam shouts. "He's not in charge. But neither are you. Just because you caused all this destruction, you think you're some hotshot. You and your dumbass dad killed Jason and Patrick. You killed everything." Tam points at Dylan with her one remaining arrow. "If I didn't have more self-control, I'd shoot this into your gut."

Dylan laughs again. "Go ahead. Use your last arrow on me, bitch."

Tam keeps staring him down. "I'll save it for something that matters." She spits into the swamp and turns her back on him.

I take a deep breath. "I'm just floating an idea. And yeah, I want to leave this wasteland. I didn't cross the river and enter the swamp for fun and games. I'm on a mission. We've been in knee-deep water for over a day." I turn to Dylan. "I'm hoping you'll keep leading us around the lake since you seem to know how to find the shore." It's all I can do to keep from adding the word *asshole* to the end of my request.

Dylan nods and says okay. Which surprises the hell out of me. And no one else says anything. Not even Tam.

I tighten the waist strap on my pack, hoping it'll ease the pressure on my shoulders.

The sun is finally breaking through the clouds, yellow rays cutting through the moisture in the air and stretching across the land. A little dry ground will do us all some good.

We start walking single file on the lakeshore—Dylan in front, me in back. But it's Max who stops us all with her shout.

The bear is crawling out of the lake right at our feet.

CHAPTER
26

I GRAB JESS AND PULL her away from the grizzly. It's moving pretty slowly but it's still moving, the arrow shaft sticking out from its snout. How long was it underwater? Maybe its nose was breaking the surface the whole time and we didn't see it because we were too busy arguing.

It's dragging its belly through the water toward us. Two slugs and an arrow, and it just keeps coming. We're all backing away from the bear, even Dylan.

Max has the pistol, but I'm not sure if she'd use it on the bear, and Tam has just one arrow. My shotgun would be good to use as a club. Mike has his spear.

The bear stops and opens its mouth and lets out a garbled growl, its four canine teeth challenging us to come closer.

"I wonder what it's trying to say," Max says. She has the pistol in her hand but isn't pointing it at the bear, which is only about ten feet away from us.

I say, "Maybe it'll be too weak to follow for long."

"It's suffering," Dylan says. "This wouldn't have happened if you'd let me do it my way."

"You didn't even have a way." I shake my head. "You would've been bear food if I hadn't stepped in."

"Big man with the shotgun," Dylan says. "What's stopping you from shooting again? Bang. Bang. Bang."

"No more ammo," I say. "I wasted it saving your crazy ass again."

The bear is lying down on its belly now, its snout with the arrow shaft sticking out just above the water.

"Quit arguing," Max says. "We just need to get through this."

I imagine swinging the gun and nailing Dylan on the side of his head. I take a deep breath and say, "Okay, let's keep walking the shore. Maybe we can outdistance the bear."

"We should end its pain." Dylan looks at me. "You started the job. You finish it." Then he laughs.

We all keep walking the shore. I wish Mike would say something to his brother. Anything. He said he would handle him but hasn't said a word since Dylan accused him of wrecking their lives.

The bear follows us like it has nothing to lose. I trade guns with Max. I want to end the bear's pain, but I also want some ammo in case we have a run-in with some people.

We start jogging, sloshing through the water, and put more space between us and the bear, but then it powers forward and closes the distance. We must have rounded a tip of the oxbow lake, because the lakeshore is starting to bend south toward the hills we agreed to rest upon.

I wish I could know what the bear is thinking. What it thought it might gain by attacking us. It is so seriously injured that it can't even walk right. I'd hate for one of us to get injured or killed by a bear today that'll probably be dead by tomorrow. I don't even wish that on Dylan. At least not all the time. Yeah, he's pretty deranged, believing that torching the land would cleanse it, but his parents are both dead, like mine. We share that. I'll have to get Mike alone and learn his version of what happened.

But right now we need to do something about this bear that's dogging us.

"Faster," I yell. "Pick up the pace."

We gain some ground, putting fifty yards between us and the bear as we reach the hills and pass the first few. Really, they're just a series of ridges poking four or five feet above the swamp, but a couple hundred feet beyond the ridges is the actual hill we are aiming for. It rises maybe twenty feet above this ash-slurry wasteland. A place where we can spread our stuff out to dry and have a look around.

"Keep going," I say, waving the pistol. "I'm going to finish this." I want Jess as far away as possible. "Max, take Jess up the hill."

Max and Jess follow Dylan and Mike through the rest of the ridges toward the hill, but Tam stays put, drops her pack, and nocks her last arrow.

I nod at her and wonder if she'd really put an arrow into Dylan if she had an unlimited supply. I remember the arrows she put in the guy at the basement and how fast he fell, and I shudder. I'm glad she's here with me.

We watch the bear enter the ridges. We've crossed six or seven of them, about ten feet of swamp separating each one.

I drop my pack, bend my knees, and hold the pistol in both hands like Dad taught me. The bear is still dragging its belly, but its legs move like they're part of a machine, a relentless killing machine set on automatic pilot.

I glance behind me and see Jess and the others on the hill, watching the show. Tam is several yards off to my right and just behind me.

Can I wait until the bear is only ten feet away? Or maybe eight feet? "I'm gonna let the bear get close before I shoot," I say. "Make sure I hit it."

Out of the corner of my eye I see Tam nod.

My heart is pulsing in my throat, pounding in my ears. I wish I had five or six shots to empty into the bear's face while Tam strums endless arrows into its torso. But all we have is one tiny bullet and one arrow.

"Three more ridges," I say, "and I'm shooting."

"Okay," Tam says. Her voice sounds tiny and far away.

The bear lets out a grunt as it crawls over the first of three ridges and then splashes back into the water, the arrow still protruding from its snout.

On the second ridge the bear opens its mouth wide and I see its sharp, bone-crushing teeth, made for ripping through moose hide and cracking bones as big around as my head.

I take a breath.

The bear slops back into the water. The pistol feels like a toy compared to the shotgun. I keep my feet spread apart, trying to stand as still as a statue, but feel my legs shaking. I can see Tam off to the side.

First, one front paw reaches for purchase on the third ridge. Then another. Long claws sink into the wet ash. Claws that can slash through skin and muscle all the way to the bone—the way a knife cuts through butter. Claws that can wipe all the skin off your face with one swipe.

The bear is halfway across the final ridge, slithering, dragging its belly the same way it has since it emerged from the lake. Relentless.

I focus on the bear's head. Ten feet of water separate me from the bear. I can almost smell its breath. I pull the trigger and the bear's head bounces back. Then there's an arrow in its neck. The bear puts a paw forward. Then another.

"Run," Tam yells.

I grab my pack and scramble across a few more ridges, following Tam. Then I stop. I wait for maybe thirty seconds. I'm waiting to see the beast haul itself up on the next ridge, but it doesn't come.

I turn toward Tam, who is halfway up the hill where the others are waiting. We've turned back this bear, but we're out of bullets and arrows. What if we run into another bear? Or some other dangerous animal?

Like a wolverine.

Or a pack of wolves.

Or people.

C H A P T E R
2 7

"IT MIGHT BE DEAD, BUT it might not be." I'm kicked back in the sun on top of the hill with everyone else. Jess has her shoes and socks off and is lying on her side, using her pack as a pillow. She's breathing the even breaths of sleep. I put my hand on her back and a little gurgle of sound escapes her lips, but she keeps sleeping.

"It's bad luck to kill an animal and let it go to waste," Max says.

Tam unties her boots and pulls them off. "Like we had a choice. And that bear might not be dead. If it is, it's underwater."

I want to hug this tiny oasis of dry ground and never let go. I rub Jess's back, dreading having to wake her up to go south, where the swamp continues. Once we get into the foothills of the Alaska Range, the walking will be drier but steeper. Maybe another sixty miles, but I can't be sure.

"I think the bear's dead," Dylan says. "I can't feel its energy anymore."

I keep my hand on Jess's back and just let that comment float past.

Dylan stands up and pulls a knife out of his pack. "I'm going to look for it." He turns to Mike. "Let me have your spear, just in case."

"I'll go with you," Max says.

Dylan smiles. "Cool. Maybe we can salvage some of it." He turns to me. "Instead of letting it all go to waste."

In my head, I cuss Dylan out, then say, softly so I won't wake Jess, "I did my job. Go do yours." I look at Max. "Just be careful." I wish she wasn't going down there, but I'm too beat to argue.

"Mom," Jess says. "Mom."

I let my hand travel up to her shoulder. I press gently and say, "It's okay," because I don't know what else to say. I don't know how to fill the void. Jess keeps her eyes closed and gets back to her even breathing.

I watch Max and Dylan walk down the hill, then scoot closer to Mike. "I think your brother hates me more than I hate him."

Mike smiles. "Dylan's pretty intense, but when he senses something, he's usually right."

I search his eyes. "What he said, about you killing your dad, and what you said happened to your mom, that was all pretty intense."

Mike looks at me, then at Tam, and says, "It was intense. But it's not the way Dylan thinks it happened."

I keep looking at him and say, "If we're going to be traveling together, we need to know. It might help me—help everyone— know how to deal with Dylan."

"Okay." Mike rubs his wrist. "I'll tell you guys, but you can't tell Dylan."

Tam and I agree, and Mike starts talking.

"Dad was going crazy long before he set the fires. Mom just kept praying for him. And she'd tell me not to give up on him. Dylan idolized him. Wanted to do everything Dad did. Wanted Dad to think he was the best. So I was kind of on the outside, except that when me and Dylan were alone, we got along. Then, he wasn't trying to impress Dad, and Dad wasn't using Dylan to try to get to me. Dad knew I didn't buy his vision, but he also knew I cared about Dylan enough that I'd do anything for him. Anything to keep him safe or happy or whatever.

"Mom, she tried to just stay out of it. She believed she could pray her way out of any situation.

"But after Dad torched the land, he became crazier. He started talking in his sleep. And when he was awake, he'd talk to imaginary people, like there were voices in his head.

"Then he started seeing people who weren't there, who were the enemy. He'd step outside the cave and just start shooting. Me and Dylan and Mom didn't know what to do. When was he gonna think we were the enemy and shoot us? But he seemed to know who we were and thought we were on his team. I was too scared to disagree with him. So was Mom.

"One day Dad sent me and Dylan on an expedition downriver to check on one of our shelters. We still had a canoe, so it wasn't that bad of a trip, but when we got back, Mom was gone.

"All Dad said was that she stepped out for a while. Like it was the most natural thing in the world for her to all of a sudden not be here.

"There were a couple of boards missing from the countertop in the very back of the cave. I asked Dad about the boards because he was particular about keeping the counters in good shape. So proud of his design. So where'd they go? *I needed them*, he said, *for something else.*

"Dylan went kind of crazy looking for Mom, but eventually my dad won him over. Convinced him that she'd run away and joined up with some religious group.

"But I didn't believe him, so I used every spare moment I had to search for her, on the outside chance that he hadn't just killed her and tossed her in the river. Maybe he'd tied her up somewhere and she was still alive.

"I found Mom nailed to a cross in a fold just beyond the coal cave. I tossed her body in the river. At first I was kind of amazed that Dylan hadn't found her, but most of his vision involves sensing the presence of living things. Or seeing the landscape in ways that other people can't.

"I couldn't tell Dylan. He was already on the edge. I knew I had to do something, and I knew it'd be hard on him, but the alternative was to lose Dylan like I'd lost my mom.

"At the same time, Dad got on this *basic* kick. He threw all the guns and ammo in the river, set the canoe on fire, and tossed most of the store-bought food he'd stockpiled over the years. Thousands of pounds of food. Into the river. Gone.

"'Basic,' he kept saying. If you can survive basic, you can survive anything. Luckily, we had lots of salmon—some canned and some dried—and berries.

"One day he came at me with a knife. And whatever voices were talking to him, he was talking back. Near as I can tell from just hearing my dad's part of the conversation, *they* were deciding whether to cut me up. He'd come at me and I'd dodge him and then he'd respond to whatever the voices were saying. It was terrifying. There was no way to live safely with him anymore. And I knew that Dylan would never leave him.

"So, when he got distracted by one of the voices, I grabbed a shovel and hit him in the head. Slammed it like there was no tomorrow. I knew if I didn't kill him that there'd be no tomorrow for me or Dylan.

"Dylan took it hard. He'd gotten so swept up in Dad's vision of cleansing the land that he was sure something pure would follow all the death. And, yeah, he still feels that way.

"That cave was my dad's life's work, so staying there afterward was hard. I mean, I felt guilty for killing him. But I felt like I'd evened the score for my mom even though she was dead, and I helped make it possible for Dylan to survive.

"I'm glad I convinced Dylan to head south. Maybe the farther he gets from the cave, from his old life, the more he'll heal. He inherited an amazing gift from my dad, but I'm hoping he can put it to good use, instead of evil. If I can just get him out of this wasteland alive."

Mike glances at Tam and then at me. Before I can say anything, he gets up and walks a little ways away and stares off into the distance.

* * *

"That's how we decided to split up our supplies," Tam says. "We wanted to be in this together and not wish we had something that the other person had. Except for common items, which we took turns carrying, everything else in each pack was the same, or as close to the same as we could make it."

We've taken all our stuff out of our packs to let the sun dry it all out. In my pack, besides some jars of salmon, the rope from the cache, the fire-starting tool, and my knife, were a pair of insulated green coveralls, a green knit cap, green mittens, a green T-shirt, and one pair of thick green socks. Jess, Tam, and Max had identical clothes in their packs.

"Jason and Patrick," Max says, "we've got them to thank for the packs and the clothes."

"And my bow," Tam says. "I wish I had more arrows." She glances at Dylan but doesn't say anything.

Max is carrying the stone spearheads from the museum, a fire starter, and a small pot. Jess has a small folding shovel.

Dylan and Mike have some interesting stuff. Besides jars of salmon, they each have some wool pants, puffy down jackets, some T-shirts and socks, wool hats, and gloves.

They also have a hammer, a couple of pocketknives, a blue plastic trowel, some rolled-up fishnet, and a fire starter like the one I have. Then there are two blue stuff sacks, each about as big as a loaf of bread, but neither Mike nor Dylan makes a move to empty them, saying it's just their personal stuff. I think about asking what that means, but I don't want to upset Dylan.

"Our dad tossed most of the good stuff into the river," Mike says. "But I managed to hide a few things behind the coal under the counter."

"None of this stuff matters anyway," Dylan says. "If we live, we live. If we die, we die. Look around. We're tiny."

"But don't you want to survive?" I ask. "You sure looked like you did when you were carrying that beaver. And then running from those guys that took it from you. And hoping to salvage the bear. Even after Max came back saying she couldn't find it, you kept searching on your own for a few more hours. And showing off the shelters your dad built, those were all about survival."

Dylan stares straight into my eyes. I wait for him to speak but he doesn't. He just keeps staring.

Finally, I turn away, but I can still feel his eyes on me. I want to get along with him and I think maybe if we just get to know each other, if we could break the ice, it'd make things easier, because crossing the land is going to be hard enough as it is. We have to work together.

The shove comes hard and quick, and I go down. Instantly,

Dylan is on my back, grinding my face into the ash. The back of my nose is on fire. I hear shouts and try to turn my head sideways to keep the ash out of my mouth and eyes and to take the pressure off my nose.

I feel my cheek getting hot, like maybe the skin is being scraped off on the jagged ground under the ash. Wet sticky blood from my nose runs over the corner of my mouth. I kick my legs and try to rotate my hips, but it feels like I'm pinned under a pile of rocks.

"Get off him," Jess screams.

I wiggle one arm free, reach up and grab Dylan's thick hair, and pull. And I just keep on pulling until I feel his face next to mine. Then I blow air from my mouth as hard as I can, hoping the ash will go into his eyes and nose and mouth. I can't see anything because my eyes are closed. I know that when I finally open them, they'll be burning and itching.

"Let go, Travis," Mike says. "We've got him."

"It's okay," Max says.

I crack one eye open and see their feet around me, but I keep my grip on Dylan's hair. I'd love to pull his head right off his body, then drop-kick it into the swamp. I can't tell if my blood is flowing from one nostril or both, but I can feel it running down my cheek. And something is grinding into my spine between my shoulder blades. Dylan's elbow, probably.

"We can't pull him off you," Tam says, "until you let go."

I feel a hand on my hand, prying my fingers. "Trav," Jess says, "let go."

I let go and feel a jab in my side as they pull Dylan off me. I push to my knees and then stand. Blood runs over my lips and I wipe it away with my hands, but it just keeps coming. I tilt my head back and take a breath through my mouth.

"Never talk about my dad," Dylan says. "Never."

I squint down at him through my burning eyes. One side of his face is covered in gray-black ash. Other than that, the bastard looks normal. "None of us have parents," I say. "We don't have anyone except each other. You hurt anyone here, you're hurting everyone." I feel blood above my lip, gathering on my mustache, and suck more air through my nose to keep it from dripping.

"Just don't talk about my dad, ever," Dylan says.

"I don't know what's in your head," I say. "I can't know unless you tell me. That's true for all of us. But if we're going to have any chance of crossing this burnt-out swamp and finding a route through the mountains, we've got to work together. All I'm asking is that you try. And that you don't attack any of us."

Dylan spits, then rubs his eyes, which I'm sure are just as irritated as mine. I'd love to clock him right between the eyes. Smash his nose so hard that it sticks out the back of his skull. I hate him.

"My dad was special," Dylan says. "He was . . ." He shakes his head. "Forget it. Just don't talk about him." He turns away.

I look at Mike and he puts a finger to his lips. I flip him off and head to the swamp to wash the blood off my face.

CHAPTER
28

TWO DAYS LATER, AND THE mountains are actually starting to look bigger. The swamp has been ankle-deep the past few hours. Dylan navigated us around a few more lakes, and we haven't seen any more bears. We haven't seen anything. Just the sun beating down on the gray slurry and on us, and some fireweed and willow sprouts on little hills poking above the swamp.

We're walking side by side, all six of us. My feet are warm but wet. And my nose is still a little sore. We left the guns back on the hill. No ammo and probably no chance of getting any. No need to carry the extra weight.

"Something's changing ahead," Dylan says. True to his word, no one has mentioned his dad and he's stuck with the group. He didn't apologize for attacking me, but I didn't expect him to. In his mind, everything he does is the right thing to do. And to me, that's what makes him scary. You just can't reason with him at all. It's better to simply let him talk. And I've got to admit, he's done a good job of navigating the land—way better than I could've done. Still, I'd like to clock him, just once, right on the nose.

Dylan stops and we all stop with him, waiting.

"We'll see it when we see it," Dylan says, then starts walking.

Slowly, almost imperceptibly, the ground begins to rise. There's less and less standing water and, suddenly, we're walking on dry ground.

I turn to Dylan. "This is a pretty nice change."

He laughs a friendly laugh, like we're best friends, and says, "This is only the beginning."

A couple miles later we encounter a fissure, where the ground has probably been wrenched apart by an earthquake. It's only a few feet wide but runs east to west as far as we can see, and it is filled with water. We jump over it and keep going.

A half mile later we hit another one. It's wider, eight feet across. Mike pokes the water with his spear and it sinks about four feet before stopping.

"It could be deeper in the middle," I say. "How about if I jump across, then you guys can throw me your packs and we'll keep them dry. Then you can each jump across."

Jess turns to me. "I don't think I can jump that far."

"I'll jump back over after the packs are across, and we'll wade across together."

"I'll wade with Jess," Max says.

Jess shakes her head. "You guys all jump. I'll do it alone." A smile breaks out on my face and I turn toward Jess and wink.

I take my pack off and hand it to Mike. "Maybe two of you could throw it. You know, each one take an end and lob it gently so I can get under it and make sure the jars don't break."

"Sounds good," Mike says.

Max, Dylan, and Jess nod. Tam has her back to us. She's always keeping watch when we stop.

"There's going to be more," Dylan says.

"One fissure at a time," I say, then laugh.

"Whatever," Dylan says. I'm pretty sure I hear him say *asshole* under his breath, but I don't even care. As long as he doesn't do anything stupid.

I get a running start and leap across with a few feet to spare. Dylan and Mike swing my pack like it's a jump rope and, on the count of three, lob it over. I catch it and stagger back a few steps.

Max takes her pack off. "I'm jumping across to help catch."

She clears the fissure with no problem.

Max and I stand side by side, arms out, knees bent, and catch one pack after another until we have all six of them. Mike jumps across, then Dylan, then Tam.

Jess wades in. The water comes up to her chin as she scrambles from one side to the other, then I pull her out.

"Good job," I say.

She sighs. "I wish I could've jumped."

I wish she could've, too. I hate seeing her all wet while the rest of us are dry. I think about jumping in too so she's not alone, but think that would only make her feel worse.

Max puts her arm around Jess. "Maybe you'll be able to jump the next one."

A few minutes later, and we're all staring at the next fissure. It's at least twenty feet across.

Mike sticks his spear in the water. "It's deep," he says. "Over our heads."

"We can't swim with our packs," Max says.

Tam keeps her back to us and says, "We could follow the fissure until it ends. It can't go forever."

I glance east and west, trying to see where the fissure ends, but can't.

"We could walk for miles and miles," I say, "and not reach the end, and have to swim anyway."

Dylan points across the fissure. "They're going to get wider and deeper."

Max touches his arm like she's his girlfriend, and he just nods without even looking at her. For part of yesterday she walked with Dylan, talking quietly to him. If Dylan goes wacko again, I hope Jess isn't too influenced by how Max sees him, because she's still close as ever to Max. I don't want to, but if I have to I'll take Jess and strike out on my own.

The sun hangs just above the mountain peaks to the south. I turn sideways to it so I can see. Our shadows stretch to the north. "We could use the rope to get the packs across. One person swims across with the end of the rope. Another person holds it taut from this side. We hook a pack into it and someone swims it across."

Tam turns. "I'll swim packs across."

Mike nods. He's barely spoken a word the last couple of days.

"Fine," Dylan says. "Whatever."

Max and Jess say okay.

We all take our packs off. I fish the rope out of mine and give one end to Jess. "Hold on to this while I swim to the other side." I wade in and the bottom drops out from under my feet, and I side-stroke across. The water's colder than I thought it'd be—freezing compared to the sun-warmed swamp.

On the other side I crawl out. I watch Dylan slide a pack onto the rope through a webbed hoop. Then he clicks the waist strap onto the rope for more support. Mike grabs the other end of the rope and we both lean away from the fissure to get the rope as taut as possible.

Tam slips into the water and shoves the pack forward. She puts her hands on it, starts kicking, and doesn't stop until the pack kisses the edge of the fissure. I haul the pack out. She flashes me a smile and her blue eyes sparkle in the sunlight. I smile back at her, wondering what her deal is and how she ended up in that group home. I know almost nothing about her life before the government pulled out.

As Tam swims back, Mike threads another pack onto the rope. Dylan jumps in and kicks it across.

At the bank, Dylan pauses before swimming back. "Good idea," he says. "About how to get the packs across."

He pushes off before I can say anything. Either I imagined that, or he's just given me a compliment. I decide not to say anything back to him even if I get the chance. I don't want to wreck whatever stability seems to be lingering between his ears.

Tam and Dylan each kick another two packs across, then Mike, Jess, and Max swim across.

We're all soaked, but we keep walking until we hit the next fissure.

"No way," I say. "No freaking way." I'm happy and sad at the same time. The fissure is at least a couple hundred feet across. And deep. But even if it was narrow enough to span with the rope, we still couldn't have used it because there's no water in this fissure except for a windy ribbon at the bottom, maybe two or three hundred feet down. And along the stream or narrow lake or swamp or whatever it is, I see the unmistakable green of plant life. Not tiny sprouts and spindly fireweed, but full-grown trees.

I want to get down there and then climb back up to the other side, but the nearly vertical walls down into the fissure, stretching as far as the eye can see both east and west, appear impossible to navigate.

CHAPTER
29

"WE EITHER NEED TO GO around this fissure or canyon, whatever it is, or through it." I pass the jar of salmon to Mike. We're all perched on the edge of the drop-off, peering down. Even Tam. Mike holds the jar until Tam nudges him. He takes a small piece and passes it to her without saying a word.

"See," Max says, "the land is healing."

I pull one of my shoes off to shake out some rocks. "I guess the fire passed over the top of this fissure."

"Even if it did," Tam says, "coals would've rained down and scorched it."

"Maybe it did burn a little, just not as hot as up here." Dylan takes a piece of salmon and passes the jar to Max.

"The Garden of Eden," Max says. "That's what it is."

The green ribbon stretches east and west. I see birch trees and willows down there. And we can hear the distant hum of flowing water.

"I wonder why this fissure isn't filled with water to the top, like the other ones," Jess says.

"It must have an outlet," Dylan says. "Maybe it empties into a river."

"Right," I say. "That makes sense. But what I want to know is how we're going to get down there."

"Maybe we could make some arrow shafts," Tam says. "And long spears for those stone spearpoints—if we can get down there. We don't want to get trapped. If we go down, we need to make sure there's a way out on the other side."

"There's a way," Dylan says. "There has to be."

"Why?" I ask. "There's lot of places people can't get to." Anger bubbles up from inside me, and I want to say that I'm glad his dad's fire of destruction missed this place. Just breathing the life in from up here would show anyone how wrong it was to set those fires. But Dylan has been so stable the last two days that I don't want to disrupt the balance.

"I just know," Dylan says. "Accept it."

"Birds," Max says. "Small birds. I just saw some flitting around down there. Well, I saw one. But where there's one, there's more." She laughs.

"The bear," Jess says. "Maybe it was coming here." She makes a growling sound, pretending to be a bear, and we all laugh. Max holds out her hand for a high five and Jess smacks it.

Big white clouds are billowing over the mountains to the south. And a breeze is blowing ash over the fissure, but before the ash reaches our side it gets caught in an updraft.

"I know there's a way down," Dylan says. "People have been down there before. Maybe some still are. I can feel them."

I glance at Mike, but he doesn't say anything.

"And that ash rising," Dylan says. "That's from warm air. All things being equal, it should be cooler than the air rising from the burnt land up here. Unless there's a heat source down there. Some hot water, or steam, or a fire."

Sometimes Dylan sounds downright scholarly. I like this Dylan, the one who studies things and talks without insulting me. Right now he's the politest arsonist I've ever met.

"Are we gonna go all the way down there?" Jess asks, as she rubs her bare feet in the ash.

I put my hand on her shoulder and say, "I hope so."

"Me too," Max says.

Dylan smiles and just keeps staring, like he's in a trance.

* * *

"The rope won't help because there isn't anything to tie it to." We've been walking east along the fissure, the green belt calling to us from below. But now the air rising from below feels cool on my cheeks, like a damp rag.

"Maybe we can cut steps into the face," I say. "Create a stairway as we go."

"Not here," Dylan says. "It's the wrong type of dirt. It'll collapse. But there has to be a way."

"This is what hell is like," Max says. "Staring at paradise with no way to get there."

Dylan turns to Max. "We'll find a way down."

She touches his arm, smiles at him, and says, "Cool." And he smiles back.

How can Max like him? I mean, he torched the land she loved. But as long as his actions don't endanger Jess, I can live with those two hanging out, hooking up, or doing whatever. I just want to keep my sister from being influenced by his type of crazy.

The clouds crowding the sky start spitting rain. We keep walking, searching for a break in the cliffs. I'm sure everyone else is as hungry as I am, but no one asks to stop and eat. Not even Jess. We'll have to inventory our food, maybe even ration it. If we keep running into big obstacles, it could take a long time to reach the coast.

The rain comes harder, soaking my hair, pressing it against my neck. Water runs down my back beneath my pack. The wind starts blowing, turning wet skin into wet and cold skin. Even though it's summer, the only way to stay warm in this weather—to keep from freezing—without shelter is to keep moving.

No one speaks as we kick our way through muddy ash. And even though fire destroyed this place, all I want right now is a big blaze to warm me up.

If Dylan and his dad hadn't burned this place, maybe we'd still be living in our house. People used to start fires in and around Fairbanks every year, but the firefighters always put them out.

Things you took for granted. Firefighters, stores full of food, a house to live in. Electricity. Gasoline.

And then later, houses, a river full of fish, few enough people that the land might be able to support them. But the fires changed all that, erased in an instant the tiny dreams of a few people. And created a desperate time. As if the land being destroyed also destroyed what was civilized in people.

But a remnant of Interior Alaska lies below us.

I have to get down there. Somehow. Just to recharge my belief in humanity. In life. My belief that even a guy like Dylan, who believes that the fires were purifying, could see that what his dad convinced him to do was a big mistake. How can I ever trust Dylan if he can't see that? I hope Mike is right, that the farther away Dylan gets from his father's cave, the more stable he'll become.

We come to a spot where the cliff has sloughed into a steep pile of dirt down into the fissure. It's still steep, but not sheer. Rainwater runs down a crack at an angle to the cliff instead of straight down.

"See that water?" Dylan asks. "I think it's running that way because people or animals or both have walked there. This is the place. The trail in."

I have to admit that—steep as it is—it does look like a trail. It's the best option for getting down there that we've seen. Really, the only option.

I put my arm around Jess but speak to everyone. "Press your body into the cliff face. We should spread out so we don't start a chain reaction. If you stumble, you don't want to fall onto someone and knock them off."

Tam slips her pack off and straps her bow to it, then puts it back on. Then she says, "Mike, just toss your spear over the edge. You don't want to walk with it. Too dangerous."

Mike turns to Dylan, who just shrugs and says, "Basic." Then he laughs, and I feel a chill travel up my spine.

"I'll go first," I say. "Just let me get about fifty yards down. And once you go, you need to keep moving. If you stop, you might screw up whoever's behind you. I'm not sure what it'll be like past this first run, but be prepared to slide on your butt or your stomach or whatever it takes to control yourself to keep from falling."

"Dude," Dylan says, "we get it. Hug the cliff, and give each other some space. Let's go. I just want to get down there. This place, it's got energy. Good energy. It's the place to be."

I cuss him out in my mind but say nothing. I really want to take Jess with me but know if I did and then fell, I'd just be endangering her.

Dylan turns to Mike. "It's gonna be a hell of a ride." He laughs. "Enjoy it." Then he slaps his brother on the arm.

Mike nods and says, "I'll try." But he isn't smiling.

Max hasn't said a word. She's just standing there, her eyes fixed on the narrow trail. "I'll go second," she says. "Jess, you follow me."

Jess just nods. If she's scared, she's not showing it.

Dylan wants to go last, and Mike just before him, so Tam is fourth.

I start sidestepping down the trail and immediately start to slide. I try to claw my way upward as my feet keep moving forward and manage to feel like I have a little control, but I'm moving about four times as fast as I want to. Out of nowhere a switchback appears, and I pivot on one foot and scramble in the opposite direction. Now I'm sure I'm out of view, but I can't stop to warn the others about the switchback because losing my momentum would increase my chance of a free fall.

I'm glad for the wet earth because it slows me down a little. I dig my hands and elbows into it and get a face full of mud but just keep dancing forward. Downward.

Up ahead I see that the cliff is eroded and almost vertical so I turn again, trying to avoid the steep part.

After I turn, I thrust my legs down and out and lean backward in an attempt to regain some control. But the cliff has other plans for me, and I start to slide straight down. I'm thankful that it's mud and not rock. I dig my palms and heels in and try to control my slide. The rain is pounding and I'm a giant mud ball sliding down the soft cliff, but I can see the green blur growing bigger.

My heels connect with something solid and I'm propelled forward. I let out a scream as my entire body catches only air, but I'm almost there. I lean forward, but not far enough, and when I hit the ground, I land on my backpack and hear the crunch of glass. I hope it's only a jar or two.

My head feels like it's still rushing forward, and I get dizzy, like I jumped out of a moving car or off a bicycle and then hit the ground. But I'm lying here, stopped. And totally covered in mud.

I hear one long scream and turn toward the cliff but can't see anything. I try to wipe the mud from eyes but my hands are muddy, which just makes things worse.

I force myself to stand up and I stumble. I slip my pack off. I have to get the mud out of my eyes, have to be able to see.

Jess, I think. *Was that her scream?* I pry my eyes open with my thumbs and index fingers. They sting like they've been sprayed with soapy water. I keep them open for a moment, staring up at the cliffs, but see no one.

"Jess," I yell through the rain that is still pounding down. I cup my hands, catch some raindrops, and rub my hands together until they feel mostly clean. Then I catch more water and splash it into my eyes until I can keep them open without too much burning.

I keep expecting to see someone tumbling down, but no one comes. I think about the lone scream I heard.

Just one scream, the word *no* all stretched out.

There could've been others. I mean, I was pretty caught up in my own descent, concentrating on trying to stay alive.

I get this sick burning feeling in my stomach.

Where is everyone?

CHAPTER
30

I CALL OUT AGAIN AND again and keep glancing up at the cliffs, but encounter only emptiness. I'm a mud sculpture melting in the rain. I turn toward the trees, wanting to take shelter, but I have to keep searching.

The light is dimmer down here, the fissure walls acting as dark barriers.

I try to replay the journey in my mind, but it grows all fuzzy after the first switchback. I was heading east and then I turned.

It was a sharp turn, I remember. A turn I almost missed. And if I'd missed it, I would have . . . I would've kept going east either in the air or on the cliff. Turning seemed like the only option, but maybe it wasn't.

And one scream was all I heard, but that was later. After I landed on my back and broke a jar, or more than one. I glance at my pack. Then I take a breath. One thing at a time, I tell myself.

East. East. East.

I shoulder my pack—it feels twice as heavy with the coating of mud—and head east, yelling for Jess. Yelling for anyone. For everyone. Even Dylan.

The rain is backing off, becoming gentler, kissing my face instead of punching it. I'm not sure how far to the west I slid but

I'm pretty sure it was way beyond the equivalent of our starting point above. I glance back. I can see the trail my feet and arms cut across the slope as I came down after the switchback. Then where I turned again and then where I plowed almost straight to the bottom until I turned into an airborne mud ball and landed on my pack.

I scan the cliff for other trails but don't see any.

The switchback. Did they all miss it? But the scream. That one scream. I feel an ache in my gut. Jess.

I keep walking—my feet sinking into the mud and making sucking sounds with every step—scanning the cliff face in the hope that I've missed something, because I don't want to believe that I'm alone down here. But that's how it feels. Did someone come? Were they ambushed after I started down?

I swallow the panic and keep walking. Then I spot something blue bumping up from the ground in front of me. Just a mound of blue maybe fifty yards ahead. I try picking up the pace but the mud keeps grabbing me around the ankles, making me earn every step.

A blue backpack. A blue backpack. I see legs, too. A blue backpack attached to a body, facedown, mostly buried in mud.

Blue. Blue. Blue.

Dylan. Mike. Dylan. Mike.

Blue backpack. They each had one.

Impact. I look up. I look down. Soft mud.

A long fall.

A scream.

Dylan. Or Mike.

I reach down and shake the backpack. Then a shoulder. But I know it's no use.

I've seen a lot of dead bodies. More dead people than live ones the past few years. I look up again. There are no marks on the cliff face. No marks of someone scrambling for a hold, for purchase. No slide marks at all. Like he jumped from the top.

I let my eyes fall to the backpack. Then to the body. The unmistakable legs as long as my own. I reach out and shake Mike's shoulder again but there's no response. The mud must've sucked in around him on impact.

Where is everyone else? I look up at the cliff again. The body is almost even with the switchback point, but not quite.

I wish it was Dylan. And then I feel bad for wishing that. But it's true.

I grab the backpack and pull. "Mike," I say, "Mike."

The resistance from the mud pulls back. I bend at the knees and yank again. I feel the body move, then settle into the mud. I pull again. The mud makes this sucking sound, and one side of the body pops free.

I keep pulling until I have him lying on his side, his back to me. I yank his free arm toward me, brush the mud from his wrist, and feel for a pulse.

"Come on," I say. "Be there."

I don't know what else to do. I mean, what can I do? I reach my hand over his head and put it next to his lips and nose, hoping to feel some air moving in and out of his lungs, but there's nothing.

I grab his wrist again, and press my fingers into the spot just below his thumb. Nothing. I feel his neck for a pulse. Nothing. I check his wrist again.

"God dammit, Mike! Wake up! Wake up!"

I wonder if anyone else is even alive. And if they are, why I haven't heard them. Why haven't they come looking for me? Max and Jess and Tam were supposed to come down before Mike. I don't understand.

I set Mike's hand down. Then gently roll him back over. I don't want to see his face. The twisted pain I imagine would be on it. The bruising. Nose probably smashed from the impact.

My legs are wobbly, but I need to keep moving to see what has become of Jess.

CHAPTER
31

I KEEP HEADING UPSTREAM—EAST. The stream bends closer to the cliff, and the hiss of flowing water fills my ears. I can see the switchback spot, and now I can see that if I'd missed the turn, I'd have had to contend with a narrow ravine that cuts the slope in two. You would definitely catch some air if you didn't turn. And if you didn't catch enough air, you'd end up in the ravine. I shudder. Are they all piled up and unconscious or dead in the ravine? But wouldn't they have tumbled to the bottom even if they did fall in there?

I check out the angle I traveled and, with my eyes, extend it to the far side of the ravine. A faint trail dances in and out of my vision in the dim light. Is it really a trail? Or is my mind just making it into one? The trail is much less distinct than mine, but maybe it's just a different kind of soil. It's lighter in color, tan instead of dark brown. Maybe the ravine is some kind of geologic dividing line.

The rain has completely stopped, but the wind has started blowing from the east, whooshing down the fissure.

I shiver.

If I was on top, I'd be in the sun, but the sun probably only hits the bottom of the fissure for a few hours a day. It's a different world down here. A narrow, green world, damp and cold right now.

Someone has to be at the end of that trail.

I keep walking along the base of the cliff. On the other side of the ravine, the trail continues down at a slightly steeper pitch. I picture my sister navigating that cliff, jumping a ravine. I know she'd give it her best shot, but maybe it was too much to ask of her. Mike's lifeless body flashes into my mind.

I spot another ravine. The trail continues on the other side of it at an even steeper pitch.

I catch a whiff of salmon and remember the crunch of glass. My backpack has to be a mess inside. Hopefully, we'll be able to pick the shards of glass out of the fish so we can eat it. *We*, I think. I hope there'll be a *we*.

"Jess," I yell. "Jess." My voice bounces back and forth between the fissure walls, with the stream gurgling in the background. My heart pounds in a panic, like it'll explode if I don't find my sister.

"Trav! Trav!"

I let out a breath I didn't know I was holding. I can hear her, just barely, like a kitten trapped way up high in a tree, but I can't see her.

I call back and stand still, waiting.

Nothing.

I run forward a dozen steps, the mud sucking at my ankles, then stop and call out again.

"Trav," I hear.

Jess. My Jess. Where are you? Images of Mom and Dad flash into my brain. And Jess.

The cliff buttresses out, blocking my view up the fissure. I scan the buttress but don't see her. I don't see anyone. Not even a trail.

I round the buttress and keep looking up, trying to imagine

her stuck on the slope, teetering on a tiny ledge. How would I get to her?

"Trav." Her voice explodes in my ears, and I jerk my head toward the sound. And there, right at the edge of the skinny birches and willows, I see her small frame standing over two muddy lumps.

CHAPTER
32

"MIKE MUST'VE FALLEN FROM THE top, or close to it," I say.

Smoke from the fire snakes upward. I never thought I'd be this happy to see a fire in the summer again. I've collected a bunch of dead willow branches, stripped some birch bark from a couple of birch trees and, with my fire starter, rained sparks onto the crumpled bark until it ignited.

"I heard a scream behind me," Tam says. "I'd just started down the trail but couldn't look back. I was too scared I'd fall."

"I think I heard it, too," Max says. "When I was jumping one of the ravines. I think it was the second one, but I'm not sure."

Nobody has seen Dylan. We called and called for him with no response. Dylan must've seen what happened. And if he did see his brother fall, why isn't he down here looking for him? Unless he's fallen too and we just haven't found him.

We've taken everything out of our packs. Broken glass, salmon, and clothes with splotches of salmon oil. We still have sixteen intact jars of salmon between us. And at least seven broken jars.

"I didn't hear anything," Jess says. "I was too busy following Max. She was flying."

My right shoulder aches. Tam has bloody scratches running up and down one of her cheeks and a sore ankle. Max says her knee throbs when she puts weight on it. And Jess is having trouble making a fist with her left hand because she's sprained her fingers.

Max takes the small metal pot she's been carrying in her pack and limps over to the creek to fill it. Back at the fire she puts some strips of oily salmon into the pot, then sets it on some hot coals off to the side of the fire.

The birches are uniformly tall and narrow, reaching for the limited sunlight that slips between the fissure walls. The willows bush out a little more than the birches, but are narrower than the willows I remember from home. Leafy green fireweed with purple flowers grows skinny, too, as does the wild rose. All this life in one little spot, stretching for sun.

I build up the fire, and we take our clothes off and drape them on branches so they'll dry. We're all sitting close to the fire and it's dim under the trees in the fissure. Max stretches her arms above her head, and I catch a silhouette of her side profile and her full breasts. I quickly look away.

Tam sits directly across from me. She's thinner than Max, more like a wild animal made to run and hunt. But there's a softness to her in the firelight.

I press my legs together. Tam and I. We each killed a man the day we met and then a few days later worked together to kill a bear when we barely knew each other. And we still don't know much about each other, but there's a certain comfort that comes when you share intense experiences. When you work together in a survival situation. So even though I don't know her, she feels familiar. She's tossed a few smiles my way, too. But that doesn't mean that it's okay to stare at her, so I try to give her space with my eyes and keep them on the fire.

"I love the feel of the heat on my bare skin," Max says. "A luxury."

No one says anything in response.

Then I say, "I think it's actually going to get dark down here for a few hours," trying to pretend I'm thinking about something other than the person sitting across from me. "Not dark enough for stars but way darker than up there." I point to the rim of the fissure.

The fire burns down. I put a few more sticks on and we climb into our coveralls.

"We need some rest," I say. "But we also need to keep watch. In pairs. I'll take the first watch."

"Me too," Max says.

*　*　*

"Your sister," Max whispers, "she's amazing. Never gives up."

Max and I are sitting in front of the coals. We talked about leaving the trees to keep watch where it's more open but decided we all need to stick together. Tam and Jess are lying down, shoulder to shoulder, on the other side of the fire ring.

"You've been a big help," I whisper. "Sometimes I just don't know what to say to her, or how to comfort her. Especially when she calls out for my mom in her sleep. There's no way I can't disappoint her." I hesitate. "It helps to have someone besides just me. She likes you."

"Jess is easy to like," she says. "She reminds me of my little sister"—Max pauses—"may she be experiencing peace, wherever she is." Max tells me about her family. About her father succeeding in killing the whole family, except herself.

"I had to move into that group home," Max whispers, "because

I had no more family. Some of the girls were tough in there, especially on new arrivals. I am not a mean person, but I had to get mean to survive that place—at least at first."

"How long did you live there?" I put another willow branch on the coals.

"About four years," Max says. "I got good at reading stressed-out people and then acting in a way that made them relax. People fighting that don't need to fight each other—that makes me sad."

A breeze shakes the tops of the trees, and water rains down from the wet leaves. I pull my knees toward my chest and catch a whiff of salmon from an oil splotch on my coveralls.

Max shakes her head. "At one point there were twenty girls living in that group home. You couldn't count on the staff to protect you, because there were so few workers. Then they fenced the whole place in and made it into a locked facility and had us do our school there, too. Not because we were all that dangerous but because that was the only way they could manage it with so few workers. About half of us would have been in foster care if that system hadn't collapsed, too. At least we had three meals a day at the home."

"So they just locked you up?" I ask. "They could do that?"

"When the state and the country are falling apart, they can do almost anything."

We sit quietly for a while and my mind switches to Dylan.

I know Max is infatuated with Dylan. And that Dylan likes her, too. And thinking of Dylan—I just don't understand where he is. He was in total agreement about coming down here. He even found the trail and talked about the good energy he felt.

"What do you think happened to Dylan?" I ask.

She turns her head toward me. Our faces are inches apart. "I think . . ." Max pauses. "I think Dylan pushed Mike off the cliff and now he's—"

"Wait," I say. I feel my forehead tighten. I go back and forth with this idea. I could see him wanting to push me, but not his own brother. "Why do you think he pushed him?"

"I can't explain it logically," Max says. "You heard him talking about the fires and the cleansing. He's crazy."

"But the way he can sense things, I thought you liked him. I mean, really *liked* him."

"At first I did," Max says. "But after seeing how flipped out he was, I didn't want to cross him. But I could tell he liked me, and I didn't want to put us all in danger by pissing him off, so I played along. I figured it was the best thing to do. Not just for me, but for everyone."

"But I thought—"

"I know what you thought," Max says. "And I did think it was super cool that he'd seen that bear, and could pick out the lakeshore in the middle of the swamp. But believing in burning the land?" She shakes her head. "I wanted to cry when I heard that."

I say, "You had me fooled."

"Look at my clothes and hair," Max says. "The only way I've survived this long is by fooling people. Until Jason and Patrick gave us these clothes and packs." She sighs. "The other four girls that didn't make it, that easily could have been me."

I nod, remembering what happened on the banks of the Yukon.

"I just want to live in a world where I don't have to pretend to be someone I'm not just to protect myself," she says.

I turn my face toward her, but then a big splash sends a jolt through my spine. I look toward the creek. I see nothing, but I know something has to be there.

CHAPTER
33

"IT COULD'VE BEEN AN ANIMAL," Max says. "Maybe a fish jumping."

"Or maybe a branch from a birch tree fell into the water," Tam says. She jumped up right after the splash.

"Or Dylan," I say.

The willows crowd the creek, making it the dimmest spot in the fissure.

I listen, but all I hear is the rush of water.

"This fissure or canyon or whatever it is, it's pretty narrow," Max says. "It'd be a hard place to hide from someone if they wanted to find you."

"Dylan," I yell. "Dylan. Come on out."

Jess springs into a sitting position. "My turn for watch yet?"

"Everyone's on watch now, sis. We heard a splash in the creek."

Jess stands up. Her coveralls are huge on her. She's like a mouse wearing clothes cut for an elephant.

"I think we should take a look." I pick up my knife. I wish I had a gun or a spear. I remember that Mike chucked his spear down from above. If we hunt around, we should be able to find it. Plus, we have all those stone spearpoints. And now we have tree branches to cut shafts from.

"I'll go, too," Max says. "If it's Dylan, I'll be able to handle him." She smiles. "You know, calm him down."

I rub my sore shoulder. "Only if he didn't overhear you while we were talking."

"Whispering," she says. "We were whispering."

"I heard everything," Tam says. "And I was on the other side of the fire ring. So if he was behind you, and just as close, he would've heard, too."

"Maybe there's other people down here," Jess says. She glances over her shoulder.

"Could be," I say. "We just don't know. All we know is that we heard a big splash."

* * *

"Just because we didn't see any footprints doesn't mean there was nobody there," I say, then add more sticks to the fire until the flames are waist-high. It's light out and we want to finish drying our mud-caked clothes.

Tam puts some salmon in the water-filled pan and sets it on some coals. "If Dylan is down here, we need to find him. If he's around, I want him in my sight."

"If he's around, he has to have seen the smoke from our fire," I say. "So why wouldn't he approach us?"

"Maybe he's hurt." Jess stretches her arms over her head and almost disappears inside her coveralls. "Maybe he can't walk."

I fold down the collar of my coveralls so it won't poke me in the neck. "It seems like I would've run into him on my hike to find you three. It just doesn't make sense. I bet he didn't even come down here. I hope he didn't come down here—if he really pushed Mike, that is. I mean, no way could we trust him then."

"Of course he pushed him. He's whacked-out." Tam yanks the pot from the coals. "Dig in. It's just hot enough."

We all pull pieces of lukewarm salmon out of the pot, then take turns drinking the oily broth until it's gone. But the small meal barely puts a dent in my hunger.

Sunlight plasters the south wall of the fissure, turning it golden. In a few hours it'll probably be bouncing off the treetops and then reaching all the way to the bottom.

We douse the fire with creek water, then kick dirt on it. We pack the loose salmon into the pot, then tie my spare T-shirt around it. It'll leak some oil, but that's our only option. We decide to take everything with us because we don't know if we're coming back to this spot. Our first task is grimmer than grim: taking care of Mike's body.

CHAPTER
34

WE HEAD WEST, DOWNSTREAM. THE ground is more solid by the stream and doesn't suck my feet into the mud with every step like it did at the base of the fissure wall yesterday.

At the second ravine we turn toward the north wall. "If we walk the base of the wall, we'll come to his body."

No one says anything in response. I feel my stomach tightening. We haven't even talked about what we're going to do. I know Jess has a shovel in her backpack, but digging a grave will take hours, hours that we could be using to keep moving south. Could we just leave him? Or would that be disrespectful? I know we're going to take the food and anything else useful in his pack, so shouldn't we do something with his body to honor him?

After a couple of minutes we run into my tracks from yesterday, so all we have to do is follow them.

I've seen a lot of dead bodies the past couple of years but it's always a shock, especially if they don't have many surface injuries. The charred bodies I encountered after the fires—it was obvious they were history.

But bodies that look mostly normal, you think there would be some way to breathe life back into them. To fix them and get them working again. They have all those cells and nerves and organs and muscles that were working one moment, then idle the next. Like someone flipped a power switch that can't be reversed even though the machine still appears to be in good condition.

"He was right here," I say. We're staring at the outline in the mud where Mike's body landed. Inside the outline are bits of blue nylon and shards of glass. And heading toward the trees is a drag path.

"Dylan?" Tam says.

"Who else could it be?" Max says.

"Look at this." Jess is pointing down just a few feet from the body outline.

I feel a chill travel up my spine. There, in the drying mud, is a pad print. Like a circle that has been stretched, or a triangle rounded at the edges. And on the wide side—the base of the triangle—are five distinct toe prints. And beyond those, little dots where claws must've pressed into the ground.

"Grizzly," I say.

Tam limps over and studies the track. "Maybe that's what we heard in the creek last night."

"Bears cache their food," Max says. "You know. They eat some and bury the rest for later. But they guard it. We need to be careful."

"Why didn't we see any tracks by the creek last night?" I ask.

"Maybe it stayed in the water for a while or walked on some rocks." Max glances back the way we came. "Maybe if we'd crossed the creek and walked a little ways, we would've seen some tracks on the other side."

Tam limps around in a circle. "That bear had to come from somewhere to get here, but I don't see a trail."

We all start looking around, studying the ground. I wonder what could support a bear in here. We still don't know the size or extent of the fissure. From the top it appeared to go on forever, but I know that on flat ground you can only see so far in any direction. Maybe it widens into an actual valley downstream or upstream. Or maybe it's tiny and ends in sheer walls in every direction, and the stream disappears underground. I hope that isn't the case.

"Here's another one," Max says. She's standing about ten yards down the drag trail.

"Maybe it dragged Mike on the same path it took to come out of the trees," Tam says.

Fragments of glass and pieces of blue nylon dot the drag trail, and stray bear tracks point in all directions along the trail, some more distinct than others.

"This track is shorter," Tam says. "And wider. Are a bear's front paws smaller than the back ones or vice versa?"

We all look at one another, shrugging.

"I've never heard that they were," I say. "But I've never heard that they weren't." Just a few years ago, I could've looked that up in a book or on a website. Now all we have as a data bank is whatever each of us remembers. And we've just lost Mike's knowledge.

"Our hands and feet are different," Jess says.

"True," Max says. "But a bear has four feet. We don't."

"It's obvious that this bear has different-sized feet," I say. "Unless there's more than one bear."

We keep going west, downstream, but stay close to the fissure wall, not wanting to surprise a bear in the willows. I remember the slugs and arrows we put into that other grizzly and how it just kept coming.

When I first looked down at the green ribbon in this fissure,

I thought that if we never made it any farther than this, at least we could live out our lives in a living place.

I wasn't counting on Mike dying and then having his body dragged off, and Dylan disappearing.

Besides looking for a missing person who probably killed his brother and a missing dead body and trying to figure out how many bears are roaming around this fissure, today has been a normal day. Jess is hanging close to Max. And, I've got to admit, it's a relief not to be constantly worrying about Dylan's influence on Jess. But it still troubles me that we don't know where he is. I'd rather see him and deal with him than have him surprise us.

* * *

"You'd think if there was a bear or two bears in this fissure, that we'd see tracks all over the place," I say.

"And piles of bear poop," Jess says. She takes another piece of salmon from the pot and leans into Max's shoulder as she eats it.

"Good observation," Tam says to Jess.

"My mom taught me about animal poop," Jess goes on. "About how you can tell what animal has been here and, if you're willing to examine it, what the animal has eaten." Jess scrunches up her face. "Sometimes it stinks." She holds her nose and then laughs.

Tam smiles. "Yes, sometimes it does." The scratches on Tam's cheek have turned red and puffy, and she's been limping around on her ankle all day, but says it doesn't hurt that much. "A bear would roam all over this fissure. If we cross at any spot from one wall to the other, we should see some tracks, at least old ones." Then Tam looks straight at Jess. "Or some of its poop."

Jess smiles and says, "Right."

Max says, "We need to move off this wall and see what we're dealing with."

I take a piece of salmon. It's pasty and oily, and has a sharpness to it that I'm not used to. Maybe it's going bad from being out of the jar too long, or maybe the T-shirt covering the pot had something on it. But I'm so hungry I'd eat rotten salmon if that's what I had. We all would.

"Let's zigzag from side to side," I say, "and see what we see."

We head toward the south wall. First we hit some thigh-high fireweed and wild rose, and some kind of silky green plant we used to call dinosaur grass. I'm sure there's more plant variety sprouting up around us, maybe even edible plants, but right now we're focused on finding tracks or bear scat and not letting anything surprise us. What would I do if a grizzly charged? All I have is my knife. And playing dead, like we've all been taught, I don't think that would work for a bear with a taste for human flesh.

Under the birches, we stop and look up. The branches start maybe forty feet up the trunks. The biggest ones must be sixty feet tall, but I can almost fit my hands around the trunks. It's more like a field of birch trees than a forest. Like they're blades of grass on a long, narrow lawn.

The willows that line the creek are more bushy than the birches, but still spindly. The creek gurgles along a mostly smooth surface at this spot. We splash through knee-deep water to the other side and pick our way through more willows and birches all the way to the south wall.

We do this three more times, slicing our way back and forth at forty-five-degree angles to the creek, but turn up no tracks of any kind. No bear scat either.

"Let's head back upstream," Tam says. "But we'll stay along the south wall and look for a way out."

I take my pack off and rub my shoulder. It's been aching steadily all day, like a giant is pressing its thumb into the spot where my arm attaches to my body. Jess hasn't complained about her hand one bit.

"We never saw Mike's spear," I say. "Remember, he tossed it over the edge."

Max nods. "I don't think a bear would walk off with that. Maybe we missed it."

And his body and pack. If a bear cached it, we should've seen evidence of digging and scraping. We didn't follow the drag trail very far, but why would a bear drag the body all that far anyway? Wouldn't it feed on the body where it found it and then cache it nearby? And that brings me back to Dylan. *Maybe*, I think, *Dylan chased the bear off the body and hid it.*

I feel a tug on my arm and turn. "Earth to Travis, do you copy?" Tam asks.

"Sorry," I say. "Spaced out." I sigh. "Tell me again, Tam."

"It's going to get dark soon. Or at least dusky. That's when bears are more active. Let's search the south wall for a way out all the way back up to where we camped last night. If we don't find a way out, we can build another fire there. We know the bear stayed away from there, so it's as safe a place as any. Maybe safer."

CHAPTER
35

WE'RE BACK AT OUR ORIGINAL campsite. Smoke drifts upward from the fire. At my insistence, we take everything out of our packs to see what we have.

Tam's bow, which somehow wasn't trashed on the trip down

Sixteen quart jars of salmon

One one-quart cook pot

One stinky T-shirt full of oily salmon strips

One one-hundred-foot length of rope

Two fire-starting tools that spray sparks

One small folding shovel

One knife

A pile of broken glass and jar lids we'd left here this morning

A jar filled with stone spear and arrow points

We each have a pair of insulated green coveralls, a green knit cap, green pile gloves, a green T-shirt (except I'd sacrificed mine for the salmon), and a pair of thick green socks.

Tam picks up her bow. "I've never tried to make an arrow. Jason gave me the ones I had. And they were metal. I'll need narrow, straight branches a little bigger around than a pencil." She shakes her head. "It's not going to be easy."

"At least there's some arrowheads in the jar," Jess says.

"I know," Tam says. "But attaching them to the shafts. Cutting a notch so I can nock it onto the string. Then finding feathers for the fletching. I—"

"Wait," Max says. "Remember, I saw birds flying when we first looked down into the fissure. But it was downstream quite a ways. There was a spot where warm air was rising. Dylan noticed it."

"We need a way to protect ourselves," Tam says. "From Dylan and whatever else."

"Why not cut a bunch of branches the right size for arrows?" Jess asks. "And just carry them with us, and we can work on them along the way?"

Max smiles at Jess. "Smart girl."

"And," Jess continues, "we can take a few larger sticks for spears."

"Okay," I say. "Before dark, we cut arrow and spear sticks. Tomorrow we head down the fissure in search of a way out."

"Why down?" Tam asks.

"Downstream is west. We want to make sure we cross the mountains more to the west than the east because we're trying to get to Anchorage, or at least where Anchorage used to be." I glance at the jars of salmon, wishing we had more. "We might even travel parts of the old Parks Highway. Even though it'll be more risky, it'll be faster. Given how much food we have, we might not have a choice."

*　*　*

We're in our insulated coveralls. The willows shake in the breeze blowing down the fissure. The sliver of sky above looks almost dark enough for stars. Max and Jess are lying down. Me and Tam are on watch, sitting across from them by the fire.

I think about my conversation last night with Max about her life and turn to Tam and say, "I know you lived in that group home with Max, but where did you live before that?"

She turns toward me, our eyes meeting in the firelight for a long moment, and I feel my heart racing.

"That's a loaded question," Tam says. She picks up a stick and pushes some coals around in the fire. "I lived with my mom until I was six. Until she died. Breast cancer. I have no idea who my dad is. After that, I was shuffled from foster parent to foster parent, never managing to stay in one house for more than a year."

"Why?" I ask. "Why couldn't one set of foster parents just keep you?"

"I would wear people out," Tam says. "I always wanted to be running or walking or playing something active. I wasn't very good at sitting still. And I'm still not very good at it." Tam keeps pushing the coals with her stick.

I think about the bear we killed and say, "When you shot that bear, you had to be still and concentrate."

"That's different," Tam says. "That kind of concentration is like movement. You are planning movement, waiting for movement, and you have to shoot at just the right time. But my foster parents couldn't or didn't want to handle someone so *intense*; that was the word they always used when they gave me back to the system. So I lived in like seven homes in eight years. The last place, my foster brother cornered me and put his hands all over me and tried to kiss me. I punched him in the balls. Hard. He ended up having to go to the doctor."

"He got what he deserved," I say.

"He was pretty aggressive. He just grabbed me out of the blue." She sighs. "If I'd known they were going to put me in the group home because of that, I wouldn't have punched him so hard." She breaks the stick that she's holding in half and tosses it on top of the coals and turns toward me. "My foster home was a few houses down from the group home, and my foster brother would walk by our yard after they caged us in and call me a bitch and laugh at me." Tam picks up another stick and rams it into the coals. Then she swallows once and says, "The last time I saw him I watched through the fence as he boarded a bus to get out of here with my old foster parents."

CHAPTER
36

"MORE BEAR PRINTS," TAM SAYS. We're all at the creek drinking some water. A sliver of blue sky is visible through the willow and birch leaves.

"A bear was this close and we didn't hear it," I say. "How can that be?"

I glance upstream and then downstream. A few prints head out of the creek and then back into it. Like the bear was walking in the water and decided to veer toward our camp and then veer back.

"Wouldn't it make all kinds of noise splashing through the water?" Jess asks.

"Maybe it's stalking us," Max says. "Bears do that. But usually, they follow a solo woman."

"How do you know that?" I ask. "You've been stalked by a bear?"

"One of our group home counselors," Max says, "this old lady, she used to hike alone in bear country. It happened to her, and once she started asking around, she found out it wasn't so uncommon."

"What'd she do?" I ask.

Max smiles. "This was back in the day. She had a satellite phone and called for help. The State of Alaska picked her up in a helicopter. It was somewhere up on the Yukon."

"I remember her," Tam says. "At the time I thought she was making it up just to get a reaction."

Once again I am aware of our lack of protection. I wonder what condition Mike's body is in. And where exactly it is. I want to get out of this place before the bear starts looking for another food source. And Dylan? Where is he?

"My dad told me that most bear attacks happen less than two seconds after the person becomes aware of the bear's presence," I say. "Usually, it's a mutual surprise. At least we'll be walking with the wind today. That'll warn the bear if it's downwind."

"We should each carry a big stick," Max says. "I know it's not much, but we don't have much else."

My knife, I think. That's it. A four-inch blade, just big enough to piss off a grizzly.

We stick to the south wall and walk downstream. We reach our turn-around point from yesterday and the wall appears sheer as far as we can see, but there's a slight bend coming up and the fissure looks like it's growing narrower. We haven't seen any more bear tracks. We've eaten the rest of the loose salmon, but I still feel hungry.

If we split two jars a day, we have eight days of food left. Not much for our journey. With what Mike and Dylan had been carrying in their packs, we would've almost doubled our food supply.

"Look how narrow it's getting," Tam says. She's back to walking without a limp, and the long scratches on her face are filling in with scabs. "If a bear passed through here, no way could we miss its tracks."

The wall is still sheer as we round a corner. Max puts a hand on my shoulder from behind and I stop.

"You guys feel that?" she says.

I turn around.

* * *

"Warm air," Tam says. "Just like we felt on top when we were searching for a way down."

Jess puts her hand on the ground. "I thought I felt something through my shoes. It's not just the air."

I bend over and touch the ground and it feels like a warm loaf of bread. I dig my fingers in and feel moisture and see a tiny ribbon of steam escape and disappear.

Max takes her pack off and puts her cheek to the ground. She pushes herself up and says, "This is a power place."

Tam's still standing, looking behind us and then in front of us. "Downstream." She points with her stick. "Steam. A lot of it."

I stand up. Down the fissure on the north side some steam filters through the willows but dissipates in the birch trees as it reaches their lower branches.

We start walking toward it, and the closer we get the more I can feel the heat penetrating the worn-out soles of my shoes.

I've gotten used to the sound of the creek, the flowing water, but now I start to hear pounding and popping sounds, too. The noise isn't as steady as the smooth sound the creek makes; it comes in bursts. The closer we get to the steam, the louder it becomes.

The south wall appears a little more jagged now, with ledges here and there, but it's still not climbable.

We decide to cross the stream to see what the deal is with the popping sounds. I step in, bracing myself for an assault of cold on my feet and lower legs, but it doesn't come. I reach down and put a hand in the creek. "Warm," I say. "Like bathwater."

We all splash our faces and scrub our hands. When I look at my hands compared to my arms, it's like they're a different color. That's how dirty I am.

Can we afford a few minutes to really wash up? Strip down and scrub up?

"Everyone," I say, "what do you all think about really washing up?"

"The risk," Tam says, "is if we all of a sudden need to move or fight, then we're vulnerable. We could have two of us keep watch and two of us bathe and then switch."

"Or," Max says, "we could all bathe at once and then we're at risk for the shortest amount of time."

We go with Max's idea and I walk downstream a little ways to give them some privacy. They are still visible but I face away from them. I quickly undress and wade back into the warm water and sit on the bottom of the creek. I scrub my arms, legs, chest, stomach, and what I can reach of my back with my hands. The popping noises that we stopped to investigate remain steady. Once we're all done, we still have to see what the deal is with those sounds.

I stick my head under and scrub my hair and beard, and then before I stand I glance upstream quickly just to make sure everything is okay. I see three heads above the water. Jess raises her hand and waves at me and I wave back.

I wish I could share this moment with them. Not just because I'm attracted to Tam but because these are my people. But I know that Tam was attacked by her foster brother, so I want to give them their space. I don't want to bring more stress into their lives and I want them to know they can trust me, absolutely, because when you're in a survival situation, trust can mean the difference between life and death.

After we're all dressed Max says, "With the warm earth and the warm water, you really could live here year-round."

A tiny bird wings by at eye level and we all jump. Max smiles. "I told you I saw birds from above."

We wade across the stream. The popping is louder and more constant, and the steam is drifting into our faces.

I push through the willows, and steam is rising from the ground all around me, like I'm inside a sauna and someone has just thrown water onto the stove.

I feel a hand on my arm and turn. Jess is hanging on my upper arm. "I don't want to go any farther. It's too hot."

Max and Tam stand next to Jess.

"Will one of you stay with Jess while I check out the popping noise?"

"Trav," Jess says, "I don't want you to go."

I look into her eyes and see the same fear I saw when we barely survived the fires that second summer. I think about saying this is just steam, not smoke, but she already knows. She's still frightened.

"Sis," I say, "we need to know what it is. We need to know everything we can know. I want—"

"I'll stay," Max says. She puts her arm around Jess.

Jess turns to Max and says, "You're my best friend ever."

Max smiles at her and says, "You're mine, too."

Tam and I claw our way through the willows. We walk under the skinny birch trees. The ground feels solid enough, but warm beneath our feet.

Just beyond the birches, but before we get to the north wall, we see it. A circular pit maybe fifteen feet across, and ten or twelve feet down the blue-green water boils, bubbles, and pops. And there's no telling how deep it is because it keeps churning constantly like a pot of boiling water.

Tam and I creep closer, the steam condensing on our faces and arms. I get down on one knee and start poking the ground, curious as to how stable it is, because steam is escaping from the ground everywhere.

Tam taps me on the shoulder.

"What?" I ask as I continue to check out the ground. Under the crusty surface, my fingers sink into sticky mud, hot to the touch. If you kept your fingers in the ground, they'd slowly cook. You could wrap a fish in foil and bury it, and it'd cook. Or you could heat up a jar of salmon.

Tam taps me again. Then she pulls on my arm. I stop poking the ground, pivot toward her, and stand up. Her face, free of dirt, is bright and beautiful, but there's a troubled look on her face. Tam's other arm is outstretched, her index finger pointing. I turn and follow it with my eyes, and my breath catches in my throat. There, along the north wall, fading in and out of view through the steam, I see bodies, more like skeletons really, slumped together.

CHAPTER
37

"I THINK THEY WERE TRYING to stay warm," Max says. "Maybe they'd run out of food."

"Probably starved," I say. We've gotten Max and convinced Jess that it's safe, and we're all standing on the side of the boiling pool.

"These bodies look undisturbed," I say. "Like they died here, in a group, together. On purpose."

"Or maybe they were sick," Jess says. "My friend Elsie died because there was no medicine for her. Her tonsils swelled up. She couldn't breathe."

Max puts her arm around Jess and pulls her tight, and Jess lets her.

Most of the corpses' clothing is worn away, but there are still pieces of gray cloth around their arms and legs. And fragments of dried skin on bones. Two of the skeletons are smaller than the others. A family traveling south? How long have they been here? Did they leave the year the buses took people north? Or had they left even before that? I mean, how long does it take for bodies to get to this state of decay? Another thing I don't know, can't know, but can only guess.

"Group suicide," Max says. "That's the only way they could've died together. Unless someone killed them all. But it doesn't look like that."

"I think they lost all their gear," Tam says. "I mean, here they are, but there's nothing else around here. Not even a junk pile. Maybe they got robbed, or their stuff sank in one of those water-filled fissures."

I shake my head. "The one thing I don't understand: If there's a bear roaming around down here and it dragged Mike's body away, then why aren't these bodies disturbed?"

The heat from the steam is making me sweat. I take a couple steps back from the boiling pool.

"I've been thinking about that, too," Max says.

"If a bear didn't drag Mike away, then what did?" Jess asks. "And what about all those tracks?"

"You mean, what about those *few* tracks?" I say.

I glance over at the pile of skeletons again and wonder what's become of Stacy's family. Did they make it to the coast? Or are their skeletal remains littering some other spot in this wasteland? Is this their family plus a few other people? I wouldn't be able to tell for sure anyway. They're literally skin and bones.

"I think we all know who might've dragged Mike away," I say. "Maybe Dylan's watching us right now."

"Or maybe he's headed back to his cave up north," Jess says.

"Or maybe he kept heading south," Max says.

"Or maybe he's dead," I say. "But if he's down here and wants to be found, he'll make himself known. We've been walking all over the place, building fires at night, screaming his name. It's not like we're invisible."

"You think he faked the bear prints?" Tam says.

"Probably," Max says. "Remember, we were confused because they were different sizes."

I'm pretty sure everyone thinks he's dangerous. And I don't know what was in that blue stuff sack that he refused to empty when we were taking stock of our possessions. Mike had one as well.

"Whatever we do," I say, "we need to be careful. And if we see Dylan, we need to be extra careful. We don't know what he has in his pack."

We keep heading downstream. Pools of boiling water dot both sides of the stream. Most of the plant life has disappeared; there's just a stray willow here and there. The ground is dark brown, flaky and moist at the same time. In some places it's collapsed and mud slowly bubbles in the depressions.

My feet start to sink and all of a sudden I'm in over my ankles. I take a couple of big steps backward, battling against the suction of the hot brown goo. My ankles are on fire and my feet are hot, like they're in an oven. I run for the creek and splash into the warm water, shaking one foot and then the other.

"Nobody walk out there," I say. "I almost cooked my feet." I try to imagine what it'd be like if I really sank in that goo and got stuck, like up to my waist. I'd basically bake until I died. I remember burning my hand on the woodstove when I was little and how painful that was. How I screamed. I rub the wrinkled skin on the palm of my hand.

I step out of the creek. My feet feel fine, but I'm still feeling warm above the ankles. I pull my pant legs up. The skin on my lower shins and calves is light pink, like I've been sunburned.

Max takes a look and says, "First-degree burn. You should be okay."

"Does it hurt?" Jess asks.

"It's a little hot," I say. "But not bad."

I'm glad it was me and not Jess. Just a little hot skin, I tell myself. But I'm shaking. You hurt your feet out here and you're screwed.

We decide to walk in the creek to avoid the hot mud. Farther down the fissure we can see where it gets green with plant life, and we figure the ground will be more stable there.

A couple miles later we stop at the edge of the willows and step out of the creek. I stare back at the narrow, steamy stretch behind us. "If you could keep yourself from being boiled, burned, or baked, it'd be a nice place to spend the winter," I say. "If you had food."

"Back in the day," Tam says, "you could've hunted up top and lived down here, climbing up and down with ropes and pulleys. With the right materials you could make all this steam and hot water work for you. But not anymore."

Max smiles. "If you built a shelter on top of the warm ground, it'd heat up nicely."

A rumble shakes the ground, causing the trees to wave. Little bits of dirt rain down from the fissure walls.

"Just a reminder that we're in a crack caused by an earthquake," I say. I wonder if it could close back up the way it opened.

The ground heaves up again, like it's trying to throw us off. I stumble and grab the back of Max's pack for balance. I hear a splash and turn. Jess is on her knees in the water.

Tam grabs Jess by the pack and pulls her up.

"I'm just glad we weren't standing by one of those boiling pools. We could've been soup." I smile, but no one laughs.

"Maybe it's not such a great place to live," Max says. "But if you could pipe the hot water down to this spot, that'd be cool. And it'd be all gravity flow."

"All you'd need is some pipe," Tam says. "Good luck finding that. And then getting it here."

"I'm speaking in ideals," Max says. "Maybe it'll be possible in the future. It could be one of several places you visited in the cycle of seasons. Maybe a good winter spot. People used to move around to survive. My ancestors were nomads."

"So are we," Tam says, "so let's keep moving. Besides the trees and the stream where we soaked, this place is a hellhole. We've already spent too much time down here. I wish we would've stayed on top and followed the edge until it was clear that, once we committed to coming down here, there'd actually be a way out. If Willa were still here, that's what we would've done."

"You didn't argue at the time," Max says.

"Trees, trees, trees," Tam says. "Everyone was taken by the trees."

"And you weren't?" I ask. I think of the trees by the Yukon River. That place felt like heaven because of the plant life. Until my parents got murdered there.

"All I'm saying is that we didn't look for a way out before we came down a route so steep we wouldn't be able to climb out the same way." Tam pauses. "We got so comfortable letting that crazy-ass lead us through the swamp, it was easy for him to talk us into coming down here before we knew how we'd get out."

An image of the skeletons at the boiling pool flashes into my mind. Why didn't they make it out of the fissure? My stomach muscles contract, and I taste old salmon in the back of my throat and swallow it back down.

Maybe there isn't a way out.

CHAPTER
38

WE KEEP HEADING DOWNSTREAM IN silence, searching for an escape. The fissure keeps narrowing and dropping. In one spot the creek tumbles over a series of tiny falls, each three or four feet high, like a descending stairway.

The steam and boiling pools totally disappear. So do the birches, leaving a thick band of willows following the stream, bordered by rock and dirt. This feels like the old Interior Alaska. It even has the old smell of freshness you get when rushing water creates its own cool breeze.

We hug the south wall, each with our big walking sticks that we hope to craft into spears.

Up ahead a spine of dirt and rock slopes down from above. The tip of the spine disappears into the creek, creating a sharp bend with willows clinging to the outside edge.

I stop and point. "Right up there. Could be our way out."

"Steep," Tam says, "but doable—probably. A little risky, but I don't think we have another choice."

"We might have to ditch the walking sticks." Max points about halfway up. "It looks like we'll need to use our hands in places."

"Let's strap them to our packs," I say. "We really might need spears."

Jess hasn't said a word. And her face is way closer to an all-out frown than a smile.

"Sis," I say, "what's wrong?"

Jess points partway up the spine we're talking about. "It looks really steep right there."

"What if we use the rope in the really steep place where we need our hands to climb?" Max says. "Not for everyone to climb on, but we could have a couple people climb up the steep part, lower the rope, and then we could tie the packs onto the rope and haul them up one at a time."

Tam nods. "I forgot we had a rope. Good idea. That way we won't have all that weight throwing us off-balance on the dangerous part."

I turn to Jess. "Do you think you could give that a try? You could even use the rope for a little support while you're climbing if you want."

Jess nods. "I could try."

We climb with our packs on about a third of the way up the spine before we hit the really steep section. Tam and I drop our packs; I put the coil of rope around my neck and start climbing. Using my hands and feet, I climb toward the spot we've picked out, about thirty or forty feet above where I started from. It's more vertical than I thought it would be. I'm glad Jess will have the option of some rope support. Truth is, I wouldn't have minded some for that stretch.

I hoist myself over a small ledge and turn around. Tam is about halfway up and moving fast. The spot I'm standing on, just back from the little ledge, is tiny. Behind me the slope rises steeply, but it's not vertical like the climb Tam's about to complete. When she reaches the ledge, I put out my hand and she takes it, and I help her over the ledge.

Now we're standing side by side, her shoulder pressing against my upper arm, her hip against my thigh. It is literally that tight of a spot for two people. I toss one end of the rope down to Jess and Max and they tie it to a pack.

"Okay," Max yells.

Tam and I start pulling, and even though our arms and hands are bumping, we get into a rhythm of both pulling at the same time, hand over hand, and the first pack comes up to the base of the ledge quickly.

I turn toward Tam and she turns toward me to grip the pack to hoist it over the ledge. It's like we're hugging, except there's a pack between our heads and chests, but with our thighs brushing and pressing against each other. I can feel my heart racing, not from hauling up the pack but from the contact with Tam.

"What should we do with this thing?" I ask.

"You let go," she says, "and I'll carry it up the slope behind us a little ways."

"Okay, I'm letting go." I let go of the pack and Tam scrambles a few steps up the slope, sets the pack down, and unties it.

Back at the ledge, side by side, I throw the rope down again.

We haul the other three packs up in much the same way. Then Jess comes up using the rope for balance but mostly climbing on her own. When she gets to the ledge, Tam and I offer our hands and help her over the ledge. When Max appears moments later, we do the same for her.

Max and Tam lead us up the last part of the spine as it starts to level out, and I walk with Jess a little ways back.

"You did a great job coming up that steep part," I say, smiling at her. "You barely even used the rope."

Jess smiles back. "I watched what you and Tam did when you climbed. I used the rope in the spots where I couldn't reach where you two reached."

"Mom and Dad would be proud of you," I say, then feel my eyes getting moist.

"I really miss them," Jess says.

"Me too," I say. I wipe the tear that's escaped from one of my eyes.

"Hey," I hear Max call out.

I turn from Jess and we both look up toward Max. She's at the top of the spine.

"There's something up here."

CHAPTER
39

"IT SURE LOOKS LIKE A bear's work, except for the stick and stone art next to it," I say. The first thing we encountered on the lip of the fissure was Mike's shredded backpack, empty, with the word *basic* spelled out with pieces of his spear and some rocks.

"Dylan knew we'd climb out here," Tam says. "But we didn't see his tracks on the trip up, so he must've climbed out somewhere else."

We're all looking around, hoping to spot him, just so we can know where he is instead of feeling like we're being watched. Stalked. If he can push his brother off a cliff, he'd probably have no qualms about killing any of us. And he was acting so normal right before we got to the fissure. At least we're armed with big sticks that we hope to turn into spears.

"I'm hungry," Jess says.

I search her eyes, wondering if I should bring up Mom and Dad again, to finish the conversation we were having before Max called out to us, but I decide to let it ride for now. We're out of the fissure and I want to make some tracks heading south. Sometimes you have to put important things off in order to do even more important things. Like the way I've started feeling about Tam—I'm not gonna bring that up now either.

We sit at the edge of the fissure and split a jar of salmon. Jess doesn't make a single fish face while we eat.

Max points down into the fissure. "I wonder if you really could live down there. You know, actually survive. I think this place is more than a fissure from an earthquake. I'm not sure what, maybe just an isolated drainage that the fires couldn't get to. It's like a window into the past and a door to the future."

I pass the jar to Tam. I think of the burnt land surrounding it for hundreds of miles. "It'd have to be pretty extensive or pretty rich to sustain even a few people."

"Maybe we've only seen a small part of it," Max says.

Tam gives the jar to Jess and stands up. "Maybe. But the part we did see had a pile of skeletons. Not a good sign." She's bouncing up and down on her toes like she's ready to run. "Why does it matter anyway?"

"When I first went to the group home," Max says, "I thought it'd be a short-term thing. But then more things started falling apart. Not just in my life, but everywhere. You know, the aspen trees dying on the heels of the spruce trees, the yellow jackets taking over the skies, people looking out for themselves so much that they didn't care who they stepped on. We were poised for a big fall. But this land, it will come back. And so will I. Someday. This fissure or valley, or whatever it is, is a seed bank for the future. It could be a place to build from."

Jess eats the last piece of salmon and says, "The only reason I'd come back is if my mom were here."

I put my arm around Jess and pull her close. *When we stop for the night*, I think, *we'll have to talk about this.* Right now we have to get moving. And we've got to keep a sharp lookout for Dylan.

* * *

We've been walking for a couple of hours, and now we're on drier ground because the land is slanting ever so gradually toward the mountains. Jess has been walking next to Max, sometimes holding her hand. Inch-high willows poke through the ash in places. These will be good browse for moose, if there are any moose left. We still hit the occasional patch of swamp, but even in those spots the water is only ankle deep. We're heading south and west for a distant notch in the mountains—the one that looks the lowest— that we hope to pass through. We spotted it when the haze covering the mountains cleared for a few minutes. We can't see the notch now, but the tops of the two peaks bordering it are poking through.

We've seen some tracks here and there, but not a continuous trail because the wind is constantly blowing and rearranging the ash. And in lots of spots the ground is rocky. No one has said much of anything, but I'm pretty sure they've been thinking the same thing I have.

Dylan. Where is he? And what the hell is he doing? Did he kill Mike? Is he watching us?

We hit a stretch where the land is pocked with craters of sucking mud. Some are only a few feet across and deep, but others span forty or fifty yards, their bottoms fifty or a hundred feet down. And there are boulders dotting the land, half-sunk into the mud in places.

"Sinkholes," Tam says. She turns to Max. "Remember the one that opened up down the street from the group home and swallowed that blue house?"

Max nods. "One day that house was there when we went inside

197

to do our schoolwork, and it was tilted sideways and smashed up at the bottom of a hole when we had our afternoon break."

Sinkholes are kind of spooky. I've never seen one open up before my eyes, and I'm sure some open more slowly than others, but still, stories like Max's make you pause, make you realize that the ground under your feet—the ground you want to be stable—just isn't.

I poke my stick into the mud covering a shallow hole, and it goes down several feet. "Like quicksand," I say. "My dad told me about big holes close to the mountains formed by huge chunks of underground ice. The ice melts and the ground caves in. Maybe that's how these holes and craters formed."

We pick our way along, poking the ground with our sticks and staying away from the rims of the larger holes.

A little while later we're detouring around a huge hole when Tam says, "Stop. I think I see that bastard."

CHAPTER
40

"DO YOU THINK HE'S REALLY under there?" I say.

Tam says, "Who else could it be?"

We're all peering into a monster of a sinkhole. At the bottom is a blue backpack partially sunk into the mud. An outline of arms and legs stretch out from the pack under the mud, like someone was skydiving.

"It's gotta be him," Max says.

Jess takes a few steps back from the edge and sits down.

"Do you think he fell in or jumped?" I ask.

"Maybe the ground collapsed underneath him," Tam says. "I don't know how to tell how old a sinkhole is."

I nod. The rim of the sinkhole doesn't look newly formed to me, but I've never studied sinkholes. If these holes formed the way my dad said they did, I think it'd take years for a chunk of ice to melt and have the ground collapse. But the edges could be unstable.

"It seems like a crazy way to commit suicide," I say. "Maybe he was standing on the edge of the hole and the rim collapsed and took him with it."

"If you're going to commit suicide, then maybe you're already kind of crazy," Max says.

I think of Willa and Randie. And Mike. Now Dylan. "Right now, we've got a fifty percent survival rate."

I think of my mom and dad, and Clint with his group on the banks of the Yukon. And all the charred bodies I'd seen after the fires. The land is consuming everyone and giving back nothing in return. Maybe that's the true definition of dead. To keep taking without giving back.

I think about our food. Fourteen jars of salmon. I'm always hungry. I look down at the partially submerged pack and the body outline beneath it, at least fifty feet down. Is it floating or settled on a solid surface? I don't know.

"Whether Dylan is buried under there or not," I say, "we need that pack."

* * *

I look Tam in the eye. "We won't let go." She's perched on the edge of the sinkhole. We are ten feet back, in a line. Me, Max, and Jess, all hanging onto the rope. We have our gloves on and the rope wrapped around our hands.

"Okay," Tam says. "Here I go." She's taken off her camo clothing because she knew it'd be a hot job. She has a T-shirt on. If she has underwear, it's hidden by the T-shirt. I swallow the lump in my throat that has formed and double down on my grip on the rope. She's lean, her arms and legs ribbons of muscle. She's beautiful. Like a wild animal.

Tam's blond hair disappears over the ledge, and we all lean into the rope to counterbalance her weight. We're too far back from the ledge to see her, but I can feel little tugs as I imagine her bracing her feet against the sinkhole wall as she scoots down the rope hand over hand.

My triceps tense each time I feel a tug. We're silent. Listening for anything Tam might shout from below.

My hands grow hot from wearing the gloves and gripping the rope. And my injured shoulder starts to ache.

"Halfway," Tam shouts.

I take a breath. I wish she were farther. I glance over my sore shoulder and see Max's face glistening. She flashes a quick smile. Behind her, Jess has her head down and is leaning back, putting all her weight onto the rope.

I feel some bigger tugs and guess that Tam's letting more rope slip through her hands before grabbing it, probably becoming more comfortable with the descent.

"I'm down," Tam calls. Her voice sounds small, like she's ant-sized, at the bottom of a tin can.

The rope goes slack for a moment, and then a big tug almost yanks my shoulders from their sockets. I stumble forward a couple steps, then lean back.

"Sorry," I say to Max and Jess. I hear a couple of grunts from them, and nothing else.

It feels like someone has stuck a knife in my injured shoulder and left it there. I roll my shoulder back and forth in little circles, but it does nothing to ease the pain. Sweat runs down my forehead and into my eyes. I work my face toward my sleeve and drag my eyes across the fabric. My eyes start burning and I realize there's ash on my sleeves.

I keep squinting and sweating, not knowing what's happening down there. The tugs aren't coming in a set pattern or direction. And every so often I don't feel any tugs, just a constant pressure, which is just as painful. How long has she been on the bottom? Four minutes? Five minutes?

Is she in the mud? Or standing on top of the pack? Is it dry enough to stand without sinking? *But if it were dry*, I think, *she wouldn't be putting so much pressure on the rope.*

There is at least ten feet of free rope that she can use to tie onto the pack.

Another jolt pulls me forward. Then another. I lean backward and try to regain some ground.

"Climbing." Tam's voice sounds far away and deeper, like her throat is clogged or her mouth is full of mud.

I dig my feet into the ground and keep leaning back. But the rope keeps willing me forward. I feel a couple of tugs and then a rest. A couple of tugs and then a rest. But the rests aren't really rests, just a constant pressure sucking every ounce of energy out of me. She feels a lot heavier coming up than she did going down.

Tam has to be more exhausted than we are. I wish we could help pull her up, but if all went as planned, the bottom of the rope is attached to the pack and no way could we pull both of them up.

Tam's risking her life. It made sense that she'd be the one to go down. I'm strong enough to climb but too heavy to be supported. Jess is the lightest, but I wasn't sure if she'd be strong enough to climb back out or wrestle the pack off Dylan. Tam is taller than Max but lighter, and maybe stronger. Back in the day, she would've been a star in any sport she chose. Now she shoots arrows at armed men and takes backpacks off of dead bodies in sinkholes.

I glance behind me. Max is a rock. She's squatting, her knees spread with the rope running between her legs. Jess is kneeling now and leaning back like she's in a limbo contest. I have one foot in front of the other and am pulling from the side.

Another big tug slams my triceps. I hear a deep grunt from the direction of the sinkhole. She must be close.

Come on, I think. *Just get here so I can rest.*

Then this dark head pops over the edge and my heart leaps to my throat. Tam is a blonde.

CHAPTER
41

I GLANCE AROUND. BOULDERS SPRINKLE the land to the south. *Lots of hiding places*, I think.

Tam was covered in mud when she emerged from the sinkhole, making her blond hair look brown. I told her I had wanted to let go of the rope when it looked like her hair wasn't blond, and if I hadn't been paralyzed by fear and confusion, I probably would have.

She told us about not finding a body even though from above it looked like there'd be one. It was just streaks of mud that radiated out from the pack. Maybe they were created by the impact of the pack hitting the bottom of the sinkhole with a big force.

Then she told us about tying the rope around her waist so she could use both hands to work on the pack. And how she could float on the mud, but at the same time it grabbed her and didn't want to let go, and it had this smell like rotting leaves.

She'd had to get her shoulder under the pack and tilt it to the side to expose the straps, so she plunged completely into the mud to get underneath it. Pretty much mud wrestling with the pack. And for a while she thought it would win.

The top of the pack had been partially open, and two small blue stuff sacks tied together by their drawstrings had fallen into the mud during the wrestling match. She'd slung the bags over her shoulder and around her neck and closed the pack as much as she could.

"Those sacks." I pick them up. "Mike and Dylan, they each had one." I stuff them into my pack so no one else has to carry any extra weight.

"The pack down there was so overstuffed," Tam says. "He must've taken all of Mike's stuff. It was a bitch wrestling that thing."

"I'm glad you won," Jess says.

Tam smiles at her. "Thanks."

Any doubt that Dylan is responsible for Mike's death and the disappearance of his body is erased from my mind.

Tam points into the sinkhole. "The pack is tied on, resting on top of the mud, but it's probably sunk down some since I've come up." She shakes her head. "I was so angry with Dylan when I learned that he'd started the fires. I wanted to kill him. And given what happened to Mike, I still do. But seeing his pack down there still kinda makes me sad. I mean, he must really be nuts. Can't last long out here with nothing."

"His dad got on that basic kick, where he chucked everything," I say. "Remember? Maybe this is Dylan's way of following his dad's vision." I glance around. "He could be anywhere. He could be watching us right now. Whether he's completely nuts or not, he's dangerous."

The wind is starting to blow. I can feel the sweat drying beneath my clothes. Tam puts her arms around her chest. She is mostly mud, with only a T-shirt on. If we were still in the fissure, she could've washed off in the warm creek water. I'm sure we'll find some water up here, but it probably won't be warm.

She starts brushing the mud off her legs. Jess steps up and helps her. So does Max. I don't know what to do. Is it okay for me to put my hands on her and help out, too? I step behind her and run my hands down her back, trying to get some mud off her T-shirt. She smells like rotting leaves, like the land before it burned. I take another sniff.

"Forget the shirt," Tam says. She grabs the bottom edge and pulls it over her head. Then she slips out of her muddy underwear. Her white backside stands out, bordered by her mud-covered neck and legs. "I'll just put my camo clothes on over the mud. I'm starting to freeze."

She bends over and grabs her pants, and I catch the tiniest glimpse of a nipple on her plum-sized breast, and that sends a jolt from my eyes to my groin. She's beautiful.

I turn away and try to focus on the next task at hand. There are supplies in that pack and we need them.

Hauling the pack out of the sinkhole is more difficult than I thought it would be. We try grabbing the rope, bracing our legs, and walking backward, but the rope digs into the lip of the hole, which creates a lot of friction and stops us dead. And the pack feels way heavier than Tam.

So I go to the lip of the hole and we get a system going. I heave on the rope, raising the pack a foot or so, and Max and Tam, standing several feet back from me, take in the slack. Since we don't know where Dylan is, Jess is keeping watch.

The wind is still blowing and it's starting to rain, but I'm warm because I'm sweating again. We've brought the pack up maybe ten feet from the bottom. I can feel the muscle strain in my neck running down the outsides of my arms. The pack is covered with mud from Tam's wrestling with it, which adds to the weight.

I count one, two, three. On three, I pull with my arms, back, and legs until I'm standing straight up, and Max and Tam take in the slack. We do this again and again. I'm leading with my good shoulder, but the injured one still stings every time I yank on the rope. We usually lose a little ground between pulls. Like for every two steps forward we end up going back one, but that'll be okay as long as we get the pack out of the freaking hole.

I glance back. "How're you two doing?"

"Just shut up," Tam says. "Keep pulling."

"Arms of steel," Max says.

I keep pulling, and they keep taking in the slack, but the pack doesn't seem to be getting much higher in relation to all the rope we're hauling in.

"Stretch the rope out," I say. "Tell me how much we've got."

I glance back. Max is holding the rope tight and Tam is walking backward with the end.

"Maybe twenty feet," Tam calls. "And another ten between you and Max."

I guess we have at least another thirty feet to go.

The pack is skidding along the sinkhole wall, getting caught below every little bump and inside every divot. Sometimes I have to let it drop a little and then yank it extra hard to clear a bump. I hate losing any ground, but there's no way around it.

Tam and Max are so tuned in to the process that I don't even have to tell them when I'm doing this. They just give the tiniest bit of slack, unless I ask for more.

The pack gets jammed below the biggest bump yet. They've given me a little slack, and when I call for more, they give me a couple more feet. I let out the slack and can see the pack edging out from the bump. I consider moving to the right a little bit, but

207

I don't want to start wasting energy moving sideways, because there are bumps and divots all over the wall.

On three, I give a huge heave on the rope, and then it gives all at once and I'm thrown backward like I've been blindsided by a grizzly bear. I keep my grip on the rope as my ass smacks the ground and my wrists pull in all the way to my chest. I dig my heels into the ground and wait for the forward tug that I'm sure to feel, hoping that Tam and Max have a good grip.

But it never comes.

My stomach clenches. And even though I know, I don't want to know. I just want to pretend that it hasn't happened. I slam the rope on the ground and stand up. Max and Tam are already standing.

All three of us walk to the edge of the hole and peer down. There, on the bottom, a tiny window of blue fabric peeks above the mud with a strand of rope snaking out from it.

"Son of a bitch," I say. "Christ." I know we don't have enough rope to get back down there. And even if we did, I couldn't be sure that it would hold anyone's weight after all the stress we put on it.

I shudder at the thought of the rope breaking when Tam was climbing. But still, I want that pack. I search my brain but can think of no way to get it. At least we have the two blue stuff sacks, whatever is in them. But all that work for the pack. All that risk.

I lift my face to the sky and feel the sprinkles of cold rain on my cheeks. We've wasted enough time and energy on this.

I turn to Max and Tam. Muddy streaks run down Tam's face and neck.

"Sorry," I say. "Maybe if I hadn't pulled so hard that last time. I—"

"Hey," Jess calls. "I think I see something moving."

CHAPTER
42

THE THING ABOUT THE LAND—it's huge. But you can see especially long distances since the vegetation burned.

The dust cloud Jess had noticed was quite a ways off. Maybe even on the far side of the fissure. I knew someone was causing it—kicking up dust as they traveled through the ash.

My first thought is Dylan, on his way back to the Sacrifice Area to live out his dad's vision. My second thought is Mom. She'd be coming this way if she'd survived. I don't mention this to Jess because it is so unlikely that she survived, since she didn't turn up before we headed south. And I know we have to keep moving forward. My mom wanted me to get Jess to a safe place. Her note didn't say *wait for me*.

We are in a spot sprinkled with boulders, so we have some possible cover if we need it. It used to be that whoever you met in the Alaska bush was probably a pretty good person. Maybe a little rough around the edges, but not out to harm you or rob you. Sure, some people ran from the law into the wilderness, but that was the exception. Most people looking to take advantage of you stuck to places where there were people.

But the abandonment and the burning have turned everyone into potential bad guys. Desperation does that. So instead of banding together, which actually makes sense for survival, people avoid each other. Max and Tam are with us now only because we somehow worked through a showdown where I was pointing a gun at them and Tam had her bow trained on me.

Even though part of me wants to believe that the dust cloud behind us presents no threat, and maybe even represents help, we can't take the chance. We need to keep moving.

I stuff the remaining rope into my pack and off we go into the boulder field, with the awareness that we could encounter anyone, anytime. The sprinkles of rain increase and now it's just plain raining.

Rolling hills stretch out ahead of us, so the boulders combined with the dips make for lots of potential hiding places. Except for the rain the land is dry and well-drained. We see a stray footprint here and there, but no continuous trails of tracks.

No one says much of anything for hours as we move southwest through the boulders toward the mountains. Occasional patches of willow and knee-high dwarf birch dot the landscape. Dylan's dad's inferno could only reach so far. We all know that stopping in the pouring rain without any shelter is a recipe for freezing, so we trudge at what I hope is a sustainable pace. It's fast enough to keep us from being chilled to the bone but slow enough that we can keep moving without collapsing from exhaustion.

When we reach the base of the mountains, the rain lets up and the sun pokes through the clouds. Dark, rocky slopes cut with green bands of vegetation rise before us. Tucked into the highest valleys, we see the dirty gray of glaciers, remnants of what were huge rivers of ice.

We eat another jar of salmon. Jess wants to open a second jar and I tell her we can't. She makes a fish face and then stares at me with sad eyes, but I hold firm even though I want to give her everything she asks for.

We all put on our knit caps.

My feet are blocks of ice, and I want to be back in the fissure soaking in the warm water. I need to talk to Jess about Mom, but I can't do it while we're freezing.

We decide to head west along the base of the mountains until we reach the low gap where we plan to cross.

But before we leave, I remember the blue stuff sacks that Tam lifted from Dylan's pack. I pull them out and what we find in them changes everything.

CHAPTER
43

"BUT CAN WE REALLY TRUST the map?" I ask.

"We can't trust anything," Max says. "But why would Dylan and Mike have carried the map if they didn't think it was valuable?"

"But why didn't they say anything?" Tam asks.

"Maybe they were gonna wait until we got to the mountains," Jess says. "Or maybe they didn't trust us."

We argue some more about which way to go. I want to believe the map will help us. I really do. Maybe it's the best option, if we can even follow it. But it has us slanting east instead of west. And it shows a settlement at what used to be Valdez, a small town a couple hundred miles to the east of Anchorage. Valdez is where the oil pipeline ended. Or at least where it used to end before it ran dry. My parents didn't mention Valdez as an option. As far as I knew, it had been downsized after the oil pipeline ran dry and then totally abandoned after a big earthquake.

There's a big black *X* marked over the word *Anchorage*.

"Dylan was pretty whacked," I say. "Maybe the map is just what he freaking imagines is there."

"It could be the best way to get through the mountains," Max says. "Remember how Dylan led us across the swamp, and how he could pick out the old lakeshores? He may have been crazy, but he also had a gift. If he imagined all that, he did a damn good job. Maybe it's his way of helping us, continuing to guide us even if he's gone back home."

"Why would he guide us?" Tam says. "I mean, he killed his brother. It's not like he's a nice person. He hated me and I hated him. Even if he's dead, I still hate him."

I stare at the map. It's an ancient highway map with some colored lines penciled in. Solid black lines show the two old highways. One leads from Fairbanks to Anchorage, the other from Fairbanks to Valdez.

"He must've been marking our progress in secret," I say. "See the red marks."

A solid red line starts at a place marked *home* on the Tanana River, cuts a jagged line south, and ends just after a place marked *fissures*. Dylan also labeled the lake we'd gone around and the place we'd killed the bear. And then at the fissures is Mike's name and, next to it, a little cross.

"I wish we could've talked to him in the fissure," I say. "Before we got to the rim he was acting kind of normal."

"I think he drew all the red lines after we separated at the fissure," Max says. "It would've been hard for him to pull out the map and not have any of us notice."

I nod. I only saw the stuff sacks once, and Mike and Dylan said what was in them was personal, and no one challenged them. One is labeled with the letter *D* and the other with an *M*.

From where the solid red line ends at the fissures, a dotted red line takes over and runs east until it meets up with the black line— the old highway route to Valdez that used to parallel the oil pipeline. Just south of the pass where the old highway used to cut through the mountains is a place marked *Uncle Mark's Cache*. From there, the red dotted line parallels the black line south all the way to Valdez, where the word *Settlement* is circled.

Everything from the sacks is spread out before us.

> From Dylan's sack:
> The map
> A small box of colored pencils
> A hand trowel
> A picture labeled "Mike and Dylan at the secret cache with Uncle Mark"

> From Mike's sack:
> A necklace with a heart-shaped locket
> Two six-packs of giant Snickers bars
> A small drawknife wrapped in a cloth
> Lures and line

"Last time I saw a Snickers bar was like six years ago," Tam says. "It was in my last foster home. I remember having to split it with my foster brother, Chris, which was no big deal since it was back before he tried to molest me."

I remember Tam's story from the night we were on watch in the fissure. I look over at her and she acknowledges me with eye contact and a nod.

"I don't think I've ever seen one," Jess says. "Until now."

Candy was one of the first things to go when the government took over food distribution. Essential goods only. So candy bars got axed, along with toys, board games, and soda, to name a few things. At least that's what my parents told me. But they had no reason to lie. We were living on the edge of collapse then, I just didn't realize it. We'd get big blocks of government-issued cheese, bags of pinto beans and rice, and powdered milk.

"They must be old," I say. "Think they're any good?"

"Only one way to find out," Max says. She glances down at the pile of stuff. "Candy. Not bad."

Tam nods and says, "Score."

The wind is blowing a cold wall of air down from the mountains. More cold means it'll take more food to stay warm.

I pick up a package of Snickers and tear the wrapper open. When I was Jess's age, seven years ago, you could pretty much get any kind of candy you wanted. Then bam, the year after that, you couldn't get anything except baker's chocolate. And a year later that was history, too.

I keep the bar in the wrapper and just feel it. "It's hard as a rock."

We pass the Snickers around. When it comes back to me, I say, "I'll cut it into four pieces."

I tear the wrapper lengthwise. The bar is bumpy and sprinkled with an off-white color. I sniff. "Smells like chocolate," I say. "But the white stuff—"

"It's okay," Tam says. "At the group home we had some ancient chocolate chips that were speckled with white, but we still ate them and they didn't make us sick."

My stomach tingles. We had chocolate that first winter three years ago. We found someone's stash in an abandoned house. But we've had none since then.

I take my knife out of my pack and saw the bar into four pieces. Little flakes of chocolate break off, but the wrapper catches most of them. We each take a piece, but before anyone eats, I hold mine up and say, "Here's to the next part of our journey, making it safely through the mountains, whichever way we go." I push my piece forward and so does everyone else. We let our chunks of stale candy bar touch, like glasses clinking in a toast. Tam and Max and Jess crack small smiles and I feel myself doing the same.

How did Dylan even know the way from here? But then there's the picture of Dylan and Mike with Uncle Mark at the secret cache. And they look young—maybe eight or nine years old. Uncle Mark has a brown beard that matches the color of the rocky bluffs behind the three of them in the photo. But why didn't they tell us any of this? And why didn't they just leave on their own after their parents were dead? They could've taken a direct route instead of wandering west with us. Is their uncle Mark still alive? Is he living in some secret place in the pass just before the Buffer Zone? And if he is, does that mean there are others?

My mind runs with all these questions as I let the Snickers soften in my mouth. I remember sharing chocolate with Stacy. Eating a hot fudge sundae made from homemade ice cream and homemade fudge after store-bought ice cream and chocolate became a memory. Two spoons. One bowl. All in secret when her parents were out.

My chest feels raw, like I've just inhaled some fragments of glass. I wonder where she is. Had her family gone east or west? I don't even know.

I glance at Jess. She has her eyes closed, concentrating on the chocolate in her mouth, like she used to when we ate blueberries that we'd picked before the fires came. Then I think of Mom and Dad, and how they would have loved to see Jess now. To see how she's adapted and how she keeps rising to every challenge that's put in front of her. My eyes grow hot. I wipe a tear away before it has a chance to run down my cheek.

We have a decision to make. Go toward Valdez like Dylan's map suggests or toward Anchorage like my parents instructed. And we need to make it soon.

PART
THREE

CHAPTER
44

WE STICK TO THE EDGE of the mountains and follow the map, walking east for three days, only stopping to eat Snickers bars and salmon, and to rest our feet, which are continually wet from creek crossings. Towers of dirty, gray ice fill some of the valleys, while others are ice-free.

The glaciers have been on a melting rampage for almost a century and will probably be gone in another twenty years. At least that's what I learned in school before it closed.

Supposedly, all the glaciers in the Brooks Range between Fairbanks and the Arctic Ocean have already melted. But not down here in the Alaska Range. No one predicted that. My dad was fascinated with how things worked in the natural world. He told me, *You just never know what's going to happen. There are too many factors involved to make accurate predictions.*

Then, once the oil started getting scarce worldwide and Alaska was in the long process of getting cut off, the science up here pretty much stopped. No one was flying over glaciers and taking measurements, and no one was getting paid to study anything, not for years. My dad said it was foolish not to put money into studying the ways the planet was changing, because ultimately, there'd be nothing to do with money if we didn't have a livable planet. It was like feeding wood into your woodstove on one side of the house while an out-of-control fire was raging on the other side and coming toward you.

We follow Dylan's route marked in red, toward the old road, as best we can. The Richardson Highway, it used to be called, before the Tanana, Delta, and Gulkana rivers chopped it into pieces, reclaiming parts of the valleys they'd carved out thousands of years ago.

"When we do get to the old road corridor," I say, "we'll have to be even more careful."

"How will we even know when we're there?" Jess asks, standing on one foot and then the other.

"Maybe we'll be able to see old sections of pavement," I say. "Or stray pieces of pipeline that weren't hauled away."

"You can always tell when people have changed something," Max says. "Even if the injury happened a long time ago, the scars remain."

"And depending on how far the fires reached," Tam says, "we might see some old buildings or fences, or cars."

"Wounds," Max says. "Like this." She pulls her shirt up and a pink scar a couple inches long runs up her side. "The skin of the land might cover a metal fence, or a pipeline, or a road, but we'll be able to tell." She pulls her shirt back down.

I think of Fairbanks. Was it just a big zit on the earth that got burned off the surface? But people are part of the planet, too. They're natural. But sometimes what they do is unnatural. Where do you draw the line? I mean, people have to live, too. But the earth doesn't care. The earth just *is*.

I put my share of the last Snickers bar into my mouth. We have six jars of salmon left. Why did I decide to haul the whole pack up at once? If we would've taken the supplies up a little at a time we'd be set. My dad wouldn't have let that happen. I hope we'll be able to find Dylan and Mike's uncle's cache.

And this guy, Uncle Mark—is he still around? And is he crazy like Dylan's dad? Like Dylan?

We haven't seen a sign of anyone since that last dust plume days ago, not even footprints, and truth is, I don't want to see anyone. I don't want to deal with the stress of figuring out who's dangerous and who isn't. And what about Dylan? What if he didn't go north? What if we run into him? I just want to find some food so we can keep going, because it's still a long way to the coast.

Well, that's not true. I want more than food. I want to take Jess and swing her around like I used to when she was little. I want to hear her laugh and scream with delight, and see her hair flying behind her. To see her being a kid.

And I want to get to know Tam, if she's into getting to know me.

I want a life. A life where I'm not constantly on the lookout for thieves and murderers. I want a life where I can lie down at night and close my eyes.

CHAPTER
45

"HOW ARE WE GONNA CROSS that?" Jess asks.

As near as I can tell, we're standing on a large floodplain at the confluence of the Delta River and a roiling creek that flows out of the Black Rapids Glacier, or what's left of the glacier. According to the map, the old road runs along the other side of the river above the floodplain for a while. If we can get across, this will be the easiest place to access the road.

But the brown-gray river water churns with three-foot standing waves tipped with dirty froth. The far side looks unreachable from this spot.

The cache Dylan marked should be on the other side of the river and down the road, on the far side of the pass that leads out of the Sacrifice Area and into the Buffer Zone. Dylan labeled these areas on his map pretty much the way my dad talked about them.

Black Rapids Creek is impressive on its own, and probably accounts for half the flow of the river.

"We could do a rope crossing of the creek, then keep hiking up the river until we find a spot to do another rope crossing," I say. "We lost part of the rope in the sinkhole, so it couldn't be too long of a crossing."

Max keeps her eyes trained on the far side of the river. "It'd be better to cross here in terms of finding the cache. Otherwise we might have to backtrack."

"That cache might not even exist," Tam says. "Even if it does, crossing here would be group suicide."

"We have to get to the other side to follow the route," Max says. "Could be food at the cache."

Tam bangs her stick on the ground. "The map," she huffs. "If we didn't have that map, maybe we would've found a quicker way through the mountains to the west, instead of walking for three extra days and then getting stuck right here. Following that crazy asshole's scratch marks on an ancient map!" She shakes her head.

"Tam," I say. "The cache—if we can find it—could have some food stored in it." I glance at Jess. She's taken off her pack and is sitting on it, staring upriver. I know she's hungry, but with only six jars of salmon left we have to make them last.

"So you're really counting on that cache?" Tam asks. "Stupid." She twirls a finger at the side of her head. "Dylan might be waiting there, ready to kill us."

"I'm not counting on anything, but if that cache exists, I want to find it," I say. "And if Dylan's there, I'm willing to take that chance. I mean, we've got almost nothing left to eat."

Tam turns to Max and asks, "What do you think we should do?"

"We all agreed to go in this direction," Max says. She puts her hand on Tam's shoulder. "We'll figure this out. We've survived this long."

"That's my point," Tam says. "We have survived this long. We don't want to screw up now by chasing something that probably isn't there." Then she walks off and sits on a rock about fifty feet away.

I want to follow Tam and try to convince her that we're doing the right thing by trying to find the cache, but part of me doesn't know if that's actually true. But another part of me knows that I can only push Jess so far. For her age, she is freaking incredible, but I can't keep expecting her to do everything the rest of us can on so little food. I want to find that cache for her.

I squat down next to Jess and say, "We'll figure out a way to cross. On the other side, that's where we might find more food."

She turns away from me so her back is to the river. I hear her sniffling and I think, *How is she ever going to cross the river if she's so scared she won't even look at it?*

Max comes over, sits on the other side of Jess, and puts her arm around her. "Remember when you climbed that cliff to get out of the fissure? That river behind us is like another cliff to climb."

Jess sucks some air in through her nose. "Yeah, but—"

"You guys," Tam yells, "I think I see something."

I stand and see Tam pointing upriver. I scan both banks and see nothing. But then I catch a flash of yellow in the water. Then red. Then green. Upriver about a hundred yards, coming around a bend. Jess and Max are standing and facing the river, too.

We all watch in silence as a procession of bodies floats by— coming from the exact direction we need to go.

CHAPTER 46

"BODIES OR NO BODIES," I say, "we still need to get across the river." We headed about half a mile up the Black Rapids tributary after the thirty or so fully clothed bodies floated by on the river.

"I'm not going to waltz into a bloodbath," Tam says. "Especially with no weapon. We need to at least make some spears. Whoever's responsible for this is beyond evil."

"More death," Max says. "Always more death. You can't avoid it. Especially now."

"Maybe they all caught some disease." Jess's voice cracks. "No one has any medicine."

"Or maybe not," Tam says. "Maybe they were gunned down."

Jess turns away from the river.

"Whatever happened to them," I say, "no matter how many there were, we can't change it. And we might never know."

"I don't want to know," Tam says softly. "I just want it all to stop. I hoped once we got far enough away from Fairbanks that the craziness would stop. That we'd be safe—at least from people. Guess I was wrong."

A cold wind is blowing down from the mountains above the headwaters of Black Rapids Creek. Snow isn't out of the question. I just want to make it through the pass before the winter sets in.

We split a jar of salmon. Then Tam and Max spend some time attaching stone spearpoints to the ends of our sticks while Jess and I climb a hill to get a better view of the river and the creek in hopes of finding a safe place to cross.

I put my hand on her shoulder. "The farther we walk up the creek, the smaller it will get. Maybe I'll even be able to carry you piggyback." I smile.

She wipes her nose with her shirtsleeve, then says, "Only if you want to. I can walk myself."

"Of course I'd want to. It'd be fun." I touch her cheek and a small smile appears on her face, and I feel myself smiling back.

I glance down at the river. More and more bodies keep coming around the bend. I turn to Jess. "I don't see any great spots to cross yet, but we'll find a place."

Jess looks me in the eye. "Trav, how do you think all those people died?"

I take a deep breath. I wish I knew who the people were and where they'd come from. Maybe I should fish a few bodies out of the river and examine them. Maybe we'd learn something valuable, something that would make the difference between life and death. Or maybe we'd catch some disease and die.

"I don't know," I say.

"Are the people who killed them going to come after us?" Jess asks.

I take a breath and say, "Whatever happened to those people, it's not going to happen to us. Not if I can help it. Let's get Max and Tam. We need to make a decision."

CHAPTER
47

"IN DYLAN'S PHOTO THE ENTRANCE to the cache looks rocky, like it's on the side of a cliff," I say. "But we don't need to worry about that yet because it's on the other side of the pass in a different valley. The river there should be flowing south, not north."

"Then why can't we just wait to cross the river?" Jess asks. "And just keep following it until it really braids out and gets small?"

"According to the map, the river bends away from the road and ends up at some lakes to the west," I say. "We can't afford to walk that far out of our way. We'll use up all our food." The pack at the bottom of the sinkhole flashes in my mind and I hate myself for not trying to haul it up in smaller loads.

Tam picks up a rock and throws it into the creek. "Quit talking like this cache is a done deal. It might not even exist."

I know she's right, but I need something to keep us moving in the right direction. If we just flail around moving east to west and west to east, we'll starve.

"Even if we don't find the cache," I say, "at least we'll be moving in the right direction. If we follow the river, besides going out of our way, we'll be going toward where the bodies came from."

Max hasn't said a word since she and Tam joined us on the hill. They used the drawknife that Mike and Dylan left us to whittle away the ends of the sticks we've been carrying until they were thin enough to split. Then they made tiny splits in the very ends and wedged a spearpoint in each one.

Now Max hands me one of our new spears.

"Nice," I say, fingering the point. It sticks out about two inches from the end of the shaft.

"Throwing them won't do much good," Tam says. "But if you have to stab something"—she pauses—"or someone. It should work okay. I wish I had some arrows. Those willow shafts we cut—they're too flimsy. And without fletchings, they're even more useless."

"Your dad," Max says to me, "he knew what he was doing when he went after these spearpoints."

I just nod. Yeah, he did know, but if he'd really known what he was doing, he would've listened to my mom and got us all on one of those buses heading north. "My dad was pretty stubborn and driven," I say. "Sometimes I felt more like his worker than his son."

"At least you had a dad," Tam says. "And now you've got memories. Since my mom died when I was six, all I've known is institutional living and running. Foster homes with people who didn't care. A group home stuffed full of girls who turned on each other for their own survival when supplies got scarce. I tried to stay out of everyone's way after that, but I couldn't. I had to fight if I wanted to eat, because some girls would take anyone's food they could. The really timid ones would just hand over part of their meal to the bullies so they wouldn't get pounded. I fought to keep mine. The counselors lost control. They called themselves *house parents*, but they were parents in name only."

"The land is my parent," Max says. "I feel—"

"Big friggin deal," Tam says. "The land is dead. You always say that kind of crap. Even when we lived in the group home, you acted like some kind of Earth mother." She turns her head away and spits.

"I can't help it if I feel connected—to everything," Max says softly. "It's a gift and a curse. That fire burned me deep, but I'll heal, just like the land."

"The land might not heal," Tam says.

Max frowns. "This place is hurting enough without your negative energy pounding it down more."

"I know," Tam says, "it's just that sometimes I can't take it. All I want is to live without being in constant danger and to have enough food to eat. I'd live in a cave if it was safe and I wasn't going to starve."

Max faces Tam straight on and says, "Girl, you're part of this place, whether you want to be or not." She points at me and Jess. "We all are."

"But you want to be here," Tam says. "I don't. When those buses left and they abandoned us, I wanted to crawl under a rock and die. Instead, I had to instantly start fighting for my life and basically haven't stopped since."

Max puts her arm around Tam. "You were a fighter long before the government abandoned us. That's why you've survived as long as you have."

Tam leans her head on Max's shoulder. They start talking softly and I motion for Jess to follow me.

"We need to give them a little space," I say as Jess falls in beside me.

"Are they going to be okay?" Jess asks as we climb a little hill.

"Yes," I say. "They're just two good friends helping each other out."

At the top of the little hill we turn and face downriver, and my breath catches in my throat.

Back from the way we've come, something interesting is going on. There must be a shallow gravel bar or some other obstruction on the river bottom, because the bodies are piling up and spreading out. Forming a dam.

CHAPTER
48

"THERE MUST BE SOMETHING STICKING up from the bottom of the river," I say. "Something that the first few bodies lodged onto, then the rest piled up behind them." The upstream end of the wall is jagged, but the downstream end is almost straight, like whatever is catching the bodies runs the width of the river. Maybe there's some old pieces of pipeline there. Whatever it is, it must be just below the surface, because we can't see it.

"When the water rises, they'll just keep going downriver," Tam says.

The bridge of bodies cuts a crooked line across the dark water, which spills through the downstream end of the body dam, creating a two-foot waterfall across the entire river where there used to be rapids a little while ago.

Max says, "There must be at least a hundred bodies. Maybe two hundred. All that potential—gone."

We've all seen bodies, especially after the fires, but I've never seen this many in one place. And I think it's more like a thousand. Some are faceup, others facedown. Limbs are tangled across one another like they were all taking part in a group wrestling match and were frozen in position mid-match.

They don't look mangled or cut up. And I can't make out any

bullet holes or stab wounds or protruding arrows from where I'm standing.

No one says anything for a while. We all just keep staring, studying, like maybe we'll see something that will make it all clear.

When you encounter charred bodies, it's easy to figure out that the people probably burned to death, or if you find a skinny corpse or two in a crawl space with no food, that they probably starved. And bullet holes are easy to spot on gunned-down people.

But this is different. I mean, the bodies look untouched.

Then Tam says what we're all thinking. "I wonder if it's stable enough to cross."

"Would they just move every time you stepped on one?" Max says.

"All that movement might disturb them," Jess says. "They might get washed downstream when we're on top of them."

"What about diseases?" I ask. "What if they're infected with something and we catch it?"

"If we just stay over here," Max says, "there's a good chance we'll starve to death."

Tam nods. "We should at least take the risk and try to get across the river."

I take a breath. "We'll have to go one at a time."

CHAPTER
49

MAX AND TAM CRAWLED ACROSS the body bridge one at a time.

I don't want Jess to go alone, but I know that two people on the bridge will make it more unstable. I want to be on the other side encouraging her, but I also want to be on this side in case she gets scared and won't cross or has to come back. And I want to be on the bridge with her in case it gives out, or she falls in and gets pinned between two bodies.

I feel my teeth grinding together. I don't like any of the options. Max and Tam are staring at us from across the river. I know the longer we wait, the more chance there is that conditions will change and make the crossing even less safe.

But she's my sister, and I've promised that I'll do everything I can to keep her safe. To keep her alive. To keep her from suffering. To do what my parents couldn't do.

"Jess," I say. "I think you need to go next. But remember, you can always turn back if it doesn't feel right." If she makes it across and I don't, at least she'll be with Tam and Max.

She nods. "I can do this." But her whole body is shaking.

"I know you can," I say, trying to believe my own words. Trying to believe that the bridge will hold her like it did Tam and Max. Trying to believe she won't slip and get pinned under the bodies by the current or be swept downriver. Trying to believe that I won't be standing here watching my sister drown among a bunch of corpses. Or that I won't drown trying to save her.

Jess unbuckles her waist strap, gets on her hands and knees, and puts her palm onto a corpse.

"Stop," I say, then I grab her leg and pull her back.

The bridge is shifting. It's swaying from underneath in the middle of the river, like something is pushing up from the bottom, or like an ocean swell is coming downriver.

Silently, we watch as single bodies become dislodged and float downstream. Then rafts of ten or twelve bodies are floating downstream.

Quickly, the bridge is gone.

"Now what do we do?" Jess asks. "If we hadn't waited so long, we would've been across."

"Wait a minute," I say. "I—"

"Waiting is what screwed us up. You're just like Dad. Just like him."

"Christ," I say.

"See?" Jess says. "You sound just like him, too."

I stand there for a minute, then finally say, "Okay. Maybe I am a little like him. But we've still got to figure out how to get across. Come on." I grab her hand. Jess drags her feet for a few steps, then starts walking.

We walk upriver to where Black Rapids Creek pours in and then follow the creek, looking for a place to cross. The creek bends away from the river, which we can still see in the distance, and still need to cross once we figure out how to cross the creek.

Tam and Max are heading upriver. At least that's what we think from our attempts to communicate by shouting and hand signals.

We hope to meet up with them on the other side as soon as we get ourselves across.

I know that every step upstream is a step farther away from the river, but the stream is a rage of silty water. We use our spears as walking sticks, keeping the pointed ends upward.

"Do you think we'll be able to find Max and Tam?" Jess asks.

"I think so," I say. "If we can cross this creek and then the river, they should be pretty easy to find."

We keep walking upstream with the wind at our face, crossing in and out of shadows cast by gray clouds scudding across the sky.

The higher we climb, the more tiny green plants poke out of crevices in the rocks. We're in a green band that's been spared by the fires, but not much grows here because it's mostly rock. If we can get through the pass, maybe there'll be actual trees.

"This is the spot," I say. The land has leveled out for a short distance and the creek has fanned into several channels across the flat spot. "A natural crossing. Too bad we had to walk so far to find it." The river is a tiny ribbon in the distance, five or six miles away, I guess.

We cross the knee-deep channels, then sit down and split a jar of salmon. I can't help thinking of my mom. All the time she spent canning this fish, keeping the fire in the woodstove hot enough to keep the water boiling, the canning jars sitting on the wire holder in the bottom of the three-gallon pot.

My mom, sweat dripping from her chin, covering her neck, just doing the job without complaining even though she wanted to be on a bus heading north, then on a ship sailing across the Arctic Ocean to a better place. She must've really loved my dad to agree to stay, to stop herself from presenting him with an ultimatum. But the sad thing is, if she'd said she was leaving and held firm, I think he would've agreed to go.

But that hadn't happened. She had given in. Now they're gone and we're here. Almost out of food, a big river to cross, and the wind blowing cold air up our sleeves and under our collars.

We finish the jar and I'm still as hungry as I was when we opened it.

I stand up and look toward the river, searching for braided spots, but we're so far away and the light's almost gone, so it's hard to see anything but an inky-black line. I don't want to go upriver any farther than needed because the river is starting to bend away from the road. Plus, the bodies came from upriver, and I'm not actively seeking their source.

I just want to cross, make it to the road, and then follow the road through the pass into the Buffer Zone, and not get killed doing it. And meet up with Max and Tam.

Simple.

CHAPTER
50

WE PICK OUR WAY DOWN the other side of Black Rapids Creek in the fading daylight.

"If you're up for it," I say, "I think we should keep walking—all night. We'll just have to be more careful in the dark."

"Can't we stop for a while?" Jess asks, then looks at her feet.

"We'll take short breaks," I say. "But if we stop for too long, we'll get cold, and there's nothing to make a fire with." I wouldn't make one even if I had the wood, because I don't want us to be seen. Those bodies are still fresh in my mind.

I feel a burning in my chest, like the salmon I've eaten wants to come out the way it went in, so I swallow and take a couple of deep breaths.

"Trav," Jess says, walking next to me, "do you think I'm a fighter?"

"A what?" I say. "A fighter? Why do you want—"

"That's what Max called Tam," Jess explains, "when Tam was so upset."

"We're all fighters," I say, "in our own ways. And you might just be the biggest fighter out of all of us."

Jess shakes her head. "I'm the smallest."

I stop walking and turn toward Jess, and she stops, too. "That's exactly why you're the biggest fighter." I pause. "Every step we take, you've got to stretch farther than anyone else, and you still keep up with everyone. You've got to be a fighter to do that. Understand?"

"I think so," Jess says. Then she tilts her head sideways a little and asks, "Trav, we take care of each other, right?"

"Of course we do," I say. "You and me have been taking care of each other for a long time."

Jess smiles. "Then we're good friends, too? Just like Max and Tam, right?"

I touch her cheeks with my hands like my mom used to do with her. "Not just good friends. Great friends." I wish my mom and dad could see Jess now, not just because of what she's done but because of how she's thinking and asking questions. "We have to take care of each other the best we can, no matter what happens."

"But not just us, right?" Jess asks. "Max and Tam, too."

"Right again, sis," I say. "In this world Max and Tam are basically family, too."

"Do you like Tam?" Jess asks. "I mean as *more* than a friend."

"What?" I say. "What makes you ask that?"

"You keep looking at her when she's not looking at you," Jess says.

Has it been that obvious? I wonder. I feel the corners of my lips curling upward. "Yeah," I say. "I think I do. I mean, yeah, I like her."

Jess nods. "She does the same thing."

"What do you mean?" I ask.

"You know," Jess says. "She keeps looking at you when you're not looking at her."

My heart does a little leap. "Really?" I say. "Are you sure?"

"Max pointed it out to me the day we found Dylan's pack. She thought it was cute because Tam's never had a boyfriend."

"Still," I say, "she might not like me the way I like her. You never know."

"No," Jess says, "not unless you ask her."

We walk in silence for a while. My feet burn with every small step, the jagged rocks poking me through my thin rubber soles. The constant rush of the creek fills my ears, making it hard to hear anything else. I think about what Jess has told me. Tam likes me the way I like her? Maybe? Not that any of it matters if we don't survive. But if we do make it to the coast and we do find a safe place to live, then maybe we could be together. My mind jumps back to our thighs pressing together as we hoisted packs out of the fissure.

And then how she stripped down and climbed into that sinkhole.

Fearless.

Strong.

And beautiful.

My chest feels tight. Like there's something squeezing it, but not in a bad way. It's like when you are hoping for something or looking forward to something. Like the way I used to feel before I'd meet up with Stacy. We'd make a plan to be alone and as the time approached, my chest would get tight in anticipation.

Me and Tam together. I like the way it sounds in my head, and the way it makes me feel in my chest, but if I spend too much time or energy obsessing over it, I might screw up and die. You don't survive out here by letting your mind wander for long.

Plus, if we don't find a way to cross the river, I may never see her again. Even if we do cross, I may never see her again. It makes me feel like I'm mourning a future without her, mourning what could have been, even though I don't know for sure what it could be.

It starts to snow, giant, sopping-wet flakes.

We keep walking and angle away from the creek just enough so its roar isn't so overwhelming. I want to be able to hear other noises—animal noises.

People noises.

The snow keeps falling but not quite sticking, and the wind, blowing down from the mountains behind us, pushes it in front of us in swirls. I hear some sounds coming from Jess, like she's crying but trying to hide it.

We stop on the lee side of a rock the size and shape of a school bus. I pull Jess to me and wrap my arms around her to keep her warm.

"We're gonna be okay," I say. "We've just got to make it through this night. That's all that matters right now."

"But that's not all that matters," Jess says. "What about tomorrow and the next day, and the day after that? What about Max and Tam? And all those dead people? And all the miles we still have to walk? What about—"

"Jess," I say. "If we don't survive tonight, none of that will matter. We can take care of each other. Focus on tonight. One thing at a time. It's too much to think about otherwise. Your mind will get so crowded you won't be able to think. You won't be able to move. Think about how you used to do jigsaw puzzles. You would focus and work on one until you got it, and no one could drag you away until you were finished. That's what you need to do now. Only instead of a jigsaw puzzle to focus on, you need to breathe and hunker down and rest so you have energy to keep going. I'm going to be right here with you, doing the same thing."

I can feel her sobs against my chest. Then her whole body shakes. I hug her a little tighter. It's true that she's a fighter and it's also true that she's only ten years old. "We'll stay right here for a little while, slip on our coveralls, and give the clouds a chance to snow themselves out. Then we'll keep moving. Maybe it'll even be getting light by then."

We get into our coveralls. I sit and lean against the rock and my back turns to ice. Jess sits in front of me and leans her back onto my chest, and I cradle her with my arms and legs, trying to blanket her from the cold. "That's the way to do it. Curl up. Lean back. Relax."

After a while I feel Jess's even breaths as sleep takes over. I sit as still as I can, hoping for her it is a restful night.

A few hours later, yellow light stretches across the southern horizon. The snow has let up and hasn't stuck, but it's a warning. Our days of surviving without winter gear are numbered.

* * *

We're standing on the riverbank, the water rushing by, a formidable barrier bending away from the road the farther upriver we walk.

"We might have to ditch our packs and swim," I say.

"No way," Jess says. "We need our stuff—all of it."

"We need to cross the river."

"So let's say we swim and we don't drown, then what?"

"Hopefully, we'll find Max and Tam, and the cache."

"And if we don't?"

"If we don't, we still need to keep heading south. And the road has to be the fastest way to go from here. Maybe we'll try to spend the winter in the Buffer Zone if we don't find the cache."

"What are we gonna eat?"

"Jess, we've got a few jars of salmon between us. We could finish these off, swim to the other side, and still be hungry. I don't want to lose everything: the coveralls, the glass jars, the rope, our spears, the arrowheads. I can put the fire starter and the knife in my pocket. And we can wear our hats and gloves, but the rest of the stuff—we'll just have to leave it. The more we carry, the more chance we have of drowning."

"I'll freeze without my coveralls."

"We'll eat the rest of the salmon, then we'll bury everything under a pile of rocks, and depending on what we find on the other side, maybe we'll be able to come back and get it. Who knows what's over there. Could be a canoe or a rowboat." I grab Jess by both arms and look her in the eye. "But most likely, we'll never see this stuff again."

Jess squirms out of my grasp and says nothing.

"We'll be able to walk faster without the packs," I say.

"Do you remember last night?" Jess asks. "We would've froze without the coveralls."

"All the more reason to move. The Buffer Zone will have wood for fires, I hope."

"I don't like this plan," Jess says.

"Neither do I, but it's the only one we've got."

"Let's stay on this side."

"That's one way to die," I say. "Is that what you want?" I pause. "If you've got a way to get our stuff across the river, I'd love to hear it. I was hoping for a braided place to cross, but there isn't one. And I'm not going to keep walking farther from the road. Those bodies came down the river. Whoever put them in the water is probably still by the river."

"You don't know if any of that is true," Jess says.

"Remember the Yukon? How fast it happened? How quickly we went from two parents to no parents?" I glance upriver. "People might be watching us right now. Evil people. Or people so bad off that they've turned evil."

"You sound just like Dad," Jess says.

"If I'd listened to Dad on the Yukon, maybe he and Mom would still be alive. I'm the one that talked him into approaching Clint. Maybe we'd all be on a boat headed across the Arctic Ocean if it weren't for me, if we'd stuck to ourselves and built our own raft. What happened on the Yukon, I can't let that happen again."

"So we're just going to abandon our stuff for something that may or may not exist? Maybe those bodies had been piled up for months and an earthquake or landslide sent them into the river."

"Didn't look like they'd been dead long to me," I say.

"Maybe the people who dumped them in the river are on the road." Jess pounds the ground with the butt of her spear. "Maybe it's safer on this side."

"If we follow this side and don't find a place to cross, we'll hit some lakes miles and miles from the road. Then we'll have to go around the lakes and cross all that land just to get to the road. And we'll miss the cache." I pull out the map and show her. "We'll run out of food way before we get to the road."

For a couple of minutes Jess just stares at the map, silent, like she's hoping to find some undiscovered detail that will make everything okay.

Finally, she turns her face toward me. "I'm scared to swim across the river."

I put my hand on her shoulder. "So am I."

CHAPTER
51

WE PICK A SPOT UNDER a towering rectangular rock to bury our packs and hide our spears. It's set back from the river about a half mile and partway up a hill, prominent enough to see because the rock rises at a slight angle and the top is about thirty feet high, the base about ten feet wide.

"All we do is bury stuff," Jess says. "First it was the cache at our place before we went north. Then Dad made you bury that stuff sack before approaching those people on the Yukon, and now this."

I force a smile. "We're kind of like dogs." I bark once.

Jess laughs and that makes my smile real.

I picked this rock because I'm pretty sure Jess could find it on her own if she needed to. I hate thinking about this stuff, about my sister being alone, but I can't help it. Even if you were as careful and cautious as my dad, you could still end up dead.

I take the map and the photo labeled "Mike and Dylan at the secret cache with Uncle Mark," and the letters from our parents, and put them into the Ziploc bag, then fold it up and stuff it into my pocket. I put the fire starter in my other pocket along with my knife.

I pick up the drawknife. It would be useful if we had to work with logs, but there's no way to take it. I think about tying one of the stuff sacks around my waist or my shoulder and putting it in there, but I don't want the extra weight and don't want anything that might snag on a rock and pin me to the bottom.

I wish we could somehow take the coveralls, but their weight, once they're soaked with water, would drag us down like we had cement blocks tied to our feet.

We finish filling in the hole, eat the last of the salmon, then pick our way downslope to the river. The wind is blowing through my clothes, and gray clouds threaten rain or snow.

At the bank, Jess and I stand side by side as I study the water, trying to figure out the best way to approach this suicide mission.

After a minute I say, "The current will pull us away from shore. Don't fight it head-on. Just swim at an angle against it. That'll move us across the current, but it will also keep us from being swept too far downstream." I put my arm around Jess and say, "See that point of land jutting out on the far side of the river and downstream a bit?"

"Yeah," Jess says softly, "I see it."

"We want to be on the other side before we reach that point," I say. "There's an eddy there, you know, where the current flows backward just before the point. If we can get in that eddy, it'll help pull us toward shore."

I turn to Jess and have her repeat what I've said to make sure she understands the plan.

"I'll stay downriver from you," I say. "If we miss the eddy, we'll be swept around that point and the current might try to pull us back toward this side because of the way the river bends. Hopefully, that won't happen."

"But what if it does?" Jess asks.

"We'll have to see where we are," I say. "If we're exhausted, we might have to just head for this side, rest a little, and try again."

"Again?" Jess says. "If we don't make it, I don't know if I could even try this again." Her face is shaking.

I put my hand on her arm. "I hope we make it on the first try. But if we don't, it's good to have an idea of what we might do next."

We put on our hats and gloves and wade into the river, the current tugging at our knees. "Remember, keep your head pointed upstream."

After a couple more steps, the bottom falls out from under us. I kick with my legs and pull with my arms and try to breathe steadily. I swim the sidestroke so I can keep an eye on Jess. The cold water is squeezing me. I feel a shiver run up my back. Even with gloves on, my fingers are already turning to ice.

Jess is keeping the angle, kicking with her legs, and doing a doggie paddle with her arms. She doesn't have much experience swimming. The few pools in town were shut down by the time she was old enough to enjoy them.

I see her head go under once, but it instantly shoots back up with her gasping, and then she's holding steady again.

I'm feeling the weight of my waterlogged clothing and start kicking harder to keep my head above the water.

"You're doing great," I call. "Just keep going."

Jess doesn't turn or say anything, just keeps kicking.

I swivel my head around, trying to get a sense of how we're doing. We're only a freaking quarter of the way across. The current is carrying us downstream at a faster clip than I hoped.

"Jess," I yell. "Kick a little harder if you can." I take in a mouthful of silty water and cough it out, but it leaves a gritty layer on my teeth.

Maybe the current is just getting stronger the farther we go from shore. I don't know if Jess can kick any harder than she already is, but if we want to have any chance of catching that eddy, we need to speed up.

I think about having Jess hang on to me while continuing to kick with her legs, but I doubt we'll be able to go any faster than we're going now.

I'm right next to Jess now. Any closer and our shoulders will bump. "Keep it steady," I say. "Don't talk. Just keep kicking and pulling."

I know she's doing her best, and she hasn't freaked out, but we're just not going to make it into the eddy at this rate. It's like we're in an express lane in the middle of the river with no exits in sight.

I swivel my head again, trying to figure out if we should head back to shore now to save our energy for the next try, or just abort this crossing idea altogether, and that's when I spot movement. One person is walking downriver on the shore we started from. I imagine our heads as dots on the water. If he didn't see us wade in, he might not know we're here.

But soon he'll come upon our footprints leading from the burial spot under the big rock to the shore. Then he'll know.

CHAPTER
52

I DON'T SAY ANYTHING TO Jess about the person on the shore. I just keep pulling with my arms and kicking with my legs. My chest and back are going numb, like they've been completely wrapped by ice packs. I know my arms are still moving, but I can barely feel them.

Jess seems to be holding up okay, but just like me, she has to be freezing.

I keep repeating the word *eddy* over and over in my mind. My legs are starting to hang straight down. I'm still kicking them, but it feels like I'm going in slow motion. One of my feet hits a rock on the bottom. I stumble and my head goes under. The current pulls my hat off and it's gone. My other foot kisses the bottom, and I push upward. My legs hang down and they bump the bottom again.

"Almost there, Jess," I call. "My feet touched bottom." Then my toes are dancing on the bottom with my head still above the water for a moment, but just as fast the bottom drops out and I go under again.

I come up coughing and spitting. *I just need to keep my nose above the surface*, I think. Just my nose. My feet hit bottom again. Now they're bouncing along and my whole head is above the water. Jess is still just in front of me, upriver. We're approaching the far end of the eddy but are still in the current on the outside of it.

"Go for the point," I yell. "With me."

I windmill my arms forward. I know the channel will cut back across the river on the far side of the point. We have to make it to shore before we reach that point.

Jess's shoulder bumps mine. I put my arm around her and keep kicking. I'm pretty sure the water is only four feet deep but it's freaking zipping along so fast you can't stand up without being knocked down.

My free hand grazes the bottom while my head is still above the water. I let my legs fall and my feet and shins bounce along the rocky bottom. I push Jess forward and let go of her.

"Shore," I try to yell, but it comes out garbled.

Now I'm in knee-deep water, crawling right for the point. My hands are unresponsive hunks of frozen meat. Through my hair, I can see Jess lying facedown in the water a few feet from the shore, just inside the point.

I crawl toward her, slipping on rounded river rocks being scrubbed by the current.

"Jess," I yell. "Jess."

I pull her through shin-deep water. *Get her to shore,* my mind screams.

She was fine all the way in. All the way to when I let go of her, she was still kicking. I drag her out of the water and roll her on her side. A little dirty water trickles out of her mouth and nose. I put my hand in front of her face, but my fingers are so numb I can't tell if she's breathing. I roll her onto her back and put my ear to her chest and feel for the thump of her heart.

CHAPTER
53

I RUB HER ICY CHEEKS and say her name over and over. Then I grab her hand and her fingers curl ever so slightly, just like when she was a baby and I'd put my finger in her hand and she'd grab it.

I put my lips to her ear and say her name again. She squeezes my hand, then lets go. Then squeezes again, and my eyes grow hot.

"Jess," I say. "My Jess."

She squeezes my hand again.

I scoot back and sit up so I can see her face. I brush her cheek with the back of my hand and see her closed eyes tighten, then relax.

"Jess," I say. "Can you open your eyes? Can you do it for me?"

The river is rushing by our feet. On the other side I can see the person. Did he have something to do with all the bodies in the river?

I look down at Jess again and see the rise and fall of her chest. Is she hurt or just exhausted? I put my hand on her forehead and start to gently pull one of her eyelids up with my thumb. She turns her head sideways and I stop.

I know we need to keep moving. Work our way to the road and then try to find the cache. Try to find anything. Find Max and Tam.

Can Jess walk? Is she in danger of freezing to death? Her face is pale but her lips don't look blue, just a light pink color. I know she can move her fingers, and she turned her head away when I touched her eyelid. Maybe she's in shock. I don't know exactly what that means, but I've heard the term.

I replay the scene in my mind. She was swimming. We got into the shallows and then I saw her floating facedown, but not for very long.

Something happened. But what? Did she just pass out in the water?

I slip one arm under her neck and another beneath her knees, and I slowly stand up. When Jess was little, I used to carry her to bed when she'd fall asleep in the family room. I used to like doing that. She almost never woke up. But the more my dad put me to work after the buses left, the less I saw of Jess. My dad thought with a simpler life we'd be even more of a family, but when I look back on it, I see that the main thing it did was divide us. Me and my dad scavenged and worked the land. Mom took care of Jess and did all she could at the house. Family time pretty much disappeared so we could focus on survival. On this journey, I was slowly getting my sister back. I can't bear to lose her now.

On the far side of the river the person is walking toward the big rock where we buried our stuff.

I turn away from the river and start walking, my eye on the small bluff I need to climb to get out of the floodplain and onto the old road. With her soaked clothing, Jess is extra heavy.

The cold, which settled into me like I was wearing a suit of icy armor, starts to fade as I warm from carrying Jess. She grunts a couple of times when I stumble, which actually gives me some relief. I mean, any response is better than no response, but let's face it, if our situation doesn't change soon, we'll end up a couple of corpses. Like the ones we stumbled upon in the fissure.

And where are Max and Tam? I could sure use their coveralls to keep Jess warm.

I'm confused and pissed off. I mean, if I'd crossed the river on the body bridge and they hadn't, I would've tried to track them along the shore, not lose sight of them, so I'd know if they made it across and where. And I think they'd do the same for us, but we'd never talked about what we'd do if we got split up with a wide and raging river between us.

The more I think about it, the more convinced I become that they would've stayed if it had been possible. Something dangerous must've been going on over here that I couldn't see from across the river. Or maybe we were gone up the creek for so long that they thought something had happened to us.

At the base of the bluff I sit down facing the river, keeping Jess draped across my lap. If only she were just asleep, like when she was little. If only she wasn't soaked and cold and barely responsive. If only it wasn't my plan that put her in this condition.

I touch her cheek, and it's chilly compared to my fingers, which have warmed from the walk. Then I put my hand on the top of her bare head—she must've lost her hat, too—and run it down one side of her soaked hair, like my mom used to do countless times when Jess would curl into her lap or grab her leg for a hug. And that's when I feel the bump.

CHAPTER
54

JESS'S BUMP ISN'T SUPER BIG and there's no blood. But she's unresponsive besides a grunt every now and then, and squeezing my finger when I put it in her hands.

Head injury, I think. Then I rack my brain for information about how to treat someone with a head injury. Not that I have anything to treat her with. My teeth grind together. I feel helpless. Why did I insist that she swim the river? And why did I have to let go of her at the end?

I replay the scene in my mind. Her swimming, then the next time I see her she's floating facedown. I don't know how long I lost sight of her. Maybe just a few seconds. A minute at the most. If she was pointing downstream, the current could've slammed her into a rock—headfirst. Hard.

The sun breaks through the clouds as I work my way up to the old road with Jess. At the road, I set her down and rest.

She is curled into the fetal position, which I take as a good sign since she did it on her own.

I pull out the map. I can pick out where we are because I can see where Black Rapids Creek pours into the river, and that spot is on the map.

The spot marked with *C* for cache is still down the road, either at the high point in the pass or just after it.

It's easy enough to follow the old road with my eyes, but walking on it is going to be just as bad or worse than traveling cross-country since it's so torn up.

"Mom," Jess says softly.

I put my hand on her forehead. Then I press my cheek against hers. Through my beard I can feel the coolness of her skin.

"Jess," I whisper into her ear. "Be okay. Please be okay."

I turn and wipe the tears from my cheeks before they can flood Jess's face.

"Mom," she repeats. "Hold me." Her tongue reaches out of her mouth and licks her lips. Then she's still again, but I can see her chest moving up and down with deep, even breaths.

My heart aches for her, for her loss. Because right now, she's with our mom, but if she's going to live, she's going to lose Mom again.

"Jess." I gently shake her arm. I take her and hold her and rock her. I put my lips to her forehead, feel her clammy skin, and cradle her tighter.

* * *

Jess is moving pretty slowly, but at least she's moving. I'd held her for maybe three or four hours before she fully opened her eyes. Then we sat for a while longer talking about what happened during the crossing. She remembers getting almost all the way across and me giving her a big push, but that's where her memory of the crossing ends.

Steep, raw valleys with ribbons of willow cut into the mountains to the east of the road. There used to be glaciers up these valleys that fed the streams, but they've mostly melted.

Because this place hasn't burned completely, it feels almost relaxing. I mean, even though we're out of food and don't know what's ahead, at least we're in a place that isn't so spent. Like it wouldn't be a bad place to die. Not that I want to die, but I'd rather try to survive here than in a burnt-out basement in the middle of a burnt-out landscape.

I'm alternating between letting Jess ride piggyback and having her walk. I carry her on the smooth sections of road, but she walks the rough ones because I don't want to take a chance of falling with her on my back.

When she's on my back, she asks into my ear, "Where do think Max and Tam are?"

I stop and scoot her up my back farther. "I hope they're around here somewhere," I say. "But I haven't seen any signs that they are."

Truth is, I'm confused. I would've waited if I had been in their position. Unless . . . unless something happened. Like if they had to run from someone or hide or fight. My chest feels raw. They have their spears, but nothing else. Two girls, alone. Not that they couldn't protect themselves as well as anyone. But my mind flashes back to the Yukon and my parents alive one moment and dead the next. I pick up the pace a little. If Max and Tam are around here, I need to find them.

* * *

"This tastes nasty," Jess says.

"Just chew on it," I say. "For as long as you can." I'm sitting in the fading light against a rock and Jess is leaning against me. We're still damp. I know the willow bark is bitter, but it's better than nothing. I peeled a bunch of bark off some shoots before stopping here.

I don't want to keep walking at night, because I don't want to miss any signs of Max and Tam. Maybe they're up one of the creek valleys and have left a marker by the road. It'd be nice to have a fire, but the glow would make us a sitting target. But then again, the glow might be seen by Max and Tam.

I follow our progress on the map. It's pretty easy because of how the river bends away from the road. We've still got some miles to cover to get to the cache, if it even exists and if it's accurately marked on the map.

A few stars appear in the sky, and I wrap my arms around Jess to keep her as warm as possible. It's a good sign that she can walk and talk, because after hauling her out of the river and seeing her just lie there, I thought she was history. Or that she'd been hurt so bad that I wouldn't be able to do anything except watch her die.

At first light I rouse Jess and we keep going down the road. The sun spills over the ridge to the east, bathing the valley bottom. I can still see the river in the distance even though it has already bent away from the road.

Jess is walking beside me, not saying anything. We hit a bend in the road. A small creek flows over brown rocks, then over the road, and plunges off the bluff into the valley. Above the creek on both sides, brown and yellow cliffs rise in front of the mountains. I glance down the road. The brownish rock runs at least as far as the next bend a couple miles away and maybe farther.

I stop and reach into my pocket and pull out Dylan's photo. I nudge Jess. "See this," I say, pointing at the photo. "The rocks are brown, just like the ones around here."

Jess stares at the photo and nods.

"I don't know how far the brown rocks go, maybe all the way into the pass, which is another thirty miles or so, or maybe they're just in this section, but keep your eyes peeled. Anything you see that's odd—anything—you tell me. We don't know exactly what we're looking for, but hopefully, we'll recognize it when we see it."

What I don't tell Jess: If we don't find that cache, we're as good as dead.

CHAPTER
55

JESS AND I ARE HUDDLED under a rock overhang about a hundred feet above the road, but because of the fog I can't see what's below. I can't see five feet in front of me. I'm raining sparks on tiny willow shavings that I made with my knife, but they just won't catch. I wish I had some birch bark or some matches. Anything that will make this stuff catch. And some food, any food.

I think about those bodies floating down the river. *No way*, I think. *I'm not that hungry. I'll never be that hungry.*

My stomach lets out a long growl.

I reach over and touch Jess's arm. I don't know how far I'd go in order to keep my sister alive. Would I insist that she eat human flesh? Or could I trick her into eating it if we came upon more bodies?

Then I hate myself for even thinking about it. But I can't control my mind, especially when I'm starving. Maybe there are caribou and moose in the Buffer Zone. And fish and berries. I mean, there are willows here. This place didn't burn twice in two years like the land around Fairbanks did. And there weren't a ton of people down here before that, people killing everything in sight just so they could eat. But I haven't seen any animal tracks either.

Some places are emptier than others, Dad had said. *Animals, they move. You can't count on them being where you think they'll be. Especially not now.*

I know what he's talking about. With the wacky weather patterns—more extreme hot and more extreme cold—some plants and animals are slow to adapt. And if they don't adapt—they die out. Moose didn't exactly die out, but the moose tick population exploded years ago because the winter temperatures didn't get cold enough to put a check on them. I saw pictures of moose covered with moose ticks. One moose had over ten thousand ticks on it, and those ticks were swollen with the blood from the moose, making it look like the moose was covered in grapes.

So the tick infestation killed a lot of moose and kept the population way down.

And you might think that you can survive anything because you have a house and a job and food at the store, but take all those things away and what have you got? The two of us huddling under a rock in the fog, starving, without any way to make a fire. Maybe Jess even has a concussion, but I don't know how to tell or what to do if she does.

This is life stripped down to basics. We are animals. And when I think like this, well, feeding on another human doesn't seem like such a far-off possibility, especially if they were already dead. Hunting and killing other people for food, I don't think I could do that. But how can you really know what you will do until you're in the situation?

Through the fog a crunching noise invades my ears, like boots on gravel. I put my lips to Jess's ear. "We have to be absolutely quiet."

I feel her nod.

The crunching sound stops, but not right away—like maybe one person stopped walking, then another did the same.

I'm not sure if we'd be visible from the road without the fog. I'm pretty sure whoever is down there can't hear my heart beating even though it's pounding in my own ears, relentless, like a bass drum.

Maybe they've spotted our tracks. Maybe they've been following our tracks all day. And all day yesterday.

A fainter crunching noise works its way into my ears over my heartbeat.

Then another.

And another.

Slow careful steps. Steps that are meant to be soft and unheard. Sneaky steps. Dangerous steps.

I slide my knife from my pocket and silently click open the blade. Three inches, maybe four. It's small, but I'd plunge it deep—and hard.

The steps stop. Just stop—like a car running out of gas or a TV being unplugged.

Are they or he or she or it waiting for me to do something? To show myself? To screw up out of fear? Part of me wants to scream or run out with my knife to show that I mean business. Maybe being on the offensive would be a good thing. Maybe it would show whatever is out there that I'm not someone to be messed with—that I'm a ruthless freaking murdering machine.

Then I hear breathing. Slow and steady—barely perceptible—but I can hear it, slicing through the fog. It has to be an animal. I mean, humans wouldn't breathe like that. They'd be doing what I'm doing—not making a sound.

Unless they aren't scared. Or are scared but trying to pretend they aren't. Or trying to psych me out, get me to choke and make a bad move.

I put my finger up to my lips for Jess to see, but she's sitting back with her eyes closed.

A slight cough, or maybe a grunt, filters through the fog. Whatever is out there could be fifty feet away—or only ten.

Now my whole body is buzzing like I've been plugged into an electrical outlet. I want to scream and run toward the sound and fight. Anything but this waiting. But I don't have enough of an idea of how far away and how many there are. People? Wolves? A bear? And maybe they don't know what we are either.

But that cough—if it was a cough from a person—either it slipped out, or they want me to know they're out there. But why?

I keep still. I'm hot and sweaty everywhere from the adrenaline, except for my feet, which are slabs of ice.

And I wait.

My fingers start going numb and feel more rubbery with each passing second. I keep listening hard, but hear nothing.

Maybe I've imagined the whole thing. The footsteps, the cough. You know how it is when you can't see anything and you think you hear something. And before you know it you're convinced that you're going to die, or be attacked, or whatever.

The fog still prevents me from seeing what is or isn't out there. And then I think about all the hiding I've done the past few years. Not just me, but everyone. And not just hiding, but trying to watch others to see if maybe they are trustworthy or at least worth taking a chance on.

The main thing I've learned is that with some people you can tell right away that you don't want to deal with them. That all they're after is what you have, and they won't hesitate to kill you for it. And the others are people who you aren't sure about at first, but at least there's some hope they aren't out to screw you, like Max and Tam, and to a lesser extent Mike and Dylan.

Jess leans forward and her head droops between her knees.

The fog thins for a moment, and I think I catch a glimpse of two people dressed in long coats. I shake my head. If they exist and I've seen them, then they've probably seen me as well.

"I saw you," I say. "You can't fool me. I've been listening to you sneak up here."

Jess's head shoots up and I put a finger to her lips.

"Do you have a little one? A child?" an old-sounding voice answers. A woman's voice. "We saw small prints."

"Just leave us alone," I say. "I'm armed."

"We want to help." It's definitely a woman's voice. And it sounds a little wobbly.

"How do I know?" I ask. "How can I know?"

"You can't," she says. "Just like we can't know that you won't try to slit our throats or shoot us."

I turn to Jess. Her eyes are closed. Just how bad off is she? I need to help her.

My chest grows tight, like my heart is going to break through the skin. I take a breath. "Okay," I say. "But we'll have to wait until the fog clears."

"Aren't you cold?" This voice is deeper but still sounds like a woman's. "I only saw you for a moment, but it looked like you didn't have much."

I want to stand up, to stand Jess up, and walk toward the voices. I want to believe that this isn't some trap we're being baited into.

"When the fog clears," I say, "we'll follow you." I pause. "At a distance."

"Okay," the woman with the deep voice says. "My name's Wendy. And, well, I guess you can't see her, but this here is my younger sister, Ellen."

"I'm Travis," I say. "And this is my younger sister, Jess."

I want to tell them that Jess has hit her head, but if this is a trap I don't want to give them any information that will help them out. As far as I know, they could be scouts from some cannibalistic group. Use a couple of grannies to bait in the kids.

How dangerous could a couple of old women be? I think I'm about to find out.

CHAPTER
56

WHEN THE FOG CLEARS, WE follow the two women on a windy trail that runs parallel to the road below for miles and miles up into the pass. Sections of the brownish-red rocks come and go. I think about the photo I have of Dylan, Mike, and their uncle Mark at the secret cache, and the *C* marked on the map. I want to run ahead and ask the old women if they know this guy, Mark, but there'll be time enough for that—unless we're walking into a trap.

The farther along we get, the less I think this is a setup, and I actually relax a little bit.

They both have these long brown coats, the same color as the rocks, and smallish brown packs on their backs. They keep a steady pace, slow enough that Jess can keep up. I wonder if they're doing that on purpose.

Jess and I have talked a little bit about the situation. We agreed that we need to see what these two people are all about. I mean, they followed our footprints in the fog. That was a huge risk. We could've been armed killers, desperate for anything—clothing, food. Actually, we are desperate for those two things, but I wouldn't kill for them. I wouldn't take a life just for someone's stuff, but I'd fight to keep my own stuff, if I had any.

The women turn off the trail and start zigzagging up a slope with loose rocks. If they live so far away from where they found us, I wonder what they'd been doing, where they'd been coming from when we met.

Now we're walking along the base of a brownish-red cliff that towers a few hundred feet above us. The cliff keeps wrapping around to the east as we rise higher and higher. The road is a scratchy line far below us. And in the distance I can make out a sea of green. The Buffer Zone.

* * *

I pull out the photo and show it to Wendy and Ellen.

"That's him," Wendy says. "If it weren't for Mark, we'd probably be dead."

"Not probably," Ellen says. "Would certainly be."

I tell them about Mike and Dylan, and how I came to have the map. And about their dad, and the fires he started, and our journey thus far.

"Mark said his brother was a little touched," Wendy says. "But he must've gotten worse."

"With all the destruction," Ellen says, "it could drive even perfectly sane people crazy. And with no one to help him . . ."

"We never met any of Mark's family," Wendy says. "But he talked about his nephews. About how he hoped they'd come back for another visit so they could see how he'd improved the secret shelter, even though he'd had a falling-out with his brother."

"We felt funny about moving in to his shelter after he died," Wendy says. "But after our place burned in a wildfire, well, it was more about survival than anything else."

We're really tucked into the cliffs. Somehow Mark moved a lot of rock and built supports with big beams. I'm not sure how he

267

hauled all the wood up here. And a small woodstove, too. Maybe with pulleys and block and tackle.

Since it faces south, you can sit just back from the opening and be in the sunshine with the Buffer Zone visible in the distance. And Wendy and Ellen said they have a way to close it off in the winter to keep the heat in, but they still sit out there on sunny winter days, the brown rock absorbing the heat from the sun.

"We're careful," Wendy says. "We still have a little store-bought food from back in the day. Canned goods. Dry goods. Thanks to what Mark had stored here. But mostly, we live off the land. We're also trying to put a garden in. We've been making trips back to our old place. That's what we were doing when we saw your tracks. We're slowly bringing some of our old garden soil up here."

"Fairbanks burned twice in two summers," I say. "You know all the new green growth you get after a fire?"

Ellen and Wendy nod.

"Most of the new green burned. The topsoil got scorched. And then the salmon didn't come back. There were still people, but no land to really live off. That's when things got ugly."

"We were already isolated years ago with the road being in such poor condition and the shortage in gasoline," Ellen says. "The more people that left, the more self-reliant we became. And Mark, he was always willing to lend a hand. It was tragic"—Ellen shakes her head—"when that bear got him."

Ellen is really fussing over Jess, which I think is great. She keeps saying it's so nice to have a *little one* around. I'm guessing Jess doesn't like being referred to as a little one, but she appears to be enjoying all the attention and doesn't argue. Ellen has wrapped her in a blanket and keeps refilling her mug with hot willow bark tea. Ellen checked the bump on her head and studied her pupils and told her everything would be okay.

Wendy, the older of the two, brings bowls of stew over to the table and sets one in front of Jess and one in front of me. I haven't had hot food since we cooked down in the fissure. There is some kind of meat in a watery broth and some mushy stuff that I figure is some kind of plant material.

I didn't see any sign of moose or caribou on our walk over here, but there were patches of willow and other ground plants that animals would feed on.

I just keep shoveling spoonfuls into my mouth. And I'm really happy to see Jess eating. Ellen keeps glancing at her, smiling. Then she looks at her sister and nods.

"This stew," I say, "it's really good. But I don't recognize the meat. I mean, it doesn't taste like moose or caribou. And I haven't seen any tracks." I think of the bear Tam and I killed. "Is it bear? Or fox? Or beaver? Rabbit? What is it?"

Wendy and Ellen look at each other. Their smiles don't exactly disappear as much as grow smaller.

"Travis. Jess," Wendy says, "when times get tough, you do what you have to do to survive. And sometimes you end up eating things you wouldn't normally eat."

I set my spoon down.

"Sometimes you eat things that would downright disgust you. Know what I mean?" Ellen asks. She glances at Jess, then turns back to Wendy.

"We don't really think about it much anymore," Wendy says. "It's just part of our life. Part of surviving. It's why we're alive. And once upon a time, I was even a vegetarian." She lets out a small laugh.

I think of the bodies floating down the river. I pick up my spoon and fish out a piece of meat. I smell it. I'm a freaking cannibal. I feel a chill travel up my spine. The bodies flash into my mind again and I blink hard. I look across at Jess and I don't know what to say. Her eyes are slits and she's stopped eating.

"We know some of the meat is tough," Ellen says. "We tried just eating the little ones. They're more tender, but there's not nearly as much meat on them. So usually we let them grow at least a little before they end up in the pot."

Wendy's smile fades and her face grows tight. "We've got a small spot in back," she says. "A holding area. And it's built tight so they can't escape."

I study the bumpy morsel of meat cradled in my spoon. Again, I see the bodies in the river but I can't put it together with what they've said. I turn to Ellen and Wendy. "Holding area? You mean they're alive back there?"

"Just like having fish in a pond, or chickens in the yard," Wendy says. She forces a smile. "I know it's not the normal thing to do, but you do what you have to do in order to survive."

I try to make sense of what they're saying and how they can be so casual about this, but I just can't put it all together. I glance over at Jess and she's got this confused look on her face. I turn back to Wendy and say, "What's back there?" I shake my head once. "I know it's not people . . . right?"

"People?" Wendy says, then she lets out a laugh. "Not people. Just voles. They run around in the rocks and eat the bits of plants we put in the enclosure and, luckily for us, have lots of babies."

"Voles?" I say, and let out a breath.

"Yes," Wendy says. She laughs softly. "Sorry for the confusion."

"You mean mice?" Jess asks. She puts her spoon in her bowl

and scoops up a piece of meat and studies it. Then she pops it into her mouth.

"Red-backed voles," Wendy says. "They're the same size as mice. Not that I haven't thought about eating a person. I'd be lying if I said that never crossed my mind. But the voles, that was Ellen's idea. There was quite a population of voles in our garden before our cabin burned and it became unsafe to live by the road."

"Those voles," Ellen says, "some years they ate more of our carrots than we did. So we live-trapped a whole bunch of them and brought them up here. And it's been our main protein source for over a year now."

"We eat pretty lean around here," Wendy says.

I glance at my bowl, and over to Jess's, then realize we're the only two eating. "We won't be staying long," I say. "Just long enough for Jess to get her strength back from that river crossing. The sooner we get into the Buffer Zone the better."

Jess looks at Wendy and Ellen and says, "Thanks for the food. And the tea." Then she yawns.

Ellen and Wendy smile at her and tell her to eat all she wants.

Truth is, if I thought they had more food, I might stay longer, but I just can't see eating up their vole supply with winter coming on.

Jess eats another spoonful of stew then puts her spoon down and just stares at the center of the table. Then she says, "I miss my mom."

Ellen sits down next to Jess, puts her arm around her, and says, "Of course you do, sweetheart. It's natural to miss her. I know that doesn't make it any easier. Nothing does but time." Ellen points to me. "And your brother there, you've got him and he's got you."

Jess snuggles into Ellen's side and Ellen gives her a gentle kiss on top of her head and we all sit in silence for a minute. I think about what Ellen said and I realize that yes, I do have Jess.

Sometimes I'm so focused on and stressed by having the responsibility of keeping Jess alive, I forget that not only is she my only family, but she's this amazing person. She's only ten years old and she's walked about six hundred miles this summer through a wasteland. She must be stronger than all of us given her age and what she's accomplished. She's even more of a fighter than I realized.

I want her to have a life, a long life, and I want to be around to see what she does with it. And I realize that it's not a burden to take care of her, it's a privilege.

*　*　*

A couple hours later, after Jess and I have had a little sleep, we're back around the table talking. I need information about what's ahead.

"The forest is really thick in the Buffer Zone," Wendy says. "We used to hunt and fish and pick berries and dig roots down there, but not for several years now. Those first two years after the government set us free, a lot of people followed the road south, so we kept off it. You're the only people we've seen trying to pass through this year. Not that we see everyone, but we've got a pretty good view of the road from up here."

We talk more about the bodies in the river. Ellen thinks they are probably from this religious commune that set up shop on the site of an old gold mine. When she points to the spot on my map, it's right next to one of the lakes that make up the headwaters of the Delta River.

And the person I saw walking downriver on the opposite shore after we'd crossed the river, she doesn't know what to make of him. Maybe he's part of the same group. Maybe not.

Wendy says, "Even though we're the last ones left around here, I just want to stay. Maybe if I were younger and looking to start a family, I'd risk traveling through the Buffer Zone, but not now. This is our home." She smiles at Ellen and Ellen smiles back.

I tell them about Tam and Max and how we got separated and hope to find them. I think of Tam and the possibility that she actually likes me, and I get this raw feeling in my chest. And I think of Max and the amazing way she and Jess have bonded. And I worry all the more that something bad has happened to them. At least they had their packs and spears when they crossed the river. But where are they?

Then I tell them about Dylan, and how unstable he is, and how we're pretty sure he went back north. But if not, he might show up here.

They pull out their map and show us which way they would walk if they were going into the Buffer Zone. Then they show me the same thing on my map.

They aren't sure what it's like now, but say to stay off the old road and use trails that parallel the road, like the one we took to get here. "The oldest stretch of highway from way back used to run next to two large lakes." Ellen points them out on my map. "Unlike the smaller lakes at the site of the gold mine to the west, these ones are huge. And when everything started melting, the lakes swallowed the road, so they moved that section of road to the east and it rejoined the highway south of the lakes. Eventually that road bent and buckled and was abandoned as well. We'll show you how to stay on the trails so you can avoid the huge swampy mess that grew out of those lakes. Follow our directions and you won't even see them."

"People looking to hurt other people always hunt on the road," Wendy says. "And after seeing all those bodies in the river, I'd be extra careful. Whoever is responsible could be in the Buffer Zone. It's a good place to hide. Trees from the south have been sprouting up for years now. Millions of maples growing thick, and some cedars and pines, crowding out the birch and spruce, which were already dying out. It's strange how quickly and completely the maples have become dominant down there. It seems unnatural."

Ellen nods. "It's easy to get turned around in there. The place is turning into a jungle. You'll see."

"After our parents were killed when we tried to go north," I say, "in a note, they told us to try going south if north didn't work out. They said to head to Anchorage, but we decided to follow Dylan's map toward Valdez."

"I don't know much about either of those places," Ellen says. "We can't feed you all winter. I wish we could. And you two are young. You have to go and meet others and try to make something of yourselves. Make something of the world. Something good. Something people will want to live for." Ellen points at Wendy. "We're two old ladies who carved out a life in the sticks. When we die, we won't be missed. But you. You've got the potential to do something significant. Both of you."

PART
FOUR

CHAPTER
57

THREE DAYS LATER AND WE are still traveling the windy trail above the road, hoping to minimize any surprise encounters with other people. The green mass of the Buffer Zone is growing bigger. I can see ribbons of yellow and red where the leaves are turning, slicing up the green. We'll probably be out of the pass and into those trees in another day.

Wendy and Ellen gave us a couple of Mark's heavy wool shirts and some vole stew in a jar, which I'm carrying in a little day pack they gave me. They marked on my map the best way to head into the Buffer Zone and where they used to go. Back in the day, they used to drive down the road, then hike to their secret spot. There is a little rock shelter that I hope to find; they left some supplies there, some dried food in a bear-proof container. No guarantees, but even if the supplies are gone, it's still in the direction we need to go.

I keep thinking about my mom and dad, wondering what they were thinking about when they told us to go south. What did they know that wasn't said in the note? And why didn't they just talk to me about it and really explain what they thought would be down here instead of just writing a vague note? And why did they say to go toward Anchorage instead of Valdez?

I wish they could send me a message now, tell me something that would help. I mean, we have an almost-empty jar of vole stew and the clouds are threatening to dump rain or maybe even snow.

Like the clouds can hear me think, the first white flakes start drifting down. A little breeze swishes them around our faces. I know it'll be easier to stay warm in the Buffer Zone because there'll be lots of wood to burn. But all the wood in the world won't take the place of food.

* * *

"Maple trees," I say, staring at the palm-sized leaves that are mostly green with hints of red. "They never used to grow this far north. Dad used to tell me over and over that things were changing fast. Too fast for people to keep up with."

Jess just nods. I've spoken to her a little bit about Mom and how proud she'd be of her, but mostly I've just been here with Jess, ready to talk if she wants to talk, but not pushing her. Also, we need our energy for walking and remaining alert. In this world, sometimes you have to put aside something important, like how you feel about missing your parents, in order to survive, and deal with it later.

And it seems like when we get quiet moments, like we had with Wendy and Ellen, that important thing—Jess missing Mom—rises back to the surface. The main thing for me is that I know it is under there and that I will help it to come back up during the times when it's right, when it won't endanger our survival.

We've been in the Buffer Zone for a little more than a day, and it's just grown thicker and thicker with skinny maples. Like Wendy said, it seems totally unnatural how these maple trees have taken over.

I wish I had a book or access to other information that would tell me how fast these maples have advanced. Not that it really matters, but still, I'm curious. And the more I understand, the more chance I have of not screwing up and getting us killed. The bodies in the river flash into my mind.

The forest is even thicker than it appeared from a distance. Now I realize why people refer to it as the Buffer Zone. It's almost impenetrable. Trees grow on top of each other with multiple branches crossing and recrossing, like a finely woven wall. The maples have grown up thick in the understory beneath the remaining birch and spruce, and there are some small cedars and pines—more new arrivals—vying for space.

We keep parting the maples and slowly work our way farther and farther into the Buffer Zone. The trees seem to capture heat, because it seems pretty warm—warmer than the pass—but we've lost a lot of elevation, too.

I try to follow the directions from Wendy and Ellen, but it's almost impossible. We're supposed to encounter two big hills with a stream running between them, then follow the stream to its source and look for some yellow cliffs, but once we got under the maples all visibility was cut off. The road has mostly disappeared, too, like it's been erased from the landscape. Wendy and Ellen said the road would come and go—that in some places it's totally gone and in others it's pretty easy to follow.

And to think that a huge oil pipeline used to run through here. Where is the evidence of that? I need to find a climbable spruce tree, then maybe I'll be able to get some perspective and spot those hills, or the yellow cliffs, or sections of the road.

The one cool thing about being surrounded by all the green is the birds. There's constant chatter when the sun rises, which continues for a while and then invades our ears again at sunset. But the forest is so thick that I've only caught glimpses of small birds flitting around.

I wonder about Max and Tam. Are they in here somewhere? They could be less than fifty feet away and we wouldn't be able to see them. Or they could be dead. It's not a good sign that we haven't seen any hints or clues about where they've gone. I can only hope that they're working their way south and are several days ahead of us. And I wonder about the bodies in the river. Are the people responsible for the massacre hiding out in the Buffer Zone?

We find a few patches of cranberries, stuff our faces with the sour fruit, then fill the empty vole-stew jar about a quarter of the way with more berries.

"The next big spruce we come across," I tell Jess, "I'll see what I can see."

*   *   *

In the distance I can spot what I'm pretty sure are the two hills and then, farther on, the upper edges of the yellow cliffs. I'm as close to the top of a giant spruce as I'm going to get. Jess is at the bottom of the tree with the pack, resting, but I can't see her because the spruce branches below me are a thick green blanket. And below those, the red and green leaves of the maple understory form another visual barrier.

It's hard to tell the distance, but it looks like we have an open area—a swampy spot—to cross just before the hills. I guess another five or six miles to reach the hills.

The hills are tiny bumps compared to the yellow cliffs looming on the far side where the stream originates. The wind is clipping along up here, and I can see the faint white cotton of seeds being carried over the trees, riding the wind.

I start to climb down to tell Jess that we're on the right track, but then I hear a noise below and behind me. Or maybe it's off to the side. Something or someone is crashing through the brush. I freeze and slowly turn my head toward the noise.

I'm about to call out to Jess, then stop myself because that would tip off whatever it is that we're here. And there's a good chance it'll just pass on by and never detect us if I keep quiet, because the forest is so thick.

I look straight down, trying to catch even a glimpse of Jess, to signal her to be quiet in case she tries to call out to me, but I can't see her.

The brush-crashing noises get louder and louder. And my heart's pounding through my wool shirt.

The noises stop. I take a breath and hold it.

Then they start up again.

I move my head in and out of the branches, stretching my neck. I want a glimpse of Jess, but I can't get one. I want to whisper to her, tell her to start climbing the tree and then sit without moving. I wish we'd made a plan before I'd climbed, or that I'd had her climb partway and wait above the ground.

My eyes start watering. Moisture drips from my nose. I can still hear the brush rumbling, the branches crashing. I'm pretty sure that Jess and I don't make that much noise when we move through the maples.

Now the noise is almost directly under the tree. But I still can't see anything.

I want to call out to Jess, but don't want to give away her hiding spot if she is in fact hiding. Instead, I try just to listen and hope that whatever is down there either hasn't seen her, or is friendly or at least harmless. Maybe it's a moose or a caribou. But I think Jess would call up to me if it's an animal or a group of animals, unless she doesn't want to be seen by them. Like if it's a pack of wolves, or a bear. *Jess,* my mind screams. *Jess. Call up to me to say everything is okay.*

I hear what I think is a grunt. And then more branches being disturbed. And then the tree shakes, ever so slightly, like something bumped it. Maybe Jess is climbing up a little ways, or maybe she's hiding against one side of the tree.

If I give myself away now, that might be even worse for Jess. I'm paralyzed. For all I know, she's taken cover and is safe.

More rustling and branch-snapping invade my ears. The sounds are moving away from me—toward the yellow cliffs.

C H A P T E R
5 8

IT ISN'T THAT HARD TO follow their trail. Broken branches and boot prints where the ground is soft lead the way. The hard part is trying to follow in a quiet way so I won't be discovered. I don't know if they're armed. I don't know if they have Jess. But where else could she be?

My sweaty clothes stick to me—like they've been glued on. I can't lose her. But maybe I've already lost her. *No,* I think. *No. No way.* My breaths come in short gasps even though I'm not winded. Why? Why did I leave her down there alone? After all this time of keeping her by my side, I mess up once and she's gone.

What do these people want with her? Did she even put up a struggle? Have they hurt her? My brain pounds with these questions while at the same time I try to pay attention to their trail and not make noise. My heart is pounding. And when I find who's taken my sister, my fists will be pounding.

Are they making Jess walk? Or have they knocked her out and are carrying her? Is she being cooperative? Have they hurt her? Then with my next thought, my whole body shakes and my eyes grow hot. Are they planning on eating her?

One thing I know: Jess didn't give me away. She is so freaking smart. I mean, if they knew about me, I'd have even less of a chance of saving her.

* * *

I stand just back from the edge of the open area I viewed from the treetop. I'm not sure how wet it is, but their boot prints lead straight across it. This is tricky. How to follow and not be seen? If there's someone on top of either hill, they might spot me.

But what choice do I have? The longer they have Jess, the more likely it becomes that they'll hurt her—or worse. But I can't walk into a trap, because that won't help Jess one bit. I want to sprint across the freaking swamp and strangle whoever has her. And I want to strangle myself for leaving her alone at the bottom of the tree.

I take a breath to quiet my mind and try to concentrate.

The open area is sprinkled with islands of stunted spruce trees, where the land is just dry enough for them to take hold. This little swamp is what the old Interior Alaska looked like. No maples, pines, or cedars invading here yet. It feels more like home than anywhere I've been since we started this journey.

I can't tell how many sets of tracks are leaving the jungle of maples and heading across the swamp. *Two or three*, I think. *Maybe they're walking single file.*

I wish I could see them, but the rolling hills make it difficult. They could be just a half mile away or three or four. I think about my dad and how hesitant he was sometimes. How he would watch things instead of acting, and how sometimes that worked to his advantage, but it wouldn't now, not when Jess is somewhere ahead with someone who's obviously dangerous. But my dad probably wouldn't have left Jess at the bottom of the tree. Or, if he did, he would've had a plan about what to do if someone came.

I take a couple of steps out of the maples. I just need to follow the tracks. Now. But I need to do it in a way where I won't be seen, so I crouch down, bending at the waist and knees as much as I can while still being able to move forward. I follow the tracks up and over a small hill, and then toward a tiny island of trees.

I slow as I approach the spruce trees, then stop at the back edge of them and stand, stretching my legs and back. The tracks continue around to the right of the trees. I keep following them.

In the distance, I can see the two prominent hills that I spotted from the treetop. And on the nearest of the two, about halfway up, are people. At least two, maybe three, climbing the hill.

It's all I can do to hold myself back, but I wait until they crest the hill and disappear from view. Then I take off in a sprint, following their path, hoping to make up lost ground without being seen.

Jess. Jess. Jess. My mind pounds over and over with each step.

I round a tiny island of trees and keep going. "You can do this," I say out loud. *Just keep closing in on them and you'll see what needs to be done when you get there. You'll figure out a way to do it, a way to make those bastards pay.*

Then something slams my back and rides me onto the ground, knocking the wind out of me.

I try to roll over but something heavy presses into my back, grinding into my spine. I push up with my arms, but it feels like a tank is parked on top of me.

I hear the clicking sound a gun makes and think, *Oh no, I'm dead.*

Dead. Dead. Dead.

"You are going to keep following those tracks, Travis," a deep voice says. I feel the metal cylinder of a gun kiss the back of my head. "All the way home."

CHAPTER
59

"HOW DO YOU KNOW MY name?" I say. "Did my sister tell you?"

But all he'll say is "keep walking." I don't know if his gun is loaded, and at this range I don't want to find out. I'm pissed at myself for falling into such an obvious trap. My stomach burns. I taste vomit in the back of my throat and swallow it down.

We crest the big hill, the one I spied Jess marching on. And now, down below, I can see circular huts. I count maybe a dozen. And a few smaller, more traditional square-shaped cabins.

I think about the bodies floating down the river, and the person I saw across the river as Jess and I crossed. I wonder if the guy with the gun to my back was involved.

"Did you see the bodies in the river?" I ask over my shoulder while continuing to walk. "Who were those people? Was that you I saw the day my sister and I swam across? You may as well speak to me. I mean, you've got the gun. And you know my name. You're obviously in charge here, unless of course you're just following orders. I'd be a fool to try to pull anything on you."

"You got that right."

"I wonder if that gun of yours is even loaded. Even if it is, why waste a bullet on me?" I let the question hang, then say, "I know you can't have a steady supply."

I walk a few more steps, then stop and turn around. "Go ahead," I say. "Shoot me."

"Just keep walking." This guy looks like he's a few years older than me. He's built like a weight lifter and is a little taller than me, like maybe six foot two or three, and has short, short hair—a buzz cut. And he's clean-shaven. Military looking. I wonder what he thinks of my long blond hair and scraggly beard.

I just stand there. He has the gun trained on my chest from about ten feet away. "Aren't you going to shoot?" I ask. Sweat's dripping from my armpits down my sides. My voice sounds shaky to me—like I'm scared, because I am.

I can see his big arms quivering a little bit.

"I'm a human being, just like you," I say. "So is my sister." Then I turn and keep walking.

*　*　*

I'm escorted into the largest of the circular structures, which appears to be constructed totally from maple logs. The walls are about eight feet tall, and the roof slants up at a steep angle from all directions, so the whole thing looks like an upside-down ice cream cone.

I wonder where Jess is. She has to be okay. Just has to be.

Some old guy with a gray beard hanging halfway down his chest sits in a chair made from maple poles in the center of the room. I guess he's in his fifties or sixties, but it's kind of dark in here.

"Where's my sister?" I ask.

"I'll ask the questions," the man says. His voice is a little hoarse, like he's worn it out by yelling or smoking.

"You don't have any right to do what you did," I say. "I—"

"You were trespassing," the man says. "Now, what is your name? Where did you come from? Who are you working with?"

"Come on," I say. "Your freaking security guard or border patrol knew my name. Quit playing with me. What about my sister?"

"I don't know anything about anyone knowing your name. And I assure you that your sister is fine. She's with the women right now."

A young guy enters the hut. "What?" I shout. I jump up and tackle him.

I feel him struggling and I drive my elbow into his ribs and hear him grunt. I want to break every bone in his body. I press down harder but one of his arms gets free and nails rake across my cheek. I punch him on the side of his head. His free arm comes at me but I knock it away and then hit him square in the nose, and I'm about to swing again when someone grabs me from behind. I push up with my knees so I'm standing and kick Dylan in the side before he can scoot out of the way. "You," I say. "Of course you're here."

Now two young guys are holding me back. Dylan stands up. One side of his face is red, blood runs from both his nostrils, and I know his ribs are hurting. But still, he smiles at me. Not a friendly smile. An *I got you* smile. Then he turns and leaves the hut.

The two guys drag me back to my chair and push me down. "What is this place?" I ask. "And what is that maniac doing here?"

"I'll ask the questions," the man says. He looks at the two guys holding my arms. "I think this young man will sit here. You can let go of him and leave us. If he moves before I tell him to, he won't see his sister—ever. And if he attacks anyone else, we'll eliminate him."

The two guys release me and leave the hut. I want to turn and follow them, finish Dylan off, get Jess, and get the hell out of here, but if I try any of that right now, I might never see Jess again.

"That was a dumb thing to do," the man says. "Real dumb. Dummies don't last long around here. Now, I'm hoping you'll answer my questions like a good boy. Like a smart boy. Like a boy who wants to see his sister." He pauses. "What are you doing here?"

"Look," I say. "My parents are dead. My sister and I are trying to get to the settlements on the coast. Where Valdez used to be. We're just passing through. But Dylan probably told you all that."

"We haven't had any trespassers in over a year." He shakes his head once.

"You don't own this land," I say. "No one does. And what about Dylan? He was trespassing, too."

"I control this land. And it can only support so many people. So, you say you're trying to get to the coast?" Then he looks me in the eye. "Now, what's your real reason for being here?"

"That's it. I'm from Fairbanks. We tried to go north but couldn't." I tell him about what happened on the Yukon.

I don't tell him about Max and Tam or Wendy and Ellen. I don't mention the cache up in the yellow cliffs because I'm not sure if he knows about it, and I might need it.

"When can I see my sister?" I ask again. I want to rip that long beard right off his face.

"Just as soon as we compare her story with yours. Then you'll get to see her—if your stories match."

"And then what?" I ask.

The old gray beard just smiles at me, but it isn't a friendly smile.

They have me wait in an enclosure outside, like I'm an animal. It's a freaking cage without a lid, a tall fence made from maple poles, a rectangle I can walk across in ten steps. My face burns where Dylan's nails scratched me, but I know he's hurting worse than me. I try to count the people. So far I've counted eight men and five women, but I probably haven't seen everyone. I pace back and forth in an attempt to stay warm.

Part of the valley is under cultivation, with rows of green plants about two feet high. I'm guessing it'll be frosting here soon and they'll need to harvest whatever they're growing.

In the village proper, if that's what you call it, there are lots of maple stumps sticking an inch or two above the ground. A couple of guys are hacking away at them, slicing the roots with axes and then working them out of the ground.

I guess firewood isn't a problem around here. But food? You can only grow so much. I wonder if there are animals besides the songbirds living in the maple jungle. And why have these people chosen to set up right here? Why didn't they go all the way to the coast, where you have the ocean to live off, and maybe some contact with other people coming and going in boats? And what the hell is Dylan doing here? And how can he be an insider? I mean, he came down from the north just like us.

I could hop the wooden fence and run, but I can't leave Jess here. I caught a glimpse of her entering the main hut to talk with the head honcho gray beard a few minutes ago.

I wonder about Max and Tam. Have they been caught, too? I study the yellow cliffs in the distance. Somewhere up there is a cave that might still have some supplies. But how can these people not know about it? Is Jess telling them about it now?

* * *

"Truthfully, with your attitude, and that savage attack on one of our young men, I'm not sure you have much to offer," Stan says to me. He's the head honcho with the big gray beard. "Except muscle, that is, if you're not lazy. But I wouldn't separate you from your sister unless you gave me a good reason to. My initial warning still stands."

"You can't split us up," I say. "And besides, neither one of us wants to stay."

Jess doesn't say anything. I have no idea what she's thinking because we haven't had any time alone to talk.

"You can't leave unless I say so. And you can't stay unless I say so." Stan rubs his chin and runs his hand down his beard. "Like I said, your sister is staying. We'll keep you, too, but you'll have to work just as hard as the rest of us."

"You can't take us prisoner," I say. "Just because you stopped in the middle of this maple jungle and decided to set up shop doesn't mean we need to stay here with you."

Stan points at Jess and says, "She's staying. We'll take good care of her. She'll be well respected. And when she's of age, she'll be married to a fine man of the Council's choosing. We strive—"

"Married? You can't decide who my sister marries and when." I turn to Jess, who looks like she is about to start crying. "I'll never let them do that to you," I tell her. "I won't—"

"Listen to me," Stan cuts in. "Marriage for her"—he points to Jess—"won't happen for a while." Then Stan looks me in the eye and says, "Don't give me an ultimatum, young man. Like I said, I don't want to split you up, but son, if you don't work out, you'll have to leave. Or if we think you're an ongoing threat, we'll eliminate you."

I take a breath. I know if I keep hammering him on this now, it'll just make things worse, so instead I change the subject. "And you still haven't told me why Dylan is here," I say.

Stan stares me down before he speaks again. "His father and I used to be friends."

C H A P T E R
6 0

WE BASICALLY LIVE OFF OF potatoes, carrots, barley, and greens. Every day, three meals a day, we have this stew. If you don't work, you don't eat, unless you're sick. Some people work in the fields, some preparing food, and some keeping watch at the edges of their territory. And Dylan—was he planning on coming here the whole time we were together?

Jess and I are digging potatoes. As I pull baseball-sized spuds from the dirt, my mind churns away at the problem at hand—how to get the hell away from here and not be recaptured.

"There's a girl," Jess whispers. "She's young. Like Max and Tam's age. Maybe even younger."

"Who is she?" I ask.

"Her name is Marcy. She's in the yurt I'm in, only she's pregnant and on bed rest."

Pregnant? An image of Jess—pregnant—pops into my head. I wipe a tear from my eye with a dirty hand and my eye starts burning. "What has she told you?"

"Her husband, the man the Council chose for her, died in a logging accident. She lived in one of those little cabins with him, but moved back into the yurt after he died." Jess rubs her eye. "But get this: Stan, the head honcho, is her dad."

I think about this as we dig. Stan married off his own daughter and he thinks he's going to marry Jess off when she's, what did he say, *of age*? And then I realize that Stan's idea about *of age* might be different than mine. We need to get out of here soon, and in a way that there's no chance of getting recaptured.

"See what you can find out," I whisper to Jess. "We need to know what the rules are. Like how old girls are when Stan marries them off. And what happens to them? Act like you want to know for yourself. I'll make an escape plan."

Jess nods but I can see the fear in her eyes. I scoot a little closer to her but keep my hands in the dirt to pretend I'm still digging. "Don't worry," I whisper. "I won't let anything happen to you." I pause, then whisper, "You and me, we'll leave this place in the dust. But we need all the information we can get. I'm going to be asking questions too, but they're already suspicious of me. Questions from you to Marcy and some of the older women would look more natural. Understand?"

Jess nods.

"Let's keep digging potatoes so we don't draw attention to ourselves." As I dig, my mind pounds away at the problem. If Stan has any morals at all, Jess will have five or six years before she's *of age*. Don't get me wrong, I don't want to stay one moment past when we can escape, but I don't want to rush an escape with a poor plan and get caught. I basically have one chance, because I'm pretty sure Stan will follow through on his threat to eliminate me if I get caught.

A whistle blows and everyone stands up. Four figures are approaching the fields from the south. Another whistle blows twice in quick succession. I have no clue what the second whistle means, but the men around me start smiling.

"Okay," one of the men says. "Back to work now. We can celebrate later."

Jess and I get back on our knees and keep working the row of potatoes. The people around here are whacked. But we are way outnumbered.

I glance back a few times, watching as the four people get closer and closer to the fields. The two in front are wearing green army fatigues.

My teeth grind together and I feel acid burning my stomach.

Tam and Max.

And I'm guessing they're *of age*.

CHAPTER
61

I DON'T LET ON THAT I recognize Max and Tam as they're brought into the village or compound or commune or whatever the hell this place is. I whisper to Jess to pretend like she doesn't know them either. That way we'll have a better chance of helping them bust out of here with us. Unless Dylan tells Stan that we all know each other, which he probably will.

We stand with everyone else as they walk through the fields. I keep my arms to my side and my face averted, but I study Max and Tam out of the corner of my eye. When I think they see me, I raise my fingers slightly on one hand.

Their arms hang free. And the guys escorting them—the same ones who caught me and Jess—aren't even keeping them at gunpoint. Tam and Max even smile a little bit at everyone. They didn't survive this long in this crazy world because they're stupid. I'm sure they are picking up the major creep-vibe that this place puts off and are sizing things up and trying to not alarm anyone. I wish I had done that when Jess and I first met with Stan.

With just Jess I had some time to craft an escape since it'd be a while until, as Stan put it, she'd be *of age*. He made it clear that no one would touch her before then.

But having Max and Tam here means I have to act as soon as possible. How long will it be until the Council marries them off?

I wonder what the older women think of this system. The men and the older women sleep separately—all of them. I mean, if they came here with their husbands, how did it affect their marriages? And if the Council assigned a young woman to be married to someone's husband, how would that work? Can a man have more than one wife here?

The system of having someone choose your husband must not be about love as much as it is about sustaining a population. Could you be forced to live your whole life with someone you don't love? Someone you might actually hate?

I glance around at the green fields and the nicely constructed yurts and the smaller cabins. It took some energy and know-how to carve this place out of the maple jungle, some real determination. And this place wouldn't be half-bad if it operated by rules that made sense. On beliefs that aren't based on control. And if Jess and I weren't trapped here against our will, and mostly kept separated.

This is the first settlement we've run into and it's whacked. The only things it has going for it are stable food and shelter. On one hand, food and shelter are two of the main things I want for Jess. What if we escape here and the settlements on the coast are even more whacked? But still, to stay here, to not try to break away, would be like saying, *Okay, I'll trade our freedom—Jess's freedom—for food and shelter.* And I'd never do that.

My mind starts concocting a couple ideas to bring this place into a chaotic panic, and fast. They're pretty far out, but they need to be for me to have any chance of pulling this off.

CHAPTER

62

"THE EARTH HAS PROVIDED TWO more creators for our community," Stan says. He's gathered everyone on the back side of the main yurt the following morning. There are benches in a circle around a huge firepit. Stan's standing on top of a little hill where dirt has been pushed up into a mound to make a speaking platform.

Max and Tam are sitting in chairs constructed of maple poles to the right of Stan. The rest of us are seated on the benches. I count nine men with big grayish beards like Stan's, along with Dylan and two guys that are a little older than me—the ones who discovered us and captured Max and Tam.

There are five older women plus Marcy.

When I add up the numbers of how many people we might be up against, it doesn't look good.

"As everyone here knows," Stan says, "except maybe for our newcomers, the Council chooses husbands for women of child-bearing age. Those choices will be shared with me and I'll either okay them or ask the Council to keep working. With my daughter"— he gestures toward Marcy with an open hand—"the Council's first recommendation was what I followed."

My stomach makes a fist and I taste this morning's stew in the back of my throat. I wish like hell that Dylan weren't here. Him and his freaking gift, being able to sense things. Right then he turns his head and smiles at me like he's just read my mind. No way would any of us be here if it weren't for him.

"Maxine and Tamara," Stan says, turning toward them. "On behalf of everyone, I'd like to welcome you to your new home." He smiles at Max. Then he focuses on Tam and his smile widens and lingers. Then Stan turns back toward the rest of us and says, "Will the Council now stand?"

My brain does a backflip as all five of the older women stand. This is the Council?

We all sit in silence as the Council members approach Max and Tam one by one, bow to them, and then return to their seats on the benches.

They didn't do this for Jess. Maybe because she isn't of age yet.

If this was some kind of game, it'd be a fascinating society to learn about, but I just need to know enough to take them down. Or at least make them scramble so much that there's no way they'll catch us.

One thing I realize is that they'll try to hunt Max and Tam and Jess if they escape. Right now, they're three quarters of the potential female breeding population. They probably won't come after me unless I do something bad. So I've got to make sure what I do will draw them toward me. And if Dylan comes after us, I'll need a way to take him down—even if he has a gun.

Basic. What a bunch of bullshit.

I wonder what Max and Tam are thinking. Since all the young women stay in the same yurt, I told Jess to try to somehow let them know that I'm working on a plan to get us out of here and to just be cooperative, so what we do will take these arranged-marriage idiots by surprise.

As soon as the last council member performs her bows and sits down, a squat man with a bushy beard stands up and eyes Stan. "Instead of having the Council decide, why don't we, the men, get to decide? We could have a contest of strength. Or the new arrivals"— he turns to Max and Tam and smiles at them—"could choose for themselves."

The man sitting next to me laughs to himself and says quietly, "If it were up to me, I'd take 'em both for myself." I suck a slow breath through my nose, and it's all I can do to keep from punching him in the face.

Stan focuses his attention on the man who asked the question. "Jim, the Council will take care of the pairings, like we all agreed." He nods toward the older women, who are seated together again. "They'll report their recommendations to me, just like they did for Marcy."

The man next to me stands up. "Jim's idea isn't half bad." He remains standing.

I want to scream at these people—at how nuts they are. When I think of one of these old men being paired with Max and Tam, my Tam, I taste bile and have to swallow it down. And Marcy's own father married her off to someone just as old. And my sister? No way. Sweat builds under my arms and my ears get hot.

I squeeze my hands into fists and just keep watching. Another gray beard stands up. Then another and another. Until all of them are standing, except for Terry and Melvin—the two I share a yurt with. All their eyes are on Stan. I want to castrate every one of these old goats. Stan included. Especially Stan.

Dylan and the young guys say nothing. The older women say nothing.

Stan stands up straighter. "Now, gentlemen," he says, "I hear your concern. You want some control over the pairings. But that control, like we discussed, will cause conflict and jealousy. Since we have no control, it's less likely to become an issue." He gestures toward his daughter with an open palm, and I think I see the hint of a tear in his eye. "With Marcy," Stan says, "a tragic accident took her Council-chosen husband from her. After she's had her baby and sufficient time to mourn, the Council will choose again for her."

A few of the gray beards start mumbling, then Jim, the first one that had stood up, says, "This isn't over. If your daughter hadn't been the first, you'd have done things differently. You wanted to keep some control because she was your flesh and blood. But these new girls, you don't even know them."

"I did what I thought was right for the community," Stan says. "So did Marcy. Maybe someday we won't need as rigid a system as we do now."

"What I'm suggesting," Jim says, "it's practical, and it'd give us all more ownership. That's all. I want this community to succeed. It's all I've got. It's all any of us have got."

I stand up. "Why did you stop here? Why didn't you continue to the coast where there are, at least how I understand it, actual settlements that might even have contact with the rest of the world?" *As opposed to this maple-jungle, arranged-marriage compound you've got here*, I think, but don't say.

All eyes go to Stan.

He strokes his long gray beard. "We didn't leave the wreckage of Fairbanks to go somewhere else, where someone or some government could just tell us what to do. We stopped here so we could create what we wanted. We picked this place because there was *nothing* here. We all know what happened over at the lakes where that other group settled. They were on top of a gold deposit. This place hasn't worked out exactly how we'd have liked, but we're try-ing. If you want to head to the coast, be my guest. I doubt things down there are as rosy as you think they are. And as for getting there from here, good luck."

Now I wish I hadn't said anything. I don't want this kind of attention. "I want to stay with my sister," I say. "And so far, she likes it here. She's better provided for here than anywhere we've been. We're grateful for the opportunity."

Jess must've caught on, because she smiles and says, "I do like it here."

"Me too," Max says. "I think we would've starved if it weren't for all of you."

Tam just nods. I'm sure she'd love to have her bow and a quiver full of arrows right about now.

"Don't listen to their lies," Dylan speaks up. "I know these people. They'll run the minute they get the chance." Then he laughs. "But even if they get away, I'll bring them back."

Tam shoots him a look that could slice him in half, but says nothing.

"We didn't run when you and your brother were in trouble," I say. "I put everyone in danger. I killed a man to keep you from being killed."

"What someone did in the past," Dylan says, "is no predictor of what they'll do in the future."

"Enough bickering," Stan says. "Another week and the harvest should be done. We've got four more mouths to feed, but we'll manage."

I wonder if there had been more women with them when they started this commune or project or whatever it is. The other two young guys haven't said a word the entire meeting. I wonder how they feel about this system.

Are any of the gray beards their fathers? Any of the women their mothers? I haven't seen anything that would suggest they are, but how else would they have ended up here?

I want answers to all these questions. More information will help me form a plan, but I don't know if I'll have time to gather it. And I could draw unnecessary attention to myself. I'm still kicking myself for standing up and asking why they hadn't gone to the coast.

One of the gray beards who hasn't spoken yet steps forward. He glances at Tam, then at Max. Then he turns and faces Stan. "You can tell us what you want us to do, but there's no guarantee we'll do it."

CHAPTER
63

I WORK THE NEXT FOUR days in the potato fields alongside Jess.
Max and Tam stay in the yurt with Marcy. The older women rotate
between digging potatoes and spending time in the yurt with Max
and Tam. Most of the gray beards dig potatoes as well, but Dylan
and the other young guys surround the yurt that Max and Tam are
in, keeping watch, no doubt.

Jess has managed to convey my message to Max and Tam that
I'm working on a plan and they should just keep playing it cool.

Jess doesn't think anything will happen for a few days at least.
She heard one of the older women say they want Tam and Max to
feel adjusted. I'm sure they talked more, but Jess can give me only
little snatches of information when I collect the potatoes she's dug.
I've started carrying her bags of spuds to the holding area. I even
carry bags for some of the older women, and for one of the gray
beards who seems like he's having trouble walking.

The weather's been pretty steady—some clouds but no rain.
You get cold if you stand around, but working in the fields keeps
you pretty warm.

I'm hoping for a fogbank or some wind, but if neither of those
materializes, darkness alone will have to do for our escape attempt.

I've whispered parts of the plan to Jess, or at least ideas about parts of it so she'll know that she's going to have a big role and will have to do some pretty convincing acting, especially with Dylan around.

I'm staying in a yurt with two of the gray beards and trying to engage them in conversation, show them that I'm coming around to liking this place, while really I'm trying to learn the layout and the schedules and patterns of everyone.

At first they are pretty gruff with me. But once I tell them a little of my story, about my dad wanting to stay in the Sacrifice Area and how long we managed to survive there, they seem to respect me more. Or maybe they can relate to wanting to do what my dad tried to do. At any rate, they open up a little bit.

Tonight I learn that these two guys have been together since the government pulled out. They had each been married but didn't want to talk much about what had happened to their wives. I think one of the wives took the kids and got on a bus headed north, and the other, childless, died that first summer.

Then these two men banded together and headed south. They had ammo, so they headed straight down the road. They met up with Stan and his group somewhere along the way.

I'm lying down on my bunk, which is maple that's been planed so it's flat. On top of that is a thin mattress. I think it's grass or maple leaves stuffed into a big cloth sack. One of the problems with running from this place is that the land is cleared for at least a quarter mile in all directions. If they see which way we go and are right behind us, Dylan and the other two young guys will chase us down. So, if I could somehow temporarily disable them, or at least distract them, that'd be good. I don't think the gray beards alone can catch us if we have a little head start.

I take a breath. I have to keep in mind what's most important.

First order of the day: Get Jess the hell out of here. Then Max and Tam.

I think a little more about the escape plan. I still don't have all the details worked out, but I'm pretty sure it'll involve some blood and some fire.

CHAPTER
64

THE NEXT DAY, ONLY HALF of the gray beards are in the potato fields. The other four are readying two of the small cabins. One for Max and one for Tam.

Terry, one of the men from my bunk, the one whose wife died that first winter, tells me they'll live separately, each with their man.

I pull another potato from the ground. "How does the Council choose? I mean, can they choose any of us?"

Terry shakes his head. "Your turn will come. When you've been here longer, and"—he smiles—"when you're older."

I just nod. I want to ask him *why* but don't want him to think I'm unhappy with the system. I don't want any more attention drawn toward me than necessary.

But the question about who is eligible keeps burning a hole in my brain. I just can't figure it out. I mean, the best way to make young guys loyal to this screwy establishment would be to include them.

"So, how about those guys?" I point to the women's hut where Dylan and the other two young guys are standing watch. "Do they have a chance of being chosen?"

Terry shakes his head. "Not yet." He smiles again. "But they'd sure like to."

I just look at him like I'm waiting for him to explain.

"Travis," he says, "young people have strong emotions. Irrational at times. We know what we're doing. We know we need to have babies to keep this place going. There are only a few women who can give birth. An older man won't be so pulled. We're less likely to take our wife and strike out on our own. The Council knows that."

I nod. "So how long do I have to wait?"

"The rule we made when we settled here, and realized the situation, was that you had to be thirty years old. Those guys"—he points toward the hut—"have a ways to go. Newcomers, we decided, no matter how old they are, need to be with us five years before they can be eligible. That way, we'll know if they're loyal."

"What about Dylan?" I say. "I mean, his father and Stan used to be friends, so does that count for anything?"

Terry sighs. "Dylan's not a newcomer, technically, since he's been here before. But he's still a long way from being thirty."

"Wait," I say. "Dylan's been here before? When?"

"He made the trip with his father the first year after the government pulled out, but his father never intended on moving here unless he couldn't make it work back home."

I get this sick feeling in my stomach and I wonder what else Dylan has kept secret. He didn't visit Wendy and Ellen in search of his uncle, but here he is in this totally controlling community.

We dig more potatoes in silence. Their system makes sense in a warped way. I mean, the five-year thing would definitely weed out the uncommitted. But the two young guys who've been here since the start, how are they handling this? I mean, being excluded from the eligibilty has to cause some resentment. Maybe they've been brainwashed to believe that they too will someday be a great gray beard of the maple compound. Maybe this is all they have. And they're getting fed and have a potentially important job—patrolling the borders. But for Dylan, this system sounds way too restrictive for a follow-your-vision-at-all-costs psychopath.

I tap Terry on the shoulder. "What if the girls don't want to, you know, pair up with the person the Council's chosen for them? What if they fight it?"

"With Marcy, there was no fighting," Terry says. "Her daddy prepared her well. But these two new ones, I guess the man-of-choice would have to deal with that. I hope it doesn't come to that. We want everyone to be happy."

* * *

"What's your deal?" I say to Dylan. "You travel with us and then work with these freaks to capture us. That's messed up."

"You chose to follow my map," Dylan says. "I didn't ask you to do that. I didn't even suggest it. You were heading toward Anchorage."

We'd crossed paths at the outhouse and when I told him about finding his pack, he just smirked. But I could see the bruises under his eyes. And I bet I'd cracked a couple of his ribs, too.

"Then you just disappear in the fissure?" I ask.

"Sometimes I just need to be alone."

"Yeah," I say. "If I pushed someone off a cliff, I'd want to be alone, too."

Dylan takes a step toward me. "You don't know what happened."

"I know that Mike didn't kill your mom. I believe him."

"You don't know anything about Mike."

"I know he didn't help capture my sister for this whacked-out, rape-the-young commune. Is this your vision? Is this your idea of *basic*? It's bas—"

"The world's changing," Dylan says. "And we're part of the world. If you hadn't come along, Mike and I would still be up north. Living my father's dream."

I shake my head. "You'd be dead. That guy would've shot you."

"You don't know that."

"I do know that. And you know it, too. Even if you won't admit it out loud. He raised his gun. A couple hours before that, one of his men killed two girls, unprovoked. I know you can sense things, but even you can't stop bullets once they're fired."

"This place isn't so bad," Dylan says. "You'll see, if you stick around. Right here, we're making something from nothing."

"Okay," I say. "Whatever."

"It was my dad's Plan B if things didn't work out up north."

"Maybe your dad was wrong. Maybe he had good intentions but somehow his actions didn't match up to his ideas. Like the guys here. They want to start a community and want it to be fair, but how is what they do fair to the girls? If your dad had a daughter, I bet he wouldn't want her to be forcibly married to one of these old men. Or if you had a daughter, how would you feel? Or a girlfriend who was married off to someone else? Think about that."

"You don't know anything," Dylan says.

"I know you like Max," I say. "You going to watch her get married off?"

Dylan stares at me for a long moment, saying nothing. Then he walks into the outhouse and closes the door.

I say through the door, "This is probably the last place Max envisions when she thinks of *basic*."

His muffled voice comes through the door. "Fuck her," he says. "I heard what she said down in the fissure."

CHAPTER
65

SHOVELS, RAKES, AXES, AND ROPE, all in the tool shed. There are also hammers, but no nails that I can see. And screwdrivers, but no screws. Even an electric drill, which is pretty funny given that there's no electricity. It's like the drill is both an antique and a future fantasy.

Stan has pulled Terry off potato duty for the rest of the day to start clearing more land, and Terry got the okay to have me help him.

"This is how we get things done around here," Terry says. "A little bit at a time. It may not seem like much, me and you against this jungle, but every tree we cut and stump full of roots we pull, the more land we'll have for planting."

I grab two axes and hand one to Terry. People are still working on the inside of the marriage cabins, but they'll be done soon. Maybe in a day or two.

"We don't waste time," Terry says. "And we don't waste energy. That's how we've survived out here so far." Terry grabs a coil of rope.

I think about the dead bodies in the fissure, and the many corpses I encountered in burnt-out basements while on scavenging missions. Sometimes surviving involves luck. But the harder you work, the more chance you have of being lucky. And it's obvious that people work hard around here. But all the hard work in the world is for nothing if you're living in a place that's so controlling that people can't even choose when and who to marry.

I follow Terry in the direction of the yellow cliffs to the edge of the maple jungle. Big red leaves grace spiny branches growing from skinny trunks. The first time my ax hits a trunk, it bounces back.

"Strike it at a slight angle until you break through," Terry says. He swings, and his ax blade hits the trunk at a slight downward angle, biting in a little bit. "This is maple. It's lots harder than spruce or birch or aspen."

We stand across from each other and take turns swinging on the same tree until we get some movement, then Terry motions for me to stop. He gives the small tree a push, and it falls in slow motion toward the jungle and gets hung up on another tree.

"We'll cut down five or six, and then we'll haul them out with the rope. By that time our swinging muscles will need a break. Alternating chores makes it so we're able to work longer. That's why we're taking turns swinging—chopping at the same tree. That little pause goes a long way."

We do what Terry says, chop down six trees, then both work the rope to get them into the clearing. Even though they're thin, they're surprisingly heavy. When I mention this to Terry, he tells me these trees have been genetically engineered for disease resistance, strength, sap production, and rapid growth.

I remember what Wendy and Ellen said about the rapid growth being unnatural. "But how did they get everywhere?"

"I don't know the whole story," Terry says. "But Stan said one of the advantages to settling in the Buffer Zone was the engineered trees and how useful they would be."

I point to the circular huts and marriage cabins in the distance. "They're good building materials, that's for sure."

Terry nods. "And great firewood. That's what these trees are for."

"Do you ever wonder what it's like in the lower forty-eight now?" I ask. "I mean, do you think there're still schools, and cars, and people using money to buy things?"

"I never much cared for living bunched up close to people," Terry says. "I'll take breathing room over a shopping mall or a grocery store any day. But my guess is they're having some pretty hard times down there. A country like the United States, if it still exists, doesn't just abandon land and people like it did up here, unless things are dire."

"Yeah, I guess. But I want to live with people. Girls." I laugh. "And I want Jess to have a happy childhood. A normal childhood with other kids her age before it's too late."

"Normal?" Terry says. "Normal changes with the times and circumstances. You live here long enough and this will become normal. You'll see."

I nod and say, "Maybe you're right. I guess I'll find out in time."

Terry smiles. "Wait till spring when we tap some trees and boil the sap down to make syrup. It's delicious. We've already finished last year's syrup, but next year we're hoping to double our take and build up a surplus."

We go back to taking turns swinging our axes. My upper arms are burning and my forearms ache, but I keep pace with Terry. I don't want to be shown up by an old gray beard. Plus, I need him to think I'm loyal. That I'm inquisitive, but settling in. That I think what *we* have here is a good thing.

Later, as we're putting our tools in the shed, Stan appears and directs us to put the finishing touches on the two identical cabins they're readying for Max and Tam. We put clean towels and water basins on small tables in each cabin. We make sure the mattresses are stuffed full with dried grass. When we kindle fires in the woodstoves, I swallow down a lump in my throat and turn to Terry. "Does this mean they'll be here tonight? With their new husbands?"

Terry nods. "Since we were instructed to light the stoves, it's a possibility. The laws we laid out are very specific. After the Council reaches consensus, the women take up residence in their cabins. The new husbands are notified secretly that same night and take up residence with their new wives." Terry starts walking and I match his pace.

"You mean, when Marcy was paired up, she didn't know who the guy was until he walked in her cabin door that night?"

"That's right," Terry says, as we walk side by side. "That way, there's no time for conflict to develop prior to the pairing. The two people have to do their best to get along for the good of the community. And the Council does its best to honor the men and women by choosing who they think will be most suitable for each other. While we've been digging potatoes this past week, the Council has been rotating its members and questioning and getting to know the new women. Today, I'm guessing the entire Council met with Stan and he okayed their recommendations. Otherwise, we wouldn't have lit those fires."

We're outside the entrance to our hut, about to head over to the kitchen hut for our nightly ration of stew, when I spot Max and Tam walking toward the cabins, each escorted by one of the young guards. My legs tense up like I'm getting ready to sprint, and my heart pounds under my shirt. Tonight's the night.

CHAPTER
66

I WAIT.

I try to appear relaxed.

The door to our hut is closed, but I know what I'm hoping to hear. And I hope what I'm going to do afterward won't destroy their food supply, but I have to hit them where it counts in order to create the biggest diversion I can. The main reason I don't want to destroy their food supply isn't because I freaking love all these guys. It's because of Marcy and her being pregnant. I wouldn't want her to starve.

Terry is sitting on his bunk, and Melvin is lying down. He's the one who I helped with carrying his potatoes since it seems like he can't walk that well. I wonder how he made it all the way down here from Fairbanks.

"It all starts tonight," Terry says.

Melvin grunts in acknowledgment, then says, "One of the chosen. I hope it's me."

"Maybe it'll be you and me," Terry says.

Melvin says nothing in response.

Come on, Jess. Come on, I think. The wood shavings jammed into my pockets don't bother me, but the ones in my underwear are starting to itch. And the hammer shoved partway down the back of my pants and covered by my shirt is starting to dig into my back. At least I got rid of the screwdrivers when we'd readied the cabins. I hope Max and Tam find them under the towels in their cabins.

"I couldn't do it," I say. "I mean, if the girl doesn't want to be paired up, isn't that like rape?"

"According to Marcy's now-deceased husband, she didn't protest," Terry says. "She knew it was for the good of everyone. She knows her role."

"But if someone does protest?" I ask. "What would you guys do? Would you try to put a stop to the pairing?" I know I'm pushing it here, but figure I can at least leave them with something to think about.

Terry looks at me. "I guess we'll cross that bridge if we come to it. Sometimes you've got to do things for the good of the community, even if they aren't things you'd do otherwise."

He sounds so high and mighty. Like marrying someone against their will is taking the high road.

"What if it was your daughter?" I ask. "How would you feel then?"

"If we want the community to thrive, we have to follow through on what we've set up. We have to give the system an opportunity to work." Terry pauses. "If I had a daughter, she'd have to follow the rules, too."

I'm thinking about how to respond when a scream, followed by a call for help, cuts through the night air.

"That sounds like my sister. Come on," I say to Terry and Melvin. Then I run out the door.

CHAPTER
67

I CATCH A GLIMPSE OF Jess running toward Stan's hut, screaming about Marcy bleeding, just as planned. I sprint toward the potato storage shed, hoping that Max and Tam will be making their getaway from their cabins as soon as I create my diversion.

I see other silhouettes of people moving in the direction of Stan's hut. The people I'm most worried about are the young guys and Dylan. I just hope what I'm going to do will draw them toward me.

Behind the potato shed I empty my pockets of wood shavings. Then I unbutton my pants and dump more shavings from my underwear. I strike a match from the box I've stolen from our hut and drop it on the shavings. They catch and start burning. The wind feeds the fire and soon it's climbing up the wall toward the roof.

I hear Jess scream "Fire," and then several shouts for buckets and water. Then I hear a couple other screams. I turn toward the maple jungle and start to sprint and my feet are swept out from under me. I hit the ground hard and roll. I'm on my side, about to stand, but then someone lands on top of me. I feel his face against my cheek, and I grab his nose as hard as I can and pull.

I hear a cry of pain from whoever it is, and I keep pulling on his nose until his head is level with mine.

"Basic," he says, his voice a gravelly whisper. I shift my body in an attempt to break free, but Dylan's not budging. With my other hand, I pull the hammer out of the back of my pants and slam it on top of his head. His body jerks once like he's received an electric shock, but he's still on top of me. I hit him on the head again as hard as I can, and his hand on my other arm goes limp.

"Asshole," I whisper as I push him off me.

I stand up. I can see people approaching the potato shed with buckets. The flames have reached the roof. For Marcy's sake, I hope they'll be able to put the fire out before it burns up all their food. But more so, I hope Max and Jess and Tam are all heading for the maple jungle in different directions as planned.

I hear more footsteps pounding my way, so I turn and start running in the darkness. A shot rings out and hot pain stabs the back of my upper arm, but I just keep going. There's nothing more I can do.

CHAPTER
68

IT'S FREAKING PITCH-BLACK DARK IN the jungle. I hope the arson, the false alarm about Marcy bleeding, and now Dylan being injured or dead will be enough to keep everyone more than busy.

Our plan was to take off, each in a different direction, but to eventually meet up at the yellow cliffs. I have no way of knowing if Jess, Max, and Tam have escaped.

Jess was supposed to cut her hand on the sly, sneak some blood on Marcy's bedding, and sound the alarm. As everyone was focusing on getting to Marcy, the fire was supposed to divert some of them. Max, Tam, and Jess were supposed to slip off in the confusion.

Hitting Dylan with a hammer wasn't part of the plan. I didn't plan on killing anyone, but if I had to choose between killing him and getting my sister the hell out of there, I'd kill him. Still, I have this sick feeling in my gut from remembering the thud of that hammer on his skull. I don't know if he's dead, but I hit him hard.

I'm moving slowly in the darkness, trying not to make any noise, and struggling to ignore the pain in my arm. I know I'm bleeding, but it doesn't seem to be slowing me down. Plus, I can't move very fast anyway because I can't see anything.

I wonder how Jess is doing on her own in the pitch-black.

Maybe we should've run off in pairs? But I figured if we all split up, they'd have a harder time coming after us. If Dylan actually survived and told his story, maybe they'd focus their hunt on the direction I took, which would be fine by me. And since someone shot at me, maybe they are already on my tail.

My initial burst of energy is fading, and my legs feel like lead as I pick my way through the maples. Branches slap my face and tangle my legs. The back of my arm has settled into a steady ache, like there's a piece of hot metal resting against it. When I touch it, my hand comes back sticky.

I'm climbing a small hill now, working my way in the direct opposite direction of the yellow cliffs. I'll have to circle back eventually, but not until I'm so far away that if someone spots me, they'll have a hard time guessing where I'm heading.

On top of the maple-covered hill I stop to rest, to observe, to listen. Steam is rising in the darkness where they've put the fire out. At least I assume it's out since I can't see any flames. And then below me, I hear something. I lean forward and cup my ears. Some leaves crinkle. A branch snaps.

They're coming.

For me.

CHAPTER
69

HOURS LATER, I'M STILL CRASHING through the dark. I don't stop to listen but just keep going. They can move through the maples as fast as I can, and stopping will just allow them to gain on me.

I feel rocks underfoot, so I run my hand along the ground and scoop one up. Then I take the rock and throw it as hard as I can, up through the branches and off to one side, hoping that the noise from the landing rock will make my pursuers change course. I do this several times in succession and then keep going.

The gray of pre-dawn is taking over the sky. The earth has worked through its rotation, and our side of the planet is coming around to the sun again. At the same time, I notice that the maples are thinning, and up ahead is a clearing. It's the big clearing I was marched through at gunpoint to get here.

If I cross the clearing, whoever is following will have a way better chance of seeing me. Plus, at some point I need to circle around and work my way back toward the yellow cliffs. I haven't decided if I'm going to go east or west to get to the cliffs. And I don't know how far away from the compound to be when I circle back. Tam and Max—one had gone east, the other west, and Jess straight south to the yellow cliffs. At least that was the plan.

The plan. The plan. The plan. Did any of them even escape?

My mouth is dry. I hope I'll cross a stream or walk by a lake. I'll drink out of puddles, too. It doesn't matter. I probe the back of my arm through a jagged rip in my shirt. It feels like sand on top of a drying mud puddle. And it burns when I touch it. I hold my arm out straight and twist it, trying to see the injured spot, but I can't. So I keep examining it with my fingers, searching for an entry hole, but don't find one. Maybe the bullet only grazed me.

My mind shoots back to Jess, and Tam, and Max. Did they get shot at? Did they get away? The more those thoughts burn into my brain, the more I need to know. What if I get to the yellow cliffs and no one is there? Or what if Tam and Max appear but Jess doesn't? Or only Max and Jess make it? Or only Tam and Jess? Would we go back and try to free the other or others, or would we move on? Can you realistically have a second chance at a thing like this?

If anyone has been caught, they'll be guarding them even closer.

I want to know what the score is before I go to the yellow cliffs. Can I sneak back and observe? If any of the cabins are in use, I'd know that Max or Tam or both of them have been caught, or never made it out in the first place. But I wouldn't know how to tell if Jess is there. What if Tam and Max are back with Stan's group but Jess isn't, and then I get caught spying? I'd be abandoning Jess. I can't do that.

Okay, I think. *I need to go to the cliffs first, wait there and see. Stick with the plan.*

I hate this. I never should've split up from Jess. At the time, it seemed like a good plan. I feel my heart beating in my ears, my empty stomach burning with acid. And where the bullet grazed me, a heated vice squeezes my upper arm.

I think a little more about the plan, and then I know that if Jess doesn't show up, I'll have to go back. But if Max or Tam doesn't show, what will I do?

CHAPTER
70

THE YELLOW CLIFFS ARE A dark mustard color in the pre-sunrise light. I picked my way through the maples all day yesterday and all last night. I'm pretty sure I'm not being followed anymore, but if Jess or Tam or Max has been followed and they are as close to the cliffs as I am, then you never know who might be around.

I'm studying the cliffs from an angle, searching for anything that might be a sign. And I'm looking for some kind of opening that doesn't look like an opening—for the place Wendy and Ellen used to come. The old road they used to take has to run close to here.

The sun pops over the horizon straight into my eyes. With my hands I make a visor to block the blinding light, and I see a tiny fold in the rocks about a third of the way down the cliff face and wonder if that's the spot. And if it is, how did Wendy and Ellen access it? Do the people in the compound know about Wendy and Ellen's natural shelter?

I know the cliffs are visible from the valley because I could see them from the potato fields, but they're far enough away that it'd be tough to pick out something as small as a person from way down there. Still, it comes down to this: Do I make myself visible for someone else to see, or do I wait and see if someone else takes the risk?

Theoretically, I had the longest route to get here since my path out of the valley was directly opposite the cliffs. Jess, who is the slowest walker, had the shortest route.

Maybe my dad would've sat and waited until someone else made the move. He'd have churned it over in his mind and wouldn't have risked getting caught, because he thought he was so vital to our survival. Maybe in this situation my dad would've made a better plan. But my plan has worked so far, at least for me. I shake my head; this is no way to be thinking. If the girls don't make it, then my plan has failed. I've failed.

I take a baby step forward. And then another, trying to be silent. I step sideways between two maples, picking my feet up and then putting them down like the ground is made of a thin glass sheet that I don't want to break. It seems like it takes me an hour to walk a hundred feet.

At the edge of the maples, the last possible place I can stop before being seen, I pause. I wipe my watering eyes, then step into the sun.

I want to walk all over that cliff top and stare into the valley, study the compound for movement. And take big gulps of air in the open space, because being in the maples is so claustrophobic. Everywhere you turn there's a leaf in your face or a tangle of branches to navigate. Instead, I continue to stand at the very edge, ready to melt into the jungle if the wrong person appears.

CHAPTER
71

COME ON, I THINK. COME *on*, I hope.

Anyone. Jess. Max. Tam. No way could they have taken as long as I did to get here. And if they aren't here now, then they'll never get here. If just one of them made it. My forehead tightens as I squint across the clearing, hoping for some kind of sign. I wish we had all left together. I resist the urge to call out their names even though my mind is screaming them over and over.

Then I see movement across the clearing—a few leaves shaking—directly opposite me. A small face materializes and my heart jumps. I'm staring at Tam's sparkling eyes and high cheekbones. I swallow the lump in my throat.

Our eyes lock. Tam smiles at me, and all I want is to hold her and tell her how much I've missed her and how much I like her. She's strong and fast and brave and has endless stores of energy. If anyone was going to escape, it would've been her.

Then, like magic, Max's face appears next to Tam's. She's beaming at me and I'm returning the smile. I've missed her, too. I don't know if Jess would've been able to slog through all that swamp without Max's support. Below Tam's other shoulder, I see some more movement, and Jess's blond hair pokes out of the jungle of branches and leaves, and I have to stop myself from screaming for joy. I want to run across the clearing separating us and swing her in the air, but I know that'd just put us in danger. I'll have to work my way around the edge, just inside the trees, in case anyone from the compound is close by.

I point with my arm, then fade into the branches behind me and work my way toward them.

I hear branches snapping and know the girls are moving toward me. Max appears first and almost knocks me over with a hug. I hug her back. She feels strong, like she could carry me the rest of the way to the coast if she had to.

Behind her Tam pops into view, so I weasel out of Max's grip, and now Tam's in my arms, her firm body pressing against mine. She just hangs on, her arms around my lower back, her head buried in my neck, her nose nudging my Adam's apple, and it feels like the most natural thing in the world and my whole body is hungry and buzzing. I want to cup her face in my hands and kiss her lips forever, but over her shoulder I see Jess barreling at me so I separate from Tam and take a step sideways toward Jess.

Tam's eyes meet mine for an instant as I move away, but before I can say anything, Jess's airborne body slams into me. She wraps her legs around my midsection and collapses into my chest. I stumble and Tam catches my shoulder so I don't fall. Now I feel like I've come home.

I hold Jess for a long minute, then set her down and whisper, "All three of you here? At the same time? That's amazing." I can't believe the plan worked out so well.

"We left together. We just couldn't do it your way," Max whispers.

"We could have," Tam whispers. "But we didn't want to."

"Glad I had the screwdriver," Max says.

"Me too," Tam says. "I wouldn't have escaped without it."

"I almost didn't follow them," Jess whispers. "I had to make a decision right then and there."

"I don't care how you got here." I wipe my eyes. "Just that you made it. I was torn over what I'd do if not everyone showed up."

"It was a good plan." Max smiles.

We have a lot of catching up to do. What happened at the river? Why didn't they wait for us? How did they get caught? What have they seen? What have they learned? But first, we have to deal with the present: getting the hell out of here.

Tam's looking toward the clearing. She scrunches up her face and points. I follow her finger and see, at the very edge of the cliff, an arrangement of rocks that from this angle spells the word *basic*.

"Impossible," I whisper. Then I tell them how I struck Dylan in the head with a hammer—twice. And how his body went limp. "I could've just knocked him out, and when he woke up he came straight to the cliffs. Or he could've left those rocks weeks ago, before he even got to Stan's."

We're all glancing around with our eyes, keeping our bodies still. I tighten my grip on the hammer. No matter what we do, it seems like Dylan is always one step ahead of us. Like he has a crystal ball and can see what we're going to do before we even know we're going to do it

"It doesn't matter," Tam whispers, grabbing my arm. "We just have to keep moving. If he tries to stop us, we'll deal with it. Now that I know what that place is all about, I'd rather die fighting than live there."

* * *

"At least if we follow the old road bed we'll know we're going in the right direction," I say. We ran into the road about a hundred yards from the yellow cliffs.

"But Wendy and Ellen said it was safer to stay above it," Jess says.

"Where Wendy and Ellen live, it's treeless," I say, "so it's easy to stay off the road and still follow it. But in the jungle it's next to impossible. I'm just glad we found it."

"Your arm," Max says. "How come you keep touching it?"

"Oh, I forgot. I guess I kind of got shot. Hurt like hell for a while. Now it just aches. It's in a place where I can't see." I hold my arm up.

Jess makes a face like she's gonna puke.

"Is it that bad?" I ask.

"Sort of," Jess says. "I mean, it's bloody."

"We need you to take off your shirt," Max says. "We'll help you."

I stand still with my arms out as Max unbuttons my shirt and Tam unbuttons the cuff on one sleeve, but when she reaches up and starts pulling the arm of my shirt, a jolt of pain in my upper arm makes me gasp.

"Your shirt was stuck to your skin," Tam says, looking me straight in the eyes. "Sorry. At least now we can see what we're dealing with."

"It's okay," I say, still feeling the warmth from her nose in my neck from when we were reunited.

My shirt hangs off my other arm as the three of them gather around my wound.

"It looks like a bloody burn," Max says. "I don't see a hole."

"Me neither," Jess says. "Does it hurt much?"

"It hurt a lot less until the three of you started checking it out." I smile.

"The bullet must've grazed you," Tam says. "Your arm is all bloody, but I think it's pretty much a surface wound. At least it doesn't look all dirty, but still, we should wash it off soon. It'll cut down the chances of it getting infected. Definitely not as bad as what I did with that screwdriver. I don't know if I killed him, but he went down. I was surprised when the head guy came into my cabin. I thought maybe he was going to tell me who I'd been paired with, but then his smile told me that I'd been paired with him. He—"

"Wait," I say, "you mean Stan was going to be your husband?"

Tam nods. "He started talking in this soft voice, telling me how beautiful I was as he closed the distance between us, and I wanted to puke. I told him to hold on and turned away from him and washed my hands and splashed water on my face. My hands were shaking when I snuck the screwdriver from under the towel as I dried off. And I thought to myself, *It's now or never.* I turned and attacked him like there was no tomorrow, because if I'd lost, there wouldn't have been a tomorrow for me. Then I heard all hell break loose outside." Tam turns to Jess. "Without you doing your part, there's no way I would've escaped, because I'm sure they would've heard Stan calling for help."

Jess smiles. "One of the Council Women told me as the new husbands were arriving at the cabins. She was watching out the door of our hut. That's how I knew when to do my part. I waited a minute or two and then cut my arm on a sharp piece of wood I'd hidden, and then I rubbed some blood on Marcy's bed while I was sitting with her. She'd gotten used to me sitting on her bed and talking to her. We'd kind of become friends." Jess pauses. "Marcy

was so convinced it was her blood that she started screaming, too."
Then she lowers her voice. "I hope she's okay. I mean, I hope all
the stress didn't damage her baby."

Max looks at Jess. "You did what you had to do and you did it
perfectly. I think she'll be okay once the older women check her
out." She pauses. "I took my guy by surprise. I was pretending that
I liked him. I said to him, I got you! You're the one I would have
chosen." She shakes her head. "It was that guy, Jim, who was so
outspoken at the meeting."

"Did he die?" Jess asks. She has a troubled look on her face.

"I don't know," Max says, "but just keep this in mind: We only
hurt people who were trying to hurt us. They didn't have a right
to take me and Tam as wives, and they wouldn't let us go
peacefully."

Jess hugs my uninjured side, and I put my arm around her and
kiss the top of her head. "You are so brave," I whisper.

Her warm body snuggled beside me makes me think of Mom.
Jess used to hug her like this all the time. If only she could see Jess
now, this combination of still being the little girl full of love that
she was at the start of our journey but now with the ability and
poise to play a major role in escaping from a dangerous place. We
all relied on her and she came through.

We decide to stay away from the rock shelter on the yellow
cliffs because that's where Max and Tam were when they got
caught. And for all we know, people from the compound are waiting in there to recapture us. It's too bad, because Max's and Tam's
packs are in there. All we have is a hammer, a box of matches, my
fire-starting tool, the map and the notes from my mom and dad,
and the clothes we're wearing.

At least we've been well-fed for a few days, and since we're traveling light, we can make good time. Or as good as possible in the maples.

I can't see them, but I know there are mountains in the distance. I remember from the map—the Chugach Range, the last set of mountains to cross before the coast. Hopefully, up high we'll get into some treeless country that will be easier to walk in, but it'll be colder, too. And when we top the pass and head for the coast, who knows what it'll be like on the other side.

These mountain ranges, I realize, are like gatekeepers for plant species. Sure, some seeds blow through the passes. There were a scattering of maples north of the Alaska Range before the fires, but I never paid much attention to them. South of the range that's almost all there are. Terry said the maples were genetically engineered. But still, how did they spread so quickly?

On the other side of the Chugach there'll be a coastal influence. It'll probably be wetter country. And if people live there, well, hopefully they won't be as whacked-out as Stan and his troop of gray beards.

*   *   *

We're resting by a stream after walking for hours. We've followed it downstream for a couple of bends from where it crosses the road. We hope to stay here until it gets light out, taking turns keeping watch. Jess is already lying down, her head in my lap.

Tam pushes more twigs into our small fire. "That pregnant girl, Marcy. She just turned fifteen. That means those psychos married her off when she was fourteen. If I had any food in my stomach right now, I'd puke."

"I was really depressed when I was fourteen," Max says. "My family was dead. I thought about trying to run away from the group home"—she bows her head—"but I didn't even have the energy to try."

"At fourteen," Tam says, "I was in what turned out to be my second-to-last foster home." She jams another stick into the fire. "My deranged foster parents were kicking the shit out of me every chance they got, when they could catch me. I tried to be perfect, to not upset them, but you know me, I need to move around, and they basically insisted that I sit still, and they grew irate when I didn't. When they'd come after me, I'd run, but I didn't always get away."

Max raises her head and looks at Tam. "Both of us, even with no parents, had it way better than Marcy at fourteen. I wish we could've taken her with us."

Tam and I nod in agreement. There was just no way to make that happen.

Tam and Max tell me about being questioned by the Council and trying to answer questions in ways that would give them more of a chance of having a gentler husband, not because they thought it'd be easier to live with someone like that but because they thought it'd make it easier to escape. But based on the choices, I think they chose Jim so he'd quit causing conflict, and I think Stan chose Tam for himself. I remember his eyes lingering on her when he met her.

I tell them that Dylan had been in the fissure and had heard us talking about him.

Then they talk about the young guys catching them off guard and holding them at gunpoint. They thought they'd have to fight for their lives, but all the guys did was march them to the compound. And that they called them by their names, so Dylan must've been involved in their capture even if he didn't show his face. Maybe he put the word *basic* in the rocks then and just stayed out of view so Tam and Max never saw him.

And before all that, back at the river, Tam and Max had waited and waited. But then they saw someone on the same side of the river that they were on, and he was coming their way so they kept moving. They tried to find the cache in the brown rocks along the road, planning to wait there for us, but obviously they'd missed it.

I tell them about Wendy and Ellen and how they live off voles.

We could sure go for a few voles now because we don't have any food and don't know if we'll find any, but just being back together makes it feel like everything is going to be okay. Just being out of that compound calms my mind, even if two of the gray beards really did die from screwdriver wounds and Dylan from hits with my hammer.

I hate hurting and killing people, but sometimes people leave you basically no choice, unless you want to stand by and watch the people you love be hurt or killed.

And now we're maybe less than a hundred miles from the coast. Maybe we're actually going to make it. A shiver runs up my spine and I think, maybe I *will* get a chance to get to know Tam better.

"This might sound corny," I say, "but I'm going to say it anyway." I hold my hands over the glowing coals, the remains of our fire. "What we've got—it's special. I mean, we've come a long way together. I know it's not over yet. And it hasn't been without conflicts. And there's no guarantee that we'll even make it. And when we get there, we might not find anything. And I'm not trying to discount any of our friends or family or anyone who has helped us out. I guess I'm saying that even if I die tomorrow, I'm just happy I've had this time with each of you."

The three of us just stare into the coals, letting the soft sounds of the creek fill our ears. Jess shifts her body a little and I stroke her hair, thankful that she's recovered from that head injury. I see Max reach out and put her hand on Tam's knee. Tam turns toward her and smiles.

Then Max whispers, "I think I hear something from upstream, toward the road. Voices, maybe."

We came down the creek a couple of bends, but now that I think about it, we really don't know if the road took a bend or not. Maybe we're closer to the road than we imagine.

The glow from the coals won't give off much light, especially with the four of us crowded around it. But the smell of burning wood—depending on the wind direction—could be a giveaway.

I strain my ears, willing the noise of the flowing water into the background. I can't be sure, but I think I hear something, too.

CHAPTER
72

WE KEEP SITTING IN SILENCE, each listening but not speaking for fear of being heard. And just what do I hear?

Voices? Maybe.

Leaves rustling? Definitely.

A splash in the water upstream? Just one.

Breathing? I'm pretty sure.

I just want it to get light out so if there is something or someone, we can see what we're dealing with.

Dylan, I think. Maybe he's toying with us. Tracking us down. Maybe he's planning on trying to kill us or recapture the girls. But I'd clocked him hard with that hammer. If it is him, I decide, I will finish the job. He is just too dangerous.

I'm not scared of the dark, but noises are definitely scarier in the dark. I turn toward Jess, alert and ready, now sitting up next to me. On my other side I feel Tam's knee pressing against mine. It's been there since we all sat up straighter minutes ago after hearing the noises. Neither of us moved to avoid the sudden contact. And next to her, Max is squatting with her hands resting on the ground, ready to spring into action. I have the hammer in my hand and I know that I will kill without hesitation to protect any of them.

* * *

We're grateful when the gray light of dawn starts filtering through the maples. We haven't heard anything in hours. The cold has crept under our skin, but what can we do? We stopped putting wood on the fire when Max first heard the noise.

We cup our hands and slurp frigid creek water, then start up the creek toward the road. My arm aches. We washed the dried blood off last night before we heard the noise.

We take small steps and plant our feet like we're walking bare-foot across a field of sharp rocks, our eyes scanning the land around us.

At the faint path that used to be the road, we pause. Has someone passed through here? We all remember hearing at least one splash. It could've been something crossing the creek while traveling the road. But who or what? And which way had it come from? And which way had it gone?

"I don't see any footprints, or animal tracks, or scuffed-up ground," I say. "Maybe it was nothing."

Jess says, "Nothings don't make splashing and rustling noises."

We talk a little more and decide that yes, we heard a splash and some rustling. The voices and the breathing—we can't be certain of those. Could it have been a bird landing in the creek, its cooing or singing sounding like voices? Or some other animal? But an animal would leave tracks—unless it walked for a bit in the water like we had.

"Regardless," I say, "we have to keep going." I feel the weight of the hammer in my hand. "The sooner we get to the coast the better, I hope."

"Let's not stop until we're out of the trees," Tam says. "Or at least till we get to the edge of them. Then we can still have wood for a fire."

"These maples," Max says, "they are beautiful. But I'm kind of tired of them."

We still need to move carefully, and stay aware of what else might be lurking in the jungle. But since we don't see prints by the stream crossing, I'm feeling better, more relaxed. Like maybe we really are alone out here. Then I think of Dylan and how potentially whacked he is and wonder if he is watching us right now.

"Before we go," Max says, "I've got this thing I want us to do."

She explains the activity. We form a circle. Then we join hands. Jess's hand in mine feels small but strong. Tam's hand is surprisingly warm. Max has us close our eyes. She squeezes Tam's hand, and Tam squeezes mine, and I squeeze Jess's, and Jess squeezes Max's.

We do this half a dozen times and then Max tells us to open our eyes and drop our hands to our sides. "When I was really little," Max says, "way before I ended up in the group home, my grandma would put everyone in a circle and do that. And she'd say, 'We need to share our energy. Together we can accomplish much, much more than we can as individuals.' I used to like that game because it was fun to pass the pulse around a circle of twenty or thirty people. I didn't really think about the energy thing, but now, I'm not sure how I'd do walking this jungle road alone. I might not make it. But all of us, I'm sure we'll make it. But even if we don't—I'm at peace because I know we're doing the right thing."

I nod. So do Tam and Jess.

It's kind of true, I think. Doing something alone, one mistake and you could be finished. And there's no one next to you to keep you going when you've been without food for a few days. Or like when that bear was chasing us: Without Tam, I would've been its lunch. And without Tam and Max disabling the two gray beards, and Jess playing her part, there's no way my escape plan would've worked.

"Okay," I say. "Together, we go."

I take a step backward and bend down to retie my shoe. And that's when I hear it. A splashing sound. Then a tinkling noise. Like pieces of pipe gently knocking together.

I finish retying my shoe and stand up. It's pretty obvious that everyone has heard what I heard, because we're all standing silent, searching one another's eyes for answers.

I point upstream because that's where I think the splash has come from. Jess, Tam, and Max all nod.

I lean forward and so does everyone else. "I want to know what's up there," I whisper.

"Let's just keep going," Tam says.

Max nods.

"No," I say. "We need to know if it's Dylan, or whoever. You can wait here if you want, but I need to know." I have my hammer out. I think again of Dylan, but I also think of my mom and how we'd never found her body and how when we first climbed out of the fissure, we saw someone way in the distance behind us. I don't mention any of this to Jess, because I don't want to get her hopes up only to have them dashed when we have miles to cover and no food to eat. She's grown up a lot on this journey, but she's still only ten years old.

I hear another splash and then a whining sound. Sharp and high-pitched, but short, like it's been cut off. Like whoever or whatever has made the sound has had something clamp their jaw shut.

I step into the stream. It twists away from the road in a lazy

S-curve, just like it does downstream. Tam, Max, and Jess all pick up rocks and follow.

Whatever it is, it can't be too far. I don't want to walk into a trap, but I don't want to leave knowing someone could be this close behind us. Whether it's a person or a group of people or a bear, I need to know what our risks are instead of just running from them. And yeah, I need to know if it's my mom.

I hear the whining sound again. And then again, only louder, like whatever is making the noise is right around the corner. I raise my hammer up and see the others cock their arms, fist-sized stones in their hands.

I don't know what to expect. A grizzly bear? A fox? An injured or crazy person? Dylan? But we'll find out soon enough.

CHAPTER
73

"THAT'S NOT A WOLF," MAX says. "It's a dog."

I haven't seen a dog, any dog, in over a year. Not since my dad killed and butchered one. No one said much of anything during those meals. It was a pretty small dog, but we made it last. I don't know what kind it was. We had dog stew for a week or so. And then my mom boiled the bones and we drank dog broth. Jess wouldn't eat any of it. I was glad when it was gone.

But now, seeing that wet, mangy thing in front of us, my first thought is food.

It has gray and black fur like a husky, but it isn't as big as I think a husky should be.

It's stopped about twenty yards upstream from us, a questioning look in its eyes. I feel the weight of the hammer in my hand. I don't know how much of a fight it'll put up, and I don't want anyone to get bitten.

It curls its back and lets out a small whine. And then it starts panting.

"It's trying to tell us something," Jess says.

"Nobody move," I say. "Maybe it'll come closer. We need it, and I don't want to have to chase it, because it might get away."

"I think it needs us," Jess says.

I don't want my sister getting attached to something that is going to turn into our dinner.

Tam is standing with the rock still cocked in her hand, but Jess has put hers down. So has Max.

The dog lets out another whine, then turns its head upstream. It looks back at us and whines again. It takes a step away from us, then turns and whines some more.

I don't want it to get away. "Okay," I say. "I—"

"She wants us to follow her," Jess says. "My friend's dog used to do this when she wanted to go outside. She'd walk toward the door and keep turning around and whining. But then she wouldn't *just* go outside even though she had one of those dog doors. She'd only go if we went with her."

I don't know any other way to put this, so I just say, "Jess." I point to the dog. "That's our next meal. Don't get too attached."

She looks at me, then at the dog. "You can't kill a dog for food. That's sick."

"I wish I had my bow," Tam says.

"I think we should see what it wants," Max says. "You know the legends about how ravens used to lead hunters to moose or caribou?" She raises her eyebrows.

"Or maybe it's a trap," Tam says. "Maybe there's people around the corner and they've trained the dog to lure their victims in."

"Okay," I say. "All these are possibilities. We might have to eat this dog. We can't just follow it blindly, hoping it'll lead us to some food. And, Tam's point is well-taken. We need to be careful. I mean, dogs live with people—at least they used to."

No one says anything. The dog whines again and takes another step upstream.

"That dog needs us," Jess says. "It does." She keeps her eyes on the dog the whole time.

"Can we all agree to follow it?" I ask. "At a distance. For just a little ways. I don't want anyone getting bitten. And, if there are people upstream, I'd like to see who they are and where they're going. I mean, if they have a dog, maybe they have food—because if they didn't, they would've eaten the freaking thing."

I still hope we'll end up eating the dog. I don't want to run into people. No way will anyone have enough food for the four of us. But if there are people, why aren't they calling for their dog, or coming for her? Maybe they hear us and are playing it cautious.

The dog takes another step upstream. We all step forward and the dog turns its head. Then it turns back and keeps going. The bend keeps unfolding in front of us. I'm scanning both banks, peering through the maples as best I can, looking for evidence of people. Anything that will give me a hint of what to expect.

The creek starts to bend in the opposite direction. The dog looks back, its tail flying at half-mast, but then the dog keeps going, never waiting for us to catch up entirely. I don't know how long to follow this thing or whether we should try to call it so it'll come to us. I think about fresh meat roasting on a fire and feel a little burning sensation in my stomach, which is so empty that it's pressed up against my spine.

We're hugging the same shore the dog's on, mostly walking on gravel, but sometimes in ankle-deep water. The maples grow close to both banks.

At the middle of the bend the dog increases its pace. It turns its head and gives one sharp bark, then keeps going.

"Everyone," I say over my shoulder, "keep an eye out on shore." We're walking single file.

The dog stops where the creek runs fast over some rocks. I slow down. I don't want to walk into a trap, but something keeps pulling me forward. I've come this far and need to know what we're up against. I haven't smelled any smoke. And I haven't heard anything but the noise from the creek, which fills my ears with a constant hiss.

I keep scanning the banks as we approach the dog. We're only about ten feet away. The dog whines again, then opens its mouth and starts panting. It takes a couple of steps toward the maple jungle and whines again.

I take another step forward, and then I see them, just beyond the dog.

Two legs sticking out of the jungle.

CHAPTER
74

I PUT MY HAND UP, motioning for everyone to stop. Then I point.

The legs are sticking out from the trees, like someone is lying on their back. Two old brown boots. And some dark green pants, thick-looking, like maybe they're wool. The dog has positioned itself so I can't see any more of the person.

I motion for everyone to come up. I feel Jess and Max and Tam crowding in behind me, peeking over my shoulders.

Ten feet between us and the legs. Are there more people just back in the jungle? Was this a setup to trap us? If it was, it's working, because we're just standing and staring, waiting for someone to blindside us.

The dog whines again, then barks. It paws at the brown-booted feet.

"Do you think he's dead?" Max whispers.

"How do you know it's a he?" I whisper back.

"Just a guess."

I take a step forward and the dog lets out a low growl, but at the same time its tail gives a little wag.

"Let me," Jess says. She looks at the dog. "It's okay. We won't hurt you. Or your friend."

Jess is standing even with me, and then she takes a step forward. The dog holds its ground but doesn't growl. Jess takes another step. Then she makes a little clicking sound with her mouth and the dog raises its head a little, tilts it sideways, and wags its tail again.

I take a step forward behind Jess, and the dog lets out another low growl. Maybe it can sense I'm not above eating it for dinner. I feel a hand on my arm and turn. Max is holding my bicep. "Let her go," she whispers. "You don't want to overwhelm the dog."

"Jess," I whisper, "be careful."

"It won't hurt me," Jess says. "It likes me."

Jess takes another step toward the dog. The husky just keeps looking at her, tail wagging slightly.

Only five more feet and Jess will be standing next to the dog. Then I see one of the booted feet move, like a hand waving. The dog couldn't have seen it but must've sensed it, because it turns toward the person and lets out a whine.

"Hello," I say. "Hello."

The dog barks at me. Jess turns and puts her finger to her lips, trying to shush me.

The foot moves again.

"Chena," a weak voice from the maples says. "Come."

The dog turns and paws at the feet.

"That a girl," the voice says. "You stay with me."

"Hello," I say again. I take a step so I'm standing next to Jess. The dog growls. Then I see what Jess is seeing. Through the maples I make out the rest of the man attached to the legs. He's got a white beard and is lying on the ground, his head propped up by a backpack.

Tam and Max move in next to me.

The man's eyes seem to notice us for the first time. He opens them a little wider and thrusts his head back.

"We want to help," I say. "Your dog. She approached us. And my sister"—I point at Jess—"she was pretty sure your dog was asking us to follow her."

The man just keeps staring. His foot moves again. "She's a good dog." His voice is strained and weak. "The best," he says, his words barely reaching beyond his lips.

"What's wrong with you?" I ask.

"I'm the last one." He takes a few shallow breaths. "Got everyone else. In the river. Everyone. Dead. Grabbed my survival pack and ran."

The hundreds of bodies we saw in the river, I think. "What happened?"

His eyes close and then open again. "Gas tent. Gas tent. The greedy gold-hungry bastards."

"Where did they come from?" I ask.

He coughs once. "Where they always come from."

"What's a gas tent?" I ask.

He coughs again and puts his hand on the dog's side. "You . . . you treat her well." Then his head slouches down and he stays that way. The dog whines again and paws at his foot.

How has he gotten here? Where was he trying to go? What else does he know?

"I think he just passed," Max says. "He couldn't go until he knew someone would look after his dog."

"I will," Jess says. "I won't let anyone hurt her."

"He's the guy," Tam says, looking at Max. "The one coming

up behind us on the road after we crossed the river. His dog must've been out of sight at the time."

"Yes," Max says. "You're right."

"We have to examine him. Maybe he's just passed out." But if he is dead? I look at the dog. I can't kill and eat a dog whose owner's last words were to treat her well. And maybe the dog will be good for Jess. Maybe it'll be good for all of us. If it'll just let us approach close enough to see what its deal is.

Gold. I tell everyone what Wendy and Ellen told me about the religious commune being at the site of an old gold mine. *Where they always come from.* I wonder where that is. And a *gas tent?* What is that?

"Chena," Jess says. "See that? Her ears perked up. That's what the man called her. Chena, come." Jess pats her thighs. "Come on, good girl."

The dog wags her tail and Jess calls her again. She comes another step and Jess keeps at it until Chena is at Jess's feet.

"Don't touch her yet," Max says. "Let Chena make the first move."

I take a step away from Chena and toward the man. Chena looks at me but doesn't come forward.

"It's okay, girl," Jess says. "It's okay, Chena girl."

*　*　*

I wish we could've talked longer to the man, learned more about where he's been and what he's seen. But Max is right. He's gone. I don't think he starved to death, because there's food in his pack. And if I got it right, he's the sole survivor from the lakes, where the bodies in the river came from.

I feel bad about not burying him, but the ground is hard with a maze of roots, and we don't have a shovel. We drag him back from the stream a ways. We don't take the clothes off his back, but we do go through his pockets, looking for some clue about who he was. We find nothing.

His dog, we figure, is named after the Chena River that runs through Fairbanks, so we're pretty sure he came from around there before being part of the community at the lakes.

I don't feel bad about taking the man's pack since we've decided to keep Chena and will try to carry out his wishes. No way could I kill that dog now even if we hadn't found the owner. Jess is in love with her.

And this guy has about five pounds of dried beans in his pack and a bunch of tea. There's an old coffee can—bailing wire strung through a couple of holes on the rim for a handle—blackened from sitting on a fire. He also has a spoon and a knife, some clothing, and a couple of rusty brown blankets.

If I have to guess, I'd say he was in his sixties or seventies. We examine his body, looking for clues about why he died. We find no wounds. Maybe he had cancer, or an infection.

We collect wood and build a fire. We put some beans in the coffee can with some water and let them boil away. We keep stirring them, adding more water by cupping our hands in the creek and dumping it into the pot.

Chena follows Jess everywhere. She warms up to the rest of us, lets us pet her without growling. But Jess is her chosen one. Chena licks Jess's hands and face and lets Jess scratch her belly and behind her ears.

We take turns eating beans out of the pot and put a few spoonfuls on a flat rock for Chena. We rinse the pot and make some tea.

Tam holds up our one spoon. "I used to share a spoon with my mom. Even when she was losing her strength as the cancer took over her body, she made eating into a game. I would feed her a spoonful and she would feed me." Tam smiles and then her face goes flat. "In my first foster home, I got slapped on the hand when I tried to share my foster sister's spoon. There was no lesson about what to share and what not to share. Just a slap and a mean look and a don't-you-know-any-better lecture. I learned from my mom to share everything and then from my first foster family to share nothing. I mean, I had just turned six."

"Some humans," Max says, "they just plain suck. No one's perfect, but look at us. Even with the tiny amount of food we have, we're sharing it with a dog." Max smiles. "We rock."

I think about how lucky it is that we found the dog. Or that the dog found us. And how if we hadn't stayed at the creek crossing to see what the noise was, we'd probably be starving. We took a risk and it worked out. And, at the same time, we helped a man die in peace. But his people had been massacred for gold. Then I remember what Stan said about choosing a spot in the maples that had nothing anyone else would want. That's one way to live. But shouldn't people be able to make choices about where to live that aren't based on fear?

We decide to stay up the creek for the night since the day is already turning toward darkness and we have hot coals for a fire. We can drink more tea and heat up water to wash our faces and hands and my gunshot wound.

CHAPTER
75

THREE DAYS LATER AND WE'RE approaching the pass. *Thompson Pass*, I remember from the map. The maples have thinned out and you can actually just walk on the old road for stretches instead of constantly bushwhacking.

Chena stays with us, like she's always been part of our group. I haven't said or done anything about my attraction to Tam, except in my mind, but I can still feel her face buried in my neck from five days ago. Between coaxing as many miles as I can out of Jess each day, rationing our meager food supply, and keeping watch at night, my mind and body are already overloaded. Still, on quiet stretches like this where the walking is pretty easy, my mind goes to Tam.

Maybe someday we'll be in a place that won't be so fraught with danger that there'll be space to have a relationship. To be with someone I like, who also likes me. Does she like me the way I like her? According to Jess, she does. But when we hit these quiet stretches, I think, *If she really does like me the way I like her, then why not start now? Why wait? Today we are alive. There could be no tomorrow.*

"What's that?" Jess asks, pointing, and my mind instantly shifts from what could be to what's right in front of me, to the girl I need every ounce of my awareness to protect.

"It looks like an old section of pipeline," I say. I thought they'd hauled it all away years ago. That's what we'd learned in school. When the Trans-Alaska Pipeline shut down, all the materials were gathered to be recycled or reused. Metals were getting scarcer and more expensive, so every scrap was coveted. That was back when there was still a transportation system in Alaska, and oil and gas were being shipped here to power heavy equipment to do the work.

We keep walking. I don't know if it's still September or if we're into October, but I know the higher up we spend the night, the chillier it'll be. I hope there'll at least be some willows to build a fire with; otherwise we'll be hungry and cold.

We have about two meals of beans left and enough tea for a few more pots.

The closer we get to the pass, the more I start to believe that we might actually make it. If there really are people living on the coast, what will they be like? Will they accept us? What kind of laws and rules will they have? Will they even let us live there? Will I recognize anyone? Are they the ones responsible for the massacre with the gas tent?

I'm comfortable with Jess and Max and Tam, and yeah, we're pretty close to starving right now, but we're together. I know how to do this, how to be moving toward something, but actually arriving—I'm nervous about that part. Scared.

All my dad wanted was to live a simple life on the land, but the land took too much abuse in too short of a time to make that possible. I remember what Max said—that the land would heal and that someday she would go back. I wonder if the genetically engineered maples will keep marching northward and cover the land all the way to the Yukon, or if the native birches and spruce will reclaim the wilderness like they used to after a fire.

I didn't notice any maples in the fissure. In some ways that fissure is a window into the past. And the seeds blowing upward from it—maybe they'll sprout in the ash and help create the future.

The sun is sinking behind a ridge. *One more day*, I think, *and we'll be at the top of the pass.*

Cars and trucks used to drive through here on a paved road. A massive pipeline used to move hundreds of thousands of gallons of oil a day the entire length of the state—eight hundred miles. I see the pictures in my mind, the ones I'd seen in the history books and videos. Alaska's heyday, from 1980 until 2040, that's what it'd been coined. Not that we're officially counting the years anymore. Well, maybe someone is. Another five and we'll be into the next century, even though the way we're living, it seems like we've gone back a hundred years from the heyday instead of forward.

A few years ago the government couldn't even sell Alaska for the original price of three cents an acre. Instead, they had to abandon most of it. But if you are power hungry, why buy anything in this world when, if you have the power and the desire, you could just take it? Like whatever those gas-tent people did to kill everyone in that commune. I guess they wanted the gold in the mine. They took it because they had the power. And in Stan's compound, women who could have children were forced to stay and get married.

I just hope whoever we find at the coast treats people—all people—with respect.

I can see up ahead where the willows peter out. We decide to head off the road to make camp while we still have willows for cooking fuel. We follow a small creek downstream, moving away from the road a quarter mile or so before stopping.

"We're close," I say. "Maybe tomorrow we'll be there." My arm still aches from the gunshot wound, but it hasn't gotten any worse. And my shoulder that I hurt on my descent into the fissure is pretty much back to normal.

"I wonder if they still call the place Valdez," Max says.

"And I wonder," Tam says, "if it's still part of the United States. That is, if the USA still exists."

"I hope they like dogs," Jess says. She takes Chena's head between her hands and says, "Good girl."

"Me too," I say. And it's true. I don't want Jess to have to part with Chena. That's something we just can't predict. But if we had to abandon Chena, Jess would survive.

"If Valdez didn't burn," Max says, "maybe it's still like a real town or something, just hard to get to from the north. Maybe ships still come into port. We're so cut off, it's hard to believe that tomorrow we might learn something about what's going on in the rest of the world."

I haven't thought much about that, or about Valdez being connected. Maybe there're phones and computers and electricity. Maybe. We just don't know.

I do know that after the pipeline closed and the fishing industry collapsed, the town decreased in size by two-thirds. And when was that, forty or fifty years ago? And after that, they had to abandon part of the town because of the rising sea level. And then there was a big earthquake and a lot of the land right around sea level sank, so more of the town ended up underwater. Maybe nothing is there. Maybe that's why my parents said to head toward Anchorage.

At one time, more than half the state lived in Anchorage. And when people had been forced out of the villages because of lack of services, most of them had gone to Anchorage. Trusting Dylan's map more than my parents' words made sense at the time we made that decision, but right now I'm not so sure. Valdez was tiny during its heyday. It could be a ghost town now.

CHAPTER
76

WE TOPPED THE PASS A little while ago and are winding down the old road. Right now we're in a narrow canyon. Waterfalls, fifty or sixty feet high, spill over the cliff tops on both sides of the road. There's so little water flowing in one of the falls that when an updraft catches the water, it blows the whole thing right into the cliffs.

"Can't be much farther now," Max says. "And this road, isn't it in a lot better shape since we came through the pass?"

"It's rockier here in the canyon," I say. "Maybe the plants can't take over as fast."

Tam and Jess and Chena are walking about ten feet in front of us.

Max nods. "Could be."

We walk in silence for a while, keeping our eyes and ears alert for any sign of life. The canyon widens, and the waters from the falls merge to form a small river cut up by sand and gravel bars, each covered in a blaze of yellow from the willows crowding onto them. Countless channels come together, then separate because of all the little islands. The road clearly stays on the right side of the river, and beyond the floodplain the land rises steeply. It's forested mostly with big evergreens, but some birches and a scattering of maples as well. Not the spindly maples choking the land on the other side of the pass, these look like normal trees even though they are probably escapees from the same genetically engineered stock. And the land under the trees is covered in a thick blanket of moss.

Chena stops to lap water out of the nearest river channel, and we catch up with Tam and Jess.

Jess looks at me. "Do you think we'll be there today?"

"I don't know," I say. "But with every step we're a little closer." I have this raw feeling in my chest. What if there's nothing there? Or people as whacked-out as Stan and his followers? I look at Max, then at Tam.

I don't want to burst Jess's bubble, but I don't want her to be let down either. The only thing I really know is that we have one meager meal worth of beans left in the pack I'm carrying. And that dog is looking more and more like a food source by the minute.

"What is it?" Jess says. I guess my face must've given away my worry.

I feel my eyes getting hot. "Jess," I say. "I'm not sure what we'll find at the end of the road. So when I said with every step we're one step closer, what I meant was we're one step closer to finding out if anyone is there."

Jess nods. Her hand reaches out and settles onto Chena's head.

"You know," I say, "we're not on the road Mom and Dad told us to take."

Jess keeps her hand on Chena's head. "We wouldn't have found Chena if we'd gone the other way."

We keep walking down the road with me and Jess and Chena in front, followed by Tam and Max.

I take Jess's hand as we walk. I say, "I miss Mom and Dad." Jess's grip gets a little tighter. "And I'll probably always miss them. But that's okay. It's painful, but it's okay."

Jess nods as we keep walking hand-in-hand, and I say, "Whenever you want to talk about it"—I pause—"about them, I'm here." I'm not going to press her to speak right now, but I hope what I've said lets her know that I know she misses them.

Jess stays silent but keeps a grip on my hand.

The floodplain narrows, and the forest closes in on the road. I drop Jess's hand. We have to climb over tangles of fallen trees and cross small streams that have cut through the road.

The road makes a big turn to the west, and we see our first evidence of people. The partial skeleton of an old house stands off the road in what used to be a clearing, which is now blanketed with chest-high evergreens. Two bare walls—nothing but studs—slant outward.

We work our way through the thick field of saplings and stand in front of the walls. Moss covers what used to be the floor of the house. It's sunk deeper than the surrounding land, like there had been a basement or a crawl space at one time.

Chena's sniffing around the outside of the walls right where they meet. She squats and marks the spot.

"This place must've been abandoned a long time ago," Tam says. "There's not even a trail between here and the road."

On the other side of the mountains I would've been relieved by no signs of people. But not over here.

Back on the road, we keep walking. I think the isolated feeling of that place has knocked us all down a notch. Even Chena's tail is flying at half-mast. We pass the long-abandoned remains of a couple more places.

We round another bend and the water comes into view in the distance. Maybe it's the overcast sky and how late in the day it is, but the expanse of water just looks gray and stagnant. My first glimpse of the ocean, ever, and it's not the blue waves rolling up a white sand beach like I'd imagined. We still have some miles to cover before we'll actually be standing next to salt water.

I put my hand over my forehead to help cut the glare. I'm looking for buildings, boats, smoke. Anything.

The land stretching to the ocean is flat and pocked with puddles and small ponds, separated by reeds and tall grasses. The remains of the road skirt the marsh. I remember on the map that the road ends at the town. Maybe it's still there, beyond the marsh, out of sight. We can see trees in the distance where the land is higher. Maybe the buildings are hidden behind the trees or are around another point.

We need to keep going, but it's going to be dark soon.

"I don't see anything," Jess says. "Nothing."

"There might not be anything," I say.

Tam shrugs but is silent. She's got this far-off look in her eyes.

"There'll be life by the ocean," Max says. "I can feel it. And smell it in the air."

Chena sticks her nose up straight and sniffs.

I don't know if Max really believes what she's saying or if she's just trying to comfort Jess. I point across the road opposite the marsh. "We can build a fire in that patch of trees and then keep going in the morning."

After finishing off the beans and having some tea, we build the fire up. Max and Jess lie down, sharing one of the old man's blankets, and Tam and I sit shoulder to shoulder with the other blanket draped over us, keeping watch. For what feels like a long time neither of us says anything.

Just tell her, I think. *Tell her that you like her.* I take a breath. *You finally have a moment.*

Right now.

Just do it.

But before I can say anything, Tam turns to me and starts talking.

"Travis," Tam whispers, "after I got sent to the group home for injuring my foster brother"—she pauses and licks her lips—"and then watching him get to leave on the bus, I was so angry. Not just at him, but at, you know, guys. All guys. I mean, his macho attitude and actions resulted in me being left behind." Tam takes a slow breath and exhales. "Then I met Jason and Patrick, and they were so into each other, it didn't really matter to me that they were guys, because they didn't act like they wanted to take something from me." Tam shoves another stick toward the fire. "I guess what I'm trying to say is, I never thought I'd like a guy from that day forward when the buses left without me. Guys were the enemy, the spoilers of everything good. Those first two years, with the exception of Jason and Patrick, all we did was fight guys to survive. Mean guys. Greedy guys. Guys who thought of us as objects to control. To violate."

She pauses and shakes her head. "But then you came along. At first, when you had that gun pointed at us, I thought you were like everyone else we'd met. I was so ready to kill you. To eliminate another threat. And then you invited Mike and Dylan to join us without knowing anything about them, and for a while I wanted to kill you even more." She pauses and licks her lips again.

"But as time went on"—she shakes her head—"I realized that I didn't hate you. And when we got separated at the river, I actually missed you. You never tried to take anything from me. And even though I still basically hate all guys"—she pauses—"I like you."

Her open palm comes to rest on my cheek, and I feel the heat from her hand through my beard. My entire body is humming. I put my hand on her cheek and take another breath and I just stare at her face in the firelight.

"I like you, too." I swallow once and whisper, "Can I kiss you?"

Tam nods and says softly, "You'll be the first."

She tilts her head toward me. Her warm breath brushes my lips. I lean in and our lips meet. Her warm tongue slides into my mouth, and we share one long kiss.

*　*　*

The next morning a foggy mist hangs in the sky. When we start down the road, we can't even see the ocean. The moisture works its way through my thin clothing and covers my skin.

We all keep moving, knowing that's the best way to stay warm. Plus, we have to see what's at the end of this road. If there's nothing, well, then there's nothing. I keep hoping to catch a whiff of smoke or hear some loud noise, some machinery or something, but everything is as still as still can be.

When I was little, I used to look at the moon through my bedroom window and try to imagine what it would be like to be there. How alone and far away it would feel. How I could walk and walk and walk and never come across anyone or anything. And I'd wonder how all that space—that nothingness—could be there with no people, no animals, and no plants.

There are plenty of plants here, but we still haven't seen any animals. Not even birds singing. Maybe when we finally get to the water, we'll see something.

The sun starts to break through the mist around midday, creating a glare that makes us all squint. The fog still sits on the ground at what we guess is the shoreline, but we can see that we're much closer.

"You hear that?" Max says.

We all stop. The sound of lapping water invades my ears. The rhythmic push of wave after wave meeting the shore. I know it doesn't mean anything beyond the fact that we are close enough to hear the water. But still, I feel a shiver run up my spine.

"Come on," I say. I actually feel happy, though I'm not sure why. Maybe it's because we've made it this far. Maybe it's because I'm with my sister and two amazing girls who I would literally kill for. Maybe it's because not only do I like Tam, but she likes me as well. Maybe it's because if we are all there is, that's better than facing the world alone. It's better than being on the moon.

The sun burns off the ground fog, and now we can see the shore. The marsh we've been skirting is coming to an end. We cover the final stretch of road, walk across a gravelly beach, and stand at the water's edge. The mountains rise steeply on both sides of the inlet.

"I think the road used to keep going," I say. "What's left of the old town is probably underwater."

Max puts her hand in the water, then brings it to her mouth and licks it. She smiles.

The beach stretches toward a forested headland, about a mile away, I guess. In the other direction, way across the inlet, what look like giant, jagged, gray teeth poke up from the water.

"Over there," I say. "Way across the inlet." I point in the opposite direction of the headland. "The remains from oil storage tanks at the end of the pipeline. That used to be dry ground, way back when."

"How do you know?" Jess asks.

"School," I say. "I've seen pictures. Plus, it's on the old map we have." We're all staring across the inlet. And I'm imagining big tankers pulling up to the docks to load. I wonder if the docks are intact underwater. The remains of a huge industrial complex, buried by a combination of the rising sea and the ground sinking after an earthquake.

"What now?" Jess asks.

I let out a sigh. "I say we follow the shore over that headland." I point in the direction opposite the industrial ruins.

"I've never walked on a beach," Tam says. She smiles at me and I remember our one kiss last night. And then just sitting next to each other, our knees touching, holding hands, and whispering. She still has a lot of anger and distrust toward guys from her experiences, but she's also starting to trust me. *Slowly*, she said to me last night. *I need to do this, to try this, slowly.*

My mind jumps back to right now. The beans are gone, and we have enough tea for a couple more weak pots. I glance at Jess, her hand stroking Chena's head, and I just can't tell her that we might need Chena for the dinner pot. I'd hoped we wouldn't have to kill Chena, but I know we will.

We walk the beach in silence and Chena runs ahead. At the base of the headland, Chena is sniffing at some rocks. She whines once, then squats.

I look back toward the road, hoping that we've missed something, that I'll see some people waving at us and pointing. Or I'll see a side road that I haven't noticed before. But no, we're alone. I pull out the map but it provides no further clues.

Chena barks once, then sits down by the rocks she peed on.

Jess walks over to Chena and runs her fingers across her head. I wish Jess wasn't so attached to that dog. I don't know what would be worse, having Jess starve and liking me, or killing Chena for food and having her hate me.

"You guys," she says, "look." Jess is pointing down.

Between the rocks lies what looks like the start of a faint foot trail leading up the headland at an angle.

I think about Chena peeing on the rocks, about dogs marking their territories. I don't want to say what I'm thinking because I don't want to get anyone's hopes up.

"Okay," I say. "How about we follow the trail Chena's found?"

I stuff the map into my pocket and let Chena lead, followed by Jess. The trail switchbacks up the headland gradually. At the top we hit thick forest, but the trail continues, cutting away from the point. I want to get to the water on the other side and see what the shore is like. Is it more cliffs or more beach? But I keep following Chena, who keeps following the trail back into the forest. I don't like the closed-in feeling I get after walking on the beach—like we could get ambushed easily by a person or a bear. Then I remember that we haven't seen any sign of people or animals.

Maybe Chena just had to pee and she chose those rocks. Maybe she wasn't responding to someone else's markings. She hasn't stopped once to pee in the forest.

We step over a few fallen trees and my hopes sink even lower. People who use a trail regularly keep it clear. The trail starts angling back toward the shoreline, then makes a big sweeping turn until we're staring down at a cove.

The hillside behind the cove is forested but there are several breaks, and in those breaks there are huts or structures that have been dug into the hillside, contoured to fit the curve of the hill. At the far end of the cove, a stream flows into the ocean.

We all just stare. I count six structures in total, but there might be more. I study the area for movement. I mean, the place doesn't look like it's falling apart or anything, but I don't see any evidence that there are people down there either.

Max points at the huts. "Whoever built these worked with the land. They didn't just level everything or cut down massive amounts of trees. You can feel the respect here."

"Let's hope they're as friendly to us as they've been to the land," Tam says.

We head down the trail and then we're standing on the shore.

"Hello," I shout. "Hello."

I tell Jess to keep Chena close by.

"Let's poke our heads into one of these huts and see what we see," I say.

We check every hut and find them empty, completely empty, but in good shape. The smallest of the huts has a woodstove in it and a couple of benches built into the walls. And under the benches there's wood cut to fit into the stove. We decide this must be a sauna.

I'm puzzled. Who would leave a place like this? And why? Unless there was no food to be had around here. Unless they were starving. But the place doesn't have that feel to it. Starving people usually can't take care of themselves, and they leave things in a mess.

We search the opposite side of the cove for a trail, but the land is steep and we can't find one. We check the forest behind the huts and find nothing.

"The water," Max says. "Whoever was here must've left by water in some type of boat." We walk along the shore, searching for any evidence of a mooring, a place to anchor a boat, but find nothing.

We decide to sleep in the sauna. It's small, but it's the only hut with a heat source. By the time we've made a couple pots of tea on top of the stove, the place has heated up so much that we've taken our clothes off just to be comfortable. Luckily, it's dark in here, because just the thought of seeing Tam fully naked is causing a major and prolonged response just south of my stomach.

Chena whines until we let her sleep outside. We hear her settle in right next to the door. I still haven't told Jess that tomorrow I'm going to kill Chena. Maybe I'll do it early in the morning before she has a chance to protest. If I let her say goodbye, I doubt I'll be able to go through with it. I already hate myself for what I'm going to do.

We talk in whispers, discussing what we should do next. Try to climb the next headland and keep going down the coast? Go back to the end of the road to see if we've missed anything? Try to head inland behind the huts, following the stream to see where that leads?

None of the options seems like the right one, but we're out of food and can't just sit here. I think of Chena again. I hope Jess will eat the dog stew. I hope she'll understand.

There's barely room for four of us to lie down together, and I end up with Jess on one side of me and Tam on the other. I'm on my back and my body is humming with anticipation. I take a deep breath and tell myself to just chill. I feel Tam's hand brush mine and our pinky fingers lock and my whole body aches for her. Tam's pinky squeezes mine and I squeeze back.

But there's no way to do anything more. Like Tam can read my mind, she lets go of my pinky and I hear her exhale. I suck in some air through my nose and relax my face.

I must've finally drifted off because I wake to Chena's barking. Maybe there's a bear or a wolf outside. Or a deer. I wish I had some type of weapon beyond a pocketknife from the old man's pack and the hammer.

I grab the hammer and open the door to see what the barking is all about. A rush of cold air against my naked body sends a chill up my spine.

Chena isn't in front of the hut but instead is down on the shore.

My heart jumps to my throat. "You guys," I say. "Look."

CHAPTER
77

I STUFF MY FEET INTO my shoes and run out the door, the hammer still in my hand. The cold air stabs me like knives, but I can't waste a moment.

"Hey!" I yell. "Hey!"

Out in the cove are two kayaks with people in them—a man and a woman.

"Come here!" I yell. "Stop!"

I realize I'm naked and put my hands over my crotch. Jess, Max, and Tam appear moments later, yelling and waving. They have their shirts and shoes on but no pants. Jess hands me my shirt as the kayakers edge their way toward shore.

"We heard the dog or else we wouldn't have stopped," the woman says, her long dark hair blowing in the breeze.

"We come here to fish," the man says. He sets his paddle across his kayak and scratches his beard, which is reddish-brown and ends in a point about halfway down his chest. "In the summer and early fall that creek is packed with salmon. One of the few left that get decent runs since the earthquake caused the ground to sink along a lot of the coast. This creek had just the right gradient to support a salmon run. We closed the place down about a month ago."

"My people," the woman says, "have lived on this coast for a long time. But the big quake a few years back destroyed my village, which used to sit about sixty miles from here in Chenega Bay. I'm one of four survivors."

Max puts her palms together and does a slight bow. "I'm sorry for your loss from the earthquake."

"Thank you," the woman says.

Max nods and then asks, "What are your people called?"

"Chugach," the woman responds, "the same name as the mountain range you are in."

"I've heard of your people," Max says. "They were the first to encounter the Russians way back in the 1700s."

"That's right," the woman responds. Then she glances at the rest of us. "Where have you come from?"

I tell her we've come down the road, hoping to find people. And that things are bad up north, as bad as they've ever been. That I don't actually know if anyone north of the Alaska Range will even survive the winter.

The man shakes his head. "No one has come down that road for a long time. A year, maybe two, as far as I know. The maples seem to stop people. If the US government hadn't screwed around with the ecosystem, it'd be a lot easier to get around through there."

"We heard that the trees were genetically engineered," I say.

"Not only that," the man says. "When we took over the Outpost"—he points with his paddle down the coast—"we found old documents detailing their experiment gone wrong. Way back, like sixty years ago, when a lot of the native trees between the Chugach and Alaska Range were stressed and dying, the government did this massive maple seed dispersal by air in isolated places. And yes, the species had been genetically modified to be fast growing and resistant to the pests that plagued the birch, spruce, and aspen.

The land managers figured they'd have a jump on reforestation if they needed it. The trees not only did well and spread, but then somehow, some of the remaining seed was stolen and dispersed in more places, which really did turn it into a Buffer Zone over time."

"Do either of you know anything about Anchorage? Or at least where Anchorage used to be?" I ask. "I mean, is anyone there?" I tell them about my parents and their instructions to head to Anchorage and how we changed our plans.

"It's about a hundred-mile paddle and then a forty-mile walk to get there," the woman says. "We've had a few refugees show up from there this past year. I think it's pretty unstable over there. In time we'd like to help stabilize that area, take it under our jurisdiction, but we can't spread ourselves too thin."

I tell them about the community we escaped from, and the old man who owned Chena and what he said before he died, about the bodies. "He used the phrase *gas tent*."

The woman scowls. "Gold raiders from Anchorage." She shakes her head slowly. "A gas tent is like a gas chamber. They're usually dropped out of the sky onto places. They're designed to kill anything they cover."

"You mean dropped, like, from an airplane?" Tam asks.

The man nods. "We'll have to bring some kayaks back for you. It might take a few days, but we'll be back. We're around the point and down the coast twenty or so miles. It's possible to walk, but there's some big mountains to cross." The man hesitates, then continues. "We'll have to talk it over with everyone at the Outpost, but I don't think there'll be any problems. We can't leave you here. And if you can get along with the others, things should work out."

"We live a simple life, but we think it's a good life," the woman says. "Everyone pitches in, including dogs." She points at Chena. "Male or a female?"

"She's a girl," Jess says. "Her name's Chena."

"Has she been fixed?"

Jess turns to me. "I'm not sure," I say.

"We'll figure it out." The woman shrugs. "One of our females died this summer, attacked by a bear on the beach you followed to get here. But we've got a male, and we could use some pups."

"Do you have contact with the rest of the world from your outpost?" I ask. "Like with the United States?"

The man and the woman look at each other.

She shakes her head. "There's a lot you'll need to know. We've been at war with the United States for over two years."

"At war?" I raise my eyebrows.

"It's a long story," she says. "The United States has continually tried to keep control of Anchorage after abandoning the rest of the state. There's a lot of internal fighting going on over there between factions, but the United States wants to hang on to Anchorage and use it as a base to extract resources, like gold. They still have some firepower, and from what you've told me, they're using gas tents on innocent people again."

The man says, "If you want to be considered for housing at the Outpost, or any place else in the North Pacific Confederation, you'll have to pledge your allegiance."

"Wait," I say. "I've never heard of the North Pacific Confederation. What—"

"We're a coastal people," the man says. "Trying to live sustainably, locally, in peace. The United States, really the Disunited States these days, doesn't always make it easy. Once you're at the Outpost and you've been questioned and we're satisfied that you're not plants from the United States, then you'll learn more about the situation we're in. And"—he hesitates—"did you walk all this way?" He glances at our legs. "Without any pants?"

We all laugh, and I say, "When I saw the kayaks, I just started running. I didn't want you to leave."

We help them pull their kayaks ashore. We talk some more, but they are hesitant to share specific information about the Outpost in case we're captured by the United States before they come back to get us. They leave us with some dried fish and tell us they hope to be back in a few days.

Before they paddle away, the man says, "If we're not back in seven days, then you'll have to proceed on foot. Stay as close to the coast as the land will let you, and you won't miss the Outpost. Hopefully you won't need to do that, but if you do, at least you know that much."

Chena runs along the shore and barks as they paddle away. I look at Jess and say, "I'm glad you made friends with Chena. If it weren't for her, we might've missed those people."

Jess smiles and says, "If it weren't for you and your plan, I'd still be a prisoner at the compound." Then she turns to Max and Tam. "And without you two, I wouldn't have made it to the yellow cliffs."

"But if you hadn't done your part so well," Tam says, "we wouldn't have had the chance to help you. We'd still be prisoners, too."

"That's right, girl," Max says to Jess. "You're the best."

I think about what Max said about her grandma and how when you work with other people, when you're committed to having everyone succeed, the energy created is way more than if each person were working alone. And no way could any of us have ended up where we are if we'd each tried to go it alone.

I hope this outpost will be a stable place even though there's a war going on. A place where we can live, where Jess can settle in and maybe even be a kid, if that's possible after all she's been through. I grab her by the hands, and even though the back of my arm throbs, I swing her around until she screams with delight. Then I set her down and Chena straddles her and licks her face, and Jess laughs and laughs.

I look at Max and Tam but they're both staring at Jess, smiling.

Chena jumps off Jess and barks.

A loud blow, like nothing I've ever heard, invades my ears and we all turn toward the water. Then we hear another and another. Dark, rounded backs break the surface and blow water skyward. A pod of orcas, six or seven whales of varying sizes, are heading toward the point the kayakers rounded a few minutes ago. I think, *Hopefully, we'll be rounding that point in a few days, starting a new life.*

Then a rumble invades my ears. We all turn and look skyward and see a formation of jets that have materialized above the industrial wreckage across the inlet. I can just make out a blue star on the side of the nearest jet as they zip by us, well offshore, and disappear around the point where the orcas are headed.

We hear the muffled report of an explosion.

We can't see anything, but we hope the kayakers are okay.

I glance at Jess, then at Max, and then at Tam.

No one says anything.

Then we all fix our eyes on the point and wait.

The jets don't come back.

I study the mountains that frame the inlet. Steep forested land gives way to even steeper rocky land as mountain after mountain stretches up the coast.

If no one shows up for us, we'll just have to walk to the Outpost.

It won't be an easy walk, but we can do it.

ACKNOWLEDGMENTS

Many thanks to all my friends who've spent time with me on wilderness trips over the past thirty-five years. All of those experiences have played into the creation of this story. Thanks to my early readers Terry Lynn Johnson, Nancy Fresco, and Elana Johnson. A big thank you to my agent, Amy Tipton, who believed in this story from the very beginning and worked tirelessly to find a home for it. Thanks to my good friend and expert scientist Carl Roland for taking the time to entertain my steady stream of natural history questions ranging from sinkhole development to hypothetical plant species distribution.

This book would not be what it is without the expert eyes of my editor John Morgan, who got behind this book early and provided valuable direction throughout. Thanks also to my publisher Erin Stein at Imprint, whose careful reading and comments helped make this book the best it could be.

Thanks also to Natalie C. Sousa, Dawn Ryan, Raymond Ernesto Colón, and Allison Hughes at Imprint and Macmillan for putting in the time and energy to make this book a reality.

And finally, thank you to my wife, Dana, for reading multiple drafts of this story and always offering her genuine and honest responses.